A
Murder
of
One

A Murder of One

by: Patti Keno

Mystic Flowur Creations, Belleville Michigan

First Edition: March 2015

Cover Design: Cheekycovers.com

All Poetry written by: Patti Keno

Crow Clip Art by: Jeneeford found on clker.com

Final Edit done by: Jennifer Friess

ISBN: 9780692388334

Dedication:

When I first wrote this novel in 1995-96 I wanted to dedicate it to my first love who introduced me to the Rave scene, but even though he inspired this novel, I cannot dedicate it to him as he is out of my life now.

There are many people I would like to dedicate this novel to. Many people helped me in the 20 years since I first put pen to paper. My mother, Nancy, first and foremost, was a sounding board for me. She put up with all my "How does this sound?" and "What's that word that means....?" She pushed me (for 20 years) to get this book published and she stood by me through the whole process.

My brother, Jeff who helped with the above questions as well as editing many of my drafts. My best friend Carrie, who helped me through the break up with my first love and has stayed with me ever since.

Most of all though this book is dedicated to my best friend Jennifer Friess, without her, this book may never have been published. She has helped me more than she can imagine, not only did she guide me step by step through the process of self-publishing, but she gave me the courage to actually go through with the process. She published her first novel: The Wind Could Blow a Bug and I said to myself "If she can do it, so can I". So thank you Jennifer for making this possible and helping me to believe in myself.

Moving onward
I seem
to be taking advantage
of this dream;
hollow and empty
I'm not the one to blame
for innocence
comes with sorrow
and sorrow only leads
to shame

6-26-96

PROLOGUE

"Are you sure that you're ready to do this?" the tender voice beside his ear inquired.

David nodded. "It's the 'anniversary'. I can't not do this, so I guess I have to be ready," he replied under his breath.

"I can't believe it's been almost 20 years," the voice whispered.

"Neither can I," David agreed. "Time just flies, so quickly now, back then it seemed to drag on forever." He shivered as a sudden breeze whipped through the cold January air.

"Are you cold?" the voice asked. David nodded and adjusted the collar of his green jacket. *"I'm sorry you had to go through everything alone,"* the voice said sadly.

"No, I was never alone, not ever!" David argued, smiling shyly, letting the voice know that he wasn't angry.

"I guess this means it's time for me to go then," the voice whispered through what could have been tears.

David flinched. He knew this day was coming, but he still wasn't prepared for it. "I know," he mumbled through his own fresh tears.

"I love you, Pez," the voice whispered tenderly.

"I love you too, Wolf. And thank you... for everything," David whispered into the emptiness of the cemetery that he was standing in.

"No Pez, thank ***you****,"* Wolf replied. David felt a kiss placed gently upon his lips, but he saw nothing. *"Good-bye, Pez,"* the voice whispered, next to his ear again.

"Good-bye, Wolf," David whispered, choking back tears. "Wolf, WAIT!" he cried out fearfully. "Wolf? Are you still there?" he inquired softly into the early morning breeze.

"Yes," he heard Wolf's voice answer.

"Will I ever see you again?" David asked, tears flowing freely now.

"Of course you will," Wolf's voice answered affectionately. The air in front of David began to shimmer; something was beginning to take shape. A vision of Wolf slowly appeared within the shimmering air. *"But it probably won't be for a very long time,"* the spirit explained to him, smiling sadly. David tried to suppress a sob at the beauty of the spirit's smile, but he failed miserably.

The spirit's smile turned into a look of concern. *"Don't cry, David,"* Wolf pleaded, shaking his head. David lost it even more when Wolf used his real name instead of the nickname he had been given in high school.

Wolf smiled again; a sad sweet smile that made David melt inside. He was sure he would never forget the feeling that the smile caused. *"Don't worry. We'll still have our dreams,"* he whispered, leaning forward and placing another cold airy kiss on David's lips. *"See you around, Love,"* Wolf whispered softly.

David nodded and watched as Wolf walked away from him through the cemetery. He lowered his head and wiped his tears away. He lifted his head for one final glimpse of his dead love, but sadly Wolf was gone.

David inhaled a shaky breath trying to fight back the tears again. In a way this was harder to deal with than when Wolf had actually died, almost twenty years ago to this very day.

"Goodbye, Wolf," David replied softly. He watched as his breath floated away in clouds and disappeared shortly after, just like Wolf had done. 'Nothing ever stays the same,' David thought. He wiped his tears away and looked once more at the empty spot where he had last seen Wolf. Even though it hurt him deep inside, he still felt a small bit of relief as he finally let go of the ghost that had been with him for so long. Finally, he took a deep mournful breath and turned his back on his pain. He forced himself to walk towards Wolf's final resting place.

As he approached the grave, he noticed there was someone standing next to it. The person standing there looked a lot like Wolf's sister, Diamond. He sighed. He had finally said goodbye to one sibling and now the other sibling was going to haunt him?

Seeing the girl standing there reminded him of the years he spent in the institution. It was a long time ago now, but he still remembered the years of hearing voices and seeing visions of things real and unreal... natural and supernatural. He spent most of his time in there trying to learn what was real (even if some people didn't believe him) and what was only in his head.

As he moved forward towards the headstones he knew that this girl was definitely **not** only in his head. She was as real as the spirit of her brother had been only a few moments ago, perhaps even more real than he was, if that was possible. The closer he got, the more he convinced himself that the person standing just between Diamond and Wolf's graves... was Diamond; or her spirit anyway.

"Diamond?" he called out to the girl.

She whipped around, startled. "PEZ!!!" the girl screamed, overjoyed at seeing him.

"Diamond?" he asked again. It seemed as if Diamond was only slightly older then she had been when she died.

"No, silly! It's me," She clarified laughing. "Mokey," she prompted, noticing his bewildered expression.

Recognition finally spread across David's face in the form of a smile. "MOKEY!" he yelled, running over to Wolf and Diamond's (still living) younger sister. He picked her up in a bear hug and spun her around.

"Jesus, PEZ!" she screamed, smiling. "Put me down!" she said through her laughter.

"I'm sorry it's just **so** good to see you," David exclaimed, smiling the biggest smile he'd smiled in a long time.

"I know. You too," she replied. "I like your hair. It's so... short. I *almost* didn't recognize you."

David ran his hair through his freshly cut hair. "Seriously? Do you like it?" he asked nervously. He couldn't remember ever having short hair, not even when he was little.

"I do, Pez. I really do," she replied, smiling brightly. "You've changed **so** much," she praised. "You're looking good, really good!" she added, afraid he would take her statement the wrong way.

"Me?" David exclaimed in surprise. "Look at you! The last time I saw you... you were this high!" he said, holding his hand up to his stomach. "Now you're a beautiful young woman."

Mokey blushed furiously. "I wasn't beautiful before?" she asked jokingly, catching David off guard.

"Yeah, you were, but you were just a k-kid then," he stammered out.

"I was just joking," she informed him. Before David knew what was happening she threw her arms around his neck. Once he recovered from the shock of her sudden display of affection, he wrapped his arms around her waist.

"I'm sorry for startling you. It's just so good to see you again," she whispered, her voice sounding almost like Wolf's. He longed for it to be Wolf's breath that brushed softly against his neck as she spoke.

"You too," he replied, barely restraining the tears. He pressed his lips together tightly to stop the tears from coming once more.

It felt wonderful to have someone's arms around him again. It felt even better to feel loved again. He had shut himself off from the world for too long and the rush of feelings he got just from one little hug was almost too much for him to handle. He sobbed once, but no tears came.

Mokey pulled back to look at him. He nodded at her and pushed his tears away. He hugged her tightly again, not quite ready to let go of her yet. Mokey understood and began gently stroking his back in a sympathetic gesture.

"How long has it been?" he asked. He couldn't remember when he had last seen her.

"Quite a while," she whispered hoarsely. "Since..." She stopped talking and choked back a sob of her own. "...the funerals," she finished.

"Uh-uhn, before that," he corrected, shaking his head. He pulled back to look into her eyes. "I couldn't go... I was 'in custody'.

They wouldn't *let me* go to the funer…" He broke off before he could finish. "I couldn't go. I couldn't even say goodbye!" he uttered desperately, losing control over his tears. Mokey cried harder with his words. He pressed his face back into her shoulder.

"I'm so sorry," she choked out. Together they stood hugging and crying on each other's shoulders. After a couple moments of tears, Mokey pulled away from David. She wiped his tears away with her scarf, and then she used it to wipe her own tears away. "We don't want to get frozen like that, do we?" she asked, smiling a quirky smile that was so unlike either of her siblings. David found himself trying to imitate it.

"What?" Mokey asked nervously laughing a little, blushing at the way David was smiling at her. The smile looked entirely different on him then it did on her. He vowed to himself never to try to smile like her again. No smile could even come close to that smile.

He couldn't help staring at her in wonder at how closely she resembled her sister.

"You just look so much…" David began, but Mokey cut him off.

"Like Diamond," she finished, rolling her eyes. "I know… It's really hard on my parents. They are so overprotective of me now. I told them I was thinking about getting my ears pierced and they totally freaked. They said they didn't want me to end up pierced all over like Diamond was. She had what, like eight piercings, or something?"

"It was more like fifteen," David corrected.

Mokey continued as if she hadn't heard him. "I couldn't even go to school dances. I had to tell them I was going to the library," she laughed.

"We used to tell our parents we were going to school dances when we would go to raves," David enlightened her, smirking slyly.

"That explains that then," she exclaimed, happy to finally understand the mystery of her parent's strange complex. "They didn't want me to get into drugs or parties or anything. They didn't want me to end up dead or crazy like y…," Mokey cut herself off and bit her bottom lip. She looked away from him, embarrassed by her babbling. "Their words, not mine," she said quietly in her own defense.

David knew she was going to say 'like you'. He was quite sure that he was the star of an urban legend in these parts. All sorts of parents probably lectured their children: 'Stay away from drugs or you could end up in the loony bin just like that Spencer boy or worse, you could end up dead just like all his friends.' Yep, that was him; a walking, talking PSA. Why didn't the judge tell him to do that? He gladly would have done any amount of public service announcements if it had eased his guilt. It probably wouldn't have though, nothing else did.

"Have you gone home yet?" Mokey asked, changing the subject as she slowly composed herself.

"Not yet. I'm not quite sure I'm ready for that," David replied, as fat snowflakes began to fall around them.

"Does your mom even know you're back?" Mokey asked.

David chewed at his bottom lip and shook his head. He took his arms from around her waist. Smiling madly, he threw back his head and stuck out his tongue, determined to catch a snowflake on it. Mokey laughed and did the same.

When David was successful at catching one, he looked back at Mokey and continued speaking, as if they hadn't stopped. "My flight landed and when I hit the bathroom I saw myself in the mirror and realized that I looked like a bum. I thought maybe it was time for a new look, so I found a barber shop." He paused rubbing the back of his neatly shaven neck again. "It was so long, they cut over eight inches off." He smiled and dug his hand into his pocket. He pulled out the tail of hair he had kept from the barber shop. "I feel weird without it. Weird and cold," he laughed.

"Do you mind... Can I have some of it, to remind me of Wolf?" Mokey asked softly, afraid he would say no. David grabbed a small chunk and pulled it out of the rubber band. He held it out to her. She smiled gratefully. She started to braid it as David finished his run down of his morning so far.

"Then I came straight here." He kicked at the duffel bag that he dropped when he had picked her up and spun her around. "I had to... It's the anniversary of their deaths," he said, gesturing to Wolf and Diamond's headstones.

"Actually, it's tomorrow," she corrected him.

"Yeah, but today is my bir... today is the day it started."

"Happy birthday," she whispered sadly.

"Yeah, exactly... Happy birthday," he replied, his eyes took on a glassy look.

"Pez, are you OK?" Mokey asked softly.

David nodded, fresh tears streaming down his face. He shivered as the wind blew across his bare neck. He pulled his scarf up higher.

"Do you come here often?" she asked. "I never see you."

"No, this is the first time I've been back to Emmerdale since I... entered the institute. Once I got out I couldn't bring myself to come back, then I got the scholarship and found myself on a lecturing tour. I guess I've been stalling coming home. Emmerdale was not a kind place to me."

"Do you think maybe..." Mokey began, but then paused. "Can you tell me what it was like?" She asked.

"The accident?" David asked.

"No, afterwards, your...," Mokey stopped at a loss for words.

"My downfall? My disintegration? My descent into madness?" David asked laughing, but also quite serious.

Mokey nodded. "Do you want to go get some coffee or something and talk about it maybe?" she asked shyly, staring at the ground in front of her feet.

David nodded. "Sure. I think I'm finally ready to talk about it now," he replied, just as shyly. This would be the first time he told his story to anyone.

"I know the perfect place. That is if you're up for a bit of a walk," she offered.

"That sounds great, but um... Can you give me a minute alone?" He pointed at the headstones.

"Sure... yeah... oh, I'm sorry, I didn't mean to... hog all your time," she apologized nervously.

"It's OK, don't worry about it. I'm just glad to see a familiar face." He smiled, hoping that she didn't realize he meant he was glad to see Diamond's face again.

"I'll be over there." She pointed to a large urn shaped headstone.

"Thanks," David said nodding. "I won't be long."

"Take your time, I'm in no hurry," Mokey replied as she turned and walked away.

David sat down on the ground between Wolf and Diamond's graves. He was glad that none of the recent snows had stuck. He wondered how many times in the past he had sat in this spot between his two best friends.

"I'm doing like you said, Wolf," he whispered softly. "I am starting over... wiping the slate clean." He paused, pulling the tail of hair from his pocket again. He separated it in half and tucked the rubber-banded chunk back into his pocket. "I cut off all of my hair so that I could bury that part of myself here with my best friends." He took a small, newly purchased switchblade out viii

of his pocket and used it to break into the partially frozen ground. "I guess I could have done this in the summer time," he said, laughing as he finally dug deep enough to place the hair in the ground.

He stood up and wiped off his hands. He stepped on the ground to pack the dirt in around the hair.

"I love you," he said, running his hand across Wolf's headstone. He turned and wiped away a tear. "Goodbye, guys," he whispered to the headstones. David picked up his duffle bag and swung it over his shoulder. He walked over to Mokey.

"You ready?" she asked. David nodded and they began to walk out of the cemetery together.

Mokey linked her arm in his and sighed. David smiled, even though his body flinched. This felt more intimate to him than when they had hugged. "Sorry, I'm just not used to this much closeness," he remarked.

"I don't have to," Mokey said, beginning to pull her arm away.

"No, it's cool, I missed it," he said, grabbing her hand before it could slip away.

Mokey smiled in surprise when David continued to hold onto her hand. They walked together, Mokey leading as David stared down at her hand. He was so much like a child to Mokey; even though he was eight years older than her. She remembered the crush she used to have on him. Her face flushed as all the old feelings came rushing back. She realized what those feelings were now. Hero worship... she worshipped him... had always worshipped him. She was glad that he was still examining her hand and couldn't see her face redden ever so slightly.

A thought occurred to her as they walked. A thought that intrigued her but frightened her at the same time. A rumor had gone around town after Pez had been sent away. It spread quickly and loudly like most rumors do in small towns. People said that Pez could see ghosts. They said that he could talk to them and that is the reason why he had to be institutionalized.

"Pez, can you really see ghosts?" she asked quietly before she lost her nerve. She wanted to ask him if he could see one ghost in particular, but she couldn't seem to bring up her brother's name.

"David, please. Call me David. Pez is... dead," he requested softly, with tears in his voice. He would have to expect to hear that name more often now that he was home. It was going to be very hard to try and break people of the habit of calling him the name he'd had since high school.

"Well, can you?" she prompted after he didn't answer right away.

He shrugged as they crossed the street. "Sometimes," he mumbled in reply. He didn't want her to think he was crazy, but chances were she already did.

He looked up as they reached the café, but Mokey sensed he wasn't quite looking at the café. In a way he wasn't. He was seeing the café not as it was now, but as it had been almost 20 years ago.

"I know this place," David stated. "The name is different, but this is the café where we used to hang out."

"My boyfriend and I love coming here," Mokey declared.

The café was definitely different than the one that David and his friends had loved. His café was a large open place with lots of soft, mismatched couches. Now, the large open space had been divided into small rooms. It made the interior look smaller, and somehow even cozier.

"What is this place?" he asked as he noticed something that looked like a gift shop, over by the counter. His eyes focused on a sign that read: "Mercury is currently in retrograde."

"It's a psychic coffee shop. I hope you don't mind. I think it's nice here." She paused, thrown off by his reaction. "We could go somewhere else," she suggested.

"No, I like it." David laughed. "It's oddly fitting. Maybe I can schedule a lecture here."

"Maybe you can rent a room... if you still see ghosts." Mokey smiled.

David stared at her blankly. "You do know what I do for a living now, right?"

"No, people don't talk about you like they used to," she laughed.

"I'm a psychic medium. I lecture, give classes on mediumship. Ghost hunt... I was on a ghost hunting show for four years in Europe. I don't think the show ever made it to the States though."

Mokey laughed. "I guess this place is fitting then."

"Yeah, life is like that. It's a series of crazy coincidences."

"I'm starting to see that. I'll get two coffees, you grab a table," Mokey suggested.

"I'll take tea, if they have it," David corrected.

"Tea? You really did spend a lot of time in Europe." She laughed.

"No, I started drinking tea long before Europe." He laughed in return.

"Any specific kind?"

"Surprise me," David looked around at the tables. "Any specific place you want to sit?"

"Surprise me," Mokey laughed, as she headed over to the counter.

As soon as they had their drinks, a song suddenly started playing from somewhere on Mokey's person. She reached into her coat pocket and pulled out her cell phone. "Sorry, I've got to take this," she explained. "Just a second." She moved a little ways away from him and answered the call quietly. Shortly after, she joined him at the table.

"Sorry," she apologized again. "That was my boyfriend. I had to take it," she explained. David noticed that she couldn't look at him when she said boyfriend. "I let him know about you. He said he's stopping by. I hope that's OK?"

David shrugged. "That's fine."

"Good." She seated herself and took off her jacket. "OK, I'm ready."

"Give me a minute to collect my thoughts," David laughed.

He stared at his tea for a long while, before he finally took a deep breath and began.

"I can't really start at the beginning. I'm not even sure when it all started. I'll just pick an event and go from there. Feel free to ask questions." Mokey nodded in agreement. "My grandfather Spencer's funeral, that's when it started getting really bad. Let's see, it was 1997 and I was a senior in high school. It was actually my second senior year, because the first one was interrupted rather violently."

"By the accident?" Mokey asked.

David nodded. He closed his eyes and slipped into the memory trance that had brought him so much grief in the past. All at once the café, Mokey, the institution, London, all of it was gone and in David's mind it was the day of his grandfather's funeral.

Part One: Sorrow

1

Pez smiled bravely in silent rebellion against the waves of sadness that broke with a vengeance upon his grief-stricken soul. The currents of his anguish threatened to pull him under and drown him in the sea of his own never-ending shame. Then again, to Pez, the ache of shame that filled his heart was nothing new.

For a split second, Pez was unable to recall where he was. He looked around. He found himself in a cemetery that was all too familiar to him. He had been here before, and he knew he would come here again many times in the days to come.

The day was cloudy, but warm. It was a day that reminded Pez of summers long gone and the one that was fast approaching.

Pez wished this funeral would hurry up and be over with. He had dealt with enough sorrow and memories for one day. Now he just wanted to go home. He just wanted to get away from all of these people and be alone. Why couldn't everyone just leave him alone?

The bright sun warmed the small crowd of mourning Spencers, but did little to cheer them. How could the sun cheer them at all when it kept hiding behind the gray clouds? Even so, Pez and many of the other mourners wore sunglasses on this sorrowful day –not for respite from the sun, but to hide their tears.

All of the vaguely familiar faces in the crowd were wet with tears. A couple of them were even sobbing loudly. The only one, besides Pez, who was not crying was Nanah Spencer. She sat in a folding chair, next to the casket of her husband. Pez's Uncle Jim stood next to her with his hand on her shoulder giving her support. They both watched solemnly as the casket was lowered into the ground. She was sitting tall and proud. She was smiling as she watched the casket disappear. The smile she wore was very similar to Pez's own smile.

She sat almost as if she wasn't even there; her eyes now closed as if she were sleeping. Pez remembered what she told him after his father died: "Whenever you are sad, just close your eyes and remember the good times and the bad times won't seem so bad anymore." He knew that Nanah was doing that now.

Loved ones surrounded Pez–correction: people who at one time were loved ones, now regretfully they were nothing more than faces in the crowd. Pez's small family had lost touch with the people standing around the gravesite (his father's immediate family) shortly after the death of his father almost eight years ago. His father's grave lay behind him and he would not… could not even force himself to look at it. Even after all those years, it was still too hard on him. He was beginning to wonder if he would ever get over the violence of his father's sudden death.

Pez looked around at his relatives. He was surprised to see that the ones who were crying the loudest were the relatives who never had a good relationship with Pez's grandfather. Could it be that they were regretting the fact that they weren't closer to Poppy Spencer?

Pez couldn't hear the priest's sermon over their loud sobbing, but he knew the sermon was about God and heaven. Pez didn't care that he couldn't hear; he wasn't listening anyway. His thoughts were on other things. Poppy wasn't the furthest thing from his mind, but God and heaven were.

The ideas parading around inside his head were by no means new. Actually he found himself thinking about them a lot lately, but now the ideas took on a new light. Today they hit him harder than ever before; they hit him with such clarity it was almost painful. The new light that guided these ideas was the fact that his grandfather died at the ripe old age of 82. He thought of all the deaths he mourned over and somehow this one seemed to be the happiest one yet. Old age seemed like such a wonderful way to die, when compared to the way all the others died; so quick, so sudden, so unexpected, and so young. Somewhere, deep inside, a new thought emerged and this thought brought a small bit of joy to a person who felt dead inside.

'At least,' he thought to himself, staring at the casket where his grandfather's body lay. 'At least I didn't kill Poppy like I killed...' He pushed that thought away quickly. He couldn't think about the others, not here, not now. If he thought of them, the voices would come back and he didn't need that. He didn't want to hear the voices now, not in front of these people, his so-called family. No one here needed to know he was crazy. 'Happy thoughts, happy thoughts,' he repeated to himself, trying to push away the sad thoughts. For once they started, there was no stopping them.

His body stood there in that cemetery, but his mind was elsewhere. His mind wandered back to the other funerals. The ones he had missed. The funerals were so recent they still brought tears to his eyes. Were the other funerals like this one? These people standing here, they could have been anyone's family. This could be any one of those other funerals. Did they have people that sobbed like the people here did? Did anyone cry for them at all? He sighed in anger and resentment; he would never know the answer to any of these questions.

Something inside him buckled, and again he was overcome with the waves of sadness and anguish that decreased only in those magical moments when he thought of nothing. So much sadness and still he smiled, almost laughing. He couldn't take this sadness much longer. Soon he was going to break and he knew it. He wanted to go home. He knew the sadness wouldn't go away at his house, but at least it would be easier to deal with when he was in his bedroom alone.

Bravely, he faced the crowd of relatives still keeping his back to his father's grave. Brave... but the bravery was false. Anyone who cared to look close enough could see that inside he was cowering, raving, confused and afraid. How could he go on living, when everyone he ever knew and loved was gone? He knew that without them he was certainly dead inside.

Lowering his wrap-around sunglasses, he turned his head to catch his mother's eye. When she looked in Pez's direction, he gestured to her with pleading eyes. She knew how much he hated funerals even before his father died, but now he hated them more passionately than ever. She glanced around, the priest was finished with his sermon and the family members were observing a moment of silence for the deceased. She nodded in response to her son's unasked question.

Pez's mother reached down beside herself with an open hand. Her youngest son automatically took her hand. Together they walked over to where Nanah Spencer sat. Pez followed a few steps behind, staring at the ground in front of his feet. He didn't dare lift his eyes to meet his relative's glares.

Pez's mother left Stevie with him and approached Nanah alone. Pez's mom, Carole Spencer, kissed her mother-in-law's cheek and whispered a few short words to her. She bid Nanah farewell and walked back to Stevie and Pez. She took Stevie's hand and stood patiently waiting for Pez to say his farewells.

Pez walked over to his grandmother, remembering how she used to hold him after his father died. His own mother had been too preoccupied with prematurely born Stevie to give Pez the love he needed so desperately. Nanah and Pez (then called D) developed a special bond as they helped each other get through David Spencer II's death. Now at David Spencer I's funeral, that bond was rekindled, if only for a few precious moments. The tears that he had fought so hard to stop began to stream down his face, as he reached Nanah's chair.

"Be strong, my littlest David," Nanah whispered to Pez as he bent down to kiss her careworn cheek. Those were the exact words she had said to him at his father's funeral. Thinking back, he was surprised at how brave his Nanah had been at her own son's funeral.

"You too, Nanah," he replied, hugging her. He just wanted to melt into her arms. He wanted her to hold him like she used to. He knew that couldn't happen. He started to turn, ready to leave, but she stopped him. She clasped her wrinkled hands around Pez's arms just above his elbows.

"You're so sad, D," she began. "You have to realize that people leave us suddenly sometimes; like your father. They leave us and it hurts so badly that you want to join them, but you have to be strong. You can't just stop living your life. You have to struggle onward because eventually it stops hurting so much, even though you never stop missing them," she instructed him. Pez smiled sadly. This was something he should be saying to her, not vice versa. Oddly enough it felt right and somehow what she said kept all the horrible memories at bay, for now. He felt regret that he couldn't say something like that to her, since it was her husband that died.

"Don't you worry about me, D," she assured him as if she had read his mind. "I'll live, just the same as you will. It hurts now, I know, but it will get better... if you let it." Pez nodded, smiling and fighting back more tears. Nanah was like that; she always put everyone else's feelings before her own. Pez thought she was so brave to be so strong. He admired that quality in her and he wished he could be more like her. He wished he could be as strong as she was.

She paused, catching her breath. She reached up with one hand and took off Pez's sunglasses. She carefully folded them up and pressed them gently into Pez's open hand. "Oh D, don't hide. Don't be afraid to let people see you hurting," she scolded him softly. "Chances are, they're hurting too." Again she lifted up her hand and wiped away his tears with a tissue that had magically appeared at her fingertips. Pez knew she always kept tissues up her sleeve to wipe away tears, his tears and her own.

Pez felt like a ten-year-old child again looking into her sweet, loving eyes. She had been more of a mother to him after his father died then his own mother had been.

Just then, her eyes took on a different look, one of haunted sadness. It was an echo of the look in Pez's own eyes, even though he didn't know it.

"You look just like your father did, when he was your age," she said as she caressed his cheek with the back of her hand. "You have his eyes," she explained, tears rolling down her cheeks. "I'm so glad we didn't lose you," she sighed, choking back the sobs. Pez's tears fell harder; he was upset at the sudden change in his Nanah. He was surprised that she didn't cry in sadness for someone who died, but she cried in happiness about someone who was still living. "God wanted you to live. He left you here on purpose, my littlest D. There is a reason He left you here. It's up to you to find out what that reason is, even if Poppy and I are gone. You have to live on and fulfill your purpose." She smiled, wiping his tears away. "I love you D. Your father and Poppy loved you too, always remember that." She heaved out a great sigh. "And your mother loves you too, even though sometimes it's hard for her to show it. Your father's death was very hard on her, you know. It doesn't help much that you look so much like him."

"I know, I'll remember. I love you, Nanah," Pez promised, hugging her again. They held each other in strong embraces for a short time. It had been so long since Pez felt the comfort of a hug like that. He wanted it to last a lot longer than it did. Sometimes he wished his mother would hug him like this, but ever since his father's death, she seemed incapable of giving him the love he needed. He never wanted this hug to end. He wanted to curl up on her lap and cling to her, bawling while she rocked him gently. Pez knew he couldn't do that. He was a man now, not a small child.

When the hug finally ended, he turned away from Nanah and fumbled in his jacket pocket. For a moment, he was afraid he had forgotten it. The thought made him panic. His mind was wild with fear that he had left it at home. He frantically searched through his pockets. All panic disappeared as his hand closed around the silver coin. He smiled in relief. This was the only chance he would get to give the coin back to his grandfather.

He glanced quickly around to find that all his relatives were too preoccupied with each other to see the lonely boy, who was almost a man, toss a half dollar into the grave where his grandfather's body lay.

"Goodbye Pops," he mumbled under his breath. "Don't spoil your supper," Pez echoed, smiling. Those were the words Poppy had used when he gave Pez the coin so long ago. He closed his eyes and almost heard his Poppy whispering, "I love you, Kiddo." He smiled sadly, so much closer to losing it again like he did in his grandmother's arms.

Pez walked back over to his mother and stood next to her. He felt the tiniest bit better and the feeling seemed to be growing. Sometimes trying to say good-bye to someone who was already gone was so freeing; other times it was the worst feeling in the world. He waited for his only sibling to say good-bye to a grandmother he hardly knew.

The situation was different for Stevie while they were growing up. Carole devoted all her attention to Stevie. She never had time for poor little D, who felt as if he had lost his father and his mother. He often found himself staying at Nanah & Poppy's house for weeks on end. His grandparents were quite happy to have a small child in their lives again. All of their own children had already grown up and started families of their own.

Looking around, Pez noticed some of the Spencers were gawking at him again. He felt very awkward wearing his father's suit. The sleeves were too long and the pants were too short, showcasing his dirty sneakers. But it was all Carole could find for him to wear, even though Stevie got a brand new suit. He knew that's not why they were staring at him. It wasn't his long hair pulled into a ponytail at the back of his neck that they were staring at either. It was the green pea coat jacket he wore. It had been his father's and he refused to go to the funeral if he couldn't wear it. He'd already given up his scarf. He'd taken it off and left it in the car, but he could never voluntarily leave the jacket behind.

He rolled his eyes toward the sky, trying to ignore the staring relatives. They were probably offended that he wanted to honor his own father's memory, by wearing the jacket his father had been murdered in. Most of the Spencers didn't even consider Pez part of their family anymore, now that his father was gone. He smiled as he absently fingered a bullet hole in the front of it. Little did they know there was still some of his father's blood staining the inside the jacket. His smile turned smug at the morbid thoughts he was having. None of these people had lost what he had. None of them could know or even fathom what it was like to lose their father at such a young age. No one here knew what it was like to grow up father-less and somewhat mother-less. No one knew what it was like to watch you own father mur… No, not that.

No one knew the pain that was Pez.

Pez tried to turn his thoughts to less morbid things. The cloud covering the sun just then looked a lot like…

"…a dragon," D finished, growling and clawing at the air, with his scary monster face on. He giggled and looked at his Daddy for approval.

"It does, doesn't it?" Daddy replied, smiling the biggest smile six year-old D had ever seen. This was young D's favorite game. Daddy pointed to the eastern sky above Johansson Park. "That one over there looks like a deer," Daddy pointed out.

"And there's the hunter, over there sneaking up on the deer. Quiet… Quiet and then POW! Just like you Daddy. Just like you. He's even got a big gun just like yours Daddy!" D looked at his father again. Daddy was looking at the same sky, but he had a faraway look in his eyes.

D waited impatiently for his father to reply. Finally D could no longer stand waiting. He looked around and spotted some ducks walking near the pond. He jumped off of the picnic table that they were laying on top of. He found a stick that resembled a gun and started walking towards them slowly, stalking them. He was a hunter. He snuck slowly towards the ducks and lifted his pretend gun. "POW!" he screamed loudly, laughing as the ducks ran. He chased after them trying to catch them, before they made it back to the safety of the water. He never saw how his father jumped at the sudden noise. He never saw the haunted look that filled his father's eyes— the terror that showed for a split second on his face. Daddy shook it off and jumped off of the picnic table.

"Look Daddy. I'm a hunter just like you," D said, showing Daddy his pretend gun.

"Guns are bad, D," his daddy informed him, taking away his stick and tossing it aside.

"But Daddy you like...," D began.

"No! They are bad!" Daddy lashed out. The words stung D as if he had done something wrong. His bottom lip began to quiver, as tears filled his eyes.

"I'm sorry, D," Daddy said, a smile spreading across his face. "You better watch out, because I'm a MONSTER and I eat hunters for dinner!" Daddy growled in his monster voice. He began to chase D playfully through the park. D squealed in joy, the ducks forgotten as his father caught him, lifted him into the air and began to tickle him. D struggled so fitfully that his Daddy lost his balance and they both tumbled to the ground shaking with laughter, gasping for air whenever the laughter would subside long enough to let them breathe.

Where did the laughter go?

sun shining through the willow trees
sprinkling the land with laughter
in the air a cool spring breeze
and here I sit dreading what comes after

people passing slowly by
stopping only to stare and chastise
I close my eyes and cry

in the distance, a million flies
buzzing, buzzing all around
the sound of stinking death

the swishing of the willow leaf
reminds me of the laughter on the ground
and I am shaken from my grief
but the laughter is gone, nowhere to be found

Pez was shaken from his memory, by the sun breaking free from the clouds. He was forced once again to face the reality of the present. He wondered how long he had been lost in the past. He looked blankly around at the graveside gathering; nothing had changed.

With sadness, he remembered what Nanah had explained to him when he asked why his daddy didn't like guns anymore. His father and some friends had been out hunting and his father's best friend somehow got caught in the line of fire. Pez's father watched helplessly as his own best friend died in his arms. That was the last time Pez's father had ever touched a gun.

He stood silently, letting the sun warm his tear streaked face. He waited for Stevie to gather all of the knowledge his grandmother was imparting onto him. Pez wondered what words were spoken between Nanah and Stevie, but from where he stood he couldn't make the one sided conversation out. He watched Nanah's lips move as she whispered words into Stevie's ear. He couldn't help feeling jealous and even a bit spiteful towards Stevie. First he had taken their mother's attention away from Pez and now he was trying to steal Nanah's. He knew that wasn't true, but he couldn't help feeling that way.

After Stevie rejoined his mother and brother, they began walking back towards their station wagon. As soon as they were out of the view of the Spencer clan, Pez's mom slapped him gently on the back of his head.

"Hey!" Pez yelped. He was more surprised than hurt. He grabbed the back of his head in a protective gesture. "What was that for?"

Pez's mom sighed and gave him a you-know-what-you-did look. "David," she began. "You could have shown more sympathy. Stevie hardly even knew Poppy, but at least he was crying."

Pez was shocked. Obviously his mother hadn't been paying attention to him while he was talking to Nanah. Stevie smiled proudly; glad to have done something right for a change. His smug little grin enraged Pez making him want to slap it right off of Stevie's cute little face.

Pez loved his brother more than anyone did, except for Carole. It was only natural for him to feel that way, the only family either of them really had was each other and their mom. Lately both of them had been getting on Pez's nerves.

"But Ma…," Pez protested, dropping his sunglasses in his coat pocket. He raised both of his hands to cover his face, forcibly rubbing his burning eyes. He didn't need this now. He didn't want to listen to anything she said, but what else could he do?

"No!" she cut him off, raising her hand as if that would stop any further protest from her son. It worked for the moment. "David," she started again after his mouth snapped shut. She was trying very hard to remain calm. "It wouldn't have been so bad if you weren't crying, but all you did was stand there with that stupid grin on your face." She paused then added as an afterthought: "You looked like you were glad that he died!" she whispered harshly; she was fuming.

"But Nanah…," he tried again to get a word in. Those were the only two his mother would allow.

"What Nanah does is her own business," she snapped.

"I'm sorry, Mom," Pez said slowly, trying to sound like he meant it. He was hoping that an apology would calm his mother down.

"What were you thinking?" she asked, no longer bothering to hide the anger she felt at her son's behavior.

"Nothing … It was stupid," Pez resigned.

"Well it didn't look very stupid. In fact, it looked pretty funny to me. Was it a joke of some sort?" Pez shook his head refusing to answer. "No, David! You are not getting out of this that easily! I want to know what was so funny that would make any child laugh at his own grandfather's funeral," she insisted; still he refused to speak. "Did you even think about how you made everyone else feel? Did you think about what they might think of you? You were being selfish, obnoxious, and rude! I want to know what you were thinking and I want to know now!" she demanded, threatening to hit him, even though they both knew she couldn't bring herself to follow through with the threat.

Pez sighed, giving up. He knew how futile fighting would be. His mother always seemed to win somehow. "OK fine!

Do you want to know what I was thinking? I'll tell you! I was just thinking that…," he paused, fighting back the tears and painful memories. He drew in a deep shaky breath. He never thought he would be voicing his private thoughts to anyone, much less his own mother. "I was thinking that maybe…," he started slowly. "Maybe dying of natural causes is better than being killed. I liked the way Poppy died! Are you satisfied now? I LIKE THE WAY HE DIED!!!" he screamed. He was quite positive the rest of the Spencers heard him. He didn't care; let all the Spencers think he was crazy. After all, she started it. She's the one that wanted to know. He just told her the truth.

He flung open the car door and slid into the back seat of his mom's freshly washed station wagon. He slammed the door shut behind him, so hard he hoped the window would break. As soon as it was shut, his carefully built walls collapsed. The tears that the walls had been holding back came pouring out of him. He threw himself down against the bench seat and cried. He cried harder than he had in as long as he could remember.

How could she accuse him of being glad that anyone was dead? Especially Grandpa Spencer; he loved Poppy almost as much as he loved his own father. He was just glad that Poppy had led a happy and full life, rather than having his life cut short like everyone else Pez loved.

Stevie looked from his mommy to the car. His mother stood in shock, looking as if she had just been slapped. Tears were beginning to form in Stevie's big brown eyes.

"Don't worry, Stevie, baby. D's just sad."

"About Poppy?" Stevie asked in a quiet voice.

"Well, that and I think he is still sad about his friends." she replied just as quietly. She was no longer angry with her mourning son.

"The ones that died?" Stevie asked. The fact that Stevie knew about D's friends shocked Carole. She decided when David's friends died that Stevie was too young to hear about such a tragedy. Somehow he had figured it out on his own. She realized with joy that her youngest son was more intelligent than the doctor's thought he would be. Stevie was diagnosed as mildly brain damaged from the traumatic circumstances surrounding his early birth and his father's death, both of which occurred on the same night.

"Yes, sweetie, that's right," she replied, looking sadly at the car where David sat crying. How could she have been so blind to his pain? How could she have forgotten about his friends? It had been just over a year since the accident. How could she expect him to be over his mourning so soon? She shook her head softly as she climbed into the car.

She glanced into the rearview mirror to check on her mourning son. He was sitting up now scribbling frantically into his ever present notebook.

aching with despair
filled with longing
but no one is there
empty and barren
the field before me
am I wrong to think
forever empty it will be
aching and breaking
down in it
down in it all
slowly sinking
my back against the wall
holding on grasping
and longing
for the love that
slipped away
yet all the while
sinking further down
this unending spiral
I am lost in my
aching nothingness
with only myself
to keep me
company

2

Pez struggled fitfully, trying to break free from the ethereal dreams the held him prisoner. He tried to scream. He tried to call out to his mother, his friends, anyone who would listen, but the words were trapped in his throat with no hopes of escaping. He tried to grab at his throat to remove the icy hands, which had enclosed his esophagus, but he could no longer move his hands. He couldn't move any of his muscles; he was paralyzed. His body shivered involuntarily as the icy hands tried to pull him under, tried to bury him in his own dreams. He struggled unsuccessfully trying to speak, but each time he tried, the hands closed tighter around his neck. They closed so tightly that at one point he could no longer breathe.

14

Finally, it was over. He sat up gasping for air, covered in a cold sweat. He tried to rationalize what just happened to him. He tried to convince himself that it had just been a nightmare; a night terror, but it felt so real, too real. He couldn't seem to stop his heart from beating so fast.

"*It's your fault, you know,*" a voice whispered within the depths of his soul. "*They're all dead and it's all your fault.*" It was true, the voice was right. He had killed all of them and nothing could ever bring them back. That was when the tears came, slowly building up inside Pez until he found himself sobbing uncontrollably.

"DAVID SPENCER!" his mother yelled from the bottom of the stairs. "GET YOUR ASS OUT OF BED! YOU JUST MISSED YOUR BUS AGAIN AND I WILL **NOT** DRIVE YOU THIS TIME!" The tone of her voice stopped his sobbing immediately.

Using his bedspread, Pez quickly dried his tears. He shook his head and shrugged. He didn't care whether or not his mother would drive him to school. If she didn't drive him, he could just call his friend Matt and catch a ride with him.

'Matt never goes to school before second hour,' Pez thought, as he picked up the phone next to his bed. It wasn't his own phone line, but an extension of his mother's phone line. The receiver was on his ear and he was dialing Matt's number before the horrid realization struck him.

"*By the way, Matt's dead,*" the voice whispered, but Pez didn't need the voice to tell him that. He knew Matt was dead. He set the receiver back down in the cradle. He was in a daze wondering how Matt died when the voice piped in again.

"*Oh, come on... You remember, don't you?*" The voice was trying to tempt Pez into a memory trance, but Pez didn't want to remember. Pez didn't want to see any of it again. He wanted to forget it ever happened. That horrid voice in his head had other plans. "*Remember how Wolf touched you? Remember how his hand grasped your shirt, pleading for you to stop the inevitable? Remember the look in his eyes... Or how about what he said to you? Do you remember what his last words were? Come on! Surely you can remember what Amber was screaming into that cold morning air.*" Just then the voice took on a feminine quality; it **was** Amber's voice he now heard ringing through his head. "*MURDERER! YOU BASTARD! YOU KILLED THEM ALL! THEY'RE ALL DEAD BECAUSE OF YOU!*" Her voice was full of such raw emotion. It made Pez whimper in shame.

"Matt's dead," Pez spoke to himself out loud, trying to drown out the screaming voice that still echoed through his aching brain. "Just like Penny and Amber and Diamond and Glenn and Wolf..." His voice broke at the mention of Wolf's name. "All of them," he murmured softly into the silence of his room.

"Isn't it funny how everyone who tells you that they love you DIES!" the voice snickered inside of his head. Pez grimaced in pain.

"Why don't you just SHUT THE FUCK UP!" he screamed angrily. He was furious that the voice was back after at least a week of lying dormant inside his psyche. Most of all, he was angry that he heard the voice at all. Normal, sane people did not hear voices.

"I'm sorry, but what did you just say to me?" his mom asked as she appeared in the doorway of his room. She was beyond pissed off.

"I wasn't talking to you," Pez grumbled with distaste, not even thinking about what he was saying. He was embarrassed that his mother heard him talking to... yelling at the voice that only he heard.

Carole massaged her temples, carefully so as not to disturb her impeccable hair and makeup. "OK, so who exactly were you talking to?" she asked, looking around the room trying to find the mysterious visitor that her son had been yelling at. Finding no one there, she glared at Pez and waited for him to answer "Well?" she asked. She was the perfect picture of anger. Her head was cocked as if she were listening to something; her arms were crossed before her and her feet were spread slightly apart. Her foot was tapping impatiently on the hardwood floor of his bedroom. Pez thought the picture would be complete if her hands were on her hips and her head was bobbing in time with her words. He stifled a giggle at that mental image.

"Hah! Now she thinks you're crazy too," the voice laughed. *"Everyone thinks you're crazy, because... YOU ARE!!"*

"Myself," Pez answered softly. He pressed his fists against his temples in a futile attempt to rid his head of the dreaded voice.

"Who?" his mother demanded.

"MYSELF!" Pez yelled, throwing back his covers.

"Are you on drugs?" she asked, automatically her hands went to her hips and her head began bobbing. "Do I have to send you back to rehab, mister?" Pez stifled another laugh. Not only was it funny that his mom had mirrored his earlier mental image, but she called him mister too. That was the funniest part of all.

"Ha-ha! If only it were as simple as rehab!" the voice whispered softly. *"She should send you back to that place. Just so they can torture you again."*

For a split second, Pez flashed on the memory of the torture hospital they called rehab. "No MOTHER!" he screamed and then lowered his voice, trying to calm himself down. "I'm not on drugs!" he claimed truthfully. Her general lack of trust made him angry. He jumped out of his bed and stumbled across his messy floor to the dresser. He pulled out a pair of black jeans and yanked them on. He grabbed a random tee shirt off of the floor and pressed it to his nose. It didn't stink, so he pulled it on.

He was beginning to feel self-conscious with his mother standing in the doorway watching his every move. "I don't need to go to rehab!" he stated as he forcefully stepped into his shoes, not even bothering to tie them. He grabbed his father's old green jacket and pulled it on. "I need to go to jail!" He grabbed his red and white striped scarf. The scarf was a gift from his father, given to Pez on the Christmas before he died.

He pushed passed his mother and stalked down the hallway, shoving Stevie out of his way. He heard his mother scrambling to follow him, so he walked even faster. He just wanted to get away from his mother's constant bickering. Bitching at Pez seemed to be her new favorite hobby. That's all she really did lately.

His mother was moving faster than he was.

"Why?" she asked as she grabbed his arm, stopping him at the bottom of the stairs. "How can you say that, David?"

He stood in front of his only salvation for the time being; the front door. He broke out of her grip.

"Because... I KILLED THEM ALL!!" he screamed in anguish, each word louder than the last. He ran out the door and slammed it behind him, right in his mother's face.

Pez thought he had time to tie his shoes, but Carole recovered from the shock faster than he thought she would. She opened the door, her mouth open as if to ask another stupid question. He opted for tucking the laces in instead of tying them.

He stood up and looked his mother directly in the eyes. "I killed the only person who's ever **truly** loved me," he said softly. He watched his mother's mouth snap shut in surprise. She was speechless. He knew it couldn't last long. Quickly he turned away from his house and ran down the street. He tried not to listen to his mother as she stood on the porch screaming.

"DAVID! WAIT HONEY! I'LL GIVE YOU A RIDE. YOU DON'T NEED TO RUN!"

Pez didn't want her to drive him to school. She would only lecture him and belittle him some more.

"YOU COULD HAVE AT LEAST CHANGED YOUR UNDERWEAR!" he heard her screaming.

Pez chuckled through his tears. He wondered what the neighbors must think. They had to be really mad; he knew **he** would be if he heard some crazy lady screaming about underwear at seven in the morning. That was the third scene like that in the past week. This was the only time she had told him to change his underwear though.

Pez couldn't wait for graduation. 'School sucks,' he thought to himself as he turned in the direction leading away from school.

3

<u>Stones of forever</u>

I listen in the air
and I can feel you there
next to me
and I long to be
in your strong arms
with your caress
infatuated by your charms

I long to be with you
but you are gone
I look across
the green, green lawn
broken only by the stones
stones of forever
marking
the place where you lie

Pez stopped. He needed to catch his breath. He stood for a moment or two staring in awe at the sight before him. The pale morning sun lit up the plot where David "Wolf" Waverly lay. It was so beautiful to Pez, as if the spotlight that Wolf enjoyed in life shone on him in death too.

Pez sat down next to Wolf's barely sunken in grave. He rested his hand on the mound and imagined that he could feel the warmth of his lover's touch against his skin. He smiled as a warm breeze blew through his just passed shoulder length blond hair. The smile faded sadly as he reached into his pocket and pulled out a picture.

Pez stared at the picture as he crossed his legs. The picture wasn't an old one, but it looked old with wear. The corners were bent, and the bottom right one had a slight rip in it. A tearstain was in the upper left hand corner just above the young man's head. It had been folded at one time, and now there was a crease running down the middle of it. The crease separated a young man and woman that stared up at Pez, who had taken the picture. They were both smiling happily.

Pez had been the photographer of the group. He loved taking pictures back then. In fact, he probably still had some disposable cameras filled with pictures lying around his bedroom, waiting to be developed.

The young man in the photo was Wolf. He had long curly black hair, which fell around his shoulders in soft, shimmering strands. Pez wished he could touch Wolf's hair once more. Wolf's brown eyes were glowing with such happiness in this photo. Pez had never before noticed that Wolf and Diamond had the same eyes, not until this moment. This photograph made their Native American heritage more apparent.

His gaze shifted to the young woman in the photo. It was Diamond, Wolf's younger sister. She had short black hair with streaks of fluorescent blue throughout. Diamond was sticking out her pierced tongue at Pez. Her right nostril was pierced and so was her left eyebrow, both sporting delicate silver hoops.

Pez rested the picture on his leg just where his left one crossed over his right. He placed his other hand on the mound that was Diamond's grave. His eyes began to fill with tears. Both of the people in the photograph were gone. They were dead, just like all of the rest of them.

A tiny smile crossed Pez's face, but disappeared shortly after it had appeared. Now no one would know that Wolf was really the one he loved. Everyone except his friends thought that Pez and Diamond were going out. In truth it was Wolf that he had been dating. He wasn't quite sure he was ready to come out about being bisexual to his mom or anyone else for that matter. Only his friends knew the truth and they were all dead. How can you talk when you are six feet under? His secret was safe. No one else would ever know now, unless Pez wanted someone to.

He closed his eyes to stop the torrent of tears that was threatening to break free. As soon as he closed them, the memories came rushing into his mind. At first, they came in flashes. Nothing in particular stood out: parties, drugs, kisses, flavors, caresses, laughter, smells, silences, angry words, passionate words, and fun; all memories of friendships now gone.

Then suddenly the whirlwind of emotions and memories gathered and melted into one giant memory. It was the kind of memory that Pez frequently lost himself in. This memory was so real for Pez that it was hard for him to realize that it was **only** a memory and not the actual events occurring again. He had to keep reminding himself that it was just a memory, a vision and nothing more.

Pez found himself in a darkened room filled with smoke. He could actually smell the smoke; he could feel it burning his eyes. He could feel it filling his lungs with every breath. The smoke he smelled was not a bad smoke... no, this was a good smoke: part fog machine, part cigarette smoke, mingled with the sweet incense-like smell of cloves. Oh, how he loved those clove cigarettes.

The room was very large, but crowded. The music was loud and the bass was shaking the building to its foundation. It did not take Pez very long to recognize this place. It was Skate 'Til You Drop, the local roller rink/night club. Pez and his friends had always fondly referred to it as "Roller E" or sometimes just plain "E". They called it that because when you took ecstasy (the drug of choice for Pez and his friends) you 'rolled'.

The Roller E had been an abandoned warehouse on the industrial side of town, up until a few years before when a group of ravers/skateboarders/inline skaters bought it. They turned it into the best underground rave scene party zone in town; hell, all of Michigan really.

It was comprised of five rooms, each named for the activity that occurred in it. The room Pez was standing in was called the Rink Room. It was a standard roller rink with a snack bar. The bathrooms were located in this room as well as a small DJ booth, which was suspended in the air just to the side of the rink. Most of the teenagers hung out here, never knowing that the other rooms even existed.

On the left side of the Rink Room was the Ramp Room where most of the skateboarders and Inline skaters hung out. In that room a miniature street course was setup for a variety of extreme sports. Also in the Ramp Room was a half-pipe where the vertical tricks were executed. Technically the Roller E was not supposed to have a 14 foot vert ramp in the back room, so they had to keep that room pretty exclusive. Pez had been in there a couple of times, but skateboarding wasn't his thing.

The other rooms were located in the basement; you weren't allowed to wear your skates down there. The downstairs contained two rooms that Pez knew quite well. To get to either of those rooms, you first had to travel through the R-cade, which was a pretty large scale arcade with many of the more recent games and many of the classics too. The usual arcade noises were drowned out by the music of whatever DJ was spinning that night in the Rave Room. The Rave Room was Pez's favorite room. That room helped to make the Roller E a second home to Pez in the years that he spent with his friends.

The last room was another of Pez's favorites. It was an exclusive room, only open to friends of the owners. It was said to be the headquarters of the owners of this whole semi-legal operation. The owners had remodeled the offices of the original factory into a small apartment. This room was essentially their living room. Pez had visited it many times before. He loved the secrecy of it. He loved the winding tunnels the owners built to keep the room a secret. It was so exclusive that it didn't have an official name, although he and his friends had dubbed it the Riot room. This was the place where you could get some of the best mind-blowing, brain-altering drugs. Pez loved the Riot room and all the drugs that came with it.

All of this came rushing back to Pez as he stood on the edge of the roller rink with the backs of his legs supported against one of the mushroom shaped benches. He knew this was the night the photograph had been taken. That night Pez and all of his friends had gathered at the E to celebrate Diamond's birthday. They were all there: Diamond, Wolf, Sal, Penny, Glenn, Eddie, Matt, Diamond's boyfriend, and Mike, Wolf's boyfriend. Glenn and Eddie had brought their girlfriends too, but Pez didn't know them very well.

It was on this night that Pez decided it was time to come clean to Wolf about the feelings he had for him. Some of the other guys in the group were bi-sexual, but Wolf was the only one who was all out men only and Pez wanted him. He liked Wolf from the first day he met him. It wasn't until the night of Diamond's birthday party that Pez worked up enough nerve to finally tell Wolf how he felt.

"Hey Diamond," Pez greeted as he skated up to the table in the snack bar where Diamond sat alone eating French fries. She looked up at Pez and smiled brightly. He tossed a small stuffed teddy bear onto the table and smiled crookedly. "Happy birthday!" Pez wished her. "I won it from the crane," he said proudly. "I hope you like it." He began rubbing the back of his neck nervously. "It only took about five dollars." The only reason Pez had tried to get it out of the crane was because he felt guilty. He didn't even know it was her birthday, so he hadn't brought her a present.

"Oh Pezzie, I do. Thanks, it's the bestest gift I've gotten so far!" Diamond exclaimed, jumping up and kissing Pez on the cheek. She neglected to tell him that it had been the only present she got that night; he found that fact out later.

"I wouldn't go that far," Pez told her, feeling embarrassed by her show of emotion and ashamed because he hadn't been thoughtful enough to get her a real present.

"Well, it's definitely the cutest." She smiled again, flashing her tongue ring as she sank back into her chair. "Look, he even matches my hair."

Pez laughed. She was right; the teddy bear was black with an electric blue nose, ears, and paws. Pez straightened his jacket and scarf in another nervous gesture. He didn't know why

Diamond made him so nervous. He took a deep breath. "I've got a question to ask..." Pez announced slowly. He didn't want to ask her, because if he did, then there would be no turning back. Pez still wasn't sure he could actually do what he planned to do. Diamond's eyes lit up in anticipation that Pez failed to notice. He was too busy worrying about what was to come. She nodded, waiting for him to ask his question.

"Have you seen Wolf?" Pez asked, not bothering to hide the smile that came to him whenever he spoke that name. Pez didn't notice her crest-fallen look as she shook her head in response, then seemed to take a greater interest in her fries.

Pez looked around and finally spotted Wolf across the crowded Rink Room. His heart seemed to stop for a minute as he took a deep breath and made his way towards Wolf. He didn't even notice the lonesome tear that rolled down Diamond's glitter-covered check.

Why couldn't he see that she wanted him? At the time, he had been oblivious to that fact, but looking back now he could see it in every move she made. She wanted him.

Pez skated quietly into the men's room behind Wolf. Surprised to see Pez's reflection in the mirror, Wolf spun around to greet him. Pez sighed as Wolf met his gaze. Pez had never been so infatuated with someone before. Not even Lisa, his ex-girlfriend, had made him feel this way. Pez felt butterflies in his stomach.

He stood there gazing at Wolf quietly, trying to remember what he planned to say.

Wolf was wearing tight black jeans and a white tee shirt. His long hair (which was usually tied back into a ponytail) was cascading freely down his shoulders in soft black curls. Pez longed to run his fingers through it.

Before Wolf had the chance to even get a greeting out, Pez remembered what he wanted to say. So he gathered up all his nerve and forced himself to ask the question that he and Sal had finally decided would be the best. "What would you say if I asked you to kiss me?" His voice faded somewhere near the last words and he was afraid that Wolf didn't hear them.

Apparently, he did hear them. His eyes opened wide with surprise as he tried to stammer out a response. Pez knew that nothing but the direct approach would work now, if there was any chance of getting together with Wolf. This is what he wanted; it was not an overnight decision on Pez's part. He didn't just wake up this morning and say, "Hey, I think I'm going to be gay today."

He had spent the last few weeks wondering what making out with Wolf would be like and struggling with the strangeness of these new feelings inside of him. He'd been dreaming of Wolf's touch ever since their first shared smile. He wanted this, more than anything. HE WANTED THIS. The only thing standing in Pez's way was Wolf's current boyfriend: Mike.

Wolf stood before Pez, still trying to work out an answer from his speechless lips. Pez didn't wait, the question was meant to be rhetorical anyway. Pez skated closer to Wolf. He took a deep breath and went for it. Pez's lips met Wolf's lips and his arms encircled Wolf's waist awkwardly. Wolf resisted at first, but then gave in. He wrapped his arms around Pez's shoulders. Surprised, Pez pulled away. "What about Mike?" Pez asked softly.

"Mike who?" Wolf answered, smiling slyly. Wolf knew the man he really wanted was here in his arms. "I love this song," Wolf whispered, and then promptly resumed kissing Pez. Pez smiled inwardly, for his lips were otherwise occupied. The song that was playing was his favorite song: "Pictures of you." by the Cure.

the feeling lingers
as our lips slowly part
my eyes are open
they stare into yours
your eyes of deep brown
sparkle so brightly
with happiness
with love
that I cannot help
but to spread my
lips again
craving for more

That moment was one of his most cherished memories. The memory of the song that had been playing filled him with deep sorrow and a sense of irony; for all that was left now were pictures of Wolf.

Thinking of Wolf and that night made him think about all of his other friends. He thought about how everyone's search for their soul mate eventually led them into the arms of another in the group. He remembered how hard it was to keep track of who was dating whom. The only two who were exclusive with each other were Penny and Sal. Their searches had ended; they found their soul mates in each other. Pez smiled as he thought of his friends. His tears faded as he drifted into another memory trance.

"I need to talk to you," Sal confessed, smiling shyly looking at Pez. They were on the roof of Sal's apartment building. Pez was beginning to get nervous. He didn't know Sal as well as he knew the rest of his crowd. This was before Pez & Sal became such good friends. In fact, it was probably one of the reasons they became such good friends in the end.

"OK, but why do we have to talk on the roof?" Pez asked, looking down sixteen stories to the ground below. He shivered. He didn't know if the shiver was caused by his fear of heights or the chilly November breeze that blew wildly across the rooftop. Pez adjusted his scarf to keep out the cold air. All at once, he was glad that he never went anywhere without it.

"It's a little more private up here," Sal replied. He smiled when he noticed Pez's tentative fear.

"Private?" Pez squeaked. The last time he heard that word, some pervert at the E tried to rape him. The man had lured Pez back into the coatroom with the prospect of drugs. Then the creepy man tried to have sex with him in the coatroom because it was so 'private'. That was one of his first times at the Roller E.

"Not for anything like that!" Sal exclaimed, laughing.

Pez missed his laugh.

"I just didn't want Penny to hear what I'm going to ask you. I AM going to ask you," he said more to himself then to Pez. He paused for a moment searching for words. "I just wanted to tell you something." He made a face that told Pez that wasn't quite what he wanted to say. "I need your advice on something, something I don't think I could ask anyone else."

"Why me?" Pez asked. He was surprised that anyone would trust him after what he did to Wolf and Mike. He was flattered that Sal trusted him enough to keep a big secret, like the one he was sure Sal was going to tell him.

"You're different... from the others. You understand what love is," Sal explained. "You love Wolf, don't you?" he

asked. Pez nodded. "Can you ever see yourself with anyone, but him?"

Pez thought hard for a minute and tried to imagine a life with someone other than Wolf, but he couldn't. "No," he finally replied truthfully, smiling at the image of he and Wolf growing old together.

"See what I mean?" Pez didn't have a clue as to what Sal was talking about, but that was partly because of the pot they had just smoked. He nodded as if he understood. It was strange he could understand the most abstract theories and stories and totally believe in them when he smoked pot, but when someone tried to talk about everyday life his mind just went blank.

"I want to show you something... and ask your advice," Sal ventured.

Pez cleared his throat, still a tad bit nervous at Sal's need for privacy. "Um...OK."

Sal looked around as if searching for something. Finally he shrugged and sat down on the ledge. He let his feet dangle in the open air. Pez fought the urge to scream and pull him away from the ledge. Instead of doing just that, he sat down next to him hesitantly, facing the safety of the roof. Pez kept his back to the vast empty space that lay between them and the ground. A cold breeze snaked into his coat somehow and gave him a violent chill. He tried to suppress any further chills, fearing that the force of them might cause him to fall of the ledge and plummet to his death.

"I love Penny so much... more than anything. You know that right?" Sal asked quietly.

"Everybody knows that, Sal." Pez smiled. He decided it would be safer for him to sit on the roof and rest the back of his head on the ledge. He moved and looked up at Sal's face as he continued.

"I was thinking...," he began quickly, but lost it just as fast as he began. He tried again slower this time. "I've been thinking about this a lot lately, a lot meaning all the time. I think I'm... what... Do you... I...," he stammered uselessly. Whatever it was he was trying to say would not come out, no matter how hard he tried or how he phrased it. He gave up trying to speak. Instead he reached into his coat pocket. "HOW?" he forced the single word out. He held something down towards Pez. Pez climbed back up onto the ledge—fear temporarily forgotten—to examine what Sal held out before him. It was a small blue velvet box.

"How what?" he asked, smiling. Sal's silence assured him his assumption about the box was correct. He opened it to

find a beautiful silver ring with a small diamond mounted on it. Pez looked at Sal who sat quietly staring down at the ground, watching Penny and the others playing in the new fallen snow.

"I know it's a little small, but she likes silver the best," Sal explained to him in a small voice, not taking his gaze off of the people below.

"You're going to ask her to marry you?" Sal nodded. "You want my advice on how to ask her?" He nodded again.

The memory shifted then to New Year's Eve that same year.

The ten friends and their boyfriends or girlfriends at that time were gathered at Sal's apartment celebrating the coming of the new year. Loudly they counted down the seconds to midnight. Everyone was smiling in anticipation of the big event of the evening. Finally, when the clock struck midnight—instead of cheering, making noise and kissing—the room dropped into a deafening silence. Pez could hear parties elsewhere in the apartment building raging with excitement.

Penny looked around in shock at the total change in character of all her usually loud and boisterous friends. She returned her gaze to Sal who was on his knees in front of her, holding out the ring. Despite all the trouble Sal had while trying to talk to Pez about the subject, he said in a loud clear voice, "Penny, I love you more than anything. I have loved you from the first day I saw you. Will you marry me?" Penny broke into tears and nodded happily. Sal stood up and put the ring on her finger. He smiled and stared deeply into her eyes with a love that Pez could almost feel. She threw her arms around his neck and kissed him.

That kiss was the silence breaker. Everyone burst into cheers at once. The apartment that would soon be Sal & Penny's was filled with cheers almost as deafening as the silence had been. Pez would never forget the beauty of that moment; a man and a woman in love, sharing that love with everyone they knew.

<u>her answer</u>

the ring
glistens
in the dim
light of

the moon
silver shining
brightly against
the blue
velvet
of the box
he kneels
before her
afraid of her
rejection
but the answer
is already there
in her eyes
as she throws
her arms
around him
in joy

The memory shifted once more to a hazy recollection of the aftermath of the accident. Sal was pulling his wife out of the burning, twisted wreckage of his car. He was sobbing as he tried desperately to revive her broken body. Her neck & back were twisted at such a strange angle; there was no doubt in Pez's mind that both were broken. Sal howled in frustration as he watched her life slip away. Sal obviously blamed himself for the accident, not knowing that Pez was the actual cause of it. Sobbing, he laid down next to her dead body. He placed his bloody head against her stomach. He was listening for sounds of the life he helped create inside Penny, but there was nothing. He closed his eyes, blood from the gash on his forehead mixing with Penny's lifeblood.

Even now, Pez could hear his muffled sobs as Sal buried his face into Penny's lifeless stomach. Pez pounded his fists against his forehead. Every memory always led him back to that one. Some people say that sometimes, when you are in any sort of trauma, your body goes into a state of shock and most likely you will block out the events surrounding said trauma. That wasn't true for Pez; he could remember every minor detail of the crash. The memory of the accident was so fresh in his mind that it could have happened yesterday. Sometimes, like this one, the memory of the accident would keep repeating in a vicious cycle that threatened to push Pez over the edge. Pez pushed up the sleeve on his left arm. He dug his nails into the flesh of his arm as hard as he could. It was the only way that Pez had found to free himself from the memory loops he would get caught in.

To Pez, every day seemed to be a constant battle for his sanity. He tried so hard not to think about the accident, but the visions, the memories, the voices kept breaking through. Quite often he felt that all of the voices and memories would drive him insane, but somehow he held on. He frequently wondered why he fought so hard to hold on when there was nothing for him to live for… anymore.

Pez took a deep breath and forced his mind away from the memories. He wiped the tears from his eyes with the back of his dirty hand. He hadn't even realized he was crying until then.

He wiped his hands on his jeans and replaced the picture to its normal spot in his coat pocket, where it would be close to his heart. The picture was safe there.

He blinked as he looked up into the sky, wondering what time it was. When he was a small boy, his father taught him how to tell time by the position of the sun, but it had happened so long ago that he couldn't remember now. His father was another topic that Pez didn't wish to dwell on.

"I wish you could hear me, Wolf," Pez whispered as he stood up. "I miss you. It's so hard now, without you." He walked over to the headstone. This was his prayer, his tradition. He closed his eyes and the words came without any thought… he began reciting the chorus to Treasure by The Cure, this was his mantra. He smiled as he remembered once again.

He was tracing his finger across Wolf's back as he read the Cure shirt that Wolf was wearing. He lifted up the shirt and traced his finger across the words tattooed on Wolf's back exactly as they had been on the shirt.

"Hey!" Wolf cried out in shock.

"What?" Pez asked. Wolf was sprawled out on his bed half dozing. Pez had been watching TV.

"I was just about to fall asleep," Wolf informed him groggily.

"I'm sorry," Pez apologized.

"Don't be. Just do it again," he said sensuously. Pez read the words again and this time Wolf joined him in reciting them. "Do it again," he said, his voice sounding sleepier. Pez obeyed and ended it with a kiss in the small of Wolf's back. "I will never get tired of hearing those words."

Pez repeated the phrase a second time into the silence of the graveyard. This time he could hear Wolf's voice repeating the lines with him. Suddenly he felt someone standing near him, he opened his eyes. No one was there.

As he started to head out of the graveyard, something or someone caught his eye. He turned to see someone standing by a headstone shaped like a giant urn. "Wolf!" He couldn't help but cry out his lover's name. He looked at the person standing by the grave. It wasn't Wolf. It didn't look anything like Wolf. It was probably just someone visiting a loved one. He could feel the embarrassment creeping up on him, making his face feel hot. He had just turned into the boy who cried Wolf.

The person didn't seem to mind. In fact, the person didn't even notice Pez. "Hello?" Pez called out to the person. He started to walk towards the man. When he got about halfway there, the man finally looked up and noticed Pez. Then he turned his head and looked down at the ground near the urn. He seemed to want Pez to see what he was looking at.

Pez took a few more steps towards him. "Who are you?" Pez asked. The man just lowered his head in shame. He pointed at the ground and then disappeared. Pez blinked his eyes rapidly and shook his head. Did he really just see that?

He walked over to the urn and looked at the ground nearby. There was a headstone that read: James Stanley Mackenzie. Next to the headstone was a tree with the name "Lisa" carved into it. His mind went into overdrive as he made the connection. The man had been Lisa's uncle. When did Lisa's Uncle die? Why had Pez seen him? He took a deep breath and made his way quickly to the gates surrounding the graveyard. He had to get out of there fast. This graveyard was starting to creep him out.

"It's a cemetery. Graveyard sounds so morbid," Glenn's voice echoed in his head. Pez ignored it. He was still too freaked out by the man he had just seen. He shook his head. Maybe he had just imagined it.

He paused outside of the cemetery and planned his next move. His growling stomach begged him to stop at the café before going to school. He turned and headed in the direction of the café, which unfortunately was in the same direction as school. He wasn't ready to face the crowded halls of his school yet, not while he was still talking to himself, he realized as the words escaped his lips.

"I thought that was you in the cemetery," Pez was saying out loud. He imagined Wolf walking beside him. He glanced around and seeing the streets empty, he continued to babble to no one in particular.

"Why did you have to die?" he said sadly, full of anger; not towards Wolf, but angry at himself. "I wish I would have died instead," he whispered. "I never liked it here anyway. You at least made living fun again, but now you're gone. You're dead and I'm dead too," Pez whispered miserably. He glanced to his side, but Wolf wasn't there.

He heard the familiar sound of rushing water. He was surprised to find himself at the bridge already. He must have been walking faster than he thought he was. He stopped in the middle of the bridge and slowly looked at the beautiful sky around him. He looked down at the tiny river below him. Everything was so beautiful. He had never before stopped and admired the beauty of nature like this. He smiled. It was wonderful. He could learn to like just standing so still and staring at the beauty.

"Too bad Wolf isn't here to enjoy this with me," he said with a sigh and closed his eyes. He took a deep breath, inhaling the stench of the river below. He wished someone would clean out the garbage in the river, and then maybe it wouldn't smell so bad. It never smelled like this when he was a child.

That is when the other voice came back, the voice he had heard earlier that day. This was the voice that above all else, forced him to believe that he was truly going crazy. Pez decided he would call the voice 'D'. D was the name of the boy who died when his father was killed. D was the name of a person who was dead. D was his name.

"You've just got to see the view from up here. It's amazing!" With his eyes closed Pez imagined he could see the form of a human standing on the hand railing, but when he opened his eyes, he saw no one there. He walked to the other side of the bridge and looked down at the rocks beside the tiny river. He was filled with sadness once again.

"*Don't be such a chicken-shit! Get up here! Come on, I know you want to,*" D urged. It was true. Pez did want to join him on the hand railing, as thin and slippery as it looked. Pez considered very carefully before making his final decision. This time Pez was prepared. This was the day he would finally do it, even without D's incessant urging. He was going to end his life and pay for his guilt with death.

"*You're so damn overdramatic, just shut up and do it!*" D commanded him. D seemed to be losing patience, if an imaginary voice could have patience. "*Now get up here and DO IT!*"

Pez rubbed his eyes in shock. He could actually see D standing up there; he looked just like Pez. "That's not possible...," he stammered. "You're not real!" he shouted out at the figure standing on the hand railing.

"*Not real?*" D asked. "*If I'm so not real, then why did you name me?*" he snarled. "*Maybe you're the one who's not real!*" D accused. Pez's mind reeled.

"No I'm real. I'M REAL!" Pez cried.

"*Look Pussy, if you're going to do this, you got to just do it. No hesitation... No thinking, nothing. You just jump,*" D scolded him for not moving faster. "*You just JUMP!*" D screamed at him. "*DO you need reasons? I can give you reasons! Do you remember how his hand closed around your shirt just next to your heart? He was begging for you to save him, begging for you to make the pain go away. You couldn't do it, could you? You couldn't stop him from dying. Do you know why? Do you? BECAUSE YOU WANTED HIM DEAD!!! YOU WANTED HIM TO DIE, so that you could become the sniveling little punk sissy that you are now. You needed him to die, so that people would treat you like they did after your precious Daddy died. Come on! You know it's true, it's just like Amber said.*"

Pez cringed in pain as Amber's voice filled his head once more. Her accusatory words alone would have been enough to make him do it, to make him jump. "*MURDERER! YOU BASTARD! YOU KILLED THEM ALL! THEY'RE ALL DEAD BECAUSE OF YOU!*"

Pez climbed carefully up onto the hand railing. He stood next to the hallucination of himself. He longed to reach out and touch the vision and see if he could feel the fabric of the identical coat that D wore. Pez could see D's face more clearly now. He looked as Pez imagined he looked last year; drug-eyed and sleep-deprived.

Pez smiled at his hallucination, the hallucination smiled back with yellowed teeth. *"That's only the first step, my friend,"* D informed him. Pez felt that he was really going to do it this time. He really was. He closed his eyes and imagined what it would feel like falling, spinning, with the wind blowing through his hair.

ℯ

sallow face
filled with hunger
angry eyes
filled with desire
a heart that is
empty
and longing to
fly
stepping over the
edge he closes
his eyes
the feeling of
fear only
lasts a moment
he soars
in ecstasy
and does not even
notice as his body
dies

He stood there balancing precariously on the edge. Once more, he looked down at the rocks below. He felt the shame and self-pity beginning to overwhelm him again. What kind of loser was he? He couldn't even keep his friends for longer than a couple of years; hell, he couldn't even keep them alive. How was he ever going to be able to live with the guilt boiling inside of him?

"Quit feeling sorry for yourself! You pussy! Just do it!" D shouted in his ear. Pez imagined he could feel flecks of D's spit hitting the side of his face. Pez half expected to feel D's hand shove him off the bridge. Pez knew that if the screaming hallucination beside him were an actual person it would have pushed Pez without hesitation. He closed his eyes. He felt like screaming. What the hell was he doing? He took a deep breath and held it, maybe then he wouldn't scream. Suddenly as he stood balancing on the railing, the dream that woke him earlier that morning came flooding back into his mind. It shook him so violently he almost lost his balance.

The dream had started with him standing exactly where he was now; on that very spot; on that very bridge. In the dream, his friends were somehow still alive. They surrounded him, standing on the bridge itself. They were begging him not to jump, not to kill himself.

(Could he hear them now?)

Still dreaming, he turned around to look down at them. He began to get angry for no reason, at least no reason that he knew of. He jumped back down from the ledge, landing amidst his friends. They cheered for him, happy that he decided to live. Happy he was still alive.

(Were they cheering now?)

He became enraged with such a feeling of hatred; one that he never felt before. He began to shove his friends one by one off of the bridge. Each one struggled, trying to break free, but Pez was stronger. He started with Wolf, his boyfriend; his love. Then Glenn, his best friend; Diamond, the girl who loved him; Sal, his closest friend, the one who asked Pez, out of all of the friends, to be his best man. And so on and so forth, until he was left standing alone on the bridge.

"Don't you get it? You're supposed to be DEAD!" he screamed as he watched the last one fall. Below him scattered on the rocks, lay the dead bodies of his only friends. He smiled and without any thoughts in his head, without fear, without pain he climbed onto the railing and stepped from the bridge. This was the way he wanted to die, the way he wanted to go: without any feeling at all. He began to laugh at the sheer rush of throwing himself off a bridge to the ground so far below him. He watched excited as the ground (still littered with the bodies of his friends) rushed

towards him. He laughed in joy knowing he would soon be with them.

He laughed even harder when he heard his mom's voice echoing through the dream, "If all your friends jumped off a bridge, would you follow them?" He laughed until he realized his friends were getting farther and farther away from him. He reached out to them, noticing then that his hands were covered with blood, their blood. That was when he started screaming. The hands that had closed around his neck were D's hands. D was trying to kill him.

Helpless

madly I grasp
at catching my past
not wanting to let go
yet wanting to move on
hating the change
reversal of roles
time flies and I watch
helpless
the shadow appears
as dark as night
I am filled with fear
knowing what will happen
he caresses me gently
I stand still
full of disgust yet
helpless
I watch in pain
as they all leave
One by One
never to be seen again
they all die and leave
me to myself
all alone

36

helpless
madly I grasp
at catching my past
not wanting to let go
yet wanting to move on
hating the change
reversal of roles
I am sad; it slips away
I am helpless
so helpless

Pez opened his eyes in horror, afraid that he did it. He was afraid that he would do it, afraid that he could actually jump, without even thinking about it. He let his breath out in a silent sigh of relief. He was still alive. He still stood wobbling uncertainly on the hand railing. He heard his mother's question repeat in his head and this time it didn't make him laugh; this time his mom actually made sense.

This wasn't right; this wasn't the way it was supposed to happen. Why was he scared? Why was he thinking twice? Why was he thinking of his mom, for God's sake? He jumped down from the railing, landing in a sprint towards the café before he could even consider climbing up there again. He ran fast, trying to leave behind the images that plagued his aching mind.

"Where are you going? WUSS!" D called after him. *"You'll never be able to do it!"* D screamed in frustration. Pez ran faster.

4

$\mathcal{P}$ez stopped just outside of the café to catch his breath. He couldn't seem to stop wheezing. When he finally recovered his breath, he walked into the café slowly, nervously. He was more than a little afraid of the memories that awaited him inside. It filled him with the pain of loneliness and remorse, to return to the 'hang out' of his long ago life and his long lost friends. Coming into the café again after all these months did not help the longing for companionship that he felt deep inside; it made him feel so much worse.

Pez smiled sadly as he looked around inside the empty café. The thick red velvet curtains were pulled back to let the

38

morning sun in.   He noticed how strange the café looked by daylight. It was so cheerful and happy, the complete opposite of what Pez was feeling inside. An image flashed in his head of those big, thick curtains closed blocking out any sounds of the small town surrounding it. Sometimes it made it seem as if the outside world didn't exist. When they were closed those curtains made the place seem dark and gloomy, but the clientele had always made the place seem happy and friendly.

Pez remembered the big soft couches with the fluffy pillows on them, which lined the walls of the café. With his eyes he searched for his favorite one, but it seemed that it was gone. It didn't surprise him. Lately it seemed like everything he knew was gone or different somehow.

His head was beginning to pound. He longed to lie down on one of the soft couches right now. He could almost feel the couch's softness pulling at him, urging him to lie down and sleep. His stomach growling pushed that idea right out of his head.

He walked slowly past a pool table. He grabbed the closest ball to him and rolled it into the other pool balls still spread out on the table. The sound of balls clicking lightly against each other brought another memory swimming to the surface of his mind.

"Looks like I won again," Eddie announced, smirking. "Don't worry, I won't tell anyone that I beat you six times out of six."

"You're just a sore winner," Pez accused, sticking out his tongue. He turned to see Wolf returning from the counter with drinks. He set them on a nearby table and joined Pez and Eddie.

"He beat you again, didn't he?" Wolf asked, smiling. Pez nodded as Eddie went to sit on the couch next to Glenn. "Tricky bastard," Wolf said, shaking his head. "He's such a hustler. He lures you in with that... 'Oh I don't know how to play pool very well,'" he mocked in a high-pitched girly voice. "Then he wins every game, rubbing your nose in it every single time," he sighed, shaking his head. He leaned forward and placed a kiss on Pez's forehead. Pez smiled brightly. He didn't mind when Wolf showed him affection at the café. It was a gay friendly place, that's why Pez and his friends loved it there.

"I'm sorry he suckered you, baby," Wolf comforted him, gently caressing his cheek. Pez melted at his touch and his use of the nickname 'baby'. "At least it wasn't for money," Wolf

shrugged and then noticed the guilty look on Pez's face. "It was for money, wasn't it?"

Pez nodded shamefully. "Can I borrow thirty bucks?" Pez asked, smiling shyly.

"I love that smile," Wolf breathed; he paused, just staring at Pez. "Don't worry about it. I'll talk to him," he said giving Pez a hug. "He needs to learn not to hustle his friends." Wolf winked.

"He got you too, didn't he?" Pez asked.

"Yeah, last night. I owe him fifty," Wolf said, laughing. Pez threw his arms around Wolf and buried his face in Wolf's shoulder. "Hey, what's wrong?" Wolf asked, pushing Pez back a little.

"Nothing, I just love you, that's all," Pez replied.

"I love you too, baby," Wolf said, squeezing him hard. Pez liked that Wolf was taller than him. He was just tall enough to nuzzle into the side of Wolf's neck.

Pez smiled. Some of his memories were good and made his heart feel happy and light. Some of the memories that plagued his mind were bad and those memories made him want to die. They made him believe that his surviving was just a fluke. They made him feel like none of this should be happening. His survival... his life was all just a big mistake. He should be dead. He wished that all of the memories would just go away. Why couldn't he just start over? Wipe the slate clean? Forget everything? Having no memories would mean no more pain or sorrow.

He ran his index finger across the soft green top of the pool table and continued on his way. Pez looked around the room at the tables. Pez had always loved the décor of this café, so gothic and decadent. He loved that every table in the room was different from the others. It was the same with the chairs and couches. He loved the eclectic look of it all. It made the café seem that much more like home.

He turned to look now at the stage, the place that drew his attention above all else in the café. He stopped in front of it, transfixed. The stage was not really a stage in the literal sense of the word. It was just a curtained off area that was used for a variety of purposes: a stage, a storage area for tables and chairs, extra room for customers. Right now the stage was set up for Open Mic Poetry Night.

"You need to go up there and read your poems," Wolf's voice urged him softly. Pez had trouble trying to figure out if this was a memory or a voice he heard now. *"I love your poetry. I'd like to put it to music,"* Wolf's voice faded softly away.

Pez's chest tightened. Wolf was the only one who even knew that Pez wrote poetry. Wolf had caught him writing one once and even though he was embarrassed, Pez shared it with him. Wolf loved it; Pez began to read Wolf every poem he'd ever written. He loved the praise that Wolf gave him. If Wolf hadn't died, he probably could have helped Pez to work up the nerve to share his poetry on Open Mic Poetry Night.

Why was he standing frozen in front of this painful area? It was like pouring salt into his gaping emotional wounds. It was the stage where Wolf played his guitar and sang. The place where Eddie, Amber and Penny read their poetry. Diamond had even read some of her's the last time they came. This was the place where his best friend Glenn would spin his records on Techno Night.

He remembered dancing with such triumph and joy as Eddie got them to let Glenn spin there for the first time. He was amazing too; he spun better than he ever had. The staff at the café loved him; they asked him back many times after that. He was on his way to fulfilling his dream of becoming a Superstar DJ. All of them had their own talents and could have been famous, if they hadn't died.

"Let's dance!" Diamond yelled over the loud music that Glenn was spinning. *The manic beats were tearing through Pez's body like electricity. He felt like he was being eaten alive by them.*

"What?" Pez asked smiling, the E he had taken was just kicking in. He loved the way he felt while he was rollin'.

"I SAID: LET'S DANCE!" Diamond shouted, taking his hand. Her touch sent shivers through his body. He found himself wanting to eat her alive, figuratively. He wanted to be inside her and her inside of him. She tugged on his arm until he finally stood up and followed where she led.

They made their way to the dance floor. On Techno Night, the café staff would clear most of the tables off the floor for dancing. All of the tables were shoved back into the curtained off area. Glenn stood just inside the curtains behind his turntables; a few feet away from the hectic dancers. His face was a mask of concentration as he tried to match every beat up exactly. His hard work paid off; to everyone in the café it seemed as if the song never ended.

Pez and Diamond danced wildly to the music for a while. Their bodies became the music and the crowd became a living, breathing creature that undulated through the room. Pez watched as Diamond danced, her lithe body moved so gracefully. She brought her hands up in front of her and waved them in and out twisting them upwards in an intricate pattern that left sparkles of light trailing behind them. Pez knew Diamond had a vial of Fairy Dust in her hand; she was letting glitter fall with each intricate twist of her hands. The effect on Pez was amazing. It was too magical for his mind to believe he was really seeing it. Her arms were stretched above her head now and the glitter fell over her head and down her arms.

Pez followed her hands with his eyes down her arms. Her armpits were shaven shimmering hollows that Pez wanted to lose himself in. Her skin was dark and luminescent at the same time, she seemed to radiate with light. Pez had never noticed how beautiful and shimmering she was.

Pez watched as her shirt shifted a little higher as she moved her body in front of him. A small part of her bra was visible at the bottom of her half shirt. Her belly button shimmered at him with the jewel that was pierced through it. He wanted to lick that jewel and feel its texture on his tongue. All at once Pez needed to touch her; he needed to be closer to her. He pulled her closer to him so suddenly she gasped. They began to dance as if they heard a slow song, even though the throbbing beats of the song playing had not changed.

Diamond melted into Pez's arms. She smiled in surprise at his sudden change. Diamond was also surprised by how close her lips were to his. She was in total shock when Pez kissed her. She knew that he was dating her brother and had been since her birthday.

She didn't care. She was in heaven and so was Pez. Every kiss was pure ecstasy to Diamond. Her knees were weak and her heart was pounding and she hadn't even taken anything that night. She pulled away from him after the kissing had gone on long enough to give her whisker burn. Pez looked too young and innocent to be shaving yet, but he was. She licked her lips languidly and opened her eyes to look at Pez.

"I love you, Pezzie," she blurted out truthfully, with a grin shining on her face. Her heart was pounding so hard she

thought it would explode. This was all she had ever longed for, to be in Pez's arms kissing him, loving him.

"I love you too, Wolf," he replied, the name slipping between his lips before he could even stop it. At first he hadn't even realized that it was the wrong name. He watched in a daze as the grin fell from her lips and tears filled her eyes. Her beautiful lips curled into a pout. Pez would never know how bad he'd hurt her that evening. He no longer cared about her feelings. He didn't even care that she was sad and heartbroken. The ecstasy in his system overruled caring. All he wanted was the feeling of her tongue ring in his mouth again. He could see the longing sadness in her eyes. Deep down she wanted it too and he knew it. He pressed his lips against hers in a clumsy attempt at a French kiss. The kiss was clumsy only because Diamond wouldn't open her mouth.

She pushed him away. "I CAN'T BELIEVE YOU!" she screamed over the music. "ASSHOLE!" She slapped him forcefully across the face and then stormed out of the café. Pez shivered at the pleasure that her slap gave him. He looked once at Penny running out of the café chasing after Diamond, and then he shrugged and started dancing again.

NO! That was a bad one; he couldn't believe that he treated Diamond like that. Pez struggled to shake the memory off.

He yanked his attention away from the stage. He walked towards the counter contemplating what he would buy to eat. He felt as if someone was in the café with him, but as he looked around he saw no one. There wasn't even anyone behind the counter. This place was a ghost town. Pez shivered at that thought.

Suddenly, soft guitar music filled the café and stopped Pez dead in his tracks. He recognized the music being played. It was so familiar. What was it? He turned slowly and looked back at the stage. Dread began to fill him as he realized that Wolf was sitting there playing his guitar. He was *really* there. Pez was torn between the urge to run to Wolf and the urge to flee screaming from the café, but he was frozen in place.

Wolf was playing his favorite song of all time, James Taylor's Fire & Rain. Wolf's voice was now accompanying the guitar.

This time it was different though, this time it really was Wolf and not just a memory. He wanted to pretend that he didn't see it, he wanted to just leave, but he couldn't. Wolf was onstage performing to an audience that wasn't there. The café was still empty, only Pez and the spirit of his lost love were in the room. Pez began to shake uncontrollably. His breathing quickened almost to the point of hyperventilating.

His mind was still trying to convince him that it was a memory that he had just forgotten about, but it couldn't have been. Wolf kept his favorite song a secret, only playing it for Pez once (after a lot of pleading on Pez's part). He swore that he would never play it in a public place. It was his special song, one he didn't wish to share with anyone.

Wolf's hair was tied back in a ponytail that fell over his shoulder in a big heap of curls. He looked up and noticed Pez. He smiled with his beautiful, white teeth.

"What am I doing here?" Pez asked to no one in particular, unable to take his eyes off of the Wolf-ghost.

"Wallowing in self-pity and torturing yourself," D answered.

Pez sighed; he had hoped to leave D behind for good, but obviously he hadn't. He shook his head trying to rid himself of the vision of Wolf. It didn't seem right somehow. The teeth were too white, Wolf had been smoking since he was thirteen and his teeth were yellowed with tobacco. His hair seemed much too curly. Wolf's hair had never looked like that had it? Oh God, he was forgetting Wolf already. What color were his eyes? Blue? Green?

I cannot let him go

I feel as though he's slipping away
I cannot let him go
everyday his memory seems to fade
I must remember
I cannot let him go
it seems as though he will disappear
If I ever forget
It seems as though he will wink
out like a candle
never to be remembered
I cannot let him go

Pez took a deep breath, trying to stop the panic attack that was slowly rising inside of him.

'No,' he scolded himself. 'I'm not forgetting him. His eyes were brown, chocolate brown.' He longed to take the picture out of its safe place and gaze at it some more. He decided against it. He knew the picture would not ease his pain; nothing would.

"Nothing can even stop the pain except for…"

"SHUT-UP!" Pez yelled, cutting D off. Why couldn't the voice just leave him alone? Pez turned and started to walk towards the side door of the café. He wanted to leave the voice and the ghost behind, but he couldn't bring himself to walk by the stage again.

"Oh Shit! I am so sorry. I was in the backroom," a new voice said, stopping Pez mid-stride. Pez turned to see a tall blond girl with freckles standing behind the counter. She was wiping her hands on her apron. "I thought I heard someone out here. Can I get you something?" she asked.

Pez shook his head.

"I didn't keep you waiting, did I? You're not angry… Are you?" she asked quickly, worry filling her face.

Pez smiled his best smile and folded his arms slowly in front of his chest. "No," he shook his head. "I've just decided I'm not hungry anymore that's all," he explained softly, his sadness aching through his façade.

"Oh good, I hate pissing the customers off, but somebody's got to do inventory," she babbled.

Pez nodded politely.

"Did you hear music?" the girl asked.

"No," Pez lied, his fake smile fading. "I didn't hear anything at all."

He walked out of the café and down the street a bit. He slowed down as he spotted a small boy crouched down in front of the store window. The boy seemed to be crying. Pez approached him cautiously. He didn't want to frighten the boy. He crouched down in front of the boy and tentatively placed his hand on the boy's shoulder to get his attention.

"Are you OK?" Pez asked. The boy only sniffled in response. "Are you lost?" Pez ventured.

The boy shook his head. *"I lost my daddy,"* the boy whimpered softly.

"I can help you find him," Pez said, smiling brightly, hoping the boy couldn't see the sadness in his eyes. But the boy hadn't even looked up.

"You can't help me," the boy said, slowly lifting his head from his knees. *"You can't even help yourself,"* the boy snarled. He shoved Pez, who was still crouched down balancing precariously on his toes. Pez fell over backwards. He lay on the sidewalk in total shock; no one had ever spoken to him like that, let alone a small boy. He looked up at the boy who was now towering over him.

The boy was wearing ripped up jeans and a Star Wars tee shirt. His dark blond hair was shaggy in a grown out bowl-style haircut. The clothes looked hauntingly familiar to Pez, but it was what he held in his hand that told Pez who the boy was. It was an old metal Transformers lunchbox. At the bottom of the front side, written in permanent marker was the name: 'D. Spencer'. That was the lunch box that he kept all his father's pictures in. Pez began to scream as the realization hit him. His body began shaking again. It was him; it was Pez as a child. It was D… little D. The boy placed his Velcro shoed foot on Pez's neck and began to apply pressure.

"You don't deserve to live," the boy D growled viciously. *"You're a murderer and you don't deserve to be alive."* He pushed down harder with his foot.

Pez struggled violently, but to no avail. The boy… the ghost… the figment of his imagination was choking him. He couldn't breathe; he was beginning to see stars. Then suddenly it was gone. The boy… Little D was gone.

Pez gasped in large amounts of glorious fresh air. It tasted wonderful to him, as he lay on the sidewalk, still shaking.

"Hey kid! Are you OK?" a familiar voice asked. Pez opened his eyes to find the girl from the café squatting on the cement next to him.

Pez nodded and looked around for the boy. He was nowhere to be found. "Where did he go?" he asked the girl.

"Where did who go?"

"The boy, the little kid that was here; he attacked me."

"I didn't see any boy," the girl replied, apologetically. She glanced further down the street. Pez followed her gaze. The boy was leaning against a building further down the street.

"That's him!" Pez yelled struggling to get up. The girl helped him and the two ran towards the boy.

"Where did he go?" the girl asked, as they reached the spot where the boy had been standing.

Pez shrugged and shook his head. "What's your name?" he asked, still gasping slightly. The girl smiled, blushing a bit.

"My name is Mercury," the girl replied.

Pez smiled a small smile back. "Well Mercury, my name is Pez... Welcome to my own personal hell," he said, holding his hand out to her.

She shook it. "Uh... Thanks?" she laughed.

"I have to be getting to school now, so... It was nice meeting you and all. Sorry about everything." He paused. "Oh yeah, back at the café? I did hear music. Sorry 'bout lying."

Mercury smiled again. "It was nice meeting you too and hey, you didn't do anything, don't apologize." He met Mercury's eyes and saw sadness there and he knew he would never learn the reason for it. Pez didn't know that she saw the same thing echoed in his eyes. Pez began to walk away from Mercury and the weird experience at the café.

"Hey, Pez!" she called out to him. He turned back to her. "Be careful kid! Watch your back!" she warned. With that, she turned and walked back towards the café.

alone I wander
through the empty streets
waiting for you
to come back to me
come back
I know you are gone
and alone I wander
on
waiting and aching
for the love that was lost
in the dying light
for the kiss
that still remains
unkissed
waiting for all the
promises
now broken
the endless nights
are gone and yet
we have never spoken

no sad goodbyes
no I love yous
no words...
nothing
and now
you're gone
forever
and I must
wander on alone
waiting forever
for you
to return to me

5

$\mathcal{P}$ez knew when he got to school that he couldn't just waltz in. He would most definitely get in trouble for truancy if he did that. Instead he snuck over to the outdoor courtyard, which was a small area surrounded entirely by bushes, where students who wanted to could go outside to eat.

He squeezed through the bushes and lay hidden on the ground to wait for the next bell to ring. Pez thought that maybe coming to school would take his mind off of Wolf, then again maybe it wouldn't.

Pez growled in anger as he flopped down next to his favorite tree in the courtyard. He took a drag off of his clove cigarette and blew the smoke out slowly. He wasn't actually old enough to be out here smoking, but he didn't care. If he got caught they would just send him home, which is what he wanted anyway. He was pissed off; he didn't feel like being at school. He wanted to be out partying, with Wolf and the others.

"Psst!" He heard someone hissing at him. He turned and looked in the bushes beside him. He saw a familiar face smiling back at him.

"Diamond?" he called out.

"Shh!" she shushed him.

"What are you doing here?" he whispered.

"I've come to rescue you." Diamond winked at him. "We're going on a road trip," she whispered. "Come on!" she urged.

"Where to?" Pez asked.

"Pennsylvania," she said, smiling. She crinkled her nose and flashed her tongue ring at him. This was before she found out that he was going out with her brother. He looked at her shocked, but all she did in reply was gesture for him to come with her.

"Hurry up! We're gonna get caught!" She started to crawl backward through the bushes. Pez flicked the remainder of his clove off to the side and all but dove into the bushes after her.

"Why are we going to Pennsylvania?" Pez asked, as they ran from the courtyard to Mike's waiting van. Pez knew there was only one reason they went anywhere lately, but he asked anyway.

"Why do you think, Pezzie?" She turned as she climbed into the van, a smile stretching across her face.

"A rave," Pez said. It was more of a statement then a question.

She nodded, touching her nose. "You got it!"

"Who's spinning?" he asked thoughtfully. They didn't usually drive that far just to go to a rave unless it was a killer line up of DJs.

"You'll never guess in a million and a half years," she informed him.

Pez shrugged.

"GLENN!" she replied, smiling a big cheesy grin.

"Are you serious? That's awesome!" he cheered.

"Mr. Spencer! Miss Waverly!" a voice called out.

"SHIT! TEACHER! GO!" Diamond screamed, reaching for Pez and hauling him into the van.

"You children are leaving school property!" the teacher yelled. Like they didn't know cutting school early was bad. "Your parents will hear about this!" he yelled after the van as it tore away. Laughing, Pez and Diamond clung for dear life to the doors of the speeding van. They watched as the teacher chasing the van slowly shrank to invisibility.

"That was awesome," Pez said through laughter as Diamond pulled the doors shut.

"I know." A quick corner tossed Diamond across the van on top of him. "Sorry," Diamond said, as Pez helped her right herself. He would never know that she had done that on purpose.

Pez started violently as the school bell rang jolting him out of that memory. That had been such a fun trip. It turned into a weekend stay. Pez could still hear his mother lecturing him after he returned.

"I don't care what was happening in Pittsburgh! Sixteen year olds don't just walk out of school and go on a cross-country road trip," his mother fumed.

"I'm seventeen, Mom, and Pittsburgh's not that far away from Michigan," he replied stubbornly.

"Not that FAR? That's a five hour drive. You were gone the whole weekend!" she screamed. She calmed herself by counting to ten slowly. "It's not about going to Pittsburgh... That's another fight all together!" Pez winced. Another fight meant another boring lecture like this one. "David, you're not even going to make it to your senior year if you keep cutting classes. I don't have the time or the money to be dragged out of work for a meeting at your school! It's hard enough being a single mother with two jobs! Now you're making me deal with you too! I can't handle it David," she paused taking a breath. "You need to get a job," she continued. "You've been suspended for two weeks. If you don't find a job by the time you go back to school," she stopped again, closing her eyes. "You'll have to move out."

"You're kicking me out?" Pez asked defensively.

"Yes, if you don't get a job. I can't afford to let you slack off anymore, David. We're not doing very well, in case you hadn't noticed. The insurance company keeps hassling me over Stevie's bills..."

Pez cut her off. "It's always about STEVIE! I know you love him more," Pez accused, trying to hurt her.

"David, you know that's not true." she argued.

"SCREW YOU!!! I don't know it's not true. If you loved me, you wouldn't have sent me to live with Nanah & Poppy for so long!!!" Pez couldn't believe the words coming out of his mouth. It was the truth; it was how he actually felt.

"David... I" His mother was in total shock.

"SCREW YOU!!!" he screamed again. He ran out the door before she could stop him.

"I don't need you or your stupid rules," he mumbled as he made his way towards the Waverly house. Pez really needed Wolf's reassurance and love. He thought Wolf would be so proud of him for standing up to his overbearing mom.

"She kicked you out?" Diamond asked, as she wrapped a piece of string cheese around her tongue. Pez nodded. "That is so harsh."

"What am I supposed to do?" he asked, only then deciding to tell them the rest of it. "She said the only way I can stay is to get a job. I don't want a job. I want to party with you guys!" he said sadly.

Wolf shrugged. He thought for a moment and finally answered. "You need to get a job," Wolf instructed. "Pez at the risk of sounding like a parent, you need to start thinking about the future... your future. Are you always going to fight with your mom? She's only trying to do what's best for you, and besides, she's pretty much all the family you've got," Wolf explained. Pez was flabbergasted.

"Plus, where would you go?" Diamond asked. "Wolf's right." She shook her head sympathetically.

Pez didn't want her sympathy. "I could move in with Sal," he responded. He was beginning to feel like a small child whining for a toy that he couldn't have.

"Glenn is moving in with Sal. It's a two bedroom. It'd be too crowded," Wolf countered.

"But I...," Pez tried to speak.

"Your Mom's right, Pez," Wolf stated.

"Look Pez, we've all got jobs," Diamond reasoned. "How do you think we pay for the partying?" she asked quietly.

"Yeah, everyone's getting tired of paying for you all the time. You have to start paying your own way. It would be different if you were like Amber. We pay for her a lot of times even though she has a job, but she lost both of her parents; she's got bills to pay and she has to support herself," Wolf explained, looking at him with a hint of sadness in his eyes. "I didn't want to be the one

to tell you that, but it had to be said," Wolf stated, looking down at the carpet under Pez's shoes.

Pez struggled out of the memory. He had to quit thinking about them. He shook the last remnants of the memory away. He was going to have to learn to control this if he was ever going to function as a normal human being again.

He stood up, casually and walked out into the courtyard as if he'd just left school for a smoke. If only he had a clove to smoke. He could use one right about now. He had about five minutes before he absolutely had to go in, so he leaned against the building and looked around the courtyard.

He spotted his ex-girlfriend Lisa sitting under his favorite tree. He could tell by the look on her face that she had just seen him sneak in. He wasn't worried. He knew Lisa wouldn't rat him out. She wasn't like that.

Lisa was sitting next to a boy. She looked happy with the boy. Maybe it was her new boyfriend. Maybe she was in love. Pez wondered how much she had changed since he had last seen her. He was shocked to see her lift a clove to her lips and inhale. She had never smoked before, not cloves anyway.

He tried to ignore her, tried to think about something else. He shifted nervously against the wall. The only thing he could think of was Glenn. He missed Glenn.

Glenn and Pez had been best friends since way back in their childhood. He knew Pez before Pez's father died, before he was even called Pez. Glenn met Wolf and the others a long time before Pez did. For a while Pez was too busy with Lisa to meet Glenn's new friends. Glenn was so excited when Pez finally agreed to meet them at a party.

Lisa and David held hands as Glenn led them down the hallway to the party. David was beyond nervous. David knew that Glenn had told his new friends all about him, and Glenn tended to exaggerate. It was hard not knowing what he was supposed to live up to. Lisa squeezed his hand knowing how shy and nervous he was.

Glenn led them to apartment 1106. He glanced at Lisa. She smiled nervously; she was as shy as David was.

"Come on!" Glenn yelled over the loud music that flooded into the hallway when he opened the door. He noticed

David and Lisa hesitating in the doorway. "Don't worry, they won't bite!" he said, grabbing David's arm and dragged him through the doorway. He dropped David's arm and led them through the crowd. David and Lisa followed, trying to keep up with Glenn. He didn't seem to have a problem with shoving people out of his way.

The only furniture David could see in the dark, people-filled apartment was a couch of indeterminable color. The couch was pushed up against the far wall. It was made to seat about three or four people, but David noticed about eight or ten people sitting on it, most of them were making out. A DJ table lit up with a small purple light was set up next to the couch. David couldn't make out anything else as the crowd blocked his view again, although the room seemed to have nothing else in it.

A strobe light began to flash madly through the smoke filled air. It seemed to light up every other person that David focused on. The people were dressed in strange clothes with a multitude of hair colors and styles. David was overwhelmed by the diversity of the crowd surrounding him. He paused, and for a moment he felt the crowd closing in around him. He shuddered, starting to feel very claustrophobic. He reached behind him and took Lisa's other hand. He needed her support just as much she needed his. He pulled her closer towards his back. They began walking again. She let go of his hands, scaring him for a second. Then she put her arms around his waist, clasping her hands in front of his stomach. David stretched his arms around behind her and clasped his hands together. In this was they gave each other more support than either could ask for. He began to calm down a great deal.

*Glenn stopped and turned around; in his hand he held a joint. He took a hit and handed it to David. David had never smoked marijuana before, but he wanted to impress Lisa, so he took a puff and coughed. He stopped coughing and nodded in approval as he took another hit. This time, to avoid further embarrassment, he choked it down. He inhaled deeply in ecstasy; the high was almost instantaneous. Before this the strongest drug David had ever taken was an aspirin. He began to feel his heart beating in every part of his body, of his very being. He handed the joint to Lisa. Expertly she took a hit and handed it back to David, who handed it back to Glenn. Glenn took another hit and handed it back to the person he got it from. David was definitely beginning to feel a **lot** more relaxed.*

"That's Joe, he's a pothead," Glenn said, leaning closer to David's ear. David liked the smell of pot on Glenn's breath and he made a vow to himself to kiss Lisa as soon as possible. He longed to know what the pot tasted like on someone else's lips.

"It's just back here," Glenn said, pushing through the crowd towards the far end of the large apartment. It seemed to take hours to travel through the crowd. He guided David and Lisa into a bedroom.

"Hey guys!" he said, as he shut the door behind Lisa. "This is David and Lisa." Shutting the door had a tremendous effect on quieting the music, but it still wasn't completely quiet.

"David, Lisa... This is Eddie and Angie." Angie was sitting on Eddie's lap. They sat on an oversized chair next to a window. They were oblivious to the fact that anyone else was in the room. Watching them kiss made David want to make out with Lisa all the more.

"Diamond and Chris," Glenn continued, gesturing to the couple sitting on the floor next to the bed. Chris was painting Diamond's toenails a lovely shade of green to match her hair.

"Hey!" Chris exclaimed. "I know you! You're Pez from my second hour." David nodded.

"Pez... What a cool name," Diamond complimented him; her voice was distorted as she craned her neck back to look at the newcomers.

"Thanks," David said. He had always hated that nickname, but he thought correcting them would be rude, so he kept his mouth shut.

"...This is Sal, the host of this party and his lovely lady Penny..." One of the couples on the bed each smiled graciously at the newcomers. Penny blushed at the compliment. She waved a henna covered hand at them. David smiled and waved back chuckling nervously.

"...Mike and Wolf...," Glenn pointed to the other couple cuddling on the bed. They were both men, which surprised David. He had never seen two men together before that. Oh, he knew about homosexuals. He had read books where the main characters in them were gay, and he had seen gay couples on T.V. But he had never come across any that he knew of. He glanced at Lisa, but there was no sign on her face that told him she was disturbed by the couple. He tried not to let his surprise show through.

"...And last, but not least, the hardest partier here... Brendan," Glenn waved a hand towards a lone boy who was *passed out in the doorway of the bathroom. Pez smiled again and waved to all of them.*

"Now, if you'll excuse me," he bowed gallantly to Lisa. She smiled, giggling and blushing. "I believe I need to relieve young Duncan on the wheels of steel, he seems to be missing beats. Perhaps the talented Duncan is a little bit too far gone to continue."

Glenn picked up a crate filled with records and left Pez and Lisa alone to get to know their new friends. He hoped Pez would like them as much as he did.

Lisa sat down on an empty patch of floor. Pez sat cross-legged next to her. Lisa slid a little further away and lay down, resting her head in Pez's lap. Pez smiled as he gazed at her angelic face and silky brown hair. She smiled back up at him, blushing again and half-closing her cat-like eyes. Her blond streak had fallen across her eyes. Pez brushed it delicately away. She shivered at his touch.

Pez decided it was finally time to kiss Lisa. They had kissed before, of course, but starting a make-out session had always been awkward between the two of them. It usually involved a lot of bumped noses and giggling, but once they got started there was no stopping them.

Pez hoped that the taste of pot would still be on her lips as he bent his head awkwardly to kiss her. He kissed her gently and went to pull back, but she lifted her head closer and kissed him back. They kissed for a few moments and, just as Pez was beginning to feel the strain of his awkward position, something was placed on the back of his head vibrating his skull. He lifted his head, startled by the sudden vibration against the back of his head. The person laughed and placed the vibrating toy on Lisa's stomach. She squealed out in laughter, covering her stomach with her arms.

"What is that?" Pez asked, looking up into the chocolate brown eyes of the person holding the toy. His eyes were so deep and beautiful. He was wearing make-up to enhance them, black eyeliner and eye shadow. Pez was intrigued by the prospect of wearing woman's make-up. He recognized the boy... the man, as the person Glenn introduced as Wolf.

"It's called a Humbug. It's for massages," Wolf explained, smiling. He ran his tongue seductively across his teeth. "So why do they call you Pez?" he asked, not taking his eyes away from Pez's. "You got some candy in there for me?" He leaned

forward and kissed Pez right on the lips. Wolf's tongue gently licked the inside of Pez's lips. Pez was left speechless.

"YUCK!" Lisa cried out. She was still lying on Pez's leg. Wolf looked down as if he'd just noticed her lying there. "You're drooling on me!" she pointed out, wiping her cheek off. It was only a little bit of drool, but she was saving David. She was afraid that he wouldn't like kissing another man.

Wolf smiled. He kissed her on the lips too. "Sorry 'bout that," he apologized. He pulled back to look at them both and smiled. He stared down at Lisa in wonder; he began moving his face closer to hers. He got so close to her that Lisa tensed in fear. He rubbed his cold nose against her eyelashes. "You have such beautiful eyes," he complimented her softly. "They look just...," he began.

"Like a cat," she finished for him. That wasn't the first time someone had said that to her.

"Yes, just like a cat," he laughed, Pez wriggling his eyebrows at him. He leaned forward and placed another kiss on Pez's lips, biting Pez's lower lip gently as he pulled away. "And you...," he started, staring straight into Pez's eyes. "You have the most beautiful lips. They taste like candy," he informed Pez. He sensed Lisa getting angry so he backed away, crawling back towards the bed like a cat.

"Don't worry about Wolf. He's had all his shots," the girl named Diamond laughed. She spun around until she was in a sitting position facing Pez and Lisa. "My brother here is on X," she said, petting Wolf as if he were an animal. "It stimulates you, makes you feel a little aroused." She bit her lip as if remembering the sensation.

"A lot aroused," Wolf corrected her, looking around. For a moment he seemed to panic. "Mike!" he called out. Mike jumped up and ran to his side. "I lost you," Wolf told him.

"I lost you too," Mike replied, standing Wolf upright. Mike seemed to be on X too. They both walked back to the bed, but curled up on the floor beside it instead.

"You guys want to have your nails painted?" Diamond asked, ignoring her brother and his boyfriend. "I have black, blue and green." She smiled, showing off her multicolored fingernails.

Lisa smiled, sitting up. "Sure," she replied. She knew the mood was ruined, but she didn't know how badly it was ruined. Pez did. He knew in that first kiss that he had fallen in love with Wolf. What he didn't know was that in that same moment Wolf had fallen in love with him too.

Pez beat his fists against his temples to clear the memory away. He had to stop doing this. He had to stop remembering, had to stop zoning out. Sometimes, like when he was taking a test, his exceptional memory was a blessing, but sometimes, most of the time, it was a curse. It caused him not only to remember things, but also to re-live them as if they had just happened. Each time he re-lived a certain memory he seemed to remember more and more details that he hadn't even noticed before.

6

$\mathscr{F}$inally he started walking towards the school. He glanced back at Lisa. She was laughing at something the blond skater boy said. Pez didn't think he knew the boy, but from the look of pure hatred in his eyes, Pez was positive he had wronged him in some way or another.

Pez noticed the boy had his arm around Lisa protectively and she was leaning into his shoulder. He felt a small twinge of jealousy, but that passed quickly. Lisa was in his past now. They hadn't even spoken in almost a year.

He sighed in angry protest as he walked into the school. He was revolted that he was back in this hellhole. He made his way to his third hour class: art. Pez liked art. It was the only school subject he cared about and, most likely, the only class he was actually passing.

If Pez was failing any of his classes, it was not because he wasn't smart enough—he was. He just didn't care anymore. He never did any work in any of his classes, except for art. That, along with his absenteeism, was the reason behind Pez's failing grades. His teachers were all very nice and supportive. They all knew what happened to him and his friends. So they were quite lenient with him.

He often wondered why he even came to school at all anymore. There was no way he could make up all the lost time in his few remaining weeks as a senior at Emmerdale High. Even if he wanted to make the work up, which he didn't. 'What's the point in coming in at all?' he wondered. 'But what else am I going to do, stay home with mom?' He snorted at the mere idea of spending that much time with his mom.

He shook his head. No, he would never do that. 'Maybe I can pick up some daytime hours at work,' he thought, but dismissed the idea, knowing that that would only lead to more lectures from his mother.

He walked into his third hour classroom and smiled as he noted the picture hanging next to Mr. Robertson's desk. It was a painting he had done before the accident once when he'd come to school tripping. His smile grew as he remembered the praise that Mr. Robertson had given him and it. Saying how deeply intense it was and so full of color. Looking at it now, all Pez saw was a big blobby mess. It was strange to Pez that at the time it seemed like a masterpiece, now to him it was just crap. What was it he was trying to paint—a rabbit? A mushroom? Maybe it was a rabbit on a mushroom? That's what Bren said it looked like anyway.

He laughed softly to himself, and walked over to the cupboard where the unfinished projects were kept. He took out the drawing he had been working on, his smile fading. Pez stared at it. He was disgusted by the simplicity and naivety of the drawing. The assignment was to draw a living object with some sort of activity occurring behind it. The small white longhaired kitten that stared back at him just didn't cut it. He didn't want to work on the kitten. It wasn't even his idea in the first place; Mr. Robertson gave him the idea because Pez was at a loss. He wanted to crumple the kitten up and throw it in the garbage. Instead he shoved the paper angrily back into the cupboard.

He walked to the back of the room to get a fresh sheet of paper. Then he sat down in his assigned seat next to Bren's empty one.

With a clean slate before him, he picked up a pencil. He stared at the paper wondering what he should draw. He closed his eyes to get the vibe. He had no idea what he wanted to draw. Finally, when he could think no more, he just relaxed and placed the pencil against the paper. He still had no idea what he was going to draw, but it didn't matter. Losing himself in memories, he let the pencil fly freely. He thought of Wolf as he drew.

Pez jumped quickly aside as Wolf stormed past him in the hallway leading to Sal's apartment. Pez was filled with anguish seeing Wolf in that much distress. He cautiously poked his head into the apartment to find Wolf sitting on the couch. There was a pained look on his face and tears in his eyes.

Sitting there

you were sitting
there you looked so
lost and alone
I looked down at you
sitting there
so innocent
and alone
I wanted to be
with you
to sit with
you and
end your obvious
pain
even as you
end mine
sitting there

Pez paused in the doorway, memorizing the image of Wolf. He was sitting on Sal's couch with his elbows on his knees, propping his head on his folded hands. He was wearing only a pair of jeans. His leather jacket lay in a heap next to the couch where he threw it.

"Are you alright?" Pez asked softly. He was afraid of the answer. He was worried that Wolf would want to kill himself. Worse than that, he was afraid that he would kill himself. Wolf was too sensitive when it came to his music.

Wolf looked up, barely able to contain his tears. He tried to be brave and conceal his pain. He smiled a fake smile and started to nod his head. Then his smile melted away and he shook his head.

"I made such an ass out of myself," he said, looking away from Pez. He covered his face with his hands. "I don't know why I even tried. I'll never be good enough." He exhaled slowly. His dream of playing the guitar for his favorite local band was shattered. Ever since the band first started three years ago, all Wolf wanted was to be a part of them. His big chance came along when Craig, the guitarist moved to California to be an actor. He had waited so long for this chance. Then, finally, when it had arrived; he blew it. Wolf thought it was because he played a song that he had written. Pez knew that it was his nerves. They had gotten the best of him and made him fumble through each of the three songs.

"I should have played a cover song," he mumbled sadly. "I should have played a Cure song. Those are the ones that I know the best. I should have stuck with something they would know." He paused to take a breath. "Why the hell did I get so clumsy anyway? I kept tripping up and messing up the riffs! I SUCK!" Wolf said and dropped into an eerie silence.

Pez's mind filled with a million things to say, but none of them would make Wolf feel any better, not with the depression Wolf was now in. Pez just wanted to kiss him, hold him, ease his pain, but he was so nervous. What if Wolf found him stupid or inadequate? Only a week had passed since their first 'real' kiss in the bathroom at the Roller E. In some ways, he was more nervous now than he had been then.

Slowly, Pez walked over to the couch. He sat down on the coffee table in front of Wolf. He closed his eyes and imagined touching Wolf's hairless, muscular chest. He could feel Wolf's heart beating beneath his shaking hand. He imagined touching the slightly raised skin where Wolf's new tattoo was. Wolf's painful intake of breath shocked Pez into opening his eyes. He was surprised to find his fingers were actually caressing Wolf's chest. Pez's hand seemed to be bolder then his mind was.

Wolf looked down from his hands, wondering why Pez had stopped his caress.

"Does it hurt?" Pez asked, gently tracing the wolf tattoo on Wolf's chest.

"Only when you touch it," Wolf replied wincing. Pez winced in response. He never wanted to hurt Wolf in any way. "I didn't say it was a bad thing," Wolf half-smiled at the look of surprise on Pez's face. A tear rolled down Wolf's cheek.

Pez immediately wiped the tear away. Slowly Pez lifted his shaking hand up towards Wolf's hair. He was still so afraid that Wolf would reject him at any moment. He was afraid that Wolf would tell him to leave.

<u>New</u>

now that I have

your heart

what do I do

(with it)

I can't help it,

I'm not

stupid

just new

(at this)

should I try to touch you

will you be there

or just another

fantasy

I've cried wolf too many

times to

believe

that this is

real

now that your heart

is real
what is this feeling
that I feel
passion, pleasure, sickness
all at once
I feel so stupid like
a dunce
or a child
I go on
not knowing what
to do

I can't help it
I'm not stupid
I'm just
new
at this

Pez ran his fingers through Wolf's hair; it was a dream come true for him. He buried his fingers in Wolf's beautiful hair and cupped the back of his head. He moved closer towards Wolf's mouth and their lips met. A single kiss; barely even passionate was all that they shared. It was in that one kiss that Pez knew Wolf would never find him stupid or inadequate. There was too much love between them for that.

Pez moved to the couch next to Wolf and opened his arms. Wolf sobbed and crumpled into Pez's arms. Pez smiled sadly and held him as he cried.

"Are you going to be OK?" Pez whispered with a shaky voice. This emotional side of Wolf was so new to him. Pez was frightened. He had never seen Wolf so upset. Wolf was the type to hide his feelings, but here Wolf was showing Pez a side that he didn't even know existed.

Wolf looked up at Pez with tears streaming down his face and smiled the smallest smile. Pez knew when he saw that smile that Wolf would recover from this devastating blow. Pez chuckled softly and kissed him on the nose. Wolf's smile grew, but the sadness remained. Together the two sat with their foreheads

pressed against each other, staring deeply into each other's eyes.
Pez had never been happier.

Again the loud jangling bell rang, startling Pez out of the voluntary memory trance that he had put himself in. It took him a few seconds to adjust himself back into reality. Sometimes he found himself wishing that reality would just leave him alone. It was just too harsh and painful for him. Why couldn't he just live forever in the memory of Wolf's smile?

He sighed softly and looked down at the picture that his unaided hand had drawn. He could not remember drawing what was on the paper before him. It was a drawing of Wolf, as he had been in the memory. He was looking up from his hands with tears in his eyes. The sadness in Wolf's eyes was captured so perfectly that Pez began to doubt that he had drawn the picture at all. He had never drawn this well before. Every detail was captured flawlessly, down to the exact pattern of Sal's couch. Even the drug paraphernalia was impeccably realistic looking. Every line of the drawing had a meaning within itself.

Behind Wolf, where his action was supposed to be, was a large swirling mass of something. Pez stared at it, wondering what it could be. As he stared, the faces seemed to jump out at him. Pez dropped the drawing in horror when he figured it out; it was his friends. All of his friends were there behind Wolf. Each of their bodies was twisted and dead or dying with looks of sheer terror on their faces. Pez whimpered softly in pain as he found he had drawn himself among the dead and dying.

Somehow, Pez had exchanged his life for Wolf's. Somehow he had taken Wolf's place among the dead. He had died along with his friends, just like he always said he wanted to—deserved to. It was then that Pez realized his whimper was not one of pain, but one of longing. He would gladly trade places with Wolf if he could.

I've lost my touch
it's drained away
so achingly far from reach
I stretch, reaching fingers
grasping
I am broken and confused

I am hated and amused
lost forever reaching
fingers flexing
fingers burning
aching and breaking
reaching, but never
quite touching what
I lost
I'll never get it back
he's lost
forever
come back
I need you
come back

The only thought running through his head as he stared in morbid fascination at the picture lying on the tabletop was: "Run away! Go home! Get out of here!" He wanted to leave school so badly. He wanted to go home and fall into the peaceful oblivion that he used to know when he slept.

Pez threw the drawing into the cupboard and ran. He was shaking so hard, that he could barely run. Mr. Robertson called a goodbye to him as he left the room, but Pez was unable to reply. Pez was in the hallway leading to the cafeteria before he got a hold of himself. He leaned back against the wall and took a couple of deep breaths, forcing himself to calm down. He could make it through the day. He knew he could. It was lunchtime anyway. Maybe if he finally got something to eat it would make him feel better.

Pez couldn't turn the drawing in, he just couldn't. The assignment was to draw something living and none of the subjects he drew were living now, none but him and he was just barely living. Most of his time he spent wishing he were dead anyway.

<u>continuations</u>

I am dead

not just slowly
dying
my soul is dead
I am dead inside
dead soul
aching for a life
living a reasonable
facsimile
living a lie
come to me
out of darkness
and revive
me
bring me back
from the dead
bring me back
to life
let me feel
your texture
let me hold
your heart
I need to feel
your texture
your taste
your love
to bring
me back
to life
again

'What kind of an action is dying? Is it even an action?' he thought to himself. 'I mean once you're dead, you're not active anymore,' he reasoned to himself. Dying was one action that Pez never wanted to see again. He had seen it too many times before.

"Oh it's an action alright. It's a morbid action, but it's still an action. You can see for yourself," D's voice answered his

unspoken question. *"You can join them, you know. I think that's the coolest thing about dying; you can do it all by yourself!"* D rationalized. Pez chose to ignore the voice. His mother always said when someone was bothering him: "Just ignore him or her and they will eventually go away."

"Yeah, but I don't think she was talking about the voices in your head. Especially the ones you name!" D laughed maliciously.

Sometimes it was very difficult to ignore the voice that only he heard. Especially when it always brought with it questions about his sanity. Pez was more than a little afraid that he was slowly losing control of his own mind.

He mentally pushed the voice away and headed over to the food line. Standing in line to purchase his lunch seemed to take forever. Pez tried not to think about Wolf, but somehow he found himself lost in memory once more.

Pez felt sad and rather alone. He didn't know anyone in his art class. All of his friends were spread out in different classes except for Wolf, who graduated the year before, and the two or three friends that didn't even go to Emmerdale High School. Bren used to sit next to him, but he left for Ireland earlier in the week. No one was sure when or if he was ever coming back.

His painting wasn't turning out the way he wanted it to. He was angered, mostly at being alone, but partly because his painting was going so badly. Violently he shoved the paint tray away.

"Hey, be nice to the paint! What did it ever do to you?" a familiar voice asked. Startled Pez looked up, only to find Wolf standing behind him with a big grin on his face.

"Wh... What are you doing here?" Pez stuttered, trying to contain his excitement over seeing his beloved Wolf.

"I'm just visiting. I couldn't wait 'til tonight to see you again," he whispered close to Pez's ear as he leaned down to admire his painting. Pez melted at the feeling of Wolf's warm breath on his neck. "Needs more blue," he advised, standing back up.

Pez looked up at Wolf, puzzled by his advice. It was a strange thing to say, considering he was working on a black and white painting. "Why do you say that?" he asked. Wolf just smiled slyly back at him.

Wolf was not in the least bit perturbed by Pez's failure to take his less than subtle hint to get more paint from the storage room. He tried a different tactic.

"I think you need to help me find my old art projects," he whispered softly. "Hey Mr. Robertson," Wolf called out before Pez could protest. The art teacher looked up from the project he was helping another student with. "This kid's gonna help me find my old art projects," Wolf said, jabbing his finger at Pez. Mr. Robertson smiled and nodded.

"Do what?" Pez asked, still confused.

"Don't worry about it, just follow me," Wolf instructed, walking away.

Pez hurriedly got up and followed him into the storage room at the back of the classroom. "What did you say we were getting?" Pez asked as he stopped in the doorway.

"My old art projects, my mom says she wants to see them. I never used to show her anything," Wolf answered, as he began to sift through the large piles of left behind artwork that cluttered the storage room. Pez moved forward, wanting to help Wolf. The heavy door slammed behind him and he jumped a little. He began to sift through the piles also, looking for Wolf's name.

"Oh my God," Pez heard Wolf gasp.

"What?" Pez asked, walking over to where Wolf was standing. He also gasped when he saw the painting that Wolf held. It was a painting of Pez or at least someone who looked a lot like Pez. Neither of them had ever seen the painting before.

The boy in the picture was sitting on the ground resting his back against a gray brick wall. In a nook beside him, a couple feet behind the gray wall, was a glass doorway with people milling around. The people were blurry. Their faces were barely discernable as human. The only object in the painting that was absolutely clear was the boy. He was hugging his blue jean-clad knees. His jeans were big and baggy. There was a hole in them that exposed his right knee. He was wearing Pez's green jacket and his red and white striped scarf, which is what convinced both Pez and Wolf that this was indeed a painting of Pez. No other person wore those two items together; it was definitely Pez. He had Pez's face, his clothes, and his shoes. His hair was the only thing that wasn't like Pez's. This boy's hair was black as night. Pez ran his hand through his blond hair, raising it a little to make sure he still knew what color it was.

"I saw the Cure lyrics and I had to look at it," Wolf explained softly.

"'To Wish Impossible Things' off of the 'Wish' album," Wolf pointed out. *"I think I've been to this place before. It looks like a club in Ann Arbor,"* Wolf said, scratching his head.

"Did you do this?" Pez asked Wolf.

He shook his head. "No, I thought you did." Wolf replied as they both scanned the painting for a signature. Finding none, Wolf turned the painting over to see if there was anything on the back of it.

"Lisa!" Pez said as he read the signature. He smiled faintly in recognition of her name.

"Lisa?" Wolf asked.

"My ex-girlfriend," he explained to Wolf.

"Oh really?" Wolf asked, as an unmistakable flash of jealousy filled his eyes. Pez had to look away. *"Yeah you know, Lisa. You met her, remember?"*

"Oh yeah... the girl with the cat eyes," Wolf said, rolling his eyes.

Pez looked at the date under her name. *"Weird,"* Pez said, his heart beating faster. *"She painted this in her freshman year."*

"So?" Wolf said.

"I didn't meet Lisa until her sophomore year. She painted this before we even met," Pez said, putting the painting down.

"That's a little creepy," Wolf announced. *"Let's just get back to looking for my projects."* He didn't want to think about Pez's psychic ex-girlfriend anymore.

Lisa's painting was completely forgotten by the time they found all of Wolf's.

"Pick one that you like and you can keep it," Wolf offered Pez as he sifted through the projects. Pez chose one of Robert Smith. Wolf smiled. *"How did I know you were going to pick that one?"* He laughed. *"You can have it after I show it to my mom. Can you believe I actually used to wear my hair like that?"* he asked, gesturing to Robert's wild hair.

"No, I can't believe that." Pez smiled, trying to picture Wolf with anything other than his lovely flowing locks.

"I'll give you a picture. I have a million. Diamond always said I looked a lot like him, but I don't think so. Mokey agreed, but she was so young then. She worshipped Diamond and me, she still does." Wolf smiled at the thought of his youngest sister.

Pez turned to leave while Wolf put his projects in his portfolio. Pez could hear the bell ringing and the kids shuffling out of the classroom.

"Wait!" Wolf's breathless voice called out.

"What?" Pez asked, spinning around to face Wolf. Wolf stood a few feet away holding up a key.

"I happen to know that Mr. Robertson is leaving school early today." He wiggled his eyebrows suggestively. "His other classes are all going to be in the other classroom, being taught by a sub," Wolf said slowly.

"And how do you know this?" Pez asked him.

"Because he told me, he gave me the key, and said for me to lock up when I'm done. Then I can just leave the key in the office for him."

"Um... Aren't we done now?" Pez asked.

"I'm not done," Wolf murmured, smiling coyly. He moved closer to Pez and cornered him against the door. "Are you?" he asked, his lips gently caressing Pez's cheek.

"Wait a minute! You had this planned all along, didn't you?" Pez accused. He put his arms around Wolf's waist. A smile spread quickly across Pez's face. They kissed then, but nothing more than kissing occurred that day.

Pez came out of that memory smiling. He tried to decide if he was hungry enough for a full meal or just a snack. He finally settled on just getting fries. They used to fill him up like a full meal would.

Once Pez got his food he headed to the table that was once filled with the laughter of his friends. Everything, no matter what, reminded him of that, everything.

left alone
to face this
room
full of laughter
full of shame
staring at me
there's no one
to blame

theres only

my aching

sorrow-filled

heart

that's the

only thing

that sets

me apart

    Despite the overcrowding of the school's cafeteria, their table—his table—remained empty. It was almost as if all the other students knew what he had done and they were all punishing him for it. Just like in *The Scarlet Letter* by Nathaniel Hawthorne, when the woman was forced to wear the scarlet A (for adultery) upon her chest, with everyone staring at her. He should have an M for murderer, but alas his own guilt was the only 'scarlet letter' that he wore.

    "You're always so damn over dramatic. If you feel that way, why don't you just kill yourself?" D's voice filled his mind again. *"I mean; you can't turn yourself in. Prison would be far worse than Rehab. So that means you should just kill yourself and get it over with. No one wants you here anyway,"* D laughed in his head. *"Besides, no one knows what you did. They all just think you're crazy, that's why no one wants to sit with you."* D's crazed laughter echoed through his head. Pez tried hard to ignore it this time.

    The truth was that they all had their own friends, their own tables and their own laughter. Tears began to fill Pez's eyes as he sat down. He never realized how lonely it was when you didn't have friends.

    He tried to eat, hoping that would push the bad thoughts out of his head. He was very hungry; it felt like he hadn't eaten in days, which might have been true. Pez couldn't remember the last time he had a good solid meal. He picked at his fries, but the guilt that was bottled up inside of him filled his stomach with a queasy feeling. He began to feel a crushing sensation in his chest, right where his heart was. He took a few deep breaths, trying to calm his stomach down, but nothing seemed to work.

    "Hey Dave," a freshman named Bruce said, planting himself at Pez's sorrow table. Pez and Bruce shared one class together; therefore, Bruce thought Pez was his best friend. Most of the time, Pez would humor him. He liked the thought of actually having a friend at school. He figured since he wasn't going to graduate this year, Bruce might actually be a good friend next year too. He liked Bruce most days, even though he seemed a little strange.

"Pez," he corrected Bruce. Pez was always reminding Bruce that his name was not Dave.

"No thanks," Bruce replied seriously.

His answer infuriated Pez. "That's my name, God damn it!" Pez growled, taking his pain out on poor Bruce.

"Sor-ry, Pez," he paused; making sure Pez heard the use of his nickname. "Shit, what bug crawled up your ass?" he asked.

"You," Pez replied.

Bruce laughed, uncertain as to whether Pez was joking or not.

Somehow, it was easier for Pez to take out his pain on Bruce; so much easier than it was to accept the fact that all his friends were dead and he was all alone. Did Bruce know about that? Did he know that the seats at this table used to be occupied by people Pez loved? Did he know that, in order to save money, only two of them would buy fries and two of them would buy drinks and then the whole table would eat from the same baskets and drink from the same cups? Bruce didn't know anything about him. He didn't know anything about his friends. He didn't know anything at all.

"They're all dead, you know," Pez whispered.

"What?" Bruce asked, when Pez didn't answer he turned his attention to Pez's fries. "Not eating?" he asked, reaching across the table and snatching a fry from Pez's basket. Pez shook his head. He was still in shock that he had said that to Bruce and Bruce didn't hear. Didn't hear or didn't want to hear? Pez wondered.

"Can I have them?"

Pez closed his eyes and nodded. Bruce's deep voice was grating on his nerves today, it usually never even bothered him. Pez rested his elbows on the table and began to rub his temples and eyes with the palms of his hands. School never used to be this stressful; then again he never used to be this sober. Wolf always made sure he was so high the night before that it would last him through the next day. Sometimes he even gave him a little something to help him get through the day. Wolf always cared about him that way. He pushed the thought away knowing full well what it would lead to.

Too late…

"I love you, David," Wolf's voice whispered in his head. The words echoed over and over again. They were louder than Bruce's idle chattering as he quickly devoured Pez's fries.

on your lips,

I hear a name

that name...

I know I've heard it before

it sounds familiar

so familiar

it sounds so comforting

that name it fills me

with joy

even though it can't be anyone

that I know

it can't be the name

I've answered to

so many times

before

could it be

I can't be sure

not even now

can it be

is it

it's too beautiful

the name on your

lips...is mine

Pez opened his eyes slowly, waiting for them to clear of the blackness caused by his forceful rubbing. He was surprised to find Wolf sitting across the table from him. He was smiling in that sly way he had, when he was about to make a move on Pez. Wolf stood up quickly, so quickly that Pez expected the chair to fall over, but it didn't. Wolf climbed up onto the table and began to crawl seductively across the surface towards Pez.

Pez expected the lunch monitor to do something about Wolf. He was fairly sure that it was against the rules to crawl across the lunchroom tables, seductively or not. The lunch monitor was looking in his direction, but he did nothing to stop Wolf. He didn't even see him. Pez looked around the cafeteria wildly, hoping that no one else saw what he saw, but deep inside he was praying that someone did. No one noticed Wolf, not even Bruce.

"I love you, David," Wolf's voice whispered, getting more and more urgent with each echo.

"STOP IT!" Pez shouted, unable to control his fear, his temper, or his sanity any longer. "SHUT UP! GO AWAY! I DON'T WANT YOU HERE! LEAVE ME ALONE!" Pez screamed, covering his ears. He was trying to block out Wolf's words, but he did not succeed. The echo still rang through his head. Pez wondered if this was another ploy of D's to drive him farther into insanity.

Bruce stopped talking and stared at Pez in shock, tears forming in his eyes. He swallowed them back and then apologized. "Sorry man, I didn't know you were in that kind of mood today." Bruce stood up and turned to leave. Before Pez comprehended what just happened, Bruce was walking away.

"No, wait," Pez called out in vain. "Bruce, I didn't mean you!" It was too late. Bruce kept walking.

Pez was reminded of the scene with his mother earlier that morning. The voices in his head were getting him in a lot of trouble lately. He noticed many of the nearby students had stopped eating and were now staring at Pez; some were even snickering behind their hands.

Pez was suddenly overcome with nausea. He ran quickly towards the bathroom. The nauseous feeling pushed a little harder and Pez hurried into a stall. He retched into the toilet, but nothing came. The retching made him feel a little better. He walked over to the sink and took off his jacket and scarf. He dropped it in a heap next to the sink and splashed some water on his face.

"Hey kid, are you OK?" a haggard, but familiar voice asked. Pez nodded. *"Cause if you're not... I got what you need,"* the voice whispered. Pez turned to find the source of the voice.

Standing next to him was a skinny boy with dirty, stringy hair and brownish fingernails. His face was sunken in and there were darkened circles under his eyes. His teeth were yellow and rotting as he smiled at Pez. There were track marks all over his arms and sores that looked like cigarette burn marks on his lips. His feet were bare and Pez could see track marks on his toes, which were the only part of his blackened feet not hidden by his pant legs.

junkie boy

he stands before
me aching
sallow face, yellow skin
he stands before
me ready to
strike
track marked arms
oozing with morphine
ready for another
hit
he stands before me
pills and paper on
his tongue
aching
and nothing can
stop his aching
nothing can
stop his longing
heroin, ecstasy
smack, acid
hash, morphine
coke, crack
nitrous
he doesn't care
they all ease
his pain
but they
can never

never

fulfill

his longing

his desire

for a greater

high

he stands

before me

aching

he stands

before me

longing

it takes forever

to realize

that he...

is me

Pez's mind began to panic again, as for the third time that day he saw a different version of himself. This one was a considerable amount less innocent looking then the little boy version he had seen outside of the café.

"*So what's your poison?*" the Junkie Pez asked, smiling his rotten smile.

"Wh-What?" stammered Pez. He was still in shock.

"*Come on kid. I ain't got all day. Choose!*" Junkie Pez demanded.

"Choose what?" Pez asked.

"*Don't be so dense. You know what I got and you know what you want.*" A small pencil box appeared in Junkie Pez's hand. He opened it to reveal more drugs then Pez could ever recall seeing. "*Now pick one!*" Junkie Pez demanded.

"I d-d-don't want any," Pez stuttered.

"*Come on, I know you do!*" He was beginning to sound a lot like D. "*Don't let the man tell you what you want. Do what you want to do. It's your choice, not theirs. Now choose.*"

"No! I don't want any! Now leave me alone," Pez said, as he finally found the courage to stand up to his duplicate.

"*Damn it kid! Just choose!*" Junkie Pez growled through clenched teeth. His eyes seemed to glow with evil intentions.

"I'm not gonna ch-choose," Pez argued. He was quickly losing his courage. He wanted to leave. He wanted to just go and leave the hallucination behind. He just had to get his jacket and scarf. Junkie Pez was blocking them from him. Slowly, he began to move towards the door.

"*Uh-unh, you're not getting away that easily.*" Junkie Pez ran to block the door. "*Choose!*" He shoved the box of drugs in Pez's face. Pez backed up until he could feel his jacket next to his feet. Junkie Pez followed him back each step. Pez lifted his hand; he held it over the box, trying to convince himself not to choose. He wanted to so badly. He couldn't stand being so sober, so clear-headed. He swung his hand and knocked the box out of Junkie Pez's hand.

"NO!" Pez screamed. He had worked so hard to stay clean. He couldn't just throw it all away.

"*Well, in that case...,*" Junkie Pez said and before Pez knew what was happening, his double's hand closed around his wrist. It was cool and scaly like a snake's skin. He felt a tingling sensation crawling up his arm from where the junkie boy's hand rested on him. Something akin to pleasure, but somewhat resembling pain, blossomed from each of his fingertips into Pez's arm. His blood vessels seemed to kick into overdrive. He was preparing Pez's vein for an injection. Pez struggled to pull away, but his doppelganger's grip only tightened on his wrist cutting of the circulation in Pez's arm.

"Stop! You're hurting me!" he begged.

"*I thought that was the point.*" A dirty and rusted needle appeared in his hand. "*I know what you want. Don't worry, this is the best kind of drug,*" he enticed softly. "*It's so hard to find a good vein these days,*" Junkie Pez said, staring at his almost vein-free arm. He tapped his wrist and switched the needle to his other hand. He looked back at Pez as he shoved the needle violently into his own wrist. He filled the empty syringe with his own blood. Pez started gagging; he had always hated the sight of blood. "Just *remember... You don't know where I've been,*" the doppelganger growled and then quickly–like the snake he felt like–he lunged forward and jabbed Pez's arm with the needle. Pez howled in pain and fear. "*Believe me kid, this is just what you need,*" Junkie Pez said, as he pushed the plunger in. Pez watched as the blood disappeared into his own arm. He could feel its poison spreading in his blood stream. "*I'll be seeing you around,*" Junkie Pez winked and disappeared, taking all his drugs with him, all of them, except for the needle that was still in Pez's arm.

Feeling light headed and weak, Pez reached over and pulled the needle from his vein. He dropped the syringe and it disappeared before it even hit the ground. The odd sensation in Pez's arm disappeared along with it. He wouldn't have believed it actually happened if it weren't for his bleeding arm. He got some toilet paper and pressed it against the hole in his arm. Pez noticed his few other track marks on his arm began to pulsate. He shook his head and rubbed his eyes as if trying to rid himself of a nightmarish dream. It had been a nightmare, but he was awake.

In a daze, he picked up his jacket and scarf, put them back on and walked back out into the courtyard. His favorite tree was not occupied so he sat under it; he just wanted to be alone. He closed his eyes. Maybe when he was a rich and famous artist he would come here and have the tree uprooted. He would have it placed in the garden outside his mansion. He smiled a little at the vision of his tree on his property. He could sleep under this tree; he wanted to sleep under it.

Unfortunately, his body had another plan. That's when he began to feel it. It started in his arm and he reveled in the sweet joy it brought. Slowly the sweet, soft feeling crawled through his arm and straight towards his heart. All his fantasies of being rich and famous were forgotten as a pain so horrible ripped through his heart. He grunted in pain. He thought he was done with all of this; maybe it had something to do with what Junkie Pez had done to him.

His stomach began to ache and cramp. His head began to pound in time with his loudly beating heart. He could feel his blood coursing madly through every vein in his body. He broke out in a cold sweat. His entire body began to shake with the effort of holding something back. Something that he didn't even know existed. He braced his back against the tree, so hard that he thought his jacket would rip, but it didn't. His jacket had been through hell and back; so far nothing had ripped it, except of course bullets.

His mind exploded with lights, no thoughts could be held in his mind; everything was in a jumble. He was losing himself in whatever form of drug that was inside Junkie Pez's veins. Little did Pez know that the drug inside the syringe was addiction. It was craving desire. It was needful longing. It was withdrawal. A withdrawal that was worse than any other Pez had ever felt. Finally Pez found it, the one thought like no other that existed within his aching skull. He clung to that one thought as if his life depended on it.

"Just one more hit," he conceded. "One more to stop this fucking pain," he wanted –needed drugs of any kind; heroin, ecstasy, special k, acid, hell he would even try cocaine to ease this horrid ache inside of him.

He opened his eyes and unclenched his jaw. He looked around the courtyard. He was trying to find someone; anyone who could stop the pain. Someone there had to have something; any of what it was that he needed. There was only one possible suspect in the crowd.

He walked over to Lisa. She was now standing alone, leaning against the wall, biting her fingernails. She was staring nervously at the door to the courtyard. He could barely see anyone else as he made his way through the crowded courtyard towards his ex-girlfriend. Her brother was one of the biggest drug dealers in all of Emmerdale.

"Shit!" he said, as if announcing his presence. Startled, she looked at him. "Lisa. Shit! Are you holding?" he asked desperately. She stared at him with a stupid blank stare on her face. She had no idea what he was talking about. This enraged Pez. "Do you have any 'E'?" he asked slowly, as if he were talking to a small child. The question was blunt and straightforward. At this point he no longer cared about secrecy or school rules. He wasn't afraid of anything, but the pain. The need was strong; it drove him. He just needed one final hit, just one.

Her mouth dropped open in anger. "What are you, crazy?" she whispered loudly. "Do I look like I carry ecstasy around with me at school? I don't think so. I'm not a fiend like you!" Pez had never seen her so angry before. Her anger didn't matter, because it only made him more desperate and angry.

"Look!" he growled. "I DON'T CARE HOW YOU GET IT, BUT I NEED IT NOW!" he yelled, grabbing her shoulders and squeezing. She gasped in fear or ecstasy. Pez wasn't sure. Pez didn't care.

"David. I can't. Please just calm down. Don't think about it," her whispering voice was soothing. "It'll be OK, just relax." It was her turn to speak slowly. She seemed to have gained some experience in helping people get over drug withdrawals and it was helping Pez. He was slowly beginning to feel better. "You look like shit." She placed the back of her hand on Pez's forehead. "You're burning up. Are you OK?"

Pez nodded, removing his hands from her shoulders. He began to smooth down her shirt where his hands had messed it up. "I'm sorry," he apologized as a wave of nausea overcame him.

Lisa's eyes popped open in fear. She was afraid that Pez was going to throw up on her.

When he could speak again, he explained: "I'm trying to lay off the stuff, cold turkey. It's hard you know." He didn't mention that he hadn't done any drugs at all in over a year. Lisa nodded, smiling a knowing smile.

"Maybe you should go home and rest," she suggested gently as she straightened his jacket for him. He had a strange image in his head as she did this. He felt like Lisa was a mother and he was her child. It was as if she were preparing him for his first day of Kindergarten. Pez found it strange and somewhat alluring that she was still concerned with his health.

"Yeah, maybe I will," Pez replied, taking a deep breath. Lisa seemed to be acting funny, but then again he wouldn't have known what acting funny was for her. It had been so long since he'd last talked to her.

"David?" she asked. His eyes widened in a questioning look. "It probably doesn't mean much to you," she said, her mouth forming a small frown. Her eyes told Pez she wasn't sure if she wanted to say what she was going to say. "I still... I'm very proud of you," she said quickly and before he knew it was happening, she kissed his lips softly. He blinked in surprise. Why did she kiss him? He looked in her eyes to see if he could find the answer there, but all he found were tears.

The tears seemed to be slightly contagious; he couldn't help it. Her kiss was so soft and innocent. He couldn't help remembering the way he hurt her. He swallowed back the lump of tears that was forming in his throat.

"Yeah," he said in response to her admission. He couldn't tell what reaction Lisa had been looking for, so he didn't know exactly how to respond to the admission or the kiss. Her words cut him much deeper then she realized. They seemed to hurt him more then they helped. He shuddered as he realized that the last person to say that to him was Wolf.

He sighed and wrapped his arms around himself. He was trying to give himself the embrace he so desperately longed for. Then he turned and walked away, too quickly to see Lisa's tears fall.

He wiped the beginnings of tears out of his eyes. What was wrong with him? Why was he so close to tears lately? Everything seemed to make him want to cry.

7

Pez slipped out of the courtyard the same way he used when he came in. Sneaking out was always so much easier then sneaking in. He smiled as he recalled that he had seen Lisa then, too.

As he pushed through the bushes, he heard what he thought was another voice in his head. This one seemed to be more real than the others though. It was someone calling his name. The voice sounded very familiar. He spun around thinking maybe it was a teacher. Teachers usually frowned upon leaving the school grounds without permission. He wouldn't be surprised if he had gotten caught again.

No one was behind him, so he dismissed it as a fluke and continued the way he had been going before. He walked out alone, lost in his own thoughts and memories, mostly of Lisa. He didn't see the small girl until she stepped out in front of him, cutting him off.

Pez was surprised, he hadn't seen this many hallucinations all in one day since Rehab and none of those Rehab hallucinations were as real as this one seemed. Standing before him now, he found his friend Amber. He sighed again, wishing that it really was Amber; the living Amber and not the barely recognizable Amber he saw now. He blinked and rubbed his eyes, hoping the ghost before him would disappear. She was still standing there. His mind went wild with panic. Maybe he was going crazy. Why else would he keep seeing things–people–that didn't exist or didn't exist anymore?

she turns to me
I start in remembrance
she turns to me
and I begin to doubt my
existence
am I dead?
or is she?

"Pez?" the Amber ghost repeated. She looked like hell. She was thin and emaciated. The sun shining on her skin gave it an eerie look of translucency. Pez could see many veins underneath her pale skin. There were dark circles under her red blood-shot eyes. In a few years this Amber ghost might look just like Junkie Pez. Did that make this ghost Junkie Amber?

Her left eyebrow was pierced and so was her nose. She had maybe ten piercings in her left ear and four in her right. Two tiny barrettes in the shape of sparkly silver ovals were in her short cropped bleached blond, almost white hair. Her hair hung limply on her head due to the fact that it was fried beyond all belief.

She was dressed in total raver garb. Her shirt was a small, tight fitting tee shirt that displayed her tiny breasts perfectly. Her stomach was showing and Pez noticed that her belly button was pierced and had a yellow sun tattoo around it. Her pants were baggy black JNCO jeans that totally hid her feet. The pants seemed to be as wide as Amber was tall, but Pez knew the style of jeans. He knew they were only forty inches wide in the pant legs. A long chain went from her back pocket to a front belt loop on her pants. It was so long it hung just slightly past her knee, or where her knee should have been.

She was wearing a baby's pacifier on a chain around her neck. Pez knew what that was for. (He had a large collection of them at home.) This Junkie Amber ghost was definitely doing ecstasy.

Ecstasy stimulated every sense almost to the point of orgasm. He remembered how good it felt to suck on a pacifier. He also vaguely remembered hospital masks with Vicks Vapor Rub spread on the inside of them. Both tactics brought extreme pleasure to the 'roller'.

'She looks different,' Pez thought to himself. 'I guess we all look different at that big rave in the sky,' Pez reasoned to himself as he turned away from the apparition before him. He wanted to leave the Amber ghost and all the memories she brought along with her behind.

"Well Pez, how does this look?" Amber asked as she entered her bedroom, where Pez was laying on the bed reading a magazine. He looked up at her. She looked so ridiculous he couldn't help but to laugh at her. "Pez!" she said with a sad look on her face, which made her look even funnier. He laughed harder.

It was Matt's birthday party and Amber was trying to dress like a raver for him. She had a pair of her father's jeans on. They were far too baggy in the waist, she had to hold them up or they would fall to the floor. The bottoms of the pants even when rolled were still too long. They were acid-washed and cut for a tall, heavyset man, not a petite girl. Her shirt was a Hawaiian shirt from her Dad's massive collection. It also was way too large for her. She swam in it. She reminded Pez of a small child playing dress-up in her parent's clothing. He laughed harder at that thought.

"Pez!" she scolded him. "Come on, help me! It's almost time for the party." Amber was having the party at the house she shared with her two friends. Pez, like an idiot, was stupid enough to arrive early. He could have been anywhere else, instead of dealing with Amber and her whiny attitude. She could be so overdramatic at times.

Pez calmed himself down. "Well, you definitely cannot wear that. What else do you have?"

"Nothing! Absolutely nothing! Matt's gonna get here and I'm gonna look like a big fat dork!!! I need a whole new wardrobe to please him," she said sadly. She was pouting again. She let the pants fall to the floor. Pez was shocked that she would do that in front of him even though he couldn't see anything because of the Hawaiian shirt.

"Matt doesn't care what you wear," Pez rationalized. Matt and Amber had been going out for about two weeks. Matt and Diamond broke up, but they were still friends. Amber was Eddie's friend from high school.

"You know, maybe he doesn't, but I do. Do you know what it's like going to these parties with you guys wearing a Pearl Jam or a Nine Inch Nails shirt and my normal cut, tight ass 'Chic' jeans while all you guys have your baggy pants and your various shirts none of which, by the way, say either Pearl Jam or Nine Inch Nails. Face it, Pez. I'm a loser!" she said, covering her face with her hands.

Pez knew how she felt; he could sympathize with her. He had once been in her position; luckily Glenn had connections and got him lots of nice clothes for cheap. "Glenn's got connections; maybe he could help you out."

"That sounds really cool, but that doesn't help me now!" she reasoned.

"Here, let me look in your closet and see what you've got." He opened her closet only to find various Hawaiian shirts of her father's and stacked up boxes.

"Where are the rest of your clothes?" he asked.

"I don't have any!" Amber said in disgust, lowering his hands.

Pez noticed a feather boa in the top box. "What's in this box?" he asked, lifting the lid. Inside he found costumes of one sort or another.

"That's all the stuff of my Mom and Dad's that I still need to go through." Pez smiled sadly, remembering that Amber had just recently lost both her parents in a horrible car crash.

"That looks like the costumes from when my mom used to work for the theater," she said, stepping out of the pool of her father's pants and walking towards Pez.

"This is good," Pez said, pulling out a silver mini-dress. "What's it from?" Pez asked, holding the dress out to her.

"I think it's an old Halloween costume of my mom's. It has matching boots," she said, pushing Pez out of the way and tearing the contents of the box out. "AHA!" she said, straightening up again. "They are kind of sixties-like." She held the silver platform shoes out in front of her in distaste.

"They're perfect! Put the boots and dress on and let me see what they look like," Pez said, and walked into the bathroom to pee. Just as Pez was pulling his zipper back up, Amber opened the door and stood there. She was wearing blue fluorescent fishnet stockings and a matching boa.

"It doesn't look like I thought it would, but it's damn sexy," she said, admiring herself in the mirror next to Pez. "I borrowed the fishnets from Anne. I thought they would help. I am so glad my mom and I are... were... the same size."

Pez nodded his agreement. He looked at her appraisingly for a moment. "It still needs a little work," Pez informed her. "Sit," he commanded her, pointing to the now closed toilet.

"Why? What are you going to do?" she asked, a worried look crossing her face.

"I'm going to fix your hair. Where are your brush and some rubber bands?" he asked, looking around.

"In the medicine cabinet," she replied.

He opened the cabinet to find each shelf was totally filled with hair care products and various make-up products. To his dismay, almost all of the shelves had at least one brush on them. "So whose shelf is who's?" he asked, scratching his head.

"The bottom shelf is mine, the middle one is Tammy's, and the top two are Anne's," she recited, as if she had that fact drilled into her head on a normal basis. Pez frowned as he noticed there was no make-up at all on Amber's shelf. His frown turned into a smile as he noticed that the top shelf was completely filled with glittery make-up of every color imaginable.

"Can we use some of this make-up too?" he asked, pointing toward it.

"I guess, I don't think Anne will mind," she replied, shrugging her shoulders.

Pez pulled her long dark brown hair up into two ponytails. The part wasn't all that good, but he didn't care. He wrapped a piece of hair around each of the ponytails and tucked it under the bands, creating small buns at the base of them.

Then he moved on to the make-up. He loved working with all the glittery make-up that Anne owned. He ended by dusting

Amber's skin heavily with the glittery powder that he found. She looked very futuristic.

"Voila," Pez said, grinning. "Amber Weber: Club Kid Extraordinaire!"

Pez stepped back. He was proud of the work he had done with the hair and the make-up. He never did tell Amber that it was the first time he had done either. In the end it was the look she was going for, and Matt loved it.

<u>vêtements</u>

off she takes her vêtements
and ever so carelessly tosses them aside
her whole life she has hid
no longer can she hide
she goes forth in freedom
ignoring the pain inside
no one around her knows the secret
which she keeps so protected; no one knows
that her
true self has died

He squeezed quickly through some more bushes and was on the other side, walking away from the school, before the Amber ghost caught up with him again.

Suddenly, he felt a hand on his shoulder. He jerked away from the hand as if it were death itself. He shivered violently, his sudden fear causing a cold chill to rip through his body.

"God damn it, Pez. Don't do this to me!" The angry Amber ghost grabbed his elbow and swung him around to face her. "I came here hoping to find you. Don't treat me like this Pez!" she pleaded with him. "I called your house, but your mother says you're still not taking any calls."

"Is it a message from Wolf?" he whispered softly, still stunned. He was afraid someone would see him talking to the apparition before him.

"What?" Amber asked, confused by his question. Then she understood what he was talking about. "PEZ! Snap out of it! I'm not dead, remember?"

All at once, the newscast from the night after the accident rang through his head, (his mom thought he would be interested in seeing it, so she recorded it for him.): *Yesterday morning tragedy struck the tri-county area. A seven-car pile-up on Emmerdale's west side resulted in the deaths of seventeen local residents. The only residents to survive the fiery crash were three local teens from Emmerdale high: David Spencer, age seventeen; Salvador Carroll, age eighteen; Amber Weber, age seventeen; and one unidentified man, age estimated at forty years old. All are listed in critical condition at Emmerdale memorial hospital. The cause of the accident is still unknown, but authorities speculate that icy roads were to blame.*

"Amber?" he asked with tears in his eyes. He was overwhelmed with shock, as reality smiled upon his world, if only for a split second. She wasn't a ghost; she was alive. He was no longer so alone. She nodded, tears filling her own eyes. Now, she too had found someone else out there that knew what she'd been through. A smile slowly spread across her pale visage. It was a goofy grin that Pez could not help but return.

She hesitated momentarily, staring deeply into his eyes. It seemed as if she were searching for something. Then she threw her arms around his neck in a hug. Pez put his arms around her and squeezed her tightly, hoping she wouldn't disappear. (He still didn't quite believe she was real.) He even went so far as to pick her up and swing her from side to side like he had done so many times in the past. It felt good to hold onto something he thought he had lost.

"You're hurting me," she mumbled into his shoulder. He set her down and took a step back to get a good look at her.

"Sorry," Pez apologized. "It's just so good to see you," he said, the smile brightening on his face.

She stood before him, smiling. It was only then that he noticed the scar that ran down her right cheek and down her neck. It was still red and puffy even after all this time.

Pez ran his finger down his arm where his own souvenir scars from the accident were beginning to ache.

"I thought you were dead," he laughed, even though to him it wasn't funny. "I thought you were dead and I was going crazy."

"Well neither of us is dead... or crazy. At least I don't think we are." She giggled, linking her arm in his. They began to walk away from the school. "So, how have you been?" she asked. She smiled brightly, but Pez could tell the smile was as fake as her previous one had been real. Pez could only assume that she wanted something.

Pez stared at her for a moment as he tried to find the shy little cutie he used to know. It was useless; she had changed so much in her demeanor that Pez could barely recognize her.

"Pretty shitty," he replied truthfully.

"You know what?" Amber asked, but did not wait for him to answer, "me too. What do you say we go somewhere and get drunk?" she asked, raising her eyebrows.

Pez shrugged. "Uh, OK," he replied and let her lead him around the corner.

She smiled too sweetly for Pez to look at. Everything about her seemed so fake now. Amber giggled as Pez looked away. "I know where we can get some 'e', if you've got the money," she stated, rubbing his arm with her free hand and smiling that fake smile again.

"No, I d-don't want any," he stammered. He was lucky that she hadn't shown up only a scant few seconds sooner. Even now, after the withdrawal had passed, it was still so hard to decline her offer. He had the money; he could just get one hit and take it next time he needed it. No, he was stronger than that; at least he thought he was.

"Come on Pez, I know you want some. I saw you with Lisa."

"Lisa's my ex-girlfriend," Pez explained, trying to hide what he was actually doing only a few minutes ago.

"Oh please, Pez! Everyone knows her brother deals. What were you doing there?" Amber asked. Her sweet facade was slowly falling away. "What were you talking about?"

"That was a mistake," he said through gritted teeth. Why couldn't she just drop it and leave him alone? Why did she have to bring drugs into it at all?

"You're damn right it was a mistake, Kenny is an asshole. He charges way too much for that shit he sells. Kenny's shit is nowhere near as wonderful as the 'e' that I can get for you," she enticed him.

Pez looked at her in disbelief. She was so different then she used to be. Before the accident, she had been a shy, drug-free little geek. Well, she wasn't actually a geek; she was pretty much a 'nobody'. Now, here she was scolding him for going to a bad dealer. She even knew the name of more than one dealer and how good their shit was.

"No, Amber, I'm clean now, really!" he claimed, trying to convince her of the truth.

"Bullshit! No one is ever 'clean'! So come on *Pe-ez,*" she whined his name. She had always been good at whining. *"Come o-on, you're all I have left. I ne-ed you,"* she begged, trying to look like a lost puppy dog. It didn't work. Pez fought back the urge to laugh in her face.

"At least come with us, you can get some for later. *Ple-ease,"* she said, sounding desperate.

"No Amber." Pez was getting angrier by the second. "I told you. I don't do drugs anymore! Why can't you just…"

"AMBER!" a male voice cut him off. Amber whipped around, she looked frightened for a second and then her sweet little mask was back. A man standing next to a blue pick-up truck gestured to her. She turned back to Pez.

"Look, there's gonna be a rave tomorrow. Be there, OK?" she said, handing him a flyer that she pulled out of her overly huge back pocket. Pez nodded dumbly, still in shock at the changes he found in his old friend.

"I love you," she said, kissing his lips gently and for a second, the old Amber was back. The feel of her scar against his lips made him impulsively stick his tongue out and gently caress the scar. As if angered by the motion, Amber grabbed his wrist. She pulled his sleeve back and gently kissed his scars. She looked into his eyes again, smiling sadly. "I gotta go," she said and gave him a quick hug. Pez smiled at her and watched as Amber ran over to the pickup truck where the guy waited for her.

Pez absently fingered the small scar on his forehead that was usually hidden by hair, as he watched her go. Sometimes he could still feel Wolf's broken rib hitting his head.

"Did you get any?" the man asked Amber.

"No, you interrupted us too soon," she scolded him as she stood in front of him with her hands on her lower back and a pout on her lips.

"Well then, why'd you leave?"

She shrugged. "Should I go back?"

"Naw, forget it. Let's go find Mike. He always gives us some of his." Watching Amber climb into the car, Pez noticed that Amber wasn't wearing any shoes. The bottoms of her feet were black with dirt and grime. He found it strange that Amber had no shoes on, but then again, the whole conversation had been strange to Pez.

Pez looked at the flyer in his hand. It was a plain white glossy piece of cardboard, with only the word 'senses' written on it in big black block letters. The text was off center and the letters were somewhat fuzzy. Pez was reminded of a poem that Amber once read to him.

Senses

I tried to touch the rose,
but it withered.
I tried to see the rainbow,
but it disappeared.
I tried to taste the rain,
but it burned my throat.
I tried to hear the birds' song,
but they no longer sing.
I tried to breathe the air,
but it suffocated me.
when will I ever come to my
senses

Pez laughed aloud, startling himself with the loudness of his laughter. He laughed because irony had reared her ugly head once more. Pez stopped his psychotic laughing as he realized Amber and her man were staring at him through the windows of the truck. He smiled in a goofy apology.

Pez sighed as he watched Amber and her man drive away. All Amber wanted was money for ecstasy. He remembered when he used to be like that. He sold almost everything he owned for drugs. It was sickening to see someone else like that.

"*Poor Amber. Somebody better straighten her out,*" Wolf's voice echoed in his head. Those were the same words Wolf had said when Matt first introduced the group to his new girlfriend Amber. Those words rang true even more now than they did when Wolf had first said them. Somebody really did need to straighten her out.

Pez turned the flyer over scanning the names of the DJs for any that he knew. Five DJs were spinning there, and for a second, he thought he saw Glenn's pseudonym mixed in among the DJs. He knew three of the five: DJ Brainchild, DJ Blow Pop, and DJ Marlin. All of them were local DJs and had been friends of his at one time. For a moment, he was tempted to go, just to see those DJs. He snorted in disgust, knowing that if he went, he would only have to deal with people like Amber pushing him to do drugs and such. He ripped up the flyer and let it fall to the ground. Angered by Amber's silent betrayal, Pez stalked off towards home.

8

His mom was at work and Stevie was still at school.
That meant that Pez would finally be alone. He thought maybe he
could try to sleep a little bit before work. Lately, he'd been having
trouble sleeping; nightmares, feelings of shame, guilt, and hatred
for himself all played a part in the problem.

He set his alarm clock for 3:30 pm and crashed into his
bed, fully clothed and ready for work, hoping he wouldn't dream.
His dreams always seemed to turn into nightmares of the crash.

In this dream, he walked slowly down a hallway with thick plush carpeting. The carpet felt good against the skin of his bare feet. He wiggled his toes in pleasure. The hallway before him was vaguely familiar, something tugged urgently at his memory. Something was missing from the hallway. For a moment he couldn't fathom what it was that was missing. Then it hit him: pictures... There were no pictures of Wolf or Diamond or even Mokey hanging on the walls of the hallway.

He paused in front of Diamond's door, wondering whether or not he should open it and step inside. He could hear the sounds of music playing softly from behind the closed door.

The words of Erasure echoed in gossamer wisps that surrounded his head and danced through his mind. Pez's heart wrenched as he recognized the song that was playing. 'When I needed you.' Diamond used to joke about that song. She would tell people that when she killed herself, she wanted that song played at her funeral. She called it her suicide song. Pez had never found that funny.

A noise coming from the end of the hallway drew his attention away from Diamond's door. It sounded like someone was calling his name. In fact, it sounded like Wolf calling his name. All of the guilt that the Erasure song brought up disappeared as he looked at the stairway at the end of the hall. A strong feeling of dread seemed to be urging him forward towards the attic; which had been Wolf's room. Wolf was in danger, horrible danger. He knew then the reason why he was here at the Waverly house and Diamond was not the reason. He would have to deal with Diamond later if he could, but right now he had to save Wolf. He no longer fought the urge that was pulling him towards the steps leading to the attic... the steps leading to Wolf.

He ran up the stairs, taking them two at a time. After six steps, he reached the landing and he spun around the corner so fast he almost lost his balance. He ran up six more steps and he was standing outside of the door. Suddenly, he stopped; he was afraid, afraid of whatever was hiding behind Wolf's door. It was the kind of fear that made his bones quake.

Not wanting to be the coward that he knew he was, he started to open the door. Slowly, ever so slowly, he inched the door open, afraid every second that something would jump out and attack him. To Pez's surprise and relief, Wolf's room was empty. No boogie men were waiting inside the room to gobble him up. But then again, Wolf wasn't in there either.

alone
the room is empty
and I cry
You're not there
not like I wanted
you to be
and I cry
I wanted to
say goodbye,
but you are
gone
this room is empty
I am alone
and I cry
alone
forever
alone

Pez moved into the center of the room. He stood there looking around the room with tears streaming down his face. Where was Wolf? Why wasn't he here? He looked around the room that had once been filled with his lover's belongings. Now it lay before him empty. Empty like his life had become ever since he lost Wolf. Empty like his life would be from now on. Empty.

There was no furniture filling that room... only indentations in the carpet where furniture had once been. No clothing filled the open closet... only empty wire hangers that once held Wolf's favorite possessions; his clothing. The hangers chimed together softly as if a breeze had just blown through Wolf's... no, not Wolf's bedroom. Pez could not think of this place as Wolf's room anymore. It was too quiet. It reminded him too much of a tomb—Wolf's tomb.

He noticed that the posters on the walls were gone too. All that was left to remind him that they had been there were darker squares where the paint around the posters had faded. He remembered each poster and where it should be. The poster of Brad Pitt used to hang on the wall above where the bed used to be. On the wall across from that was his Pet Shop Boys poster that he had to search the Internet to find. A framed photograph of the ten friends used to hang to the left of the Pet Shop Boys. Sadly, it had only hung there a few weeks before everyone in the photo had died (everyone except for Pez, Sal, Amber and Mike).

A poster of Robert Smith from the Cure hung to the right of the boys. Pez remembered Mike buying it for Wolf at the Cure concert that they all went to see. Next to that was another poster from that same concert. It was a picture of Robert's hands folded together, fingers entwined as if in prayer. The words written on that poster were from a Cure song, the same words that were tattooed on Wolf's back.

He gazed at the wall across from the door. He couldn't remember what had hung there. Then it hit him… That was where Wolf had painted a giant mural of Brandon Lee from the movie "The Crow". It had taken him well over a year to finish it. Pez remembered him putting the finishing touches on it. Now it had been painted over. If he looked close enough, he could almost make out the life-sized figure walking towards him, arms spread as if he was actually a bird ready to take off into flight.

For a moment, Pez wished that Wolf could 'come back'. He wanted a big black crow to come and bring Wolf back to have his vengeance, just so Pez could see him once more. It wasn't as if something like that could actually happen. He knew that. If it did happen though, Pez would be the one that Wolf would come after for vengeance, for it was Pez's fault that Wolf had died.

Now, here he stood alone, without Wolf. He had no one to hold onto or to love like he once loved Wolf. He had no one to kiss, no one to share his thoughts and his dreams with. He was all alone… ALL ALONE.

A strange, muffled-sounding scream drew Pez's attention to the side of the room closest to the door. He noticed the carpet there was moving. It began to boil and bubble upward, in a sickening, blistering fashion, filling Pez with horror. He screamed, but he couldn't run. He could only watch as Wolf's dead body slowly came up out of the carpeting, directly in front of him. A puddle of blood began to form around Wolf. The floor was filling with blood, Wolf's blood, just like the ground outside Pez's car had done. Pez found himself slowly backing away from the blood. He didn't want the blood on his bare feet.

out of the darkness
he emerges

struggling
to keep his head
above the
over spilled
Ocean of Dark

Pez's feet were frozen once again as the body jolted vilely and came to life. Wolf struggled and pulled himself out of the carpeting, coughing and sputtering.

"Pez!" the reanimated Wolf whispered hoarsely, as if he had been screaming for a century. "Help me." He reached out to Pez. "Please Pez," he begged. "Oh God, don't let me die, Pez. I'm not ready to die. Help me!" Wolf begged in the exact words and voice he had the night of the accident. Pez could only stand paralyzed and watch in horror as flames rose out of the carpet and began to consume Wolf.

"Pez!" he screamed in horror and pain. "Pez! HELP ME!" his voice rose to a dizzying pitch. Pez watched in astonishment as his own arms reached into the flames to save the older boy, even though he was already dead.

Pez's arms were burned as he pulled his lover out of the fire and dragged him over to the safety of the doorway. He cried out in pain as he used all his strength to pull Wolf down the first six steps and onto the landing.

Pez watched in wonder and awe as Wolf's wounds and his own began to heal, right before his eyes. Wolf smiled up at Pez lovingly. Pez couldn't help but to smile back. He was so happy that Wolf was back where he belonged; in Pez's arms.

"You're not real," Pez murmured softly studying the face of the man he held in his arms.

"Oh but, I am," Wolf whispered back. "I knew you would help me, Pez." Wolf sat up and pulled himself up so he was sitting next to Pez. Wolf put his arms around Pez and let him cry. It was exactly what Pez needed, exactly what he had been longing for.

When Pez calmed down, he backed away from Wolf slightly. Wolf smiled again. His smile was intoxicating to Pez. It filled him with love and the familiar longing of the past.

"You're not real," Pez whispered again.

"You already said that," Wolf pointed out, still smiling.

"But you're not!!! You can't be!!!" Pez cried out.

"Hush," Wolf held a finger to Pez's lips. "Don't say that," he looked around. "You helped me, David, and now I'm going to help you." He leaned towards Pez and softly kissed Pez's awaiting lips. He pulled back a little and Pez felt him whisper the words 'I love you'.

Lingering traces of Wolf's breath clung to Pez's lips as he fell into oblivion, but this was a good oblivion. It was an oblivion that felt much more like Wolf's arms cradling him.

<u>Dream</u>

cold like a river

dead like a sea

in the darkness I begin to shiver

where can my lover be?

I reach out to touch him

he is so cold

so...lifeless

and limp

God, How limp he is

cold like a river

dead like a sea

his eyes, still open stare up at me

I gaze into the heavens

where can my lover be

it's been so long

my lover gone

my Lover...

cold as a river

dead like a sea

Part Two: Joy

9

$\mathcal{P}$ez slept dreamlessly until his alarm went off. He wasn't jolted awake by the sound of screeching tires and breaking glass, like he had been every other night since the accident. At least this time he woke up like a normal person.

Pez realized that for the first time in a long time he was actually hungry. He was actually craving food. He fished around in the fridge for leftovers. Finally when the food was heated and in front of him, he thought of nothing but eating it, which he did. It was his first good meal in a very long time.

He took a shower, feeling more relaxed then he had in ages. His short walk to the bookstore was replaced with a vigorous jog. The jog left him out of breath and wheezing, but he smiled. He felt somewhat happy for the first time in months. Maybe his heart was finally healing. What he didn't realize is that he hadn't thought of the accident since his dream of Wolf.

After he caught his breath, Pez walked into the bookstore feeling alive and happy to be at work. He loved his job at the bookstore. He loved reading books. Reading seemed to be his only escape from the harsh realities of this world.

He loved going to work the most when Rachael worked with him. He loved working with her, being there with her. He loved the way she looked and the way she smelled, just like baby powder and soft, sweet femininity.

she is beauty
essence divine
only how I
ache wishing
she were
mine
male and female
intertwined
she is innocence
so aching
and sublime
realistic pleasure
standing the test
of time
aching my ache
rhyming my rhyme
she is the one
it's a pity
she can never
be mine

Not only did Pez find Rachael beautiful, but he also loved her sense of humor. She was the only thing that kept him going after the accident. They would usually laugh all night until they were closed, but he could never work up enough nerve to ask her out.

Rachael was sitting behind the counter shuffling a deck of Magic: The Gathering cards. She looked up when she heard him walk in.

"Well you certainly seem happy today, Davie. Are you sick?" Rachael quipped. She never called him Pez and with her, he didn't mind it. He actually kind of liked it. Pez shrugged. He smiled shyly at her for a moment. He was slightly embarrassed about his thoughts of the way she looked and smelled.

"What?" she asked nervously. She reached her hand up to smooth down her hair. Then she ran her finger quickly under her nose. She thought something was wrong with the way she looked.

"Nothing," he smiled and shook his head. He tossed his coat behind the counter and punched in. Trying to avoid any further embarrassment, he asked, "Did we get any new books in Rae?" He looked around, everything seemed to be done.

"Nope," Rae shrugged. "Boss left us a work list to be completed this evening," she replied, with emphasis on this evening. She crinkled her nose in dismay at the mere mention of Boss. Boss was one of their co-workers who thought she ran the bookstore.

"What did the manager say to do?" Pez asked, echoing her dismay.

"He didn't say anything at all. Come on Davie, we've both been working here long enough to know what needs to be done and Jason knows that! He never gives us a work list."

"True," Pez nodded. "It's like insulting our intelligence or something."

"Well, there really is nothing else to do, so we might as well do Boss's list then. It would make her happy." Rae rolled her eyes.

"HEY! Maybe she'll give us raises!" Pez said in mock excitement. Rachael laughed. Her laughter was music to Pez. He decided he would definitely ask her out... someday.

"Well, then it's settled. We'll do it quickly though, so we can play Magic," she continued to shuffle the cards.

Pez laughed. "You said 'do it'," he pointed out jokingly.

"You know what I mean!" she defended.

"I know." He smiled at her.

She stuck her tongue out at him in response.

"First, let's modify this list a little," Pez started. "We're not going to move the shelves to sweep underneath them. That's dumb! Boss can do that herself," he said, crossing the first job off of the list.

"Dust off the top of the lights? I don't think so," Rae declared, shaking her head.

Pez crossed that off the list.

"Mop the floor," Pez read the next job on the list. "We do that when we close anyway," Pez explained, shrugging as he crossed that job off of the list.

"And that leaves... Wash the windows. We can do that Davie!" Rae said smiling. "I think it's just up to our intelligence level."

"Duh, I don't know, do ya think we can handle it?" Pez asked in a stupid voice.

"We can do it," she said, nodding her head emphatically. "We're really smart... I think," Rae answered. Pez laughed as she gathered the cleaning supplies.

"Rae?" he asked.

"Hmm?" she responded as they walked over to the windows.

"Do you believe in ghosts?" Pez asked. He was surprised when her eyes lit up.

"Absolutely, why?"

"I thought I saw one today," he said. He was so close to telling her about his day.

"Really?" she asked, truly intrigued.

"Yea, but it turned out to be my friend Amber. She survived the... She was in the car... when...when...," he stumbled close to tears about the near mention of the accident.

"I know," Rae nodded, saving him from the misery of having to finish his explanation. She looked a little disappointed that he hadn't seen a real ghost.

"It was so weird Rae, like I was going crazy. I thought... I mean, somehow my mind told me that I was the only survivor and that I killed all of them," he gasped in a quick breath of air as the words slipped out. No one except for Pez knew exactly what he was doing that night, not even Amber.

"Davie, you didn't kill them, it was a car accident. Accident is the key word there."

"I know," he replied, humoring her. It was the only way she would leave him alone about the accident. He learned that was true about everybody a long time ago. Let them believe what they wanted and they would leave him alone. So that's how it had been since the accident. Pez never let anyone in and he tried so hard to never let any of it out.

Just then, she noticed a customer who needed help. She turned and went over to the counter to help the customer. "I guess," he said softly so she wouldn't hear.

Finishing one window and moving on to the next, he heard Wolf's voice whisper, *"Don't tell her Pez. Don't tell anyone, they'll all just think you are crazy."*

"Rae would believe me," he whispered back softly.

"No, baby, no. No one is going to believe you, not about this. I don't want people thinking that you're crazy," Wolf reasoned.

"Yeah, but they already do think you're crazy," D's voice contradicted Wolf.

He nodded, agreeing with his own crazy mind. Pez knew he was losing it. He knew that he was slipping out of reality faster and faster each day.

"Oooh! Look how shiny they are," Rae said in a cute little girl voice, as she walked back over to the windows. She reached out not quite touching the window before her. "Boss will surely give us raises when she sees the good job we did," she smiled.

Pez exhaled slowly, watching in bliss as her eyes crinkled at the edges when she smiled. This feeling that he felt about Rae was nothing compared to what he had felt for Wolf, but at least it was something.

"Hey, whaddaya say I go pick up some snackies for the game?" she asked, gesturing towards the door.

Pez nodded, cleaning up the paper towel mess that lined the floor underneath the windows.

"Anything special you want?"

Pez shrugged. "Whatever you want is fine with me."

"OK, be right back," she said, grabbing her coat and heading out the door.

Pez planted himself behind the counter and began to search through his Magic cards to make a deck. He left his cards at the bookstore because Rae was the only one he ever played Magic with anymore.

"Pez?" a voice asked.

The voice automatically shifted Pez into a memory.

He was sitting on the couch at Wolf's house watching movies with Diamond, Eddie, Mike, and Wolf. Eddie had gone to the bathroom and Diamond was popping homemade popcorn in the kitchen. The between movie silence was deafening. Wolf looked at Pez and smiled.

Pez smiled brightly in return. "I'll be right back," Wolf said, leaving the room.

"So, Pez," Mike said, looking directly at Pez. "When are ***you*** *going to tell Diamond?" he asked, smirking.*

"Tell her what?" Pez asked, confused by Mike's sudden attention. Mike hardly ever talked to Pez.

"About you and my boyfriend," Mike said half- laughing. He rolled his eyes at Pez. His smile was turning malicious. Pez's mind went wild. How did Mike know about Wolf and him? Pez and Wolf had decided to keep their relationship quiet. They were going behind Mike's back. Somehow, Mike had found out about their secret. How could he know? There was no possible way. He must have heard something. He must have seen something. Either that, or Wolf had told him, but Wolf promised he wouldn't tell. He promised.

"What about him and Wolf?" Eddie asked, walking back into the room.

Mike continued to stare at Pez. Silently, he begged Mike not to tell Eddie. Pez didn't want Mike to hurt him or Wolf, even though they both had hurt Mike with their relationship. Mike disregarded the pleading look that filled Pez's eyes. "Wolf and Pez are an item now," he informed Eddie in a singsong voice.

"What happened to you...?" Eddie began, but Mike cut him off before he could add the words "and Wolf."

"Seems they've been together since Diamond's birthday party," Mike announced, looking now at Eddie. Pez relaxed a little without Mike's eyes burning holes into him. "What a wonderful gift, don't you think? Diamond's gonna be real happy about that." He turned his icy glare back on Pez. "You sure know how to hurt people don't you, Spencer? It's bad enough that you stole my boyfriend, but just imagine how crushed Diamond is gonna be when she finds out."

"Youch! I forgot about that," Eddie said. "Better not tell Diamond," he advised Pez, crashing onto the easy chair next to the couch.

"What do you mean 'I crushed Diamond'? I didn't do anything to her!" Pez said, shaking his head. "Why are we all so concerned about Diamond anyway? What does she have to do with me and Wolf?" Pez asked naively.

"Because, Dip-shit. She's got a crush on you. She's had a crush on you since you first met, you are just too stupid to notice," Mike spat.

"What about Matt?"

"She told me she'd give him up in an instant if she even remotely had a chance with you," Mike explained.

Eddie nodded in agreement, rubbing his newly shaven head. It seemed to be an epidemic with his friends. So far, the only guys who hadn't shaved their heads were Mike, Wolf and Pez.

"You bastard! You're lying! She didn't say that!" Pez was lost in confusion. "I'm not lying, Spencer. That's what she said," Mike stated matter-of-factly.

"I did tell him that, Pez," Diamond said, carrying a huge bowl of popcorn in the living room. She had tears streaming down her face. "You weren't EVER supposed to tell him that, MIKE! You weren't supposed to tell ANYONE!" She dropped the popcorn in his lap.

"I'm sorry, Di," Mike whispered.

"SHUT-UP ASSHOLE!" Diamond demanded.

"Diamond... I didn't know. I'm sorry I...," Pez began, but she cut him off.

"How could you? How could you lie to me? YOU TOLD ME YOU WERE STRAIGHT, GOD DAMN IT! How long have you known? No, don't tell me, I don't want to know. I DON'T EVER WANT TO SEE YOU AGAIN! You broke my fucking heart," she yelled at him, ending in a whisper. She turned and stalked from the room. Pez heard her door slam shortly after she disappeared.

"Why are you doing this to me? Can't I just be happy for once in my life? Why do you have to go and ruin it for me? WHAT DID I EVER DO TO YOU?" Pez screamed. He knew what he had done, but somehow he thought maybe it wouldn't matter. Mike would see how much they loved each other and he would be OK with them getting together. He knew he was being selfish, but he didn't care. He just wanted to get out of there. He grabbed his coat and ran from the Waverly's house.

"Come on Pez! It's just a movie!" Mike yelled after him. Mike looked at Eddie and put a finger to his lips, indicating that Eddie shouldn't tell anyone about the conversation. He nodded, but later let Pez know what had happened after he left. "How *irritable can you get?" Mike asked as Wolf sat down on the couch in the living room.*

"Where did Pez go?" he asked. Mike pointed to the front door, which was still open. "Dammit Mike! I told you he was nervous! You swore you wouldn't say anything. Pez!" Wolf called out as he jumped up and chased after Pez. "Pez!" Wolf called again, but he never did catch up with him. "PEZ!" Wolf screamed out as Pez disappeared around a bend in the road. Wolf's voice slowly changed and morphed into Mike's and the word was less like a call and more like a question.

He looked up. Mike was standing in front of him.

"Yes?" he said wondering if he should pretend like he didn't know who Mike was. He decided against that. "Mike?" he asked, trying to smile at his old friend.

Mike nodded.

"I haven't seen you in ages," Pez pointed out, shaking Mike's outstretched hand. Mike pulled him close for a quick one-armed hug.

"Yeah. Since the funerals, no doubt," Mike speculated, smiling.

Pez couldn't tell if it was a real smile or not.

"I didn't get to go to the funerals," Pez said accusingly. He knew it wasn't Mike's fault that he didn't get to go. He just felt there was something inside Mike that he couldn't trust.

"Right, sorry." Mike nodded. "So, how have you been?"

<u>to share</u>

if you do not wish to know me
then quit asking me to share
if you do not wish to befriend me
then quit pretending that you care
do not hold your arm out to me
while your arm is bare
your attempts to befriend me
have only caused a scare
if you do not wish to know me
then quit asking me to share

"Oh, I've been alright, and you?" Pez responded politely.

"About the same, no complaints here," he looked around. "Look, I can't stay. I've got to get to work myself, but I was wondering if you were going to the rave tomorrow. It's gonna kick ass."

"No, I don't think I can m-m-make it," Pez stuttered, shaking his head. He hated that dreadful stutter that plagued his childhood, starting just after his father died. He had stuttered constantly until just before freshman year, when his mom finally sent him to a speech therapist. It came back every now and then when he was nervous or angry.

"Spencer, if you fell off the horse, you gotta get back on," Mike pointed out.

"Not if the horse is dead!" Pez argued.

Mike stared at him, horrified. "Sorry, I didn't mean it that way. It's just that there've been so many parties and raves since the accident and I haven't seen you at any."

"Well I've been b-busy... with rehab and stuff," Pez explained, wishing Mike would just go away.

"Yeah, I heard about that. I'm glad to see that you're doing so well."

"It wasn't really my choice. It was either that or jail," Pez said testily.

"Come on man, you really need to get out."

Pez shrugged; maybe he did need to go out. "I guess," he confessed reluctantly.

"Spencer, it wasn't the rave that killed them," Mike pointed out.

"How would you know that? You weren't even there. Besides, I know the rave didn't kill them, because I did. I killed them!" Pez laughed as he counted up the times that he'd admitted his guilt today and still nobody believed him.

"You didn't kill them either." Mike sighed and looked away. "I'm sorry. I didn't come here to hurt you," Mike clarified truthfully.

"Then why did you come here?" Pez demanded, angered that Mike was even there. "Was it to gloat about your phenomenal psychic powers that kept you away that night?" Pez pursed his lips and stared at Mike.

"Screw you Spencer! You know I had a wedding... You know what?" He threw his arms up. Pez flinched. He was afraid Mike would hit him. "Forget this shit! I don't care! Think what you want to! Amber and I thought it might be good for you to get out and do something other than moping and sitting on your ass all day, but obviously you're not mature enough to want that!"

Pez ground his teeth and took several deep breaths. He hadn't realized how close to crying he was. He felt his bottom lip beginning to quiver, betraying his wish to hide his tears. He swallowed angrily. Deep down he did want to go with Mike. He missed everything about the life he used to lead. He wanted to have everything back, but he knew that if he went, he might start feeling alive again and he didn't deserve that. He didn't deserve to be alive. He wiped away a single tear that escaped past his walls.

"Mike, it sounds like fun and I'd really like to go, but... but I c-can't," he protested.

"Spencer, you need to just forget about what happened. You have to get over it. Don't think about it," Mike encouraged, genuinely trying to help.

"Get over it? You weren't there. You can't know what it feels like," Pez spat, more tears spilling over. He wiped them quickly away. How could Mike suggest he forget about his friends? How could he tell him to just get over it? Pez couldn't forget anything, but this... this he didn't want to forget. "Besides, I can't forget," he said softly, not looking at Mike.

"Pez, I'm sorry, I really am," Mike confessed. Something in the way he said it made Pez believe him. "Just be there, OK?" Mike held out a flyer. Pez reached forward and took it.

Mike turned and left the bookstore. He waved a quick goodbye as he disappeared out into the street.

Pez looked around. There were no customers left in the store, so he put his head down and tried not to cry. He closed his eyes; it was so hard not to fall asleep. He kept jumping awake at every sound, thinking it was a customer, until he heard a voice within his half-formed dream.

"Pez, it's OK, go to sleep, we have to talk." He looked frantically around the bookstore to find the source of the voice. When he found no one there he realized that it was Wolf's voice echoing inside his head.

He closed his eyes again and drifted quickly into a light doze.

When he opened his eyes he was somewhere else standing next to Wolf. He looked around. Although he could hear no music or noise, the people all around them were dancing. They were at a rave.

108

"What is it?" Pez asked, no longer concerned with how crazy talking to a dead lover would seem.

"Mike's right," Wolf pointed out.

"What?" Pez asked in surprise.

"You need to get out and have fun. You need to forget about... things for a while," Wolf advised. Pez was surprised that even Wolf had trouble talking about the accident.

"I'm not ready. I don't want to forget," Pez argued softly. "I don't want to forget you," Pez explained, almost begging him. "I don't want to forget any of it," he stated with a finality that left Wolf with no room to argue.

"Amber and Mike, they're not gonna leave you alone, you know. They are going to keep bugging you until you go."

"Why?" Pez asked, almost whining.

"Because that's where you belong," Wolf insisted.

"NO! I belong with you!" Pez protested, anger putting daggers into his words.

"No, you don't. You belong to the world," Wolf asserted cryptically. "You are alive, Pez. You've got a life, now all you have to do is live it... instead of dwelling in the past," Wolf pleaded. It was his turn to beg.

Pez only nodded. "I love you," Pez whispered, choking back tears.

Wolf took Pez's face in his hands.

"Oh baby, I know you do, and I love you too," he said, gently kissing Pez's forehead.

"I never got to tell you," Pez said, the tears now falling. Wolf gently wiped his cheeks. At first he was afraid that he wouldn't be able to touch the spirit before him, but he tried anyway. Pez caught Wolf's hand and kissed the inside of his wrist.

Wolf laughed softly. "I knew it all along," he answered, a tear rolling down his own cheek.

Your questions

I cry for you on lonely nights
I ache for you, but I have no
right
I never knew you
I miss it
the sweetness of your

touch
even though I've never touched
you
I hear the rise and fall of
your chest
but I cannot feel the breath
as
you whisper in my ear
I hear the words
pouring from your
lips
but it's only the past
you are frightened
when you see a tear
fall down my
cheek
you are afraid
you do not
understand
"I cannot hear a
word you say"
I whisper
"That's funny."
you laugh
I feel your
smile against
my cheek
"You haven't heard
any of my
questions,
but you've answered
them anyway"

"Hold me," Pez demanded. He opened his arms to the
Wolf spirit that haunted his dreams and sometimes even his waking

hours. Pez knew as Wolf's arms encircled him, that this is where he truly belonged. No matter how hard he tried, he couldn't stop the tears that now fell. "Don't ever leave me again," Pez sobbed into Wolf's shoulder. He could feel Wolf's chest heaving as he shared in the sad joy that Pez felt inside.

Pez wished that this were real and not just a dream. He didn't want to go back to the cold cruel world, not alone... not without Wolf. "Please," Pez begged. If only he could stay here forever with Wolf.

"I won't," Wolf replied, softly whispering into Pez's hair, when his own tears had subsided enough to let him speak. Pez sobbed once more at the truth he found in Wolf's voice.

"I can't live without you anymore. I just want to die, so that I can be with you again," Pez uttered truthfully, tears streaming down his cheeks.

"NO!" Wolf insisted forcefully. "Don't ever say that. You have been given a gift, David. The gift of life. Don't waste it on me. If you want me to be happy; then live your life," Wolf begged, but Pez didn't hear any of it. He was staring deeply into Wolf's eyes.

Lost in their depths, he leaned forward and kissed Wolf's lips. It was the softest, deepest, sweetest kiss the two had ever shared. The kiss broke gently, leaving Pez crying. "Do you promise that you'll never leave me?" Pez whispered hoarsely. Wolf nodded, tears streaming down his face also.

"I promise, I won't leave until you're ready," Wolf vowed hugging him. "I love you," Wolf whispered as the two held onto each other for dear life and death.

I cry silently

or when I'm

alone

you're there

next to me

but you're not

the silence

is aching;

bleeding

and my

heart is

twice as bad

my heart is twice

as bad

aching because

I'm here

but

you are

not

     Pez wanted to see him once more before he woke, but when he opened his eyes the Wolf-spirit was gone and Pez was once again alone in the bookstore. He wiped his eyes just as Rae walked in.

     "Are you OK, Davie?" Rae asked.

     Pez nodded. "Allergies," he lied in response.

     "Did you turn the open sign to say closed?" she asked.

     "Uh-uhn," Pez replied. 'Who would want to turn the sign over?' he thought, and with that thought, he knew that Wolf had done it.

     They played Magic until it was time to close the store. At 9:30, the store was closed and Pez found himself walking home alone again. Rachael got a ride with her friend and they were going out. All the way home, Pez kicked himself for not asking her out. He knew it was his fault that she hadn't realized he was in love with her. All he had to do was say something, but it what so hard. He was so shy.

10

On the way home, Pez started thinking about Mike. Something about what Mike said was bothering him, but he couldn't quite put his finger on it. He thought about Amber and the way she had changed. He wondered if Mike had changed as much as she had. He didn't seem very different. Then again, he really hadn't lived through any life altering traumas lately. Sure, he'd lost his friends too, but at least he hadn't watched them die.

He was still thinking about Amber and Mike when he arrived home. Pez walked into his living room to find his mother waiting for him. She was sitting on the couch pretending to read a magazine. She had a very angry look on her face, but when she saw Pez walk in, the anger disappeared and she actually smiled at him. She hadn't done that in so long. Pez did a double take. He eyed her warily as she stood up and walked over to block his path.

"David, I want to apologize," she said, her smile fading a little. "I'm sorry for being so hard on you. I know what you've been through and I should try harder to be more sensitive to your needs," she sighed and continued with more bullshit about how she was going to try to change, but he had to try to change also. He was beginning to hate that word... change.

Pez didn't hear a word of it. He was too busy watching what went on behind her. Wolf was standing behind her making faces and goofing off. Pez's eyes popped open wide. He didn't know whether he should laugh or cry. He noticed Stevie in the hallway behind Wolf. His mother stopped talking and followed his gaze. She turned to look behind her at Stevie. "Steven, I thought I told you it was bedtime," she scolded. She seemed to look right past Wolf, or through him. Stevie didn't seem to see him either. Pez suddenly began to feel very nauseous.

"Honey? Are you all right? You look pale," his mom asked, feeling his head to see if he had a fever.

"I... um." He swallowed his fear and tried again. "No, I'm not feeling good at all. I'm going to go to bed now." She had given him the perfect excuse to leave. Pez pushed past her and ran into his bedroom, locking the door behind him.

"Leave me alone, Wolf," he whispered deliriously to the Wolf apparition that had followed him into his room. "I'm going crazy. I know it. I'm just going crazy," he repeated to himself, closing his eyes. He used the words as his own personal mantra and slowly calmed himself down. Luckily, when he opened his eyes the apparition was gone.

He curled himself up into the fetal position in his bed and began to cry. He cried wretched tears, sobbing so hard at times he gagged and heaved, but never threw up. He cried himself to sleep that night, like so many other nights since the accident. Hoping as he slipped into slumber that it would be a peaceful night, but it wasn't. The nightmares plagued his sleep once again.

these dreams...
haunting, lifelike
filled with death
that I cause

with my own hands
these dreams...
they fill my mind
with disillusionment
and fear
bringing doubt
where peace of mind
once rested
these dreams...
so achingly familiar
they are here
every night
repeating
I fear
knowing now
I will never
escape
these dreams

In this nightmare, Pez found himself at his last rave. He was dancing alone amidst the press of bodies. He was himself, but he could also see, across the crowded room, another past version of himself surrounded by his friends. He watched them from afar; they were talking, discussing plans for that morning. He could hear their voices louder than the music, drowning it out. Their words hammered against his ears until he wanted to cry out for mercy, but he couldn't move his mouth. He tried to move his hands to block out the sounds of their voices, but he couldn't move; all he could do was dance. He tried to stop but he couldn't. He listened as his friends decided to leave. Again he tried to cry out. He needed to stop them, but he couldn't. They were all going to die and all he could do was stand there and dance.

Just then, Pez noticed a small ball of light coming towards him from the direction of his friends. It jumped and danced swiftly through the crowd. He was startled as a small voice called out his name. Moving his eyes to look around, he could see that no one was paying any attention to him or the ball of light that glittered directly towards him. The light began to circle *around Pez's head and he longed to swat at it, but he still couldn't move.*

"Pe-ez... Pez!" the light said as it stopped in front of his face. He squinted into the light and saw a silhouette of a girl's body. It seemed to be a fairy; he blinked, but he still saw it. The fairy flew forward quickly and placed a kiss upon his nose. He swatted it away, overjoyed to find that he could move again on his own. He stopped dancing. Somehow the fairy had set him free. He wiped the sweat away from his forehead and was surprised to find his sleeve came away bloody. How long had he been forced to dance? It felt like an eternity.

"I have to stop them!" he beseeched the fairy and started to run towards his friends.

"Stop!" the fairy commanded.

Pez stopped, frozen in mid-step.

"You can't help them. This is just a dream," the fairy informed him. "Follow me, Pez!" the fairy whispered into his ear. It flitted away through the crowd. He hesitated a moment, not wanting to follow. He was weighing his options. He could stay there and live out the rest of his nightmare or he could follow the fairy. It didn't seem like that hard of a decision, but Pez was afraid that following the fairy could lead him into another deeper, darker nightmare. His nightmares seemed to operate like that; promising something nice and pretty, something better than what was, but then giving him something so much worse.

"Hurry, Pez, hurry," the fairy begged as it flew back to him. The fairy's voice took on a much deeper, louder, and more menacing quality as Pez still refused to follow. "We can do this the easy way..." The fairy pointed off into the darkness of the direction it had flown away in. The fairy seemed to be growing before his eyes. "...Or, if you prefer, we can do it the hard way." Pez shivered at the purely evil tone the fairy's voice had taken on as she grew. She pointed towards his friends.

"I have to try and stop them," Pez whispered. He stood there staring in the direction of his friends, as they started to walk out the door. He longed to be with them. He had to find a way to stop them. He ignored the fairy and started walking back over to them.

"Dammit! You asked for this!" the fairy that had grown into full human size said. He stopped again, puzzled by her words. She stood behind him as he watched his friends. Pez felt the fairy place her hands on his back and shove as hard as she could.

"Hey!" Pez yelped, stumbling forward to catch himself. He felt arms catching him, supporting him, helping him stand. It was Glenn.

"You OK?" Glenn asked. Pez nodded and smiled. Finally, he was back with his friends. Even though this was still his nightmare, at least this nightmare was familiar to him. He looked around for Wolf and couldn't find him. Somehow this didn't seem right, maybe this wasn't his nightmare, maybe this wasn't the accident, and maybe, just maybe, his friends wouldn't die this time.

He followed Glenn out to Sal's minivan. He realized in shock that Matt was making out with Lisa as they leaned against the car. This definitely wasn't the accident. Lisa wasn't supposed to be here, she didn't even know Matt. Pez still felt a little hurt even though Lisa was in his past. He had left her for someone better.

He looked closer, just behind the minivan was another familiar car; Wolf's Buick Century. Wolf didn't drive that night. Wolf was walking towards the car with Mike. That wasn't right either; Mike wasn't there that night. This was all too weird for Pez.

"Wolf! Wait!" Pez called out to him. He started to move towards the other car, but Glenn grabbed his arm. Pez turned to look at his best friend. He stared at Glenn's fuzzy shaven head and his sad eyes filled with love. Love... Pez had never seen that in Glenn's eyes before.

"What?" Pez asked, trying to break free of his grip, but Glenn would not release his hold.

"Why can't you just forget about him? Can't you see he's in love?" Glenn pointed out, gesturing towards Mike and Wolf getting into Wolf's car. "They are a couple. Just forget about him. You can go out with me. I love you," Glenn proclaimed with such desperation and love in his voice that it almost broke Pez's heart. Wait a minute! What was Glenn saying? Glenn wasn't gay, but before Pez knew it, Glenn kissed him gently on the lips.

Pez ripped his arm free and ran towards Wolf's car. Wolf and Mike couldn't be a couple; Wolf loved Pez and only Pez. He climbed into the back seat of the car and sat in the middle. That was when he caught a glimpse of himself in the rearview mirror.

He stared in shock at the image that was reflected back at him. It was Diamond's face, wide-eyed with fear. He **was** Diamond. A movement in the front seat caught his eye. He looked and saw Mike's hand reaching out across the seat of the car.

Wolf's hand met it in the middle, where the two hands clasped and fell to the seat. It was true; Mike and Wolf did love each other. They were back together.

The seat that the clasped hands landed on was no longer maroon and fuzzy. It was dark blue and shiny. Pez realized in horror that they were in a totally different car. They were in Pez's Plymouth Horizon. He looked at Wolf and Wolf's image flickered violently between Wolf and Pez's own image. He looked quickly at Mike who was also flickering violently between an image of Wolf and an image of Mike.

Pain filled Pez's head as he tried to focus on one image only, but he couldn't. Everything kept flashing rapidly between the two scenes; the accident as it happened and the crazy nightmare that Pez was having. Pez was filled with nausea.

Suddenly, the images stopped. Pez was in his own car, in the back seat. His past self was driving and Wolf was in the passenger seat. He was seeing the accident—everything—from Diamond's point of view.

"Are you OK, Dime?" Pez's past self asked from his seat behind the wheel.

"You don't look so good, sis," Wolf remarked to the Pez that watched helplessly from Diamond's body. Wolf had no right to love Pez. Diamond loved Pez.

"Maybe you should lay down, Pez," Wolf's voice said. Pez looked back at the driver. It was Wolf again. Pez did not like this nightmare at all. Silently he begged for it to be over.

"Yeah, lay down," Mike's voice commanded. He obeyed immediately, hoping his nausea would go away. Hoping he would soon wake up from this horrible nightmare, this worst one yet. He closed his eyes, trying to block out the flashing that began again. He threw his arm over his eyes. He could feel Diamond's piercings pressing into his arm; this was way too real for Pez. He moved his tongue around inside his mouth and felt the pressure of Diamond's tongue ring inside his mouth.

"Don't worry, we can drop her off first," Wolf's voice whispered. Pez moved his arm a little and cracked his eyes open to see Wolf leaning towards the past Pez. He closed his eyes quickly, knowing what was coming next.

"He's asleep already," Mike's voice sounded, echoing Wolf's words from the night of the accident. Pez fought the urge to open his eyes and watch. Then he realized it wasn't his urge, it was Diamond's, and he was helpless to stop it as her body opened

its eyes all the way and watched Mike lean over and whisper into Wolf's ear.

Pez felt Diamond's body as it sat up, filled with rejection. He felt the denial that was holding her together slipping away as Mike started kissing Wolf on his neck. Mike moved his way slowly to Wolf's mouth. He wanted to scream out and tell them to stop, but all he could do was sit there and cry. So he sat crying and watching, knowing that when their lips met... too late. He felt the impact as the car collided with another car. Pez screamed as Diamond's body was jolted forward and then thrown through the windshield. Pez felt instant pain jar his body as he landed between his car and the other cars that began to smash into Sal's minivan. He watched, unable to move, as Wolf pulled Mike out of the car.

"No!" Pez said, with all the breath left inside Diamond's dying body. "This isn't right," he whispered softly. He watched as Wolf lifted Mike's head into his lap and started crying. "He's supposed to be holding me," Pez cried softly. " I love him," those words came out in Diamond's voice. He watched in understanding as Wolf turned into Pez's past self and Mike turned into Wolf. "I love you, Pez," Diamond's voice said softly. The past Pez looked up for a split second, but he looked through her, not at her. He never even heard her. She sobbed once painfully. Her spirit was slowly slipping away, leaving Pez inside a dying body.

He heard a nearby explosion and more crashing. He felt the flames licking at Diamond's back, but all he could see was the picture of Wolf holding Mike. This is how Diamond died; alone and crying, staring at the only man she had ever loved; the man who had never known just how deeply she loved him.

"I'm gonna die," Pez whimpered through Diamond's already dead lips. He saw the fairy circling him again, just before he closed his eyes and started crying. He never knew; everyone tried to tell him, but he never knew how much Diamond loved him.

"I'm sorry, Pez," Diamond's voice said.

"What?" Pez asked weakly, surprised he could even talk. He opened his eyes. He was laying on Diamond's waterbed in her bedroom.

"I said I'm sorry. I'm sorry I did that to you. I shouldn't have, but I had to!" Diamond murmured softly.

She was leaning against her bedroom wall away from Pez. He could see her pressing her forehead against the wall in anguish for what she did.

She had purple hair and she was still dressed like the fairy. She was wearing her Halloween costume from the last

Halloween before she died. It was all the same as that day, except this time the gossamer wings were real. The beauty of her wings mesmerized Pez. He couldn't take his eyes off of them. They fluttered gently, as if she couldn't stand to have them still. They moved with such fluid motions that they sent currents of air around in a soft breeze.

"Why?" Pez asked, sitting up in her bed, collecting his thoughts.

"Don't tell me that you still don't get it," she said in an exasperated tone.

"N... No," Pez stammered. "I g-get it, but why did you have to do it?" Pez asked.

"I tried to tell you, but you wouldn't listen. I told you we could do it the easy way, me telling you. Or the hard way, you feeling it for yourself. You chose the hard way," she said turning towards him. In a blink her outfit switched to a tight black tee shirt and baggy blue jeans. Her hair went back to its normal jet black with blue streaks, but still the gossamer wings remained. She noticed Pez staring at them.

"I can't help it. I like them," she smiled.

Pez noticed how beautiful she was and the wings only enhanced that beauty. "Why didn't I see it before? Am I really that dense?" Pez asked, holding his hands out in front of him.

Diamond laughed. She walked over to Pez and cupped his cheeks in her hands. She forced him to look up into her eyes. "I used to think that Pez. But I realized you weren't dense, you were in love," she said, tears welling up in her eyes. "I was the dense one. I never realized how much you loved my brother. Glenn tried to tell me, but I wouldn't listen. I couldn't listen. I didn't care. I thought you came over all the time to see me, not Wolf. It didn't help that everyone thought we were going out." She started crying. "I'm so sorry I made you hurt like that," she apologized again.

Pez stood up and pulled her into a tight embrace. "Don't be sorry Dime." Pez used the nickname that she allowed only him to use. "I'm sorry," he explained to her. "I'm sorry I didn't see it sooner," Pez comforted her.

"This is all I ever wanted Pezzie," she said, using her nickname for him that he allowed only her to use. "I just wanted you to hold me. When I was lying there dying, I saw you holding my brother. I was crying and wishing I were him. I just didn't want to die all alone."

120

"I'm sorry I let you die alone," Pez apologized sadly. "Please forgive me," he begged. He was crying now. He didn't need another thing to feel guilty over. She had to forgive him or else he could never forgive himself.

She smiled and looked up into his eyes. "You know I do," she assured him. Her smile was intoxicating. "I love you, Pez," Diamond announced.

Pez shook his head vigorously. "I can't...," he began.

Diamond quieted him with a finger to his lips.

"Don't say that Pez. Please, just let me pretend. Just tell me you love me," she whispered.

"I do love you, Diamond," Pez informed her truthfully. "It's just that I saw him first and..."

"Shh, don't explain," she said softly, shaking her head. Pez looked at her softness with new eyes. He was always too busy with Wolf to realize how much he really did care about Diamond. She stood in front of him, overtaken with the love that he had never seen before. He lowered his head and kissed her lips.

She pulled back away from him, shaking her head. "No, please don't," she begged him. Tears were streaming down her face in glittery trails. "Not unless you mean it, Pez."

He was surprised to realize that he did mean it. "I do mean it, Dime," he said at last and kissed her again. "I'm sorry I never knew it before," he whispered into her ear.

"I love you Pez," she repeated.

"I love you too, Diamond," he whispered, burying his face in her hair.

"You have to go back now," she said softly.

"Can you make the nightmares go away?" he asked in terror.

She shook her head. "No I'm sorry, but I can do something else." She bit her lip. "Get ready," she warned, kissing him quickly on the lips. Then she pushed him as hard as she could.

Surprised at her strength, Pez fell backward...

...and landed in a bed. When he opened his eyes, he was awake in his bedroom alone. It was three o'clock in the morning. He laid in complete stillness for almost two hours, too scared to even close his eyes. It was almost five before he finally fell asleep again. This time his sleep was lighter and dreamless.

11

$\mathcal{P}$ez's alarm woke him up in time to get ready and catch the school bus. He sighed, as he stood isolated from the other, younger students who were waiting at the bus stop. He was different from them; he had different problems. He had a different life. He was more grown up, or maybe he was less; it didn't matter. He didn't belong with them anymore, but then again he never really belonged with them before either. It was only in standing there, watching them chat idly about who was dating whom and which teacher was the nicest, that he realized he had changed. He was an alien in a strange world; this place called school was no longer his. He no longer belonged to that world, but what world did he belong to? None. There was no place for him anymore. He was too different; he had changed too much.

He was startled from his thoughts by the bus as it stopped loudly in front of him. He waited as the other kids climbed on, and then he followed. He looked for an empty seat, but the only one was the front seat.

He sat down sideways in the seat so he could keep an eye on the kids behind him. He still remembered what it was like in junior high, when everyone picked on him all the time. Back then it was so cool to sit in the very back seat, but if you sat in the front seat you were asking for an ass kicking. Pez silently hoped someone would mess with him. He could get into a fight and be suspended from school.

Watching the other kids goofing off, he remembered how much he hated riding the bus to school. It was so loud and noisy. The only good thing about riding the bus to school was that everybody seemed to ignore him. Despite his earlier wish, he didn't really want to get in a fight; he just wanted to be suspended. On the bus it was almost as if he didn't exist, which was fine with him. If it were up to him... he wouldn't exist.

"You know what?" D's voice filled his head once more. *"You are such a fucking wuss! You talk about it and you talk about it, but you are never going to kill yourself. You don't have the balls! Besides even if you did kill yourself, you wouldn't get to see your precious WOLFIE. You don't deserve that after you..."*

'SHUT-UP!' Pez thought to himself. He turned and faced forward in the seat. He bit the back of his fist and whimpered softly. He began to rock gently back and forth. He couldn't lose it; not here, not now, not in front of all these people.

These people on the bus, at school, they all thought he was crazy. They thought that he should be crazy, after all the shit he's been through. At least that's what Pez thought. Why would any of these people care about little lonely Pez, most of these people probably didn't even know what happened to him or his friends.

Pez needed something sharp; he was going to prove to D that he did have the guts, that he could actually do it. He pulled out his car keys, useless now, even though he still carried them. He could have taken them off the ring, but he didn't. He took the key and scraped it across his wrist. The feeling it gave him, took away some of the pain inside. There was no way Pez could kill himself with a car key, no way that he would. D was right. He didn't have the balls. He closed his eyes and lay back against the seat, still rocking slightly.

"What's wrong with the retard?" he heard a malicious male voice ask.

"Shut-up!" a female responded. "He's not a retard!" she defended. Pez wasn't exactly sure whom they were talking about until he heard the female explain. "He was in a car accident. All his friends died. So you leave him alone!" she whispered, but Pez could hear every word. "Most of them went to our school, you know," her voice took on a different tone. "This one guy, he was so HOT! He used to play guitar at the café that I hang out at. He was so good. I loved him. His name was Wolf." She seemed to be talking to someone else now.

"I remember him. He went to school with my brother," a quiet female voice spoke up.

"Oh yeah, the FAG!" the male voice said with disgust.

"Shut-up Kyle, you're such a prick. Who cares that he was gay? His songs were so beautiful," she said in a dreamy voice. Pez imagined her clasping her hands and closing her eyes.

burned flesh
and singed hair
are all I can smell
an army of flame rising
around me
are all that I
can see
I scream outward
nothing comes out
but blood
life blood
it pours out of me
faster with every
stone you
throw
it pours out of me
I hear your words of hate
above the flames that lick

my ears

and tempt my fate

burned flesh

and singed hair

are all that's left

of me

Pez squeezed his eyes shut tighter, trying not to cry. Everyone did know what happened and they did think he was crazy. He bit his fist again.

"I think he can hear us," the quiet voice spoke up again.

"Don't you dare mess with him, Kyle! If you do I will kick your ass!" the female voice said again. Pez opened his eyes. He turned around to see who had spoken up for him. A boy, probably a freshman by his attitude, was creeping down the aisle towards him. A girl was standing blocking his way, her fist in front of her in warning to Kyle. Pez stared at Kyle with ice in his eyes. Kyle backed away immediately. The girl turned to see what Kyle was looking at. She was startled when she found Pez looking at her. He smiled his thanks to the girl and she smiled back. He nodded and turned back to face the front of the bus. At least some people tried to understand what he had been through. Pez smiled again and closed his eyes. He dozed all the way to school knowing the girl had his back. Knowing that at least there were some people out there who understood his fragile state.

Pez woke up when he felt the bus jerk to a stop. He shook his head and rubbed his eyes. Silently he wished this day would just go by and be done with as he always did, now that he had nothing to live for.

He suffered his way through first hour: Hooked on Books–what a joke. Did they really need to teach a course on how to read books? Pez had been reading books since he was four. Basically he took the course as a senior fluff class. He knew he would do well in it even if he didn't try.

On the way to second hour, English, he decided he couldn't stand to deal with Miss Baranaider, (or Miss Barf-a-nator as some students called her behind her back), so he slipped into the empty auditorium. He walked onto the stage and through the curtains into the backstage area. The auditorium was off limits during school hours unless you had drama class and your teacher was with you. Pez didn't care. If he got caught he knew he would only get suspended and that's what he wanted anyway.

Pez stopped just in front of the scene shop, a room behind the stage where they prepared the scenery for the drama productions. He sometimes used to join his friends there in smoking a joint during some of their more tedious classes. Together, he and his friends had skipped many classes hidden away in this little alcove.

The pain of loss washed over Pez again and he fell to the ground. The tears couldn't come fast enough. D was right with all he had said. Pez was a wuss; he was a crybaby. He would never be worthy of anyone's love. He didn't even deserve to live, but even more he didn't deserve to be with Wolf. Pez rolled onto his back. He wished he had something to take away this pain, some sort of drug, anything to make him forget.

"*I can give you that,*" a familiar voice said. Immediately, Pez stopped crying. He looked up to find Junkie Pez standing in front of him, flicking the tip of a hypodermic needle. Junkie Pez turned to look at him with his yellow, blood-shot eyes. "*I got what you neeeeeedddd,*" he growled seductively. The look of craving in Junkie Pez's eyes moved Pez into action. He struggled up into a sitting position. He tried to scramble out of the way, but there was a wall behind him stopping him. He pressed against the wall in sheer panic, kicking his feet helplessly against the floor.

"No… No… NO…," Pez chanted. "You're not real! You're not here!" he shouted at the hallucination when his mouth finally allowed him to form words.

"*I may not be real, but this is…*" He showed Pez the needle filled with blood. Pez began shaking his head wildly.

"No… No… NO…," Pez continued chanting.

craving, lusting
whore's breath
why do you want me so?
aching, yearning
demon Spawn
because of you; I can never let go
trapping; catching
hunt to kill
you've caught me, Now I wait to die

regretting, hurting
lying to yourself
you ask yourself why?
and answer in lies
craving, lusting
whore's breath
kill me, don't let me suffer so
aching, yearning
demon spawn
because of you, I can never let go
I can never die

"*Open wide and say Ah,*" Junkie Pez whispered menacingly.

"David, is that you?" a voice asked. Pez looked towards the voice. It was Lisa. She was walking out of the scene shop.

"Lisa," Pez squeaked out, "help me."

"Come on, Lisa. Let's go!" a male voice said. Pez watched as the boy from yesterday grabbed her arm and tugged gently.

"No, Gabe, something's wrong with him," Lisa said, pulling away from the blond skater boy.

"Who cares?" Gabe said angrily.

"I do, Gabe!" Lisa said. "Just go ahead without me, I'll catch up," Lisa instructed him, moving over to Pez.

"Lisa?" Pez asked. "Can you see him?"

"Gabe's gone, David," Lisa assured him, looking around the backstage area.

Pez shook his head violently. He pointed in the air at Junkie Pez.

She shook her head. "I don't see anyone."

"*She can't see me, only you can,*" Junkie Pez said, slithering closer to him. Pez screamed and pressed himself closer against the wall.

"David! QUIET! We're gonna get caught!" she scolded him.

"But he... I...," Pez tried to piece together a coherent sentence.

"Listen to me, David," Lisa said. She cupped his cheeks in her hands and forced him to look at her, just like Diamond had done. "Nobody is there. It's OK. You're safe," she assured him.

"But…," Pez protested, looking wildly around the empty room, but Junkie Pez was gone.

"No buts," Lisa whispered softly. Her breath was sweet and smelled like bubble gum. Pez smiled and leaned forward. His lips touched hers gently and he felt her fall into a sitting position on the ground next to him.

"Thank you," he whispered, "you made it go away."

"What's wrong with you David?" she asked softly, not wanting to kill the mood.

Pez laughed out loud, startling both him and Lisa. "Didn't you hear? I'm going crazy. I thought the whole school knew it by now."

"You're not going crazy!" Lisa scolded him. "You're hurting. I can feel it. I want to help."

"You can't help me," Pez said.

"I can too! I know what you're going through. I can feel it. Come on David, I know you. If you keep it all inside it will kill you," Lisa warned him desperately.

"You don't know me," Pez rebuked.

"Yes I do, I know what you're really ashamed of," Lisa alluded.

"Shut-up!" Pez demanded. Lisa had always scared him with her uncanny way of knowing things that no one was supposed to know.

"I know the truth, David," Lisa disclosed. "You didn't kill…," she started. Pez couldn't think of any other way to shut her up other than to place his lips on hers, in a very passionate, but very meaningless kiss.

She pulled away, surprised. "Oh David," she breathed smiling.

"David's dead," he informed her spitefully.

Her smile crumbled before his very eyes.

"Fuck you, David!" She slapped him and struggled to stand up. He stood up with her.

"Lisa! I'm sorry. I didn't mean it like that!" he called after her as she ran off. He chased her and grabbed her arm to stop her. Before he could get any words out, he was knocked off of his feet.

"Gabriel!" Lisa hollered. "Leave him alone!"

128

Pez was pinned underneath the skater kid who had tackled him. The kid began to repeatedly punch him in the stomach.

"Gabriel!" Lisa shouted one more time, grabbing one of Gabe's arms and pulling him off of Pez.

"Don't you ever touch Kat! If you hurt her again, I'll kill you!" Gabe said as he brushed off his pants.

"Kat?" Pez asked, still confused by the sudden attack.

"Yeah... Kat, that's my name, Pez! ...Haven't you heard? Lisa's dead?" she said coldly. She turned to leave, but something made her turn back around to look at him. "You are going crazy, Pez," she spat out. "You're the only one who can stop it, but you're still going to end up in a hospital and I think I'll be there with you," she foretold with a faraway look in her eyes. "Until then, stay away from me. I won't stop Gabe next time." She turned and walked away from him.

"Freak!" Gabe said and spit at the ground next to Pez's head.

"*Well that's just great, push everyone away,*" Pez heard a small voice coming from above him. He looked up and saw young D sitting on the catwalk, dangling his feet over the edge. "*Come on up.*" The little boy gestured for Pez to join him. Pez looked up at the boy in terror. "*Don't worry. I won't hurt you. I'm not real, remember.*" He smiled.

Pez climbed up into the catwalk and sat next to the boy.

"*Why does everyone gotta pick on us anyway?*" the boy said. He had his lunch box in his lap.

"Why are you here?" Pez asked him.

"*I don't know,*" the boy replied, as he opened the lunchbox. He looked at Pez, still smiling. His two bottom teeth were missing. Pez tried to look in the box, but he couldn't see what was in it. "*I don't think you're ready for that yet,*" he said closing the box.

"I am ready... I am," Pez assured him. Hesitating, the boy handed him the lunchbox.

Pez held his breath as he opened it. He looked in the box with shock. Inside was a coil of rope; his hand was shaking as he touched it. He moved slowly as if it were a snake ready to bite him. His hand closed around the rope and he lifted it out of the box, only to find that it was fashioned into a crude noose.

why do I always
listen to you?

look what you made

me do

you made the plan

put the gun in my hand

where were you when I did it

when I pulled the trigger, when the

bullet hit

there's no place to hide

so I spread my arms open wide

this is the only way

to go now

oh God, why couldn't I fly?

"You said you were ready, so I guess it's up to you." The boy took his lunch box back and wandered off, leaving Pez to stare at the rope in wonder.

"So what did you think about the hanging scene?" Wolf asked, spinning around the fake gallows and miming being hung. "Was I good enough?" He took the joint from Eddie. He was speaking about his performance in the school play the night before. "Or was it too dramatic?" he asked, trying not to exhale. He blew the smoke into Pez's face and winked. Pez smiled and inhaled the herb filled air. He had only known Wolf and the others for a couple of weeks. This was his first time hiding out in the scene shop, so he was a little nervous.

"You were fabulous, Wolf. Just fabulous," Diamond complimented. She was wearing a faux mink stole, an overly large hat and every jewel and bauble the four of them could find. She was Miss Rondleshiffer of St. Clair Shores. Pez didn't quite understand that aspect of her yet, but she loved to dress up and name each character that she created. Sometimes she would even make up an entire history for each character. She held up a gold painted chalice and toasted Wolf with her grape juice.

Pez was even more nervous because this was the first time he had been around any of them without Glenn. Still, he thought he should at least make an effort to get to know Glenn's friends. "I liked when James's pants fell down. He's such a prick! He deserved that!" Pez said laughing. He was talking about the captain of the football team who had also been in the play.

Diamond, Eddie and Wolf looked at him in mock horror. At first he almost believed he had offended them, but they shared in his laughter. Wolf was the only one not laughing. He sank down next to Pez on the desk. (The room was also used to store old school furniture.)

"Wolf, what's wrong?" Diamond asked, dropping her Miss Rondleshiffer character and crossing the room to her brother. She knelt down in front of where Wolf and Pez sat and rested her elbows on their knees.

"James and I had a 'fling' once," he said slowly, biting his lip. "In secret, we saw each other a few times, because homosexuality is frowned upon on the football team," Wolf said the last line with an accent not unlike Diamond's previous accent. "He told me he loved me." Wolf sighed. "He broke my heart!" Wolf said, covering his face with his hands. Pez put his arm around him, not knowing what to say. Diamond rubbed his leg, tears in her eyes.

"I'm so sorry, Wolf," she said sadly.

Eddie started snickering. Diamond and Pez glared at him.

"Talk about RUDE!" Diamond said, disgusted.

Wolf shoved away from both of them and stood up, still covering his face. He walked a few feet away and turned around smiling.

"ACTING!" he shouted out in the same accent.

"You son of a bitch!" Diamond said, throwing her mink stole at him.

"I'm telling mom that you called her a bitch!" Wolf said, sticking his tongue out at her.

"Not if I kill you first!" Diamond said, tackling him to the ground. He quickly pinned her beneath him.

"Say you're sorry or I'll make you kiss... Eddie!" Wolf shouted.

"NO WAY!" Diamond answered. "Pez! Help me!" she called out. Only wanting to be part of the group, Pez couldn't resist the invitation. He jumped on Wolf's back and started tickling him.

"Oh shit! We got a TICKLER!" Wolf yelled and the three of them rolled around on the floor wrestling and tickling anyone they could get their hands on. Eddie sat on the couch laughing and finishing off the joint.

"I thought I'd find ya punters 'ere," Bren yelled out in his Irish brogue. He was born in Ireland to an American father and an Irish mother. They divorced and Bren was forced to move with his father to a brand new country. He had hated it here until he found his friends. "Anyone could find ya with all the noise you're making!"

"Sorry Da!" Diamond answered in a perfect Irish accent. "We'll try to keep it down."

"Aye, getting better with that accent, Lassie."

"I'm not a dog!" Diamond defended.

"Ah, shut up and hand me the joint, will ya? Hey you, what's your name? Candy-Boy, you got a bloody nose," he said, gesturing to Pez.

Pez smiled at his memory of Brendan calling him Candy-Boy. He missed Bren. Shortly before the accident he was sent home to live with his mom in Ireland. Pez looked down at the length of rope in his hand. He must have untied it as he reveled in his memories. He let it drop to the floor.

He sat staring off of the catwalk until he heard the bell ring, not caring about the tears that fell.

12

$\mathcal{P}$ez's thoughts turned back to his friends and the accident as he walked to his art class. The only reason he came to school today was so that he could rescue the picture that he had drawn the day before. He didn't want anyone to see it, especially Mr. Robertson. If Mr. Robertson saw it, he would probably send Pez to the school counselor. Pez hated his counselor. He had spent way too much time with her since the accident, and even before the accident as well.

He entered the art room and went straight to the cupboard, much like every other student who walked in. All the students were crowded around the cupboard struggling to get their art projects out. Pez couldn't get near it. He hung back to the side of the room and waited. Finally when he could get to the cupboard, his drawing wasn't in there at all. He couldn't find it anywhere. He noticed a couple other students still looking around for their own projects.

"Could everyone please be seated?" Mr. Robertson shouted over the clamor of the class preparing to work on their projects. "I have an announcement to make," he said, gesturing for the students still standing to sit down. Like the others, Pez obediently took his seat.

Now I know that some of you haven't been able to find your projects in the cupboard. That is because Mrs. Donnyl and I went through last night and chose certain ones to be entered into a statewide art contest. We chose four paintings, all were signed and looked completed or near completed. We chose the projects by: J. Adamms, T. Micheals, L. Juliette, and D. Spencer."

A few members of the class giggled at the mention of his abbreviated name. It was the reason behind his nickname: Pez Dispenser. Pez didn't hear the giggles. He just kept thinking to himself, 'How could Mr. Robertson do this to me?' Pez hadn't wanted anyone to see his drawing at all. Now the entire state was going to see it.

"I hope you students are not upset that we didn't ask your permission, but the contest was sprung on us and we were pressed for time. The projects will be returned at the end of the contest, but it's too late to withdraw them now."

Pez couldn't take any more of this. There was a burning, aching pit growing inside his stomach, making him feel nauseous. He tried to wait it out to see if it would go away, but it didn't. Pez walked over to Mr. Robertson's desk.

"David, I was really impressed with your project," Mr. Robertson commented.

"You didn't think it was too... morbid?" Pez asked quietly.

"Morbid? Not at all David, I think it's your best work yet. It's so raw and full of emotion."

Pez didn't want to hear any more of this. He didn't want to hear Mr. Robertson raving about his portrait of death.

"I feel really sick. Can I go, Mr. R.?" he blurted out, interrupting Mr. Robertson. Mr. R. finally looked at Pez who stood with one hand on his stomach and the other on his mouth. Shocked and afraid that Pez would be sick all over his desk, Mr. Robertson let him go.

Pez ran, not stopping for anything. He snuck out of school again, taking the same way he took yesterday. This time he headed to the city bus stop. He needed to talk to Sal. He sighed, wishing Sal could talk back to him.

"I have a secret." Pez whispered.

"Yeah?" Sal asked. "I have a few too, you gonna tell me yours?"

Pez nodded. "I think I'm in love," he said quietly.

"Oh, that kind of secret. Really, who's the lucky girl?"

"It's not a girl," he whispered again. They were sitting in the café. Penny and Diamond were playing pool near the table. The others hadn't arrived yet.

"Oh." Sal paused. "It's not me, is it?" he grimaced.

"Are you gay?" Pez replied.

"Wolf?" Sal guessed.

Pez nodded.

"How do you know? When did you decide this?" Sal asked in shock.

"The first time I met him," Pez said quietly. "It's been eating me up inside. I've never had feelings like this before. Sal, I wouldn't be telling you if I hadn't thought long and hard about it."

"So, you're gay?" Sal asked.

Pez shrugged. "I don't know, I think I'm bisexual. I like girls, but I can't stop thinking about Wolf."

"What about Lisa?" Sal asked.

"We broke up."

"What? When? Why?" Sal asked.

Pez laughed.

"Yesterday at school. She wrote me a letter. She couldn't even talk to me she just handed me the letter and walked away," Pez explained.

"What did it say?" Sal asked.

"It was the lyrics to 'Wonderwall' by Oasis."

"That's it?" Sal asked.

"Yup."

"That could be a good thing," Sal argued.

"Yeah, except it's true. I just don't feel the same about her, you know? Like, I grew and she's still stuck in the past. I don't know. After the next class she found me, all she did was look in my eyes. Then she stormed off like I hurt her somehow."

"Well, I guess that frees you up to pursue Wolf," Sal suggested.

"What about Mike?" Pez asked.

"Mike's an asshole. Maybe you can break them up. God knows we've tried," Sal laughed.

"He's not all bad," Pez defended him.

"Trust me,he is. Look, the only way Wolf is going to take you seriously is if you use the most direct approach. Here's what you're going to do..."

Pez shook himself out of the memory trance. He found that he had exited the bus and walked into the hospital all on autopilot. That's how often he had come here in the past year. He made his way to Sal's room. He stopped at the closed doorway to the room, afraid to enter for some reason. He'd been here at least twice a week since the accident and he'd never been afraid to see the comatose body of his friend. The burns on his face and chest were almost healed, and the room no longer smelled like charred flesh, which was a good thing. Pez's visits had gotten a lot longer since that horrid smell went away.

He gathered his nerve and pushed through the door. Sal looked the same as he did the last time Pez was here. The same pale ashen face covered with burn marks. His burnt chest was uncovered, but Pez was used to the sight.

"Hey Buddy," he greeted as he walked in. He walked over to the window and opened the curtains so the sun could shine on Sal's comatose body. "I wrote a poem, I thought you might like. It's a morbid one." Pez rolled his eyes. "Aren't they all?" he whispered the words he knew Sal would say if he were awake. He sat down next to the bed and pulled out a piece of paper from his pocket.

The abyss

the silence before
me is
aching and
so far across
the abyss
I can see

136

you standing
there before
me, before
my heart
I want to
be
with you
but I cannot
cross the
abyss
so achingly
open it
tears at
my soul
and makes
me lose
control as I
throw myself
carelessly
into the
abyss,
because
I couldn't
be with
you

"Well I guess it's not that morbid, just sad," Pez amended. "Can you even hear me?" he begged, reaching out and touching Sal's hand. "I miss you. I wish you would wake up." He squeezed Sal's hand gently.

"You know he's not in there, right?" a voice from the doorway said.

"What?" Pez asked, horrified that someone would say that. He turned to find a man not much older than him standing in the doorway. "Why would you say that?"

"Because it's something you already know," the man replied. "I'm Jon. I'm the counselor here."

"Well, you kind of suck at your job," Pez pointed out.

"Sorry, but it's the truth," Jon replied.

"How do you know?"

"Can't you 'feel' it?" he paused, looking around the room. He walked in and stood next to the window. "He is present here in this room, but he's not in that body."

"Who the hell are you? Why would you say that?"

"David, please calm down."

"How do you know my name? You're not a counselor! Who the hell are you?"

"I am the counselor here, but I know what you are. I know you can see things. I can see them too."

"I don't know what you're talking about." Pez stood up and backed away from the chair, moving slowly towards the door.

"You're not alone, David," he said sadly.

"Stop it! That's not my name. Leave me alone!" He pushed through the door and ran out into the hall. Jon followed him.

"Pez, wait," he called out.

Pez stopped in his tracks and turned to look at the strange man.

"Are you a gh-ghost?" Pez asked.

Jon shook his head. "I'm a friend."

"I don't have any friends!" Pez shouted and ran from the hospital. He ran out to the bus stop hoping the creepy man wouldn't follow him. He watched while he waited for the bus, but Jon had apparently decided to leave him alone.

As soon as the bus reached his stop, he jumped down the steps and ran. He only stopped running when he reached the so-called safety of his own bedroom, where he stood for a while, wheezing. It felt like his lungs were on fire, burning from the sudden exertion.

He wanted to sleep until three, when he had to work, but he was restless and full of energy. He knew he needed to sleep, so he slipped into the bathroom and helped himself to one of his mother's prescription sleeping pills. He barely made it back to his bedroom before the pill kicked in. He slept a dreamless sleep. Mercifully, no nightmares haunted him in the afternoon silence of his bedroom.

Part Three: Girl

13

Later in the day, he awoke peacefully for once instead of fear-filled, sweat-soaked fits of remembrance. He glanced at the clock; it was 4:15. He had forgotten to reset the alarm. He was late for work.

"Shit!" he screamed, jumping out of bed. He searched for a clean shirt or at least one that smelled cleaner than the one he had on. He grabbed his coat and shoes and ran out the door.

When he arrived at the bookstore, Rae was standing in the doorway looking helpless. It was almost as if she was getting ready to leave. Her eyes widened with relief when she saw Pez.

"What's wrong?" Pez asked, as he ran towards her.

"I've been hearing noises. I thought it was you, but you weren't here," she informed him in a slightly breathless voice.

"What kind of noises?" Pez asked, throwing his jacket behind the counter.

"All different kinds of noises, bumping and thumping, it sounds like books falling, but I've been alone since Boss left at one."

"Maybe Boss is trying to scare you," Pez suggested. He put his hands on his lower back and hooked his thumbs over his hips looking around nervously.

"I don't think so. I feel something, something different," she shivered in fear. Pez lifted his eyebrows. "Almost like there's a presence here," she whispered slowly, as if she didn't want to say it. She began shivering. Pez longed to put his arms around her and calm her fears.

"Sorry I was late," Pez changed the subject, walking passed her and over to the time clock.

"That's OK, Davie. I punched you in after Boss left. I wouldn't have minded so much if it wasn't so damn freaky in here right now."

"Thanks for punching me in," Pez smiled happily. Rae knew if Pez was late again, he might get fired.

"I'm glad you came in." She smiled brightly, looking suspiciously around the room. "I'm spooked out of my mind."

"I know how you feel," he admitted.

"Have you heard things too?" she asked.

"Not quite," Pez responded.

"*Don't tell her Pez*," Wolf's voice sounded by his ear, leaving the side of his neck with a chilled feeling.

"What then?" she inquired. She sounded genuinely interested.

"Nothing," Pez replied. Then noticing her disappointed look, he amended it to "Later."

She nodded, thinking that he didn't want to tell her because she was already scared. He let her believe that. "OK, is it cold in here or is it just me?" she asked, walking towards the backroom.

Pez turned to look where Wolf's voice had come from. Nothing or no one was there. "We got some new books in, Davie!" Rae called to him from the backroom.

"Cool, I'll be right there," Pez called back to her.

He froze in fear as he heard a loud thumping noise.

Pez swung quickly around, but saw nothing. He opened his mouth as if to ask Rae if she had heard it.

"Davie? Was that you?" she called. He walked quickly to the backroom where the new shipment of books awaited him.

"No, I thought it was you," he blurted out. She jumped, startled by his sudden answer. "Sorry."

"I thought it was you," she replied, laughing nervously.

"What was it?" Pez asked, feeling like a small child. He wanted to hide somewhere and cuddle with Rae.

"I don't know, but it was the noise I've been hearing since I got here."

"That's just freaky," he said. "So what kind of books did we get in?" He was trying to forget about the noises they had been hearing.

"I don't know. I was waiting for you to get here before I opened it."

"Well that was very nice of you... Thanks." Pez smiled at her. "Where's the box cutter? Let's open this sucker," Pez said, eager to know what was in the box.

Just then the customer service bell rang. Someone was at the counter waiting to be checked out.

"I'll get it," Rae said, heading back into the main part of the store.

Pez looked down at the box. Somehow it had gotten smaller. It was in his lap now.

"Are you excited?" Wolf asked. Pez looked over at Wolf who was driving the car that they were sitting in.

"Excited, but nervous," Pez replied.

"Go ahead open it." Wolf nudged at the box with his elbow. He smiled and glanced at Pez.

Pez smiled back and lifted the cover of the box. He pushed the tissue aside to find a shirt that read: 'I'm not gay but my boyfriend is!' He shuddered.

"I can't wear this!" he replied.

"Why not?" Wolf asked.

"I'm not gay," he pointed out.

"No, but I am," Wolf replied slyly. "Come on, it's perfect! Besides it's National Coming Out day. You have to wear it."

"I'm scared."

"You shouldn't be. You are what you are."

"I'm still scared," Pez said, shaking a little.

"Here try this," Wolf said, pulling something out of his pocket. "It'll take the edge off."

"What is it?" Pez asked, shyly.

"Ecstasy," Wolf replied. "Go ahead, you won't be scared anymore."

"Are you sure?" Pez asked, even more frightened as he took the pill in his hand.

"I'm positive," he said as Pez downed the pill. "Oh, and by the way, Pez," he heard Wolf say as the background of the car faded away and the bookstore returned into view.

"Don't tell her. I know you want to." Wolf's voice faded away.

"Damn it! You're driving me crazy! You're dead! Dead! DEAD!" Pez screamed.

"Davie, what's wrong?" Rae asked, walking back into the back room.

Pez shook his head.

"Nothing, I just, I…" He stopped talking. "What did they want?"

"This day has just been too freaky… There was nobody out there, and now the weather's getting really bad. It looks a thunderstorm is coming. The electricity might go…," she explained, cutting off abruptly as the lights went out. She screamed.

Pez felt a hand on his shoulder. He screamed. He didn't know whether it was Wolf or Rae or maybe it was someone else.

"Davie, chill out, it's just me. I'm trying to make it to the door."

Thump-Thump

"Was that you, Rae?" Pez asked, more frightened than he had ever been.

"No," she whimpered, "Davie, come with me." Pez stood up from his crouched position. He took Rae's hand. It felt soft and cool. She latched onto his arm and together they moved towards the door.

"I think I got it," she announced as the small, windowless room flooded with light. It wasn't the brightest light, but the dying light that lit the outside of the store.

Thump-Thump

Rae turned to look back at Pez. She was just as frightened as he was. "Let's go get the flashlights," he suggested. They moved towards the counter, neither releasing their hold on the other's hand.

Pez gazed around the darkened bookstore. The huge shelves were casting ominous shadows in the aisle ways. He concentrated on the desk. He was afraid if he looked around he'd see Wolf somewhere. Or someone else he didn't want to see.

After they got the flashlights and turned them on, the noise sounded again.

"I've had enough of this!" Pez said, turning towards the darkened bookshelves and saying a silent prayer that none of this was real. "STOP IT!" he screamed. "WOLF YOU'RE DRIVING ME CRAZY! YOU'RE DEAD! SO KNOCK IT OFF!" He turned to look at Rae. She had a puzzled look on her face. "I'm sorry," he uttered sheepishly.

"Oh no, it's OK. Really," she replied skeptically. "Who were you talking to?"

"Do you remember when I asked you if you believed in ghosts?" he asked. She nodded. "I told you I would tell you later." Again she nodded. "I believe the ghost of my best friend is haunting me," he disclosed slowly.

"What? Why?"

"I see him." Pez paused, trying to see if she thought he was crazy. "He talks to me," he murmured.

"What does he say?" she asked. She seemed truly interested; maybe she wouldn't find him crazy.

"He told me not to tell you about him."

Thump-Thump

"WOLF!" Pez screamed in anger. Wolf appeared next to Rae. He looked around bored.

Thump-Thump

"It's not Wolf," Pez said, searching the darkness for the sound with his eyes.

"How do you know?" Rae asked shivering.

"Because he's here."

"He's here now?" Rae asked, looking around. Pez nodded and pointed at Wolf. "I can't see him," she pointed out.

"He's right next to you."

Thump-Thump

"If he's here, then what the hell keeps making that noise? What is that?" Rae asked in a voice near panic.

"I don't know," Pez replied.

Thump-Thump
MEE-OOWWW

"Oh my God, it's Petey!" she cried, running through the darkness to the back of the store. She followed the noise to a cupboard at the back of the store and let Petey out. The bookstore's 'mouser' ran straight for the litter box. "Well that mystery is solved," she pointed out.

"What the hell was he doing in there? That's what I want to know." Pez shrugged.

"It was probably Boss. She hates Petey," Rae explained as they returned to the counter where Pez stopped and stared at Wolf. "He's really there, isn't he?" Rae asked softly, still not seeing him. Pez nodded slowly.

"What does he want?" she asked him.

Pez only shrugged.

"Well ask him," she spat out.

Wolf's face was growing crosser by the minute. "*I told you not to tell her*," he said, angry that had Pez disregarded his demand.

"Why can't I see him?" she asked sadly.

Pez shrugged again, tears forming in his eyes.

Wolf began to illuminate the room making the shadows between the shelves even darker. He showed himself to Rae before he disappeared.

"Was that him? Is he gone?" she asked in awe, already knowing the answer to both questions.

Pez nodded. "He's angry, because I told you."

"Why?"

"I don't know," he answered as the phone rang.

Rae, who was closest to the receiver, answered it.

She said a few things and then hung up. "That was Tony. He gave us the OK to close the store early," she relayed.

"Good, this place is giving me the creeps," Pez said and began counting the money.

"You're telling me," she stated. She followed his lead and began closing the store. "We'll talk about this Wolf thing later. OK?" The phone rang, scaring the crap out of Pez. He didn't want to answer it.

"Do you want me to get it?" Rae asked, walking back over towards the phone. Pez nodded as if the phone would distract his counting. Rae picked up the receiver. "Hello... hello... HELLO?" she called loudly. "Huh, no one there. They must have hung up. Oh well, if it's important they'll call back."

Pez nodded again, not letting on that he had already lost count. When Rae went back over to the other side of the store, he started over.

After they had closed, Pez began walking home. The rain had slowed to a drizzle and only the occasional thunder echoed in the sky. Pez jumped when he heard Rae's voice echoing across the empty street.

"Be careful! See you next time you work!" she called.

"You too," he replied. She climbed into her car and started the engine. Pez watched as she drove off in the opposite direction. When he was out of Rae's hearing range, he squealed in joy. He glanced around, hoping no one had heard him squealing like a schoolgirl.

He walked slowly home, even though he felt like skipping. He thought about what a great day today turned out to be. He got to hang out with Rae, which was always fun. He got to say goodbye to Diamond, which was something that they both needed. Finally, he felt happy to be alive, happy that Rae wanted him to be careful. He felt wonderful; better than he had in weeks, months.

When he walked into his living room, all his happiness came shattering down. He found Mike, Amber and the guy from the pick-up truck sitting on his couch watching cartoons with Stevie.

"David," his mother greeted him. "Your friends are here. They were concerned about your well-being, so they want to take you to a school dance. Isn't that nice of them?" Pez nodded, trying to look more eager than he felt. He had forgotten that he had agreed to go to the rave with them.

"We called the bookstore, but no one answered. We drove by and it was closed, so we came here," Amber said gesturing to his house.

your innocence
so apparent
leaves it's mark
on my soul
I arise
offended
and out of

control
is it just
a mask
or is it really
who you are
your innocence
so sublime
it reaches out
and pulls me in
is this a trap
or who you
really are

"Well Pez," Mike said, smiling deviously, "go and change. The 'dance' starts soon."

He remembered what Wolf had said earlier. Wolf was right; he knew they wouldn't leave Pez alone until he went out with them.

'Oh well, might as well go. What can it hurt?' Pez shrugged to himself. "Be right back," Pez said and ran out of the room. He was going to go and try and have fun, despite the pain he knew he would feel, this being the first rave since the accident.

'Maybe one day I'll take Rae to a rave,' he thought as he tore apart his room looking for his old raver garb. It had been so long since he had last worn those clothes.

"Here, try these on," Wolf said, shoving a pair of JNCOs under the door.

"Are you sure? I could fit this pant leg around my waist."

"That's the style. Now just put them on," Wolf urged.

Pez obediently put the pants on. "I think I could put a 2 liter of pop in these pockets," he joked. "They feel like they are going to fall off," Pez pointed out.

"They will if you put a 2 liter in them." Wolf laughed. "Let me in, I want to see how you look in them," Wolf warned.

Pez unlocked the fitting room door for him.

Wolf walked in and smiled, as Pez stood before him in his wide legged jeans. "They're perfect," Wolf assured him. "Now all you need is a belt, to keep them from doing that." He pointed at the pants now around Pez's ankles. Pez laughed and bent down to pull up the jeans. Wolf locked the door trapping Pez in the fitting room with him.

"David?" A voice interrupted his memory trance.

"Yeah, mom?" he asked.

"Hurry up. Your friends are waiting."

"OK ma."

Even though he was afraid of going to another rave, a part of him missed it all: the music, the drugs, the E, the little raver girls, the little raver boys, everything! He missed the way it used to be. Above all else, he missed the way it made him feel deep, down inside; that's what he missed the most. He missed the feeling that he had finally found a place where he belonged. Where people understood him and accepted him for him... a place that he could finally be himself... a place where he didn't have to care what anyone else thought.

He pulled his jacket back on over a big oversized tee shirt. He was wearing the pants that Wolf helped him pick out. He found them stuffed in a box in his closet.

Pez couldn't get down the stairs fast enough. He almost tripped over his pant legs as he tried to take them two at a time. He smiled as he realized that he no longer needed to pretend he was eager to go; he actually was.

"David, be back by two," his mom called from the kitchen. He looked at the others and laughed. He knew he'd probably get home sometime tomorrow morning; at least that's how it used to be.

"Let's party," Pez said holding the door open for his old friends and the stranger they brought with them. "Does it really start this early?" he asked.

"No," the stranger replied. "We wanted to go out to eat first."

"Right, and who are you?" Pez asked.

"I'm Phil, Amber's man," he explained. Amber giggled.

"Hey Phil," Pez greeted him. "I'm Pez." They shook hands. Pez hesitated and then pointed out, "Um, I don't really have any money. Most of my bookstore money goes to my mom for room & board."

"Don't worry, Spence. The evening's on me," Mike said, pulling a wad of bills from his pocket and replacing it quickly.

"Why Mike darling, where did you get so much money?" Amber asked, sidling up to him.

"Don't you worry your pretty little head about that," he replied.

She laughed and looked at his pocket longingly. "Is there enough money in there to buy some E?" she asked in a seductive voice. What the hell happened to Amber? She was straight edge before the accident and that meant no drugs or cigarettes or even alcohol. Pez wondered and watched in shock as Mike answered.

"Why do we need to buy E when I have some right here." He tapped his coat pocket.

"For us, Mike?" Amber begged, dropping her seductress act.

"For whoever wants it, but I have to charge you." Amber's face fell. Pez was appalled as the realization hit him. Mike was selling drugs? What the hell happened to everyone he knew while he was away? It was all some kind of weird *Twilight Zone* episode or something. "But Wait," Mike yelled, startling both Amber and Pez. "I did say the whole evening was on me, didn't I? Well, OK, I'll charge myself, but wait, that just doesn't matter, so yeah, but only one for each of you."

"If Pez doesn't want his, can I have it?" Amber asked, looking hopeful.

"Nope, Sorry. I have to sell the rest," Mike replied. He seemed to get joy from watching her face fall into a frown. He moved ahead of them and unlocked his car.

The angel's world

the angel lays back
relaxes her wings
let's the world go by
without her help
she falls asleep
and sleeps for
a century
she wakes in fear
she slept too long

the world went on

and look what

happened

while she dreamed

of peace

the world has turned

and no one

told her

she tries to adjust

but is slain

in the attempt

the angel dies

her wings wilt

and she falls into

nothingness

such a simple mistake

'Stupid bunch of E-heads,' Pez thought shaking his head. Pez vaguely remembered a time when he would have done anything for some E. In fact now that he thought about it, the longing started again.

"Shit," Pez breathed through gritted teeth.

Amber & Phil climbed into the back seat, so Pez reached for the passenger door. He closed his eyes as he climbed into the front seat next to Mike. He leaned his head back and tried to concentrate on breathing.

At Denny's, he couldn't eat anything again, although he drank three cokes. He felt so dehydrated and weak. He rested his arms on the table and laid his head on them.

"Hey Spence, you doing alright?" Mike asked.

Pez nodded sleepily. "Just a little tired. I don't sleep that well anymore."

"We better get going. We got a ways to drive before we reach the party," Phil pointed out, throwing his napkin into the empty food basket ahead of him.

Pez gulped down the rest of his Coke and the rest of Phil's, which hadn't been touched. Phil gave him a strange look, but continued on his way. They waited in the car for Mike to pay the bill. Amber and Phil had started making out in the backseat.

Pez closed his eyes and drifted into sleep. Pez dreamed of the accident again.

"No!" he screamed in horror as he woke–the sounds of tires screeching and cars exploding still echoing in his head.

"Jesus Christ, Spencer!" Mike swore. He was carefully moving the car back into the correct lane. "You scared the shit out of me. I could have hit someone for Christ's sake!"

Pez just sat there gasping for breath. Trying desperately to remember where he was. Trying desperately to grasp onto which reality he was really in.

"Spence, are you alright?" Mike asked, reaching over to feel Pez's brow. Pez couldn't answer. His heart was racing too hard. "Shit, Spencer, you're burning up," Mike said.

"I'm f-fine," Pez stammered.

"No matter, it's too late anyway 'cause we're here now and there's no turning back. Sorry Pez," Phil said, sympathizing with him.

"I said I'm fine!" he said angrily. Pez wiggled out of his jacket. He stepped out of the car and into the chilly air. He hoped it would get warmer soon, but for now the cold didn't bother him. It woke him up and chased away the memories that lingered in his head.

People were already lined up to get into the rave. Mike, Pez, Phil and Amber joined the inbound crowd. While waiting in the line to get in, Pez felt excitement filling him.

Pez entered the rave with high expectations. Everyone who knew him greeted him happily. They were all glad to see him back. Pez didn't know why he never considered these people his friends before this. They were all his friends before the accident. He tried to think of them as friends now, but his heart wouldn't let him. He knew the doom that lie ahead of each and every one of them. He knew they would all die like his friends did. He tried his hardest to push the sad thoughts from his head. It was hard to do that, because nothing had changed since his last rave. Everything was the same as that fateful day so long ago.

He was having trouble trying to separate that past rave from this present rave. He watched as the rest of the group took their E from Mike. Mike held one out for him, but he refused, just watching him pass them out like candy sent him spiraling into a memory trance.

"OK everyone, gather round!" Wolf called out to his friends. Pez wondered what he wanted. He joined the rest of the friends that had gathered around Wolf. "I've got a surprise for Pez on this auspicious occasion." He held out his hand to the group to reveal that he had seven pills resting in it.

"Ecstasy," Penny cooed softly, staring longingly at the pills resting in Wolf's hand.

"And I have one for each of you, not including Penny and Amber, of course," he smiled sweetly.

"Thanks, Wolfie," Amber said, twirling one of her long brown ponytails. She smiled brightly, glad that Wolf respected her wishes on not doing drugs.

"Yeah, thanks Wolfie," Penny said sarcastically.

"Sorry baby, my bad." Sal apologized, hugging her gently.

"You must have miscounted, Wolf," Eddie complained.

"There isn't enough for all of us," Glenn pointed out.

Wolf smiled. "Sure there is look," he answered and began to hand the pills out.

When he was through, Pez looked around. "I don't get one?" Pez asked disappointed.

"Now that's where you're wrong, Pez. You do get one," he said cryptically.

"But, I didn't get one," Pez said, tears in his eyes. How could Wolf have forgotten him, especially today?

"Well, let me see Pezzie, maybe there's another one in my pocket." He reached into his pocket. Pez felt like a child. He hoped that there was another one in Wolf's pocket, but at the same time he knew there was. The child in him won out.

"Is there Wolf? Is there?" he asked, getting excited as Wolf's face lit up.

"Look what I found!" He pulled something out and held out his hand. Pez looked at the pill that rested in Wolf's palm. It had a little bunny stamped on it. "I could only get a hold of one of these," he explained to the others "Since it is Pez's birthday, I thought he should have it. It's one of my birthday presents to you; you'll get the other one later." He winked at Pez.

No, not that memory, not now, he pushed the memory away and tried to concentrate on the current evening.

Pez was surprised at how fast the E seemed to kick in for his friends. They were all out dancing. They disgusted him, so he began to walk around. In the corner of the room that he was in, he saw a couple making out. They reminded Pez of Penny & Sal on another night, thankfully not the dreaded night.

Sal glanced up at Pez and smiled. Penny followed his gaze. She saw Pez and waved him over. Pez smiled back at them and began to walk towards his newly engaged friends. Penny tried to hurry him up. He could tell by the way she was smiling that she was excited about something. He crouched down in front of where they were entwined together in a sitting position.

"What?" he said, putting his ear near where their mouths were.

Penny whispered something in his ear that he didn't hear.

"What?" he repeated loudly.

"We're gonna have a baby," she announced to him.

"What?" he repeated a third time. She repeated herself a third time, shouting over the loud music.

"You're pregnant?" he shouted, excited for them.

"Two months," she said proudly.

"I am so happy for you guys," he cried out in joy. He stretched his arms around them and gave them both a bear hug. He lost his balance and fell over backward. Sal and Penny both tried to catch him, but missed. Pez lay on the floor, laughing madly.

Pez's pain inside was getting unbearable. He had to do something about it. He walked up to the closest person. "Hey man, are you carrying?" he asked, not caring if the person was a cop or not.

"What do ya want? I got everything. Special K, E, Meth, acid, smack, coke, crack. What's your pleasure?" the man asked, smiling a smile not unlike the one that Junkie Pez sported.

"Never mind," Pez said. Those weren't the drugs he had in mind. He didn't necessarily want to get messed up. He just wanted something to take the edge off of his inner torment. He walked away, sniffing the air. He would smell what he wanted before he would see it. He caught the faintest whiff and followed it. He soon came across a small group of people smoking pot. They were more than willing to share what they had. He sat with them for a while and smoked a bowl. He was beginning to feel better. He passed the pipe back and thanked his new friends. He walked back over to the makeshift dance floor. He started to dance. It made him happy to be dancing again. Thinking back, he realized that this was the first time he had danced since the night of the accident. He could feel another memory lulling him, calling him to let go and get lost in the past, but he wasn't going to; not this time. He continued to dance and that seemed to effectively keep the memory at bay.

After about two hours of dancing on and off, he began to feel tired and out-of-breath. He decided to walk around again and this time the memory snuck up on him from behind. He didn't even see it coming until it was already upon him.

"Pez!" a familiar voice called. He turned around to see Amber standing behind him, smiling. He stared at her open-mouthed, waiting until she finally explained to him what she wanted.

"I'm really tired, I was wondering if we could go now?" she asked shyly, already knowing what the answer was. Pez shook his head and tried to tell her that they still had three hours. Nothing would come out.

"You know it's so much better when you guys don't do drugs. When you do, there's no one intelligent to talk to, and when you do talk, you never shut-up," she accused angrily and stormed off. Pez watched her walk away. He glanced around to see if anyone was staring at him. When he made sure that no one was; he started to dance again.

He tried dancing again, but almost immediately the smoke and the music started getting to him. He looked around and it began to feel like the room was closing in around him. His heart was racing, making it hard for him to breathe again. He couldn't take it anymore. He had to leave.

He made his way over to Mike even though he knew Mike would not want to leave. Mike, Amber and Phil were walking towards the bathroom. Pez followed.

"Hey Mike," he called out as he got closer to them.

Mike turned to see Pez and smiled. "Hey Pez, we're going to smoke a pipe want to come?" Mike asked.

"Sure," Pez replied, not really wanting to smoke any more pot. He followed them into the dirty grimy bathroom. Mike pulled out a pipe and by the shape of the pipe he knew it was for smoking crack. "I kinda wanted to go now," Pez requested.

"We just got here," Amber rationalized.

"I'm not feeling good at all," Pez announced.

"One hit of this and you'll feel right as rain," Mike offered.

"Yeah, no thanks," Pez snorted.

"Come on, you know you want to," Amber whispered seductively into his ear.

"N-no I don't!" Pez said, filled with anger. "Can't you guys see what the drugs are doing to you?"

"Please Pez, they must have brainwashed you in rehab," Mike coaxed, reassuringly, trying to force him to take the pipe from him.

"They did not! Drugs brainwash you!" Pez said. He was seething with anger now. He wanted to punch Mike.

"I don't think so," Mike argued. Phil and Amber nodded in agreement. "You're just being stupid."

"No I'm NOT! You're the one who's being stupid!" Pez accused. "I saw it happen! I was there. I watched them die! Drugs killed them!"

"Drugs didn't kill them Pez, fate did," Mike explained calmly.

"And fate left us alive," Amber added softly. He seemed to be getting through to Amber for a second, until Phil handed her the pipe.

"SCREW FATE!" Pez screamed. "If there was such a thing, how could it separate two people who were in love?" he asked through gritted teeth.

"It let you take Wolf away from me," Mike retorted, finally seeming angry. "If fate was fair, I'd be with Wolf and you'd be with Diamond."

"Fuck you!" Pez spat out in anger.

"No, Pez, Fuck you! You hurt people too! You think you're the only one in pain and you're not! There's a world full of people who have lost people they loved!" He paused as he took a hit off of his pipe, "And three of them are standing right in front of you."

"I just want to go," Pez explained quietly.

"Too bad, I got the keys and I say we stay," Mike announced, blowing smoke into his face.

Pez coughed. "Then just let me have the keys so that I can go wait in the car," he said, coughing again.

"I don't think so, Pez. You might be tempted to steal my car and drive yourself home."

Finally the rage was so great Pez couldn't take it anymore. He reached out and shoved Mike as hard as he could. Mike stumbled backwards looking surprised. Pez moved forward and slugged him in the stomach.

Phil threw himself at Pez, knocking him to the filthy ground.

"Stop IT!" Amber screamed. She held Phil back as well as she could. "Get out of here Pez," she demanded.

"But...," he started.

"Just GO!" Amber screamed.

"FINE!" Pez yelled and stormed out of the bathroom. He pushed people out of his way as he made his way to the door, almost causing at least three fights on the way. He pushed through the doors and stopped just outside, breathing in the cold air, trying to calm down. The cold air cleared his head and his lungs. Mike and Phil had been so wasted they probably wouldn't even remember the fight they had in the bathroom. He still felt weak and feverish, but he stood out there waiting. He looked at his watch; it was only midnight. The rave would probably last for about six or seven more hours, standing outside for that long without a jacket wouldn't do him much good health-wise. He walked over into the parking lot and looked longingly into Mike's car. He checked the doors, but they were all locked. He could see his jacket lying on the front seat where he left it. It looked so warm and inviting. This is why he never took it off. The one time he does and it gets trapped. He sighed, biting his lip to stop the tears. This night was not turning out to be as good as he had hoped it was going to be.

He heard someone calling out to him. Startled, he turned quickly around.

"Hey man, can you help me?" the male voice asked. Pez nodded and walked over to where a man stood supporting his near catatonic girlfriend.

"Unlock the door for me, please." He handed Pez the keys. Pez obediently took them and unlocked the doors. "OK, now help me get her on the backseat." Pez helped him. "Do you think you could drive us to Ann Arbor? I'll give you money for a cab ride home," he slurred. Pez could barely understand him.

"My license is suspended," Pez explained to him. He didn't want to be around these two people much longer. He looked back at the door to the rave as someone walked out, but it was no one he knew. It wasn't anybody who could save him from having to answer the wasted man's question. When he looked back, the man had slumped over against the car and was ready to fall onto the blacktop.

"Shit!" Pez said as he caught the guy and pushed him into the passenger seat of the car. He climbed into the driver seat and put the keys in the ignition. He glanced longingly in the opposite direction towards home then slowly, he backed out and headed for Ann Arbor.

As he drove on in silence, he wondered what Mike and Amber would do when they realized he was gone. They probably wouldn't even notice he had left.

The road seemed long and his eyes were getting blurry, but he pushed, on making sure he kept the car going the speed limit at all times. He yawned and rubbed at his eyes, what he wouldn't give to be at home in bed right now.

Suddenly, he felt a hand slowly rising up his thigh. He looked in horror at the passed out man in the passenger seat. The man's image faded away and Wolf's image took his place. It was Wolf's hand that was slowly rising up his thigh.

Pez closed his eyes and shook his head, when he opened them Wolf was still there. He checked the rearview mirror. There was no one behind him on the road.

He watched as Wolf unbuckled his seat belt and leaned toward him. He heard the words again, sweeter than they had ever sounded or felt. He could almost feel the words fluttering around his ears like tiny butterflies.

He slammed on the breaks and pulled onto the shoulder of the road. Jumping out of the car, he started to run down the shoulder of the empty road. He would not let that happen again.

After Pez slowed down to a walk, his conscience kicked in. He realized how rude it was just to leave them there. He thought maybe he could go back, then he realized even if he did, go back it wouldn't have mattered because he had locked the car doors and he wouldn't be able get back in.

He started walking in the opposite direction towards home. At the rate he was going he'd never make it. His long blond hair kept blowing in his face. He shivered violently and wished he had somehow been able to get his jacket out of Mike's car.

A couple of cars passed by him, but none of them seemed willing to stop and pick him up. He stuck his thumb out and kept walking. Finally, after what seemed like an hour, a car pulled onto the shoulder ahead of him. He jogged over to the passenger side window.

"Where you headed?" the blond behind the wheel asked, looking past the girl in the passenger seat, who was trying to make herself as flat as possible so the driver could see past her.

"Emmerdale," Pez replied.

"That's where we're heading," the blond replied as a voice from the back seat shouted, "Davie? Is that you?"

"Yeah," Pez replied, smiling brightly at the sound of Rachael's voice.

"Well get in here, you must be freezing!" Rae scolded. Pez folded himself into the back seat. He huddled into Rae's warmth. She giggled and threw her arms around him.

"What are you doing way out here?" Rae asked. She pulled her jacket off and covered him with it.

"My friends dragged me out to a party, but I left early. What are you doing out here?" he asked, just as surprised to see her, as she was to see him.

"We went to a club over in Ann Arbor." Pez nodded as he burrowed deeper into the warmth of her.

"Thanks for the ride and the jacket," he slurred, closing his eyes thinking only to relax them just for a moment, but exhaustion took over and swept him into slumber.

He awoke to someone gently shaking him. He opened his eyes to find he was lying with his head on Rae's leg. Rae woke up when he lifted his head and looked around sleepily.

"Where do you live, kid?" the blond asked, returning her attention to the road as the light turned green. Pez was too sleepy to take offense at being referred to as a kid.

"Around the corner from the book store," he replied, rubbing his eyes and sitting up so he could give better directions once they reached the bookstore.

When he arrived home, his mother was on the couch sleeping as if she had tried so hard to wait up for him. He smiled at the sight of her sleeping there so peacefully. He reached across her and pulled the blanket from the back of the couch and covered her up with it. Even though they fought constantly, Pez couldn't help but love her. She was, after all, his only family.

He sniffed and rubbed his eyes. He was still wearing Rae's jacket. He would have to return it tomorrow at work. He slowly ambled towards his room.

"David?" his mother called out. He stopped on the steps.

"Yeah mom," he replied.

"You're home early," she pointed out. It was almost 1:30.

"It just wasn't the same as before."

"I'm sorry."

"That's OK though. I don't need to do that stuff anymore."

"Good for you," she said smiling.

"Well, I'm going to bed."

"Goodnight, D."

"Night, Mom." He smiled and wearily made his way to his room. He collapsed onto his bed and pulled up the blankets. He just wanted to be warm. He dozed off, but was awoken by the feeling of someone sitting behind him on his bed. Thinking it was his mother, he didn't move and kept his breathing regular. That was the trick (he had learned) to pretending to be sleeping. The breathing had to be rhythmic.

"*D, Honey,*" a familiar voice whispered. "*I need you to wake up, sweetie,*" the voice urged.

He felt her hand on his shoulder gently shaking him awake.

"Nanah?" Pez asked.

"*Yes, my littlest D, it's me,*" she replied.

"What are you doing here? It's so late." he whispered.

"*I came to say goodbye.*"

"Goodbye? Where are you going?" Pez asked.

"*I think you know where,*" she whispered back.

"This isn't a dream?" Pez asked.

Nanah pinched his shoulder. "*Did you feel that?*"

Pez nodded. "Are you dead?" he asked, fearing the answer.

"*Yes,*" she paused. "*I couldn't leave you without saying goodbye.*"

"No... I don't want you to go," Pez begged.

"*Yes D, it's time for me to go and be with Poppy.*"

"But you're here. How can you be dead?" Pez argued.

"*I'm not really here... anymore,*" she whispered. He could feel her breath as she leaned over and placed a kiss on his head. "*You need to get more rest,*" she urged. "*And you need to let your mother in. She loves you, David.*"

"I know." Pez started to turn over. He needed to see her one last time.

"*No, Please. This is very hard for me. Don't look,*" she begged. "*You need to tell your mom that I loved her like she was my own daughter.*" Her voice seemed to be fading away.

"No, Nanah, please don't go," he begged.

"I'm sorry," Nanah said quietly.   *"I love you,"* she whispered directly into his ear. He could feel her breath tickling his ear.

"Nanah?" Pez asked. When she didn't answer he turned to see her, but there was no one there. And the pressure on his bed was gone. "Nanah?" Pez called out again, his voice breaking a little. He sat up and turned on his bed side lamp. He looked around his empty room. He could still smell her perfume, but she was nowhere to be found.

"I love you too, Nanah," he whispered and turned off the light.

14

The next day, Pez's dreams woke him up rather early in the day. He couldn't even remember what the dreams were about and he didn't want to. He rolled over and tried to go back to sleep, but he couldn't. He growled in frustration and threw the covers off. It always pissed him off when he couldn't sleep in on Saturday.

He looked out the window and sighed. It was a beautiful day outside. It seemed like the perfect day to visit someone who couldn't enjoy the weather. He got dressed and headed for the nearest city bus stop.

He got off the bus at the hospital and walked in. The nurse behind the desk, Heidi, nodded at him in greeting. He came here so often that a lot of the nurses knew him by name. Heidi was his favorite though. He went on break with her once. She was only slightly older than he was, but she was married.

He sat down in the chair next to the bed.

"I'm back," he said softly. He always felt strange talking to someone he knew couldn't talk back. "I didn't bring anything this time." He usually brought music or food or a book or something to provide sensory stimulation for Sal. "I just needed to talk to someone." He paused, closing his eyes.

"I didn't mean to interrupt you and Penny, but I just needed to talk to someone," Pez said, trying to keep his eyes on the road as they pulled away from Sal's apartment complex.

"Where are we going?" Sal asked.

"Nowhere really, it's just more private here," Pez said, using the same words that Sal had used when he had needed advice.

"Is it about Wolf?" Sal guessed.

"How did you...,"Pez began, but stopped himself, knowing it must have been apparent to Sal. "It's just that, I love him a lot and I want to have sex with him, but...," he sighed.

"But?" Sal asked.

"He just doesn't seem to want to... make love... with me."

"Maybe he's saving it for a special occasion?" Sal offered, shrugging his shoulders.

"I don't think that's it. I mean, there's more to it than that. I'm afraid that... maybe he still loves Mike," Pez said, finally admitting to his true fear.

"I wouldn't worry too much about that. Wolf's totally crazy about you," Sal assured him, smiling.

"Well then why won't he have sex with me?" Pez said, very close to whining.

"I think that Wolf feels sex cheapens the relationship. He and Mike didn't have sex until after almost a year of going out," Sal pointed out.

"Really?"

"Yeah. Also, I mean, it's your first time. Maybe he just wants it to be special. Just give it some time."

The memory shifted then to a point shortly after that, back at Sal's place.

Penny regarded Pez with awe at the speed and accuracy with which he rolled the joint. He had only learned to roll a joint the week before.

"You're really good at that you know," Penny said, giggling a little. She was already stoned.

"Thanks," Pez replied, licking the paper and sticking it together.

"What are you gonna do about Diamond?" Sal asked. "She's got it really bad for you."

"I don't know. What should I do about her?" Pez said, lighting the joint.

"You have to talk to her," Sal advised seriously.

"She feels really stupid about what happened. She's not really mad. She's just embarrassed."

"Really? I thought she never wanted to talk to me again," Pez admitted. "I don't know what I'm supposed to say to her."

"Tell her that you're sorry; that you were a jerk for not telling her," Penny advised him as she took the joint from Sal.

"I think I can do that," Pez replied. He was not looking forward to talking to Diamond, especially not after what happened earlier that week at her house.

Pez opened his eyes numbly. He wondered how long he'd been in the dozing memory state. He stared at the body lying in the bed, mentally willing for Sal to be healthy again. He wanted his friend to be awake and aware, no more of this coma shit.

"I've been seeing these strange things lately." He paused and lowered his voice. Sal was the only person he could talk to about this stuff without fear. If he talked to anyone else about it, they would definitely think he was crazy. Not Sal, for even if he did think that Pez was crazy, he couldn't do anything about it. "I keep seeing Wolf everywhere I look and I mean he's actually there. He can touch me. I've felt him and he feels real. I don't know what to do, I feel like I'm going crazy," Pez said as tears spilled down his cheeks.

"You are not going crazy, Pez. You've been given a gift," Sal's voice sounded. Pez stared in horror as he watched Sal's face become free of burns. He began to shake in fear as a totally healed Sal sat up in the bed, even though the burnt shell of Sal still remained unmoved.

He wanted to run. He wanted to scream. He wanted to hide, but he couldn't do anything. He was paralyzed with fright. He sat unable to move.

cold; like a river
like the dead
envelops my mind
and circles my head
I hear your voice
it fills my brain
Is it really you
or am I just going insane

"Please, Pez. Don't be frightened," Sal's ghost begged. His voice broke the spell of fright that held Pez. He stood up so fast that the chair behind him fell over. He ran out into the hallway of the hospital. He felt dizzy as if the world around him had begun to spin. He glanced at some of the people in the hallway. They looked like normal people, but somehow he knew that they were dead.

"Can you see me?" the one closest to him asked, "You can, can't you?" the man asked, moving closer to Pez.

He turned and ran from the hospital, vowing never to return, Sal or no Sal.

15

When he arrived back at home he felt weak and fever-chilled, so he called off work and slept until around six-thirty, when Stevie woke him up.

"D, someone's at the door for you, it's a gi—irl," he said, laughing. "D's in LOVE!!!"

His first thought was that Amber had come to visit him, which reminded him of Sal and what had occurred at the hospital. Maybe he wasn't crazy, maybe it was all just a nightmare, and maybe he didn't even go to the hospital that day.

He took the stairs two at a time, he was feeling slightly better. He rounded the corner into the living room. He was shocked to find Rachael standing in the doorway holding a covered bowl.

"Call me corny...," she started. "I stopped by the bookstore and found out you called off because you were sick, so: I brought chicken soup," she said, her face turning a slight shade of red.

"Thanks," Pez said, stunned beyond all belief. "Ummm... Come on in," he invited, taking the soup from her.

"Tony said some guy dropped your jacket off and I brought it over for you." She held out his jacket for him.

"Thanks again. I've got your's too. It's over on the couch." Pez took the soup into the kitchen. He walked back into the living room.

"I'm... um.... going to go put some c-c-clothes on," Pez stammered as he realized all he had on was a pair of boxers. "I'll be right back down." He turned and ran up the stairs.

When he came back downstairs, he found Rae and Stevie talking. They stopped when they noticed Pez was coming into the room.

"So, you want to go for a walk or something? It seems like a nice day," Pez asked looking uncomfortably around the room. "I can eat the soup later... I don't feel as bad as I did."

"It's a beautiful day and I would love to go for a walk," she said, standing up. Together they walked out the door. Pez sensed that Stevie wanted to come along, but Pez silenced him with a look.

"So, what were you guys talking about?" Pez asked, closing the door behind them.

"Nothing important," she shrugged it off.

"Why did you stop talking when I walked in?" he asked, refusing to look at her.

She took a deep breath. "We were talking about your friends... the ones that died."

"Oh, is that all?" Pez asked nonchalantly, covering up the sting that thinking of his friends always brought.

"You don't talk about them much," she pointed out, turning to look at him.

"Well, there really isn't that much to say. We were all rolling. We got into a car accident. Everyone died, except for Amber, Sal and I. Amber's some sort of space cadet now. Sal is in a coma with no hopes of waking anytime soon. And I'm just me, lonely ole me."

"Is Amber the one with the big scar down her face?" Rachael asked, tracing a line down her face where Amber's scar was. Pez nodded. "She came into the bookstore looking for you, when I stopped in. She said that if I saw you, I should tell you that she apologizes for last night. She said 'She's very sorry and she hopes you aren't angry with them for making you go last night.' I hope I got that right."

"Last night?" Pez asked. All the strange stuff that had happened at the hospital had made him forget about the rave.

"She implied that you were sick, but they made you go anyway."

"Oh yeah, I was a little sick then."

"So... yesterday at the bookstore was crazy," she pointed out, trying to change the subject, sensing that Pez was mad. Pez **was** angry that Rae had found it necessary to talk to his little brother about his private life.

"Yeah, that was pretty funny. All that time we kept freaking out and it turned out to be the cat," he said, trying to laugh.

Rae nodded smiling. "I was so scared. I thought I was going to piss myself."

"Yeah, me too," Pez replied, smiling back. They had stopped again and were facing each other. Pez felt them getting closer for a kiss. Suddenly, Rae turned and started walking again.

"So, how long have you been seeing him?" she asked. Pez froze momentarily. How could she have found out about his bisexuality? Maybe Mike or Amber told her; if they did, he'd have to kill them. Maybe that's why she didn't kiss him just now.

"Who?" he asked, running to catch up with her. He looked at her face. Maybe she didn't know yet. Maybe no one had told her.

"That person who was at the bookstore," she replied.

"What person?"

"The gho... the one who died," she stammered.

"Wolf," Pez sighed in relief. She didn't know.

"Yeah."

"Just a couple of days now."

"Has he come back at all since...," she paused searching for words to describe what happened, "...he left?"

He hesitated before answering. He was debating whether or not to tell her about the hospital incident. He finally decided not to.

"No... um... not really," he finally answered her question.

Again the conversation dropped into silence. For some reason, Rae couldn't leave the way his friends died alone.

"Forgive me if I sound naive, but what is 'rolling'?" she asked.

"Taking ecstasy," Pez replied.

"Do you 'roll' anymore?" she asked with big eyes.

"Nope, I've been clean since I killed them all." The words just slipped out. He didn't regret saying them because he truly felt that it was his fault that they died.

"Davie, you didn't kill them," she argued.

"Yes I did. You weren't there. You don't know. I KILLED THEM! IT'S ALL MY FAULT!" Pez screamed at her, then turned and ran towards home.

"Davie, WAIT!" Rae called, but Pez ignored her. He ran home with Wolf's voice behind him the whole way. He couldn't concentrate on what Wolf was saying. He didn't want to hear it.

He ran all the way up the stairs to his bedroom and slammed the door behind him. It was useless. Wolf's face was everywhere he looked. He threw himself onto his bed hoping that sleep would take Wolf's voice away.

fading memories

I cannot get used to
this fading memory
by my side
always there
protecting me
from foolish people's pride
I miss you
I cry and I cry
since the day that you died
but you are steady
you never seem to notice
how much I have cried
because it's not just
you that died it's a part

of me
I believe that deep
inside

Sleep would be nice.
Sleep would be soothing.
Sleep would be wonderful.
Sleep would not come.

He lay on his bed staring at the picture of Robert Smith that Wolf had given him. He remembered once Lisa asked him if he wanted to go with her to see the Cure in concert. For some reason he didn't go... Oh yeah, the big rave in Toronto. Wolf took him to a Cure concert shortly after the Detroit one. They had to drive down to Toledo for it. Wolf said that was the best way to see a concert—in Toledo. The venue was smaller and there was more of a chance to meet the band after the concert.

He turned his thoughts back to Lisa again. He remembered how he felt when he kissed Lisa; at least he thought he did. He could have had something great with Lisa, but at the time he had other interests.

First there was Wolf.
Second there was partying.
And third there were drugs.

He was so heavily into the party scene at that time that he hardly remembered anything at all about the times he spent with Lisa. He thought some more about it and finally realized how cruel he had been to her. He promised himself that he would talk to her about it next time he saw her. He would apologize for treating her like shit.

He stood up and stretched. His body was sore from dancing the day before. He had a pounding headache from sleeping all day. He needed a cigarette badly. He went downstairs, checking twice for Rae, just in case she'd be waiting for him; she wasn't. He left the house and headed for the corner store down the street from his house.

He knew what he needed to do. He knew what aisle it was in. He went to that aisle and looked cautiously and covertly about. When no one was looking, he grabbed what he wanted and pocketed it. He grabbed his brand of cigarette and pocketed them too. Then he turned and walked from the store.

I've been caught
stealing
so cut off my hands
I've no use for them
anyway

He walked slowly in a daze. The voices were gone, but he was still afraid to go home. He lit a cigarette and headed towards the cemetery. He sat down in his usual spot between the two graves. He said nothing, just sat. He stared at a fence where wild strawberries grew. David closed his eyes remembering.

"Come on, Daddy," little D Spencer called to his father as he stopped and waited for his Mommy and Daddy. "Quit playing around! Hurry up!" he yelled. The two stopped kissing and followed their only child.

"Why are you in such a hurry, Davie?" his father asked. "The strawberries aren't going anywhere." He turned to his wife. "Are they Carole?" She smiled and rubbed her protruding stomach. She shook her head. D was so amazed that there was a baby growing in his momma's stomach.

He screamed as his Dad picked him up and began to tickle him. D laughed and laughed. Soon his mother joined in on the tickling and the three ended up laying on the ground laughing.

He was still lost in the memory when a voice spoke up.

"I thought you quit smoking?" He looked up. Mike was standing above him.

"I did." Pez stubbed out his cigarette; it was mostly ash anyways. He looked up at Mike, lifting his hand to offer it to Mike.

"So, you come here too?" Mike asked, taking the pack from Pez. "I've been coming here since the accident," Mike admitted.

"Me too," Pez agreed quietly.

"Sometimes it helps." Mike sat down in front of Pez resting his side on Wolf's head stone.

"Yeah, sometimes," Pez agreed, standing up. "I have to go now, I'll catch you later," he mumbled. All he wanted was to be left alone.

"Look, Pez." He stopped and looked at Mike. "If you're interested, Amber's having a party and we'd be happy if you showed up. It's at her house tomorrow," Mike said softly.

"I'll try to be there. I am feeling a little better," Pez lied as he turned and walked slowly home. He had no intentions of going to Amber's party.

16

His mother was standing in the kitchen when he arrived home. She was leaning on the counter near the sink with tears rolling down her cheeks. She looked up when Pez walked in. Quickly she wiped her tears away and tried to smile, but it turned into a frown.

"David, I've got some bad news," she announced.

"What?" he asked, as he got a plate out of the cupboard. Something jolted deep inside of Pez.

"Nanah... died early this morning," she said, tears rolling down her cheeks. Carole was closer to Nanah Spencer than she was to her own mom who had left her when she was about ten years old.

"I know," Pez responded, putting the plate back in the cupboard. He was no longer hungry. He sank into the kitchen chair.

"How do you know?" Carole asked. "Jimmy just called to tell me. They found her about an hour ago."

"She came into my room last night and told me," Pez replied.

"What?" Carole asked in shock.

"After I went to sleep last night," Pez began. "I woke up, because it felt like she was sitting on my bed, just like she used to do when I stayed at her house." He smiled a sad smile. "I opened my eyes and she was there."

"In your room?" Carole asked.

"Yes. In my room, on my bed," Pez explained.

"You must have been dreaming," Carole rationalized.

"No, Mom, I was wide awake. She was there. She said goodbye. She asked me to watch over you and Stevie," Pez rambled. He couldn't believe that he had forgotten about it.

"Is that all she said?" Carole asked, but Pez knew she was humoring him.

"She told me to tell you that she loved you like you were her daughter," Pez repeated numbly.

Carole looked as if he had slapped her.

"You shouldn't have told her," Wolf's voice sounded, even though he didn't appear. *"She'll never believe you. No one will,"* Wolf warned.

"It really happened, Ma," Pez implored, wishing she would believe him.

"Don't do this, David," Carole pleaded with tears in her eyes.

"You're hurting her. Look in her eyes. She doesn't want to believe you," Wolf pointed out.

"The funeral is on Tuesday," she choked out. She held her arms out for Pez. He took a deep breath and stood up. Carole put her arms around him in an awkward hug. He started crying and she squeezed him tightly, sobbing into his shoulder. He couldn't believe it. He didn't want to believe it. Nanah couldn't be dead, she just couldn't be.

"Her heart gave out. Jimmy said that she just didn't have the strength to live after Poppy died. Poor Nanah, she's been through so much and now she's gone," Carole whispered, pulling away from Pez. "I'm sorry," she said, wiping her tears away. She swallowed them back and turned her attention to the dishes in the sink.

"It's OK, Mom," Pez said sadly, holding back the tears. "I'm gonna go jump in the shower," he whispered, barely able to speak.

He ran up to the bathroom and stripped off his clothes. He climbed into the shower and collapsed to the floor in tears. He made sure to keep his sobs quiet as he sat on the floor of the tub bawling like a baby. Nanah was dead. Nanah was gone. What was he going to do?

Pez dried himself off and went into his bedroom, closing the door behind him. He pulled out a razor blade from his nightstand drawer. He was going to do something that he had promised Wolf he would never do again. He opened the blade and dragged it across his legs a bunch of times. He cut just deep enough for tiny beads of blood to form on each cut.

He thought of Lisa as he cut. Lisa's arms were always covered in cuts just like these; sometimes she even had words carved into her flesh. Pez had never gone that far with it, but it was still strange to Pez when he found out that Lisa was a cutter too. It was weird to realize that he wasn't the only one who did it. A lot of people did. When Wolf found out about, it he made Pez stop immediately. He explained to Pez that it was a horrible thing to do to yourself, but Wolf had never done it. He didn't know that it took all the pain that was hidden deep inside and made it go away; made it disappear, if only for a short while.

Pez put the blade back in the drawer and curled up in his sheets. He pulled on the extra blanket that he kept for those cold Michigan winters. He wrapped himself in the warmth of them and curled up crying again. He felt like he was in a cocoon. He felt like when he emerged he would be a different person living a different life. He fell asleep knowing that when he woke up he would be the same person filled with the same pain and the same guilt.

Part Four: Boy

17

He woke up Sunday, late in the afternoon. The house was empty; Stevie was at his scout meeting, which his mother was a part of.

Pez heated up the soup that Rae had brought over and ate it. He watched TV for a while and then went into the bathroom. He brought the small box that he had ripped off from the corner store into the bathroom with him. He tore open the box and spread the contents on the floor. He sat down and read the instructions.

"Strand test? Who cares?" he mumbled to himself as he mixed the chemicals together. Then he began to rub it into his hair. It took him a while to make sure he covered all of his hair with the dye. He looked at himself in the mirror; the color of the dye looked a lot like poop to him. He laughed about that, but then he got nervous. He was afraid that it would turn out that color and not jet-black like it was supposed to be.

When he finished, there was hair dye everywhere. As he threw out the instructions, he noticed that there had been a pair of gloves attached to them. He looked at his hands; sure enough, they were black. He tried to wash the dye off, but it wouldn't come off.

He washed out the bathtub and the sink. He threw the towels into the wash, hoping the washing machine would take away the dye. He concentrated on cleaning up the mess. His mother would kill him if she saw the bathroom in this state.

Finally, when everything was clean, he got up enough nerve to look in the mirror. He was shocked at what he saw.

A pale figure stared back at him. He had dark circles under his eyes. His hair was jet black, just like he wanted it to be. Jet black hair dye was all over his hands and his ears. A few streaks ran down his face. It looked like he had been crying black tears. Next time he would be more careful when dying his hair.

An image appeared in his head. The image was of him dancing at Amber's party. He checked the clock; it would be just starting.

He grabbed a tube of black lipstick from his multi-colored collection. He put on a black tee shirt and his black oversized jeans.

He ran down the hall, pulling on his jacket and scarf as he went. He ran out the door, locking it behind him. He slowed to a walk as he felt the warm spring wind blowing through his newly dyed hair. He needed to see his hair again. He stopped next to a car and tried to see himself in the reflection of the window, but he could only see a pale faded blur. He leaned his head closer to the side view mirror. He smiled a goofy smile and stuck out his tongue. He just couldn't get used to seeing himself that way.

"Hey! What are you doing to my car?" a voice called out.

Pez whipped around to see a large man stalking towards him.

"N-n-nothing," Pez stuttered. He turned and ran as fast as he could, not even waiting to see if the man was chasing him. He was laughing by the time he got there. He collapsed on the ground outside of her house.

After he finally caught his breath, he slipped into the party quietly. No one seemed to recognize him. He started to dance. Dancing wildly at first, then he calmed down a little, but as he calmed down something happened.

He stopped dancing and noticed everyone who was dancing was either 'rolling', 'tripping', or just plain drunk. As he watched, he began to see all of their bleak futures, all of their deaths. This prophecy of death overcame him. It pushed him over the edge.

He covered his face with his hands and began to shove his way to the bathroom. He closed the door behind him and leaned on it for support. When he could move again, he took out the tube of black lipstick and began putting it on his lips to calm himself down.

Pez watched the mirror in shock as his blackened hands began to smear the lipstick all over his face. He watched until it covered his entire face even his eyelids. He threw the empty tube in the garbage. He stared at the shadow of himself in the mirror. Tears were streaming down his cheeks making pale skin colored lines. He rummaged through the bathroom until he found what he needed.

He returned to the party and walked over to where the DJ was spinning records. He unplugged the system with his foot. The room fell into complete and total silence as the music stopped abruptly and everyone froze in shock at the sudden absence of music and light.

"Hey, what's the big idea?" the crowd began to shout questions at the shaking Pez. Pez stood his ground, standing on the cord so no one could plug it back in.

"Who the hell are you supposed to be?" one person shouted. Someone turned on the light in the kitchen. It lit him from behind, making him seem more menacing.

"It's the Crow!" another replied, half-joking and half-serious.

"Just who the hell do you think you are?" Amber demanded from the back of the room. She was pushing her way through the crowd.

"Be careful, he's a psycho mime!" someone yelled out to Amber.

"Shut-up!" Amber snapped back. "What do you want? Who are you?" she shouted.

"Some have called me a miracle; for I have survived more deaths then you've seen in your lifetime. Some have called me a menace and a murderer. For I have also killed more people then you have ever dreamed about… I am death," Pez answered quietly.

He picked up more confidence and volume, as some of the people seemed interested in what he had to say. "I have come," he began again, much louder this time, "to bring a message of death to all of you." He pointed at the crowd in front of him. His madness had taken over and Pez was helpless to stop what he was doing. "Each night that you party is another step closer to death, another step closer to ME! And I am waiting with open arms." He spread his arms momentarily as if to embrace them all. Then he reached into his pocket for the razor blade he had taken out of Amber's bathroom. He was prepared to do it finally. He was ready to join his friends wherever they were. A few people in the crowd screamed as Pez pressed the blade against his wrist and began to slash upward at it. He paused momentarily, thinking of Rae.

"PEZ!" a voice called, breaking through his insanity. Pez looked up. "NO!" Mike called out, he had been crying. He came up and took the razor blade from Pez. He tossed the blade aside, took Pez's arm and led him from the party.

"Why'd you stop me?" Pez asked in a small voice as they walked out to Mike's car. Pez clutched his arm to his chest.

"You weren't actually going to go through with it, were you?" Mike asked, opening the car door for Pez.

Pez climbed into the car. He waited for Mike to join him, when he did Pez showed him that he really meant to do it. He held out his wrist, which now had a thick trickling of blood dripping down it. He poked at it experimentally and they both watched as his blood started to flow faster.

"YUCK!" Mike yelled, fighting the impulse to throw up. "We have to get you to a hospital." He handed Pez clean tee shirt. "Here, wrap this around your wrist tightly," Mike instructed. "Apply pressure here," he said, pointing to a spot on Pez's arm. Pez did what Mike told him too. "We'll be at the hospital in five minutes."

"No," Pez said quietly, feeling weak and slightly nauseous at the sight of his own blood.

"What?" Mike asked.

"No hospital!" Pez shouted.

"Why not?" Mike asked, puzzled.

Pez gave him a dirty look.

"You're bleeding all over my car! I'm taking you to the hospital!"

"I'm sorry, but no you're not. Seven of my closest friends just died at that hospital and I refuse to go!" Pez would have felt stupid telling Mike about what he saw at the hospital the last time he had been there.

"OK, OK. Calm down. You need medical attention. My sister's a nurse. I'm gonna take you to her apartment, is that OK?"

"That's fine, just no hospitals, please. I hate…," he broke off in a groan.

"What's wrong?" Mike asked, his attention torn between the road and the slowly dying passenger in his car.

"It hurts," he said. His voice sounded foggy. Everything started to cloud over.

"Aw, shit!" he heard Mike whisper as he faded out of consciousness.

No Escape

I hate this world
and all the pain
I've slit my wrist
and gone insane
yet I am still here
doomed to live for
eternity
no escape from Reulily
no Escape from the pain
no going back
no returning to peace
you comfort me
in your gentle way
trying to stop
this pain

18

$\mathcal{U}$pon waking, Pez heard far away voices that seemed to be talking about him.

"If he doesn't come out of it soon, we're gonna have to take him to the hospital," a female voice said.

"He doesn't want to go to the hospital," Mike's voice answered the woman.

"Why not? He could be dying if this bleeding doesn't stop." Pez felt a pain in his wrist and he wanted to flinch away from the pain, but for some reason he couldn't move.

"He's afraid they'll keep him there for psychological reasons," Mike lied.

"They will."

Pez wanted to scream out to them. He wanted to tell them to let him die. Hadn't he suffered enough? This was it, he had finally done it and now they were trying to save him. He wanted to scream out and let them know how he felt, but he couldn't.

"Hold that rag tighter," the female voice spoke again.

"That's not a rag; it's a brand new tee-shirt."

"Hold it tighter," she demanded.

The pain in his wrist grew and he began to think that maybe he would die now, finally. He waited for death to take him in warm embrace.

"*Not yet, Spencer,*" he heard Matt's voice echo from somewhere. "*It's not your time, man. You need to go back. You survived for a reason you know.*"

Suddenly and abruptly, he returned to his senses, the change frightened him so much that tears began to roll down his lipstick-covered cheeks. He could feel reservoirs of tears forming near his ears.

"This should bring him around," a strange male voice said.

Pez opened his eyes, afraid he would find himself in a hospital. He stared up at a peach colored ceiling. Four figures stood above him, but as his eyes focused on the faces, two of them faded away. The silhouettes that faded away had reminded him of Matt and Wolf. Another figure came into his view. The only one of the three he recognized was Mike.

"Is he gonna be alright, Doc?" Mike's voice asked. Somehow it didn't quite match the way his mouth moved.

"He should be fine, now that the bleeding stopped. He's lucky he didn't cut deep enough to hit any major arteries. He really should have been rushed to the hospital. He has lost a lot of blood. Hopefully, he'll be alright."

Pez wanted to laugh. The doctor's voice was not matching the way his lips moved. It was as if he were watching a Japanese flick with the English words dubbed in. Then suddenly, sickeningly the voices snapped back into place.

"I...," Pez tried to talk and let them know he was going to throw up. Before he could the nausea overcame him and he threw up all over himself. Luckily, he had a chance to turn his head before he threw up. With his good hand he wiped his mouth, smearing the lipstick all over his hand and the comforter.

"MICHAEL!" the woman screamed. Then she seemed to calm down. "Take him into the bathroom and clean him up. Jack and I will change the sheets," she sighed.

Mike helped Pez out of the bed and led him into the bathroom. He still felt somewhat dizzy.

"What is all this crap?" Mike asked, pointing to a smear that had gotten on his shirt. Pez looked at Mike who had moved to the sink. He was washing his hands.

"Lipstick," Pez replied weakly. Mike sat him down on the toilet and began to wash his face with some sort of cream. "Sorry about your shirt," Pez offered softly. He still felt woozy and he had a hard time talking.

"If you're that sorry about it, you can buy me a new one," he said with a hint of disgust. He didn't believe Pez.

"What's your problem?" Pez asked.

"No, I want to know what your problem is!" Mike demanded.

"What do you mean 'my problem'?" Pez asked, getting angry.

"Ever since that day at the bookstore, you've been treating me like shit and I don't even know what I did," Mike said sadly.

"Well, you've always treated me like shit and I don't what I did," Pez lied. He was quite sure Mike was upset about losing Wolf to Pez.

"I asked you first!" Mike said.

"No you didn't!" Pez pointed out. "I just want to know exactly where you disappeared to that night."

"What night?" Mike asked warily. He was afraid he already knew the answer.

"The night when... w-w-when... e-everyone...," he stuttered. He couldn't finish saying the words.

"Died," Mike finished, unsure whether to be angry or sad. "I keep thinking that maybe, if I was there that night I could have stopped you guys from taking the E. Maybe none of them would've died, or maybe, just maybe, I would have died too. That would have been better than this... this suffering. This endlessly wondering if I could have changed things." He stopped talking, not by choice. A single tear rolled down his cheek and Pez could see he was fighting not to cry.

'Wait a minute,' Pez thought, 'I'm supposed to hate him. Why am I feeling sorry for him?'

`You feel sorry because you know what it is like to hurt.
You know what he doesn't. You were there. He wasn't,'* Wolf
answered his unasked question, even though he didn't appear.

"So where were you?" Pez asked softly. He was a bit
more sympathetic to him now.

"My Grandfather died and my family went to the funeral,
out of town. I begged my parents to let me stay, but they
wouldn't." More tears rolled down his cheeks. Something in
Mike's confession struck him as odd, but he chose not to dwell on
it. He was still too woozy to concentrate on one idea for long.

"I'm sorry Mike, I never realized you could have had
other …," Pez started to apologize.

Mike cut him off. "Well maybe you should have," Mike
said, wiping the tears away.

"OK, so why do you hate me so much?" Pez asked. He
had wanted to know the answer since that day at Wolf's house, so
long ago.

"I don't hate you."

"Then why were you so mean to me all the time?"

"I don't hate you. In fact I don't think I could ever hate
you," Mike said thoughtfully.

"What do you mean by that?" Pez asked warily.

"Because you have to be special; you just have to be,"
Mike explained sadly.

"Why?" Pez asked, not believing what he was hearing.

"He broke up with me, just so he could go out with you."

"How… How long… were you…?" he tried to ask.

"Four years."

"Four years," Pez repeated, trying not to cry himself.
"I'm so… so… I don't know what to say."

"He died in your arms," Mike sobbed. "He died in your
fucking arms. It should have been me. I should have been there
for him. I could have saved him," Mike whispered through his
tears.

"You couldn't have saved him. He died…," Pez stopped
talking and began to wonder if Mike actually could have saved
him. If Mike had been in the car, Wolf wouldn't have leaned over
towards Pez. He wouldn't have tried anything with Pez. He
wouldn't do that in front of Mike. "His neck was b-broken; his
skull shattered. There was nothing that you could have done."

"I could have stopped you guys from taking drugs," Mike
speculated.

Pez snorted. "No you couldn't. How many times did you try before that?"

"You're right." He paused, wiping his tears away. "Maybe there was nothing I could have done."

Satisfied with the cleaning of Pez's face, he glanced down at Pez's clothes.

"Take your shirt off. Oh God, your pants too. You puked all over everything," Mike said disgustedly.

"It's on my boxer's too," Pez said quietly, feeling like a small child again.

"How did that happen?" Mike asked.

" 's blood," Pez slurred.

"Oh well, take those off too, and climb into the tub."

Pez slowly climbed out of his pants and boxers with Mike's help. He stood naked in the middle of the bathroom, but he was still too weak to feel self-conscious in front of Mike. Mike guided Pez towards the oversized tub. Mike helped him climb in and Pez sat down in it, feeling more and more like a child with every second.

"What did you do to your hair?" Mike asked, the disgust barely hidden in his voice. He ran his fingers through Pez's black strands.

"Dyed it," Pez replied and shivered violently.

"Sorry," Mike apologized for making Pez shiver. "I liked it better blond," he remarked, making sure the water was warm enough. "Keep your arm out of the water. We don't want to get the bandage wet."

Pez scooted over in the tub until he was able to comfortably hang his arm over the edge. He relaxed as Mike began to soap his body. He took down the showerhead and rinsed off Pez's body.

"Hold this," Mike directed, handing him the showerhead.

Pez took it numbly and thought it might be funny to squirt Mike with it, but he was too tired to try. He sighed in pleasure as Mike massaged in the shampoo.

"OK, now lean your head back," Mike instructed softly, waking Pez from the dozing state all the warm water and head massaging had put him in.

Pez leaned his head back and opened his eyes. He watched as Mike rinsed his hair. He no longer felt like a child. He felt a stirring of emotion for his rescuer. He could tell that Mike felt it too as their lips met.

"I want to give you something that Wolf never had a chance to give you," Mike said, as he began to take off his clothes. He replaced the showerhead and climbed into the tub with Pez.

19

$\mathcal{P}$ez awoke to a sharp pain in his wrist. He wondered if what had happened was all just some sort of dream or if indeed it had been real. The painkillers he had been given made everything feel so surreal. He started to believe it really had been all a dream as he looked around the unfamiliar room. He spotted a silhouette against the window and focused on it. He hoped that it was Wolf standing there, but he was disappointed to find Mike standing by the shaded window with tears in his eyes.

"That shouldn't have happened," Mike pointed out, proving that it had really happened. "I...," he started again. "I have a boyfriend. This should not have happened; Wolf wanted...," he paused, thinking of a way to phrase his words, "...to be your first."

"How do you know that?" Pez asked, surprised.

"He told me. He talked about you all the time. He talked about how you looked; how you smelled. He was right. You were perfect for him but, you're just not right for me."

"I know," Pez replied.

"You do?" Mike seemed surprised that Pez felt the same.

Pez nodded. "There's this girl at my work...," Pez began.

"Oh, that one girl, you like her?" Mike asked, smiling slyly.

"I've liked her since she started working there," he said, unable to hide the smile that crossed his face whenever he thought of Rae.

The door opened and Mike quickly dried his eyes. Instinctively, Pez looked at himself to make sure he was wearing clothing. He was dressed in an old pair of Mike's sweats and a tee-shirt.

The doctor walked in. He gave Pez some last minute instructions and a few packets of prescription pain killer samples. "Legally, I can't prescribe a drug to you, so these free samples will have to do." Pez nodded. "Here's my card. Just tell the nurse you need to talk to me. If we keep this quiet, I won't charge you, but you really should look into getting counseling of some sort."

"I will," Pez lied. "Thank you."

"You're welcome and take care of yourself," the doctor said, then left.

"Come on Pez, I'll take you home," Mike offered.

"Who is that guy?" Pez whispered, wondering what doctor would come over and see him in secret.

"It's my sister's boyfriend. He's a good guy," Mike explained.

The ride back home was silent. Neither boy wanted to talk, especially after what had occurred the night before. Pez dozed lightly through most of the drive.

"Pez?" Mike shook his shoulder gently. "Are you alright?" he asked.

"I was just sleeping," Pez murmured, smiling.

"I thought you were unconscious again," Mike said nervously.

"Thanks for the ride, Mike," Pez said as he began to climb out of the car. Suddenly, he turned back to Mike. Mike raised his eyebrows in a questioning look. Pez leaned over and kissed him passionately.

Once again he started climbing out; he turned briefly and smiled at Mike.

"Oh and Mike, thanks. Thanks for... everything. I needed it."

Mike nodded.

Pez closed the door and ran into his house to get ready for work. As he was changing out of Mike's clothes and into his own, he had a sudden revelation. He decided to call off work and find Rae. It was her day off.

He called the bookstore and informed Tony that he was still ill and couldn't make it in. Tony was sympathetic and hoped he felt better soon. Tony was cool.

He opened his address book to look for Rae's number. While he was looking the phone rang.

"Hello?" Pez asked.

"Hello. May I speak to David Spencer, please?" the voice asked.

"This is," he replied slightly paranoid. He thought that the unknown voice was out to get him somehow.

"David, this is Mr. Robertson. Why didn't you come to class today?" Pez no longer cared about school or if he got in trouble for not going.

"I'm sick," Pez explained, not really lying. His wrist ached.

"I hope you feel better before Wednesday."

"Thank you, but what's on Wednesday?"

"It's the award ceremony for the art contest I entered you in."

"Oh that."

"They haven't announced the winners yet, but only you and one other student were invited to the banquet."

"Where at?" Pez asked.

"Bayberry Hall. Six pm. Wednesday," Mr. Robertson replied.

"I'll be there."

"OK, I'll see you then."

"Yeah, see ya." Pez hung up the phone. He didn't really care if he won or not on the outside, but deep inside he was very excited. He wondered who the other student was.

He dialed Rae's number, forgetting about the contest. He had copied her number down from her application. This was the first time he had gotten up enough nerve to use it. He held his breath as he dialed the numbers.

Three rings… no one answered. He wanted to hang up. It was always like this when he was trying to ask a girl out. A burning nauseous pit began to develop in his stomach. Four rings and a recorder picked it up. After the tone Pez stammered out a message.

"Hi. Um Rae… this is Pez… I m-mean Davie, from the bookstore. I… um called off today and I was wondering if you'd like to do something…my number is…"

He was cut off by a click and then a voice asking why he had called off.

"Are you still sick?" Rae's voice asked, when he didn't answer her first question. The burning pit in his stomach got deeper.

"Kind of," he replied. He was going to ask her, he really was. "What are you doing…?" No he wasn't. "Screening your phone calls?" he finished.

"Of course, I don't want to be called in on my beautiful day off," Rae said.

This was it! He was really going to do it. He was going to ask her now. 'Here goes everything,' he thought to himself.

"Well in that case," he began, almost chickening out again, but forcing himself to go through with it. "You ought to leave your house. That way you're positive that they won't be able to reach you."

He bit his lip, hanging on her response.

"Where would you suggest we go?" she asked, to his surprise.

The pit inside him exploded like a volcano. He was so filled with joy and expectation that he couldn't think of anything to do.

"I don't know," he replied, his heart falling.

"I've got the perfect place. I'll be over in twenty minutes," Rae said and the line went dead.

Pez gawked at the receiver in surprise. Then quickly he threw together a different outfit. He picked out an outfit that he hadn't worn since before the accident. As soon as he was dressed the doorbell rang.

"I'LL GET IT!" he screamed, not remembering that he was the only one home.

Rae stood on the front porch in cut off shorts and a half tee shirt. On her feet she wore a pair of old raggedy sandals. Her hair was pulled back into an unkempt ponytail. Her expression was of great surprise. Her face was lit up and her eyes were wide.

"I love your hair!" she cried truthfully.

"Thanks," Pez replied, smiling a big cheesy grin. He had forgotten all about dying it even though his hands still had dye all over them.

They walked in silence towards a destination unknown to Pez. She led Pez to a park on the other side of town. Pez knew the place well.

"My dad used to take me here," he said in a near whisper.

"My mom took me," she said just as softly as he had.

"My dad's dead," Pez informed her, still resentful over losing his father.

"So is my mom," Rae replied.

Pez remembered when Rae's mom died; it had happened quite recently. She missed a whole two weeks of work; which was nothing when compared to the two months Pez had missed after the accident. It's a wonder they hadn't fired him for that.

A hurtful silence had fallen over the two as they walked through the park. Each lost in their own memories of the parent they had lost.

Finally, Rae could take it no longer. "Davie, what did you do to your wrist?"

Pez took a deep breath and sat down on the closest park bench. Rae sat next to him; watching him expectantly, although she already knew what he was going to tell her. She could see it in his eyes.

"I um... I...," he stopped, unable to tell her the horrible truth.

"Go on," Rae urged impatiently.

"I tried to kill myself last night," he confessed quickly.

"Why Davie? You've got so much to live for," she admonished.

"No Rae. I don't. I have nothing to live for," he said, desperation breaking his voice.

"Yes, you do. You have your family, and me," she pointed out.

"*And Mike*," Wolf's voice added. Pez turned to see Wolf sitting on the other side of him. "*Besides, how can you say that after what happened last night?*" Wolf asked. He ran his fingers through Pez's hair. All of the sudden Pez remembered everything about the night before. The whole night came back to him in a flood of memory that was almost painful. In his memories it was not Mike that had made love to him. It was Wolf. "*I was there the whole time. It was me. I promised you I'd be your first and I never break my promises.*"

Pez found himself leaning closer to kiss Rae. He hadn't even remembered turning back towards her. Her kiss was soft and elegant, just like a girl should feel.

"Now I have something to live for," he whispered softly, kissing her again.

"Davie," she said, pulling away as he tried to put his arms around her. "Don't get me wrong. I don't want to offend you or hurt you in anyway."

'*Here comes the big letdown,*' D's malicious voice filled his head. '*Too bad, I wanted her to tell you that she loves you. I want to see her die too.*'

Pez braced himself for the worst and tried to ignore the voice in his head.

"That was... nice. I liked it," she replied breathlessly. "I liked it a lot. It's just that... God this is so embarrassing. I... I thought you were gay," she stuttered.

Pez's eyes popped open in surprise. Wolf burst into laughter. Pez ignored Wolf. "You thought I was gay?" he questioned, smiling a little. He was unsure of what to do next.

She nodded smiling. "That's why I never approached you. You aren't, are you? Gay I mean."

Pez shook his head. "No, I think I'm bisexual," he speculated softly.

"Oh, you just think you are?" she questioned, a smile spreading across her lips. Pez's face turned red.

"I've never had sex with a girl before," he whispered blushing slightly, embarrassed that he was telling her his big secret.

"Oh," she said loudly. "Well, now that that is settled, do you want to go with me to a club tomorrow after work?" Rae asked.

"I don't know," Pez said warily.

"Come on, Davie. It'll be fun!" she said smiling.

"No, I don't really want to," Pez protested.

"Yes you do!" Rae argued, smiling.

"You don't get it! No one gets it! The fun party Pez that everyone loved is dead! I'm all that's left!" Pez shouted.

"But Davie, he's not dead! He's just hurt and hiding," Rae began, tenderly caressing his cheek. "He's just hiding," she

190

assured him. "He's not dead," she whispered softly and kissed his lips gently.

"OK, maybe I'll go," Pez replied, "if I can have another kiss." He smiled and leaned forward to kiss her again. After she pulled away, he glanced at Wolf who was beaming. Suddenly the feelings of pain, loss, and guilt pushed away the feeling of love that had surrounded him only seconds before. His smile melted away as quickly as it had come.

"Davie?" Rae asked. "What's wrong?" She was concerned with his sudden mood change. "Did I say something wrong?"

"No," he laughed a little. "You said everything right, but my life just can't be fixed up like that. I don't deserve someone like you," he said, suppressing the urge to run away.

"How can you say that, Davie?" she said, angered.

"Because I killed them ALL!" he yelled, his hands beginning to shake.

"No you didn't, Davie. It was an accident. Calm down," she explained, taking his hands in her own.

"No it wasn't. It's all my fault they died," Pez sobbed, but Rae wouldn't give up.

"Why? Tell me how it's your fault. Convince me. What happened that night? Tell me the story from the beginning."

let them pour out
ever so gently
the teardrops of
your soul
make us pity you
make us lose control
pour out the
heavy drops
of rain
from the storm
clouds
clouding your
brain
save us with
your rain

let us drown
in your sorrow

"Wolf and I had been going out for about eight months," Pez began slowly.

"Nine," Wolf corrected him.

"Nine months, it was my birthday. He got me some ecstasy from somewhere. He got some for everyone. He handed it out. Amber was the only one who wouldn't take any."

"*Penny too*," Wolf corrected.

"Penny didn't take any either. She was pregnant," Pez repeated Wolf's unheard comment.

He closed his eyes. Instantly upon closing them, he was at the rave again. That's how clearly he could remember the night of his last birthday.

Amber was dancing next to him. She had her long brown hair in ponytails. She was wearing a too small shirt and jeans that swallowed her legs. Matt had bought her the outfit earlier that day. She was smiling brightly at Matt who was across from her. They had been going out since Halloween; shortly after Diamond and Matt broke up. Wolf was across from Pez next to Matt. Diamond was next to Wolf. She had her back to Pez. Eddie and Glenn were nowhere to be found. Pez had just spotted Sal and Penny in the corner making out.

He looked around at his friends. The cloud of ecstasy he was rolling on made it hard for him to concentrate on them. Little did he know then that it would be the last time he saw any of them... alive.

The music stopped and the lights came on. It was over; the people were being ushered out.

He didn't want to continue telling the story. He wanted to lie to her, tell her everything was fine. He didn't want to tell her how it really happened. He didn't ever want to tell anybody, but once he started with the story he couldn't stop himself. He sighed and continued as the memory swept him away again.

Pez smiled as his friends all began to climb into Sal's minivan, all still wasted from the ecstasy and other various drugs that they had separately done. Everyone but Diamond knew what Wolf and Pez planned to do that night. Diamond turned away from Sal's vehicle, a hurt look in her eye. Matt and Amber were leaning up against the car, making out. She saw Pez and Wolf climbing into Pez's car. Glenn grabbed her arm whispered something to her; she jerked her arm away from him and ran towards Pez's car.

"Wait guys!" she called, climbing into Pez's car. Wolf covertly rolled his eyes at Pez. They hadn't actually planned on going home after the rave, a nice little hotel room waited for them at the end of their journey.

"Don't worry, we'll drop her off first," Pez told him quietly. Wolf nodded, smiling.

Pez tried to keep his eyes on the road, but it was hard to concentrate, with the ecstasy and Wolf's hand rising slowly up his thigh. Pez glanced in the rear view mirror. He couldn't see Diamond.

"I think she's asleep," Wolf said, as he unbuckled his seat belt and leaned towards Pez.

Pez could feel Wolf's sweet breath in his ear.

"I love you," Wolf whispered. Pez's eyes rolled back in pleasure as Wolf began to breathe the sweet breath of angels into the hollow of his neck. He had time to notice that the sun was rising as Wolf kissed his way to Pez's lips. Pez's feet stretched languidly and his toes curled up causing the car to accelerate.

The moment was lost in a split second as his car barreled into something. Opening his eyes, he saw Wolf still in front of him turning his head in shock to see what they had hit. They had two seconds to notice Sal's minivan had spun around and was now teetering on the edge of an early morning rush hour intersection. Pez saw all of his friends turning to look at him in shock. Two seconds later and then another impact sent both cars into the intersection.

"And the rest... they say... is history," he finished off his story. The two sat in silence, pondering his words.

The first to speak was actually Wolf. He had listened and recalled the whole scene with Pez.

"You didn't kill them Pez," Wolf clarified, "I did." Tears rolled down his cheeks.

"Wolf says he killed them," Pez related to Rae. She still could not see or hear the spectral image of Wolf. She didn't even seem surprised that Wolf was there.

Rae thought for a moment, then began, "No, neither one of you did. No one died at all when you hit Sal's van right?" Pez nodded slowly. "They died after the other car hit yours and knocked both of your cars into the intersection. So the guy who hit your car killed them all," she stated more as a question than a fact.

Pez nodded frowning. "I still don't understand why I survived and no one else but Sal and Amber lived."

"That's easy, where did your head hit?" Rae asked smoothly.

Pez closed his eyes thinking for a moment. "Wolf's chest," he replied, unable to stop the tears from filling his eyes.

"Right, so Wolf actually saved your life," she rationalized.

Pez glanced at Wolf, but he was gone. He wondered if Wolf had heard her last statement.

"Thanks Rae. That's the first time I've ever really talked about the accident since it happened. I think that's all I needed," he hugged her tightly.

"No problem, Davie. That's what I'm here for," she replied, smiling brightly.

"Did I tell you that my grandma died?" Pez asked.

"No, you didn't," Rae replied, "I'm sorry."

"You didn't kill her," Pez told her matter-of-factly.

Rae laughed a little. "I guess that is kind of a dumb thing to say. I want to take you somewhere," Rae announced, jumping up.

"OK," Pez said warily as he followed Rae.

They walked in silence, through the breezy afternoon air. After a few minutes, Pez began to recognize where they were going. She was leading him to the cemetery where his family plot was. She led him through the cemetery in the opposite direction of his family's graves.

"This is my mom," Rae said softly, as she stopped in front of a headstone. "Mom, this is Davie," she introduced Pez to the stone. He rubbed the back of his head not knowing what to do.

"Um... Hi," he said quietly.

"I know she's probably not there, but I still like to talk to her anyway," Rae stammered. Suddenly, she turned to Pez. "I've never been able to feel her here. Can you feel her?" Rae asked.

"I don't know," Pez answered.

"Can you try?" Rae requested, sitting down next to the headstone.

"How would I try?" he asked.

"Just close your eyes and concentrate," Rae suggested.

Pez shrugged and sat down on the other side of the headstone. He placed his hand upon the headstone.

"What do you see?" she asked anxiously.

"Nothing... wait... I see a bowling alley," Pez said, trying to make sense of the images bombarding his mind. "I see a swimming pool," he whispered.

Rae was completely silent, hanging intently on every word Pez said.

'Wolf, help me find her,' he whispered.

"*I'm here,*" a woman's voice answered his silent plea.

"She's here," Pez informed her. He wanted to break the connection. He wanted to run away, but this is what Rae wanted.

"Tell her that I love her," Rae said.

"She knows. She loves you too. She is sorry that she left you so soon," Pez repeated what the voice told him.

"Me too," Rae agreed. Pez could hear the tears in her voice.

"She doesn't want you to take out your pain on your father anymore," Pez instructed her. "She wants you to find her jewelry box and take out the heart locket that you liked so much. She says to do it when your dad is not looking. He'll get upset if he sees you with it."

"Tell her I miss her," Rae said through sobs.

"She knows," Pez said. "She's gone now, but she wanted me to give you something from her." Pez leaned over and kissed Rae on the cheek.

"That was weird, I didn't know I could do that," Pez admitted.

"Neither did I," Rae said, wiping her tears away.

"I'm sorry I made you cry," Pez stated.

"No, it was a good cry. I needed to hear it," Rae assured him, smiling. "I'm sorry that was rude of me. I shouldn't have asked."

"It's OK," Pez said, shrugging.

"No it's not. I feel really bad, like I used you or something," Rae explained.

"You could make it up to me," Pez suggested.

"How?" Rae asked suspiciously.

"You could try it at my father's grave," Pez suggested.

"OK," Rae replied. "I don't know if I can do it as well as you did, though."

"It still would be cool to try," Pez persuaded her. "Who knows? Maybe you're as crazy as I am."

"You're not crazy," Rae defended. Pez stood up and reached out his good hand to help her up.

"Look, a crow!" Pez said, pointing at the black bird perched on a grave stone just a few feet away from them.

"Just one?" Rachael asked.

"Did you know a group of crows is called a murder?" Pez quizzed her.

"Yes, did you know that certain cultures believe that a crow carries a soul to the other side?" Rae asked.

Pez nodded. He paused, trying to remember the poem that his father had taught him.

"One crow for sorrow
Two crows for joy
Three crows for a girl and
Four crows for a boy
Five crows for silver
Six crows for gold…"

He paused, not sure he remembered what seven was for.

"Seven crows for a secret never to be told," Rae finished.

"You know that?" Pez asked in surprise. "My father taught me when I was little," Pez explained, his voice trailing off. Rae was staring off into the distance.

"If I ever decide to get tattoos, I am going to get seven crows in honor of that divination rhyme," Rae announced.

"It's funny that it was just a silly little thing my dad taught me when I was young and here we are years later talking about it," Pez told her. He stopped mid step.

"What is it?" Rae asked.

Pez couldn't find the words to tell her. He was staring at the hole where Nanah was going to be buried. "Nanah," he breathed, his voice barely above a whisper.

"Is that where they are going to put her?" Rae asked.

Pez nodded. He felt like that open grave was his own gaping wound.

"Do you want to just go?" Rae asked.

Pez nodded. They turned and started to walk home from the cemetery. "It got cold," Pez said shivering. He noticed the dark clouds that had descended upon them. "We should get home."

They walked at a quick pace towards Pez's house. About halfway there, the rain set in. They were soaked almost immediately. They ran the rest of the way to Pez's house. Pez began to look for his house keys as they stood on the porch. He couldn't find them anywhere.

"I don't have my house keys!" he yelled to her over the rain. "We're locked out." He frowned at the prospect of waiting in the rain until his mom got home.

"Since we're already soaked, let's go to my house. No one's home," Rae said, pointing in the opposite direction that they had come from Pez followed Rae as she ran through the rain towards her house.

"So, who all lives here?" Pez asked as they walked into her house. He was surprised at the spotlessly clean look of her house.

"Just me, my Dad, and Lorraine, she's my dad's girlfriend. She's a neat freak," she replied, leading Pez into the bathroom. "Let me see if I can find some of my dad's clothes for you. For now, there's a bathrobe hanging on the back of the door."

Pez nodded as she closed the door and disappeared. Pez began undressing by pulling the wet bandage from his wrist. The cut was gruesome looking, not too deep, but with big black threads sticking out. They looked like thick, nasty hairs growing from his arm. He experienced a moment of vertigo as he stared at it, finally acknowledging how close to death he actually had been.

After he recovered from the vertigo and stopped staring at his wrist, he peeled off his clothing—underwear and all. He laughed a little at the fact that he was stripping in an unknown bathroom again. He dried himself with a towel. Then slid on the soft pink terrycloth robe that he was hoping was Rae's. He stepped out into the hallway.

"Rae?" he called softly. "Rae?"

"In here, Davie," her voice sounded softly through the darkened hallway. He followed it to a room with the door closed. "Come on in," her voice came from behind the door.

He opened it, and walked in to find her standing in front of a mirror drying her hair. All she had on was a lacy bra and matching panties.

Pez quickly turned his head.

"It's OK, Pez. I've waited for this for a long time. I'm ready."

"Waited for what?" he replied dumbly.

"Waited for this… for us," she replied.

"No Rae, this is wrong."

"What's wrong? You don't want me?" she begged, her face falling.

"It's not that," Pez blushed. "It's not that I don't want you... I do," he chuckled nervously. He looked guiltily down at his crotch. "It's just that I'm not ready," he paused. "I do want to have sex with you, just not right away. Wolf and I didn't have..."

"Get out!" Rae demanded, cutting him off.

"Rae, just listen to me."

"No, Davie, just get out so I can get dressed."

Pez nodded in agreement and left the room, tears filling his eyes. He sunk down onto the floor just outside of Rae's door. He knew exactly how she felt. The incident had brought back memories of Pez begging Wolf to have sex with him. The tears began to flow.

Rae stepped into the hallway, fully dressed.

"Davie?" she asked, looking down at him smiling a bit. "I'm the one who was embarrassed, but here you are crying."

"I didn't mean to hurt you," he said looking up at her through tears.

"Oh Davie, you didn't," she assured him, bending down to kiss him on his nose. "You were right. It would have hurt us more if you had taken advantage of the situation," she said softly. "We should definitely wait." She smiled and helped him up. "Come on, I'll find you some clothes."

She led him to a room down the hall. "I'll get old clothes so my dad, won't notice that they are missing," she said, pulling underwear and a pair of socks out of the bottom drawer of the dresser. She laid them on the bed and stepped into the walk-in-closet. Pez followed her cautiously into the closet.

She found a blue bowling shirt that had "Ted" embroidered on the chest above the pocket. She held it up to Pez's chest to see if it would fit.

"Wow, I never knew how soft that robe was," she said, rubbing her hand up and down the fabric covering his chest. She dropped the shirt and put her arms around Pez, still rubbing. Then she looked up at him to see if he liked it or not. She was surprised to find his lips enclosing hers. They kissed intimately, standing in Rae's father's closet until they heard a door open and they pulled apart.

"Here, take these." She handed him the clothes she had found. "Throw them on in the bathroom. I'll stall my dad. We can pretend like we were just watching movies and you went to the bathroom." She handed him the hooded zip-up sweatshirt she was wearing. "Just to make sure your wrist is covered up." It was her favorite sweatshirt, which she lovingly referred to it as her zippy. She shoved him into the bathroom.

He caught the door before she could close it on him. "What do I do with my wet clothes?" he asked quickly.

"Stuff them under the sink. I'll wash them and give them back to you later," she instructed and shut the door before he could protest.

When he finally went out to the living room, he was introduced to Rae's father and soon to be stepmother. He made sure to keep his wrist hidden while shaking their hands.

Her father asked how the movie was and Pez almost blew it by saying it was very intriguing and thought provoking. Rae informed him later that she had told her father that they watched Beauty and the Beast.

Before he got ushered out, he asked Rae where his shoes were. He knew where they were; he was just hoping she would walk him out so he could kiss her again. She didn't pick up on the hint. She pointed out that they were on the porch were he had left them.

He walked home barefooted, carrying his sopping wet shoes. He was happy; happier than he had been in weeks. All he could think about was Rae. It had finally happened; he had finally admitted to her how he felt about her. He found that he was unable to stop himself from smiling.

When he reached his house, he walked into the kitchen through the back door. He thought maybe his mother would be in the living room and he could just sneak up the back stair without her knowing. No such luck. She was in the kitchen cooking dinner. His wet black hair fell into his eyes and he pushed it belligerently back.

"David?" his mom asked, looking up from what she was cooking. "DAVID?! What have you done? Look at your hair! Why are you wet? Why aren't you at work? Was there an accident at the bookstore?" Pez had expected this reaction from his mother.

"I didn't go to work," he said, rubbing his temples trying to calm the headache that her unending questions brought.

"Oh God, what happened to your wrist?"

"I called off work 'cause of that."

"What is it? What happened?" A look of fear and recognition crossed her face. "Oh David, you tried to kill yourself, didn't you?"

Pez just stood there staring at his mother, not knowing how to answer.

"Why didn't the hospital call me? You told them not to, didn't you? You were going to keep this a secret, weren't you?" Pez's mouth dropped open in surprise, he hadn't expected that.

"I didn't go to the hospital," Pez mumbled.

"Why didn't you go to a hospital? You could have died!"

"I know," Pez said, dropping his shoes by the door. He folded his arms across his chest and held back his next thought: 'That was the point, dumb ass.' Instead he said, "My friend knew a doctor who took care of me."

"You should have been at home in bed. Where were you if you weren't at work?"

"I was at a friend's house," he replied softly.

"What friend?" she asked nicely.

Pez gasped, "You think I don't have friends?"

"No, David, that's not what I said," she explained.

"You said it. You think I can't make any new friends." His mother just stood there with her mouth gaping as she stared at him.

"And you wonder why I tried to kill myself!" he said spitefully and stormed out of the kitchen.

"DAVID!" she yelled after him. "David, I didn't mean it that way. DAVID, I'm sorry!" She followed him to his bedroom and knocked on the door. "David, open the door, please," she begged. She couldn't stand to see her son still hurting like this.

"Why should I? You're just gonna hurt me more," Pez replied resentfully.

"David, please, I want to apologize," she pleaded. Something in his mother's voice made him open the door. She stood outside the door with tears in her eyes.

"My baby's hurting and I want to make it better. I do, David. I want to help you, but I don't know how. You keep on shutting me out and it gets so frustrating."

"Why does it have to hurt so much?"

"Because you loved him," she offered tentatively, hoping her suspicion wouldn't offend him.

"How did you know?" Pez asked, surprised that his mother knew his secret.

"A mother knows. I also know how you feel, that is if you loved him half as much as I loved your father."

"I think I did," Pez admitted, smiling through his tears. It felt good to know his mother knew his secret. It felt good that he no longer had to lie about himself anymore. His mother wrapped her arms around him and he fell into her, crying like he had never cried before. She sat on his bed, rocking him until his tears ended.

"So, whose house were you visiting?" she asked cautiously.

"A girl from work, Rae," he said, smiling brightly at the memory of her touch.

"And she's just a friend?" his mother asked, raising her eyebrows at the contagious smile on her son's face.

"No, she's different... special... I think I love her. I think I always have," Pez admitted to his mother.

"Oh honey, that's so good to hear. I'm glad you're a little bit happy," she smiled.

"I'm not happy," Pez said sullenly.

"Then why are you smiling?" she laughed, hugging him closer for few moments. "You know I love you, don't you?" she asked. Pez was surprised to hear tears in her voice.

"Yeah," Pez nodded. "I love you too, mom," he whispered in a voice thick with tears.

"We have to stick together, now that Nanah and Poppy are both gone," she whispered. "You have to let me in, David. You can't keep it all inside, OK?"

Pez was silent, thinking about her request. Should he tell her about ghost-Wolf? Should he tell her about D, or Junkie Pez?

"OK, D?" she asked, squeezing him tight.

"OK!" Pez laughed.

"Good!" She gave Pez a peck on the forehead and stood up. She walked towards his door, but paused and turned around. "Oh, by the way your friend called... Mike, I think. He said for you to call him as soon as you got in," she informed him and then she was gone.

Pez picked up his bruised feelings and dialed Mike's number only to find out that Mike wasn't home. So he left a message on his answering machine.

Pez lay down on his bed trembling. He couldn't believe the changes that had so recently occurred in his life. Now if only Sal would wake up from his slumber. He would be even happier.

He started to think about the hospital where Sal's inanimate body lay. Pez tried to imagine what it would feel like if he were in a coma and Sal was the one being alive. He imagined it so vividly, Sal putting the gun to his own head and pulling the trigger. Pez started as if he had actually heard a gunshot.

The phone rang again.

He heard his mother yelling something from the front part of the house as he reached out to answer the phone.

"Hello?" he asked. Mike was on the other end. "Hold on a minute, OK?" Pez said and set the receiver down on the nightstand. He jumped out of bed and ran into the kitchen to see what his mother was yelling about. He found Stevie and his mother in the kitchen, finger painting. "What?" Pez asked.

"I asked you to answer the phone, because I'm all covered in paint," she replied holding up her hands to demonstrate how paint covered she was. "Who is it, sweetheart?"

"It's for me. It's Mike."

She nodded as Stevie began to explain the picture he had painted.

"This is me..." He pointed to a small figure. The figure was dressed all in red. "This is D." He pointed at the figure dressed in black. "This is mommy." He pointed at the larger pink figure. "And this is Daddy up in heaven with God watching over us." He pointed to the two figures standing on a cloud.

Pez sighed and went back to the phone. "Mike?" Pez asked and waited until Mike responded before continuing. "Sorry about that. My Mom was yelling and I had to go see what she wanted," he explained to Mike, not knowing exactly why he felt he needed to explain himself to Mike.

"No problem, I can't talk long. My boyfriend's taking me out to dinner for my birthday. I was just calling to see how you were doing."

"I feel a lot better," he replied and then decided to add "physically and emotionally... You know that girl from the bookstore?" He asked, the smile returning to his face.

"Yeah," Mike answered in anticipation.

"I talked to her about everything. Then I told her how I felt. Then I... I... kissed her," Pez rambled on excitedly.

"Cool!" Mike exclaimed genuinely. "Hey listen, the reason I wanted to call was on the day after tomorrow there's going to be a rave at the warehouse. We are gonna celebrate my birthday there. I was thinking maybe you want to bring the girl."

"That sounds cool. I'll definitely ask her. I'm sure she'll go, if she's not busy," Pez assured him, eager to see if going to a rave with Rae would be better.

"Alrighty then, see ya there," Mike said, hanging up the phone.

Pez walked back into his bedroom and closed the door. He took a deep breath to calm himself down. He realized he was still wearing Rae's zippy. It still smelled like her. He lay down on his bed and gathered the zippy up to his nose. He fell asleep breathing in the sweet smell of Rae.

Dreams of her soft and delicate touch followed him through the night.

20

He awoke feeling more refreshed then he had in months. He was happy for a few moments until he remembered that Nanah had died. It was strange he hadn't even thought about it all yesterday. He'd been too busy thinking about Rae.

'Speaking of Rae,' he thought to himself, 'might as well call her and see what she's up to.' He looked at the clock; it was noon. He had four hours before work. He had pretty much decided he wasn't going back to school. He called Rae and invited her out for breakfast or lunch or just coffee. She agreed and they met at the cafe.

Pez was nervous going in, afraid he would see Wolf's ghost again, but he didn't. He and Rae had a marvelous time. They talked until it was time for work; they were both scheduled in at four. They walked towards the bookstore together. Just before reaching the bookstore, Rae stopped.

"Hey Davie?" she began.

"Hmph?" He squeezed her hand gently, the hand he had been holding since they left the cafe.

"Maybe we shouldn't let people at work know about us. If they know, they'll stop scheduling us together." Pez nodded, reluctantly releasing his hold on her hand. "I'll go ahead. You've got time. Wait a while then follow, OK?" Pez nodded as Rae ran ahead to the bookstore. He followed her slowly.

"So you're actually coming in today huh, David?" Boss greeted Pez as he walked into the store. "Oh and look at that, you're actually on time. My, my, maybe that new hair color made a new man. You got a little on your ears. Who did your dye job, a blind woman? Oh it's all over your hands too. You must have done it yourself, no wonder it's such a shitty dye job," she paused a minute, looking around. "They ought to hire more people to close this damn store. So I don't have to stay and help that Tony boy when one of you decides to take a joy day."

Pez wished he could throw up all over Boss's shoes right then and there.

"I swear, you two have missed so many days..." Pez found himself actually trying to make himself throw up as Boss rambled on. He couldn't make himself throw up, so he cut her off.

"Isn't it time for you to punch out?" he asked. He was sick of her listening to her bitch already. He hated the days he was scheduled to work with her. All she ever did was gripe constantly about everything. She would bitch about anything from the shape of the store to Pez and Rae's personal hygiene, of which she was one to talk. Pez and Rae would joke about her rank breath, saying she used a dead rat as a pacifier while she was sleeping.

"You're probably right. I should be punching out now." Boss punched out and Pez punched in. "That damn cat's been howling since I put it in the cage," Boss said as she walked towards the door.

Pez looked at Rae, feeling cocky. "Doesn't that tell you that maybe the cat doesn't want to be in the cage?" Pez said loud enough for Boss to hear. She turned around, her mouth open as if she were going to say something then decided against it.

Rae laughed. She was trying to quiet the cat until Boss left.

After the door was safely closed behind her, Pez looked at Rae with a twinkle in his eye. "Did you see how she tried to kill us with her breath before she left?" Rae burst into gales of laughter. She was laughing so hard that she couldn't even get the cage open to let the cat out, which made her laugh even harder. Pez walked over and opened the cage to let the cat out. "Want to play Magic?" he asked.

Rae looked up, seeing that Pez was no longer laughing. She gathered herself up and tried to stop laughing. She nodded between giggles.

They sat behind the counter at the desk and pulled out the decks that they kept at the bookstore. Pez tried to shuffle his deck, but his wrist ailment made it very difficult.

"Um, I think you need to shuffle this for me." He set the deck in front of her.

"Wh...," she started, but stopped as she realized the reason he asked her. "OK." She set hers aside and began to shuffle his. They lapsed into semi-silence.

"We can talk about it," Pez said, not exactly sure that he could talk about it.

"Talk about what?" Rae asked.

"That wasn't the first time I tried, you know," Pez sniffled. He hadn't realized how close to tears he was, but he had to get through this. He had to tell Rae. He had been trying to tell her all day. "I've tried four times before."

"Davie, I don't want to hear about it," Rae said with near panic in her voice.

"But Rae, you need to hear about it. It's important to me that I tell someone and you're all I have right now, Rae. The only reason I didn't succeed in killing myself is because of you."

"Because of me?" she asked in a small voice.

"I loved you from the first time we met. I know it sounds corny, but I can't help it. It's just the way I feel."

"Nobody's ever been so honest with me before," Rae said, tears rolling down her cheeks. She had stopped shuffling so she could hear Pez's small voice.

"When you've seen so many people die, you learn to speak your mind. You never know when your last chance to tell them is."

"You never got to tell him you loved him, did you?" Rae asked.

"I did, but I never got to tell him how much I loved him," Pez clarified, trying to hold back the floodgate of tears that threatened to explode with every word.

"I'm sure he knows," she said, smiling and choking back tears of her own.

After a few minutes of quiet with the two of them gazing at each other, Rae shattered the silence.

"I want you to come over early tonight, so I can help get the hair dye off of you." Pez nodded. "I can't believe Boss said that to you. She's such a bitch."

"You're telling me," Pez said, nodding in agreement. "Or how about when she referred to the owner as that Tony boy? Does she thing she owns the store?" He laughed.

"I think she does, that bitch." She agreed, shaking her head. She set his shuffled deck in front of him. "Now, are we going to play or are we going to chat?" she asked winking at him.

21

"My mom taught me a really cool way to get rid of hair dye. Well it's not really all that cool, but it does the job," Rae said to Pez, who was sitting on the toilet, with his hair pulled back into a ponytail. "It's only one certain brand. I've never seen anything else work, that's not to say that nothing works, just that this is the only thing I've seen that works. It's called a Friday Night Mud Mask."

"But it's not Friday," Pez joked.

Rae just smiled. She stepped up to Pez and began to spread the stuff around his ears and the side of his face. He couldn't help, but notice her breasts. He barely even realized he had reached up to touch her breast until she swatted his hand away. "Not now, Davie. You've got the mask on. Now give me your hand." Pez had the strange feeling that she was going to smack his hand, but she didn't. She began to spread the mask on his hands. "My mom never got it on her hands, but I'm sure it will work there too. Hold your hands still. It needs to get hard. It can't get hard if you keep wiggling them around like that," Rae scolded him.

Pez giggled. "Just think what that would sound like if you only heard the last part of that conversation."

Rae laughed. "Now we let it dry for a half an hour; then we wash it off. Are you hungry?" she asked. Pez nodded. "Do you want me to reheat some macaroni and cheese?"

"That sounds good." Pez said. To him, his voice sounded weird and his face was beginning to tingle. He followed Rae into the kitchen and sat down at the table. He watched her get the food ready, never once wondering how he was going to eat it.

Rae thought about it as she was getting two forks out of the silverware drawer. "Are your hands hard yet?" she asked.

"No, but they're getting there," Pez replied. "Do you have any gloves?" he asked. He was surprised to find himself hungry.

"Don't worry about it, Davie. I'll feed you." She smiled and set the microwave dish in front of him. She took turns feeding herself and then him. When they were finished, she announced that it was time to take the mask off.

After the mask was off, she painted Pez's fingernails black to hide the dye that had gotten underneath them. Then she changed into a short black dress, black and white striped nylons and black platform Mary Jane style shoes. She assured Pez that he wouldn't feel stupid for not dressing up; that she always dressed up for the bar even though no one else did.

"Before we go to the bar, there's something I want to do," Pez said softly.

"What?" Rae asked nervously.

"There's an open m-m-mic night at the café." Pez explained. "Nevermind," he said in disgust.

"What, Pez, why not?" Rae asked.

"This stupid stutter… I thought I got over it, but when I get nervous it comes back." He paused. "That's why I never wanted to do it before."

"But it's important to you?" Rae asked.

"Yes, but I don't want to get up there and stutter like a moron."

"Don't worry about that," Rae suggested. "If you need to do it then you should. I'll be there, and if anyone at all laughs at your stuttering I will kick their ass," she threatened.

Pez smiled. "OK," he agreed.

Part Five: Silver

22

Pez and Rae arrived at the café just as Poetry Night was getting started. Hardly anyone was there yet, so Pez confidently put his name in the line-up.

They sat at a table farthest from the door so Pez wouldn't be tempted to flee.

"You sure you're OK?" Rae asked.

"Oh yeah, I'm good," Pez replied sarcastically. He held his hand out so she could see how badly he was shaking.

"Maybe we should get you some tea," Rae suggested.

"Tea? I'd rather have a valium," he joked. He had never drunk tea before. He'd always thought tea was a ladies drink. "My Nanah drinks tea," he laughed.

"Tea is actually quite helpful in relieving stress. Certain kinds are like nature's valium," she explained. "Chamomile for example is very soothing. It's always worked wonders for me." She flagged down a waitress who was zooming by.

"Hey Pez!" the waitress greeted. Pez smiled nervously. It was Mercury from the other day. She turned to Rae. "Can I get you something?"

"Yeah, my boyfriend here is about to do his first poetry reading and he's very nervous. Do you have anything to help calm him?" Pez showed Mercury his shaky hand.

"Chamomile tea works pretty good," Mercury suggested.

Rae nodded. "That would be perfect," she agreed.

Mercury moved in a little closer as if she were going to tell them a secret. "Also I have a trick of my own. Just dab a little of this on your wrist," she instructed, pulling a vial out of her apron. "While you're up there, if you get nervous run your hand through your hair. The ladies love that, but it also will hide you sniffing your wrist. It will help calm you down."

"What is it?" Pez asked. He took the lid off of it and sniffed it gingerly.

"It's lavender oil. It's aromatherapy. All you do is inhale it and it calms your nerves."

"Really?" Pez put his finger over the opening and flipped his hand. He rubbed the oil on the inside of his wrist. He capped the vial and handed it back to Mercury.

Mercury nodded as she took the vial and deposited it back into her apron pocket. "Don't break too many hearts up there." She winked at Pez and walked away.

"Do you know her?" Rae asked after Mercury was gone.

"I met her a couple days ago. She helped me after one of my episodes," Pez explained.

"After you saw a ghost?" Rae whispered.

"Something like that," Pez replied as Mercury returned with the tea.

"How much do I owe you?" Rae asked, grabbing for her purse.

"Nothing, hun. The tea is free here." Mercury smiled and disappeared into the much larger crowd.

"Holy crap!" Pez exclaimed, looking around. "There's a lot more people here."

"Don't worry, you'll be fine," Wolf's voice sounded from beside him, startling him. He was sitting beside Rae, smiling. Pez hid his reaction by taking a sip of the tea. To his surprise he rather liked it.

"Don't worry about them; pretend I'm the only one here," Rae offered.

Pez nodded. "Thanks. This is good." He pointed at the tea.

"You should try it with honey," she suggested. "That's you," she announced as they called Pez's name.

Pez sighed. "This is it." His stomach was in knots, but he needed to do this. The tea seemed to be helping a little. He stood up, Rae squeezed his hand, and Wolf gave him a thumbs up sign.

Pez walked to the stage, concentrating on not tripping on anything. He sat on the stool behind the microphone. He tried to adjust it to fit him, but it slid down too low. He fumbled with it for a few seconds, which felt like minutes to Pez, until he finally got it at the right level.

He glanced up at the crowd and immediately regretted it. They were staring at him expectantly. He looked over at Rae and she smiled and mouthed the words "I love you".

He couldn't stop the smile that spread across his face. He unfolded the paper on which he had written his poem.

"My n-n-name is Pez," he began, the stutter returning as he knew it would. He glanced back at Rae. He was surprised to see the spirits of all of his friends sitting at her table watching him. He realized then that he had written the poem for them and they were giving him the strength to share it with this crowd. "My poem is called 'Car Crash' and it's a true story," he annunciated clearly.

Car crash

I kissed you then
on our last morning
I heard her screaming
I heard her howling
and I kissed you again
as you lay there
with your head in my lap

I held onto you and begged
you not to go
I told you everything
would be alright
you looked up at me
with pain in your eyes
my blood running
down your cheek like a tear
you looked up at me
and lifted your hand to
my cheek
I cried then
as you said goodbye
I cried then
as I heard your words
I cried then
as I felt you die
regretting that I never
got the chance
to return those words to you
dreading the fact
that now I never will
get to say those words to you
those words
so hard to say
make me st-st-st-stutter
make me shake
I tried to say
"I love you"
but I could never get it out
I tried to say I love you
and now you'll never know

every night I dream
and in those dreams

those nightmares
I watch you
die in my arms again
over and over
until there is nothing left
of me
I died too,
that morning
the morning that I couldn't
say those words
the morning that I couldn't say
"I love you too."
I couldn't say goodbye
all I could do was
LIE...
"Everything will be alright.
Everything's gonna be fine.
Just stay here with me,
Please don't leave."

Pez ended the poem by wiping away the tears that had fallen. He looked up at the silent crowd. Did they like it? Rae started clapping and the rest of the crowd followed. Pez smiled as the room erupted. He stood up and starting walking back to the table. He was stopped by people along the way who wanted to talk.

"That was so beautiful," Rae whispered more to herself than anyone.

"*It was*," Wolf agreed. "*I always told him his poems deserved to be heard, but he never listened.*"

Rae turned in the direction his voice came from, but she didn't see anything.

"Rae?" Pez asked as he finally made it back to the table. "Are you OK?"

"That was beautiful, Davie, just beautiful," she praised. She picked up his tea and took a big gulp.

"You sure you're OK?" Pez asked, sitting down.

"I think...," she began. "I think I just heard Wolf."

"What did he say?" Pez asked. He scooted his chair so he was right next to her. He put his arm around her.

"He said that you deserved to be up there," Rae repeated.

"That sounds like him," Pez agreed.

"Is he here now?" Rae asked.

Pez looked around; he didn't see Wolf or any of his other friends. He shook his head. "No, but he was when I was up there, all of them were."

"All of them meaning, the ones that died?" Rae asked.

"Yep," Pez answered. "I wrote the poem for them."

"Let's go now," Rae urged. "I'm getting a little freaked out."

Pez hugged her close and kissed her head.

"Welcome to my world," he whispered.

"It's a little scary here," she whispered back.

"Drink some of my tea," Pez laughed.

Rae stuck her tongue out at him, but finished his tea.

"I'll meet you out there. I have to hit the bathroom," Pez told her.

"OK. I'll get the car and bring it around," Rae replied, kissing him quickly as she ran out.

After Pez came out of the bathroom, Mercury stopped him.

"Is your girlfriend OK?" she asked. "She looked a little shook up when she left."

"Yeah, she'll be OK. She just heard something other people couldn't," Pez replied.

"Oh, got ya," Mercury said, taking the hint.

"Like when we saw that boy the other day," Pez said nodding. Something told him that Mercury was skeptical. "You did see him, didn't you?"

She shook her head. "I'm sorry. I didn't, but you did and that's all that matters right?" She noticed his crestfallen look. "Look Pez," she began, placing her hand on his shoulder. "Everyone sees spirits differently. I didn't see him, but that doesn't mean he wasn't there."

"What if it wasn't a spirit?" Pez asked nervously.

"What do you mean? What else could it have been?"

"Nothing, nevermind. I gotta go." He escaped her hand and ran outside, where Rae was with the car.

"Are you OK?" Pez asked as he climbed into the car. "I mean, is it too much?"

"Is what too much?" Rae replied.

"My world... you know... the ghosts," he said the last word almost in a whisper, as if saying the word would conjure a spirit.

Rae laughed. "Oh God no, I asked for this. I wanted proof of the afterlife and now I have it. It's not too much. My mind is just a little blown that's all." She smiled her infectious smile and kissed him on the nose.

He smiled back.

"Good." He replied and settled back into his seat.

23

"Is this the bar you were at that night you picked me up?"

Rae nodded. "It's not really a bar; it's more like a dance club. You like to dance right?" Pez nodded. "You'll like this place a lot then."

They walked into the bar, which was in the main part of town. Pez didn't notice the name of the bar. He only saw a sign that stated Gay Night. That frightened him very much. He had never been to a bar on gay night before; in fact, he had never been to a bar before at all. He expected the worst. When he walked into the bar, he saw to his surprise, normal guys doing normal guy things; dancing, drinking, and having a good time. The only two who were doing anything out of the ordinary was the couple on the dance floor making out, but that didn't bother Pez. In fact, it aroused him a little.

There were a couple of scary older men, but the rest looked completely normal. Most of them were gorgeous model types.

"This is the first time I've ever come here without Georgette," Rae yelled to him. "I want to go downstairs, the music is better down there."

Pez nodded, still a bit weary. He thought the music here was just fine. As he followed Rae down the stairs into the other bar, he found himself in a mini-rave surrounded by ravers galore. Some of them he even knew.

"This is cool," he shouted over the music.

She nodded smiling. "It's my favorite place to be," she shouted in reply.

"Well, if you like this place, you'll love a rave. They play the same music there, only it's bigger."

"I've always wanted to go to one," she admitted.

"There's going to be one tomorrow, if you want to go?" Pez asked.

"Sure, I'd love to," Rae replied smiling. "Let's dance." She pointed to the dance floor. They danced for a little while. Pez even heard some new songs. After a while, a young man came up to Rae. She stopped dancing to hug him. He handed her a Zima and she took a generous swig of it as he whispered something in her ear. Pez pushed back the jealousy he felt. She turned to Pez.

"Do you want to stay here, or go to a party?" Rae asked.

Pez shrugged. "Either is good with me."

"OK, let's go then," Rae said, taking his hand and leading him from the bar.

"Justin said it's over on Church Street," she said, shivering in the chilly air outside of the bar.

"Here, have my zippy. You must be freezing," Pez said, wrapping his zippy around her.

"Thanks," Rae said, snuggling up in his zippy. Pez wanted to put his arm around her to keep her—and himself—warm. He was freezing. Finally, when he could take it no longer, he took a deep breath and put his arm around her. She sighed and snuggled into his warmth. Pez smiled. He was happy she was warm and that she didn't mind having his arm around her.

"You're so warm, Davie," she said, stopping in the middle of the sidewalk. She reached over and put her hand to his forehead. "You've got a fever, Davie," she said, turning around. "You're sick. Let's go home," she said, waiting for him to join her.

"We don't have to go, I'm alright," Pez lied, not wanting to be away from her again.

"You need your rest, Davie. You are never going to get better if you don't get any rest."

"You sound just like my mother," Pez laughed as they began to walk back to the car.

"You should listen to her. She's a smart woman. I never listened to mine and look where it got me," she said.

"Where?" Pez asked, not realizing she was near tears.

"I never got to say goodbye. I never got to tell her… that I love her. She was gone too fast, just gone."

"How did she die?"

"Drunk driver killed her," she replied through her tears.

"You hate me, don't you?" Pez asked, afraid of the answer.

"No, why would I hate you?" she asked, stooping to unlock the car door.

"Because I was wasted when my friends were killed."

"Davie, I've already explained it to you. It's not your fault they died. I don't hate you because they died. I don't hate you," she paused, looking over the car at him. "You've got to stop thinking that everyone hates you. Nobody hates you."

"Mike does," Pez mumbled.

"I'm sure that's not true. Why would he hate you?"

"Well I sort of stole his boyfriend," Pez admitted.

"OK, well maybe he hates you," Rae said laughing, "but no one else does, OK."

"The thing I don't get, is why is he always acting so nice to me? I can feel this hatred oozing off of him, but he acts like it doesn't exist."

"That is weird," Rae agreed.

"Do you think it would be alright if we didn't go home just yet?" Pez requested.

"Why not?"

"Sometimes it's hard to sleep. I'd rather spend more time with you, if that's OK?"

Rae smiled. "Yeah, that sounds great. But you need to take some aspirin. I don't want you staying out here if that fever doesn't go down."

"Of course," Pez leaned up against the car as Rae dug through her purse for some aspirin. He leaned his head back and stared up into the sky. "Wow I think I just saw a shooting star," he exclaimed.

"Oh yeah, there's supposed to be a meteor shower tonight." She paused in her search and looked up at the sky. "Hey! I've got an idea. Let's drive someplace with less light and we can watch it. Maybe we could grab some food on the way?" She glanced over at Pez, who was still staring up at the sky. "That is, if you're up to it."

Pez looked at her and nodded. He watched as she walked around the car towards him. "Yeah, I'd like that. I should be fine if I take some aspirin. I mean I don't feel sick, just a little chilled."

"OK, but you let me know the moment you need to go home," she commanded, handing him a bottle of water. He took it and held out his hand for the aspirin.

"Aye aye, Captain," he smiled, and then tossed the aspirin in his mouth and washed them down with the water.

They drove for a while listening to a mix tape that Rachael made. They were quiet, but there was no awkwardness in their silence.

"What about right here?" Rae asked, pulling her car over next to a cemetery.

"Looks good to me," Pez approved, unbuckling his seatbelt.

"Not too creepy?" she asked, glancing over at the headstones a few feet away from the car.

"Naw, we'll be alright," Pez replied.

"You don't 'see' anybody, do you?" she asked shivering.

Pez laughed. "No there's nobody here but us."

"Good." She stuck out her tongue at him and walked to the back of her car.

Pez got out of the car, still looking at the cemetery making sure that he really didn't see anyone in there.

"I'll get a blanket out and we can lie down on the hood." She stuck her car key in the trunk.

Pez's stomach growled. "You know we forgot to get food," he pointed out.

"Should we get some?" Rae asked.

Pez was anxious to lie down next to Rae. He weighed his options and finally decided food could wait. "I think I'm OK for now," he finally answered.

"Me too," Rae said, spreading the blanket out across the hood of her Buick Century. "This way 'Ye Olde Cow' won't get any rust on us."

"You named your car Ye Olde Cow?" Pez asked.

"Of course. It's got spots, doesn't it?"

"But it's blue."

"So!" Rae laughed.

"How old is this car anyway?"

"It's only about 10 years old. It's a hand me down from my Uncle."

"I'm not going to fall through, am I?" Pez joked as he climbed up.

"No... Ye Olde Cow is solid," Rae laughed as she shimmied up next to him. Pez offered his arm for her to use as a pillow. Rae smiled and laid back.

"It's beautiful out here," Pez commented once they were settled.

"There are so many stars," Rae agreed. She pointed up to the sky. "That one there is Cassiopeia."

Pez squinted up at the sky, trying to see what she saw. "Where?"

"It's the one that looks like a W," Rae pointed out. She traced the W with her finger.

"Oh, I see it now," Pez replied.

"And over there is Orion. That one's my favorite."

"You have a favorite constellation?"

"Yes," Rae replied. "Orion was a great hunter, but he was very boastful. He was in love with Diana, the virgin huntress. They were planning to marry, but Diana's brother Apollo, thought that Orion wasn't good enough for her. So one day Orion was out in the ocean and Apollo dared Diana to shoot at the black dot they could see very far away. Diana, being such a great huntress, took up the challenge. She pulled back her bow and let her arrow fly. It hit her target easily. When Diana found out that it was Orion she had killed, she put him up in the sky so he could live forever."

"Wow, that's sad." Pez replied. "Where is it?"

"See the two stars with three stars close together under it, then 2 more under that?"

"Yeah."

"The 3 stars closer together are Orion's belt."

"So the two stars above would be his shoulders."

Rachael giggled.

"What?" Pez asked, looking down at her.

"I just remembered the name of the star to the left... I think. Its name is Betelgeuse."

"Like the movie?" Pez asked.

"Yeah, but it's spelled different. Betelgeuse means 'armpit of the great one'," Rae laughed.

"Did you say...," Pez asked, but Rae didn't let him finish.

"Arm pit of the great one," she repeated. "At least that's what my mom taught me. The laughter disappeared from her face as she said the words.

"Mom and I used to love stargazing," she smiled sadly. She glanced at Pez only to find he was staring at her instead of the sky. "It's good to know, I have someone that knows what I'm going through." She closed her eyes, pushing back tears.

Pez wasn't quite sure what to say, all he could do was stare at her lips. He leaned in closer for a kiss.

Rae pulled away suddenly. "Your nose is cold!" she squeaked, grabbing her nose. She paused for a second as she registered what just happened. "Oh," she said softly as Pez tried again. This time she didn't pull away from him.

"I love star-gazing," Pez whispered as he pulled back from the kiss licking his lips. Rachael's lips tasted like bubble gum, from the flavored lip gloss she wore.

"Me too," she breathed, kissing him again tenderly. Then she pulled back biting her lip.

Pez noticed that there were tears streaming down her cheeks.

"Rae, what's wrong?" Pez asked, pushing himself up on his elbow.

"I'm sorry." She wiped at her tears. "It's not you. I just remembered something my mom told me about shooting stars." Rae looked away from Pez and stared up at the sky as she continued. "Mom always said when you see a shooting star it's because the spirits up in heaven miss us so much that they spread the sky apart to look down at us. She said sometimes when they spread the sky, stars fall through the gaps and that's what we see."

"You're mom told you that?" Pez asked shocked "My Nanah used to tell me that exact same thing." He smiled "It must be true then."

"Must be," Rae agreed.

"They're looking down at us right now." Pez smiled.

Rae nodded, but her tears began to fall.

"The last thing I said to her was that I hated her," she confessed.

"She knows you didn't mean it," he soothed.

"Is she here now?" she brightened at the thought.

Pez shook his head sadly. "I don't see her." Pez wiped a stray tear from her cheek. "I'm sorry."

"It's OK," Rae replied.

"Rae, listen to me. When I 'talked' to her the other day, I didn't 'feel' any anger or pain or resentment. All I felt was love. The love I felt from her was like no other love I've ever felt. It was all encompassing. I thought I knew what love was, but all of the love I've ever felt pales in comparison to what she felt for you. You were her world." He paused taking a breath. "She's always with you, Rae. Always," he finished.

"Thank you," Rae whispered through her tears. "Hold me?"

Pez snuggled back down next to her and wrapped his other arm around her. He pulled her close and buried his nose in her hair. She smelled like cotton candy and cigarettes.

"I think your fever's gone," she whispered.

"Me too," Pez smiled.

24

"You know it's time for bed when the birds are chirping," Pez pointed out as he got in the car after they ate breakfast at Denny's.

"Or when the mail trucks are on the road," Rae laughed.

They drove for a bit before Rae got up the nerve to ask a question that had been nagging her for a long time.

"If you don't mind me asking, how did your father die?"

Pez looked at Rae. He wished she would just start the car and they could be off, but she wanted the answer to her question first.

Instead of answering, he lifted up his shirt to reveal a scar on his stomach.

"What's that?" Rae asked.

"I got shot."

"With a gun?"

Pez nodded. "When my father was killed," he explained. Her mouth dropped open in shock.

"He was killed?" Rae asked.

"He was murdered."

"And you saw it all?"

"So did my mom," Pez replied, nodding.

"Who did it?" she asked

"Some people my dad knew."

"Did they get arrested?"

Again, Pez was unable to speak. It was still hard for him to talk about his father's murder. "I had to... testify against them." He stared out the window as he talked. He couldn't bring himself to look at her. "They were like my uncles... It was really hard," he said softly.

"I'm sorry," Rae apologized as she started the car and pulled out of the parking lot.

Pez said nothing. After a few minutes of silence he closed his eyes and fell asleep.

He dreamt again that he was walking down a hallway. He walked quietly; he didn't want to wake anyone up. He knew people were there this time. He knew that they were sleeping. He walked up to Wolf's bedroom as silently as he possibly could.

This time there was stuff in Wolf's room. The posters were in their usual places and someone was lying in his bed. Pez walked over to the bed, only to find out his suspicion was true. It wasn't Wolf sleeping in the bed. It was someone else.

"That's my cousin," Wolf's voice informed. It was coming from behind him. Pez smiled and spun around to find Wolf standing there.

"Wolf," Pez said out loud.

Wolf shushed him. "Unlike other dreams Pez, this one is real. If you wake up my cousin, we're both screwed," Wolf whispered.

"What do you mean this dream is real?" Pez whispered back to him.

"I don't have time to explain it. I have to warn you, you're almost home. Watch Amber at the rave, keep a good eye on her," Wolf said, beginning to fade away.

"How do I know this was real?" Pez asked as Wolf's room began to fade away, leaving him in darkness. He felt something being placed into his hands.

"Take this, you'll know," Wolf said, disappearing.

He tried to lift up the object so he could look at it to see what it was, but it slipped through his hands. Now he would never know if the dream was real or not.

"Wake up sleepyhead, you're home," Rae's voice woke him. When he opened his eyes, he found Rae had parked the car in the street in front of his house. "Are you feeling any better?"

"A lot, thanks to you," he replied softly. He leaned over to kiss her goodbye. They kissed for a while, until Rae pulled away and placed her finger on his lips.

"Rest," she commanded.

Pez nodded. "I'll call you tomorrow... later today," he promised as he climbed out of her car and walked slowly towards his house. He turned and waved from his porch.

25

Pez found himself walking down a long hallway.

"Pez! Hey Pez!" Glenn's voice called out to him.

"Glenn?" he asked, walking in the direction of the voice.

"Over here Pez!" Glenn called from the end of the hallway. Pez saw him standing there and smiled.

"Glenn!" he called out, picking up speed as he made his way to the end of the hallway.

"What are we doing here?" Pez asked as they stood outside a green colored door.

"Someone wanted to talk to you. She had trouble getting through so I had to help her," Glenn stated. *He stood aside so Pez could walk through the door. Pez stopped as he read the door.*

"The morgue?" Pez asked. "I don't want to go in there," Pez said, remembering the last time he had been in there. Nanah told him it was important that he see his father. She had led him down that hallway; she had shown him his father's corpse. *"I'm not g-going in... in th-there,"* Pez stuttered in shock, mad that his cursed stutter followed him even into his dreams.

"Don't worry Pez. It's not really the morgue." Glenn opened the door to reveal a fragrant garden.

"Is that heaven?" Pez asked.

Glenn smiled. *"If it is, it's her heaven,"* Glenn said, nodding towards a young woman that stood in the middle of the garden. She looked up at Pez smiling.

Tears began to fill Pez's eyes. *"Nanah?"* he asked, taking in a deep shaky breath.

The woman nodded.

"You never knew me this way," she explained, gesturing to her thirty-year-old body. *"Would you prefer me the other way?"* she asked.

"No," Pez answered quickly. *"This is how I always saw you."*

"You little charmer, you," she said, laughing. *"Come give your Nanah a hug."* Pez ran over to her and threw himself into her arms.

"Well, my job is done. Have a nice reunion," Glenn said. *"See ya, Pez! See ya, Nanah!"* Glenn said, waving his hand. *"Say goodbye to Poppy and Sierra for me!"*

"Bye Glenn. Thank you!" Pez called out to him.

Glenn smiled and slowly faded away.

"Who's Sierra?" Pez inquired.

"She's your sister," Nanah answered him slowly.

"My sister?" Pez asked dubiously.

"Your mother never told you anything, did she?" she sighed. *"Stevie had a twin. She died during child birth. Your mother named her Sierra."*

"Her grave is next to my father's, the lamb statue. That's her grave, isn't it?" Pez deduced.

"Yes."

"Can I meet her?" Pez asked.

"You will soon enough," Nanah assured him, *"but first we need to talk."*

"About what?" Pez asked.

Nanah reached out and took his hand; she turned his wrist up towards him. "About this?" she said.

Pez looked away from her nervously.

"You can't try that again," she warned him.

"Why not? If I do, then I can be with you here," he reasoned.

"No, you can't," she informed him.

"Why not?" Pez asked.

"If you choose to... kill yourself, you go somewhere else. I don't know where, but it's not here," Nanah answered. "So don't do it D." She smiled, wiping away his tears.

"You better listen to her, Kiddo," a male voice warned. Pez turned and found himself staring at a young man that looked almost exactly like his father. He too seemed to be in his thirties.

"Dad?" he asked, excitement filling his voice.

"Sorry kid, it's just me, Poppy," he chuckled a little.

"Poppy!" Pez said. He ran over and hugged his grandfather.

Poppy laughed and swung him around in a circle. "Man, it's been forever since I was able to do that," he said, laughing. He led Pez back over to Nanah.

"Why did you leave me?" he demanded of the both of them.

"It was my time," Poppy said, "and your grandmother just couldn't bear to be without me," he laughed, hugging his wife.

"It was my time, too," Nanah agreed. "I tried to warn you."

Pez thought back to what she had said at Poppy's funeral. "Even if Poppy and I are gone; you have to live on and fulfill your purpose," Pez whispered softly.

Nanah nodded. "Always remember that and remember that some things that happen are beyond your control. Not everything is your fault," Nanah explained.

"But I...," Pez began, but he was interrupted by a child's laughter. He turned and looked where his grandfather had come from. There was a girl standing there giggling.

"Don't be sad about Daddy's death," Sierra implored him. She smiled and laughed. "He plays with me sometimes." She walked closer to Pez. "You look like him," she pointed out.

"Sierra?" Pez asked. The little girl nodded.

"Tell Mommy that it's not her fault I died," Sierra requested. "I have a secret," she whispered.

Pez leaned down closer to her.

"Stevie's not sick. He doesn't have brain damage." Sierra laughed. *"Daddy says that Mommy's depressed and she coddles him too much," she informed him.*

"Is Daddy here?" Pez asked in a child-like voice.

"I'm sorry kiddo, he's not," Poppy answered.

"He's earthbound," Nanah added.

"What does that mean?" Pez asked.

"He's stuck there, silly," Sierra clarified. "Something is making him stay. I keep telling him to come and see Nanah and Poppy, but he won't. He won't come here and when they go there, they can't see him." She paused, looking at Pez. "I know why he stays there," Sierra confided.

"Tell me," Pez begged.

"You can help him," Sierra assured him.

"Sierra, how?" he asked, but the garden was slowly fading away.

"Sierra?" he called out, but his young sister was gone. "SIERRA!" he screamed.

"David!' He felt someone shaking him. "David! Wake up!" He opened his eyes to find his mother standing about him terror-stricken.

"How do you know that name?" Carole demanded, with anger in her voice.

"What name?" Pez asked sleepily.

"You know what name. You were yelling it in your sleep," she let him know.

"Sierra?" he asked. His mother flinched.

"I met her, Nanah introduced us," he said, smiling.

"Don't ever say that name again!" she told him. "Get up, it's time to go to Nanah's funeral," she declared and tossed his father's suit on the bed. "And you better behave!" She stormed out of the room.

"Who's Sierra?" Stevie asked. He was standing in the doorway watching as Pez pulled on his father's suit. He was dressed in his new suit.

"She's your twin sister."

"She's fun," Stevie said to Pez's surprise. "She likes to play. I always thought I made her up, but I never knew her name." He shrugged and left Pez gaping at him.

Pez dressed slowly and walked down the stairs to find his mother in the kitchen.

"It's nice to see you're not wearing that ratty old jacket," Carole complimented.

"No, I'm just wearing this ratty old suit, today," Pez retorted.

"That suit was your father's!" she informed him.

"So was the jacket," Pez returned, feeling proud of the way her mouth snapped shut.

"What time is the awards ceremony?" Carole inquired, changing the subject.

"How did you know about that?" Pez asked.

"Travis told me," she replied.

"Travis?" Pez asked.

"You know, your art teacher?"

"You call him Travis?" Pez asked in shock.

"Well, I can't go calling my date for the evening Mr. Robertson," Carole stated. Pez could tell she was feeling proud of the way his mouth snapped shut.

"Date?" Pez asked. His mother hadn't dated anyone since his father died.

"It's been a long time," she said. "Are we ready?"

"I guess," Pez replied.

"Can Sierra come too?" Stevie asked.

Carole gave Pez a look that clearly read 'See what you started.'

"I didn't do it," Pez protested. "The kid says he's seen his twin sister all his life. All I did was tell him her name."

"I wish you wouldn't have," Carole sighed sadly.

"I really did see her, Mom," Pez asserted.

"I don't want to hear about this!" Carole exclaimed, picking up her purse and holding the door open for her boys to exit the house.

"Whatever!" Pez said, storming past her and out to the station wagon.

26

$\mathcal{P}$ez stood near the same spot he had stood for Poppy's funeral. This time his back was to Poppy's and his father's graves. He looked around at the faces of the people standing around the graveside. There were twice as many people for Nanah's funeral as there had been for Poppy's.

Pez saw Sierra standing next to Stevie. She looked up and smiled at him. Pez was too sad to smile back. His Nanah was gone. Even though he had seen her twice since she died, he had this terrible feeling that he was never going to see her again. He stopped fighting the tears and let them fall.

this pain that grows
inside of me
ever outward does
it flow
threatening to
send me falling
into my ocean of
black waiting below
I try so hard to
push it aside
but it keeps coming
back to me
threatens to leak its
way outside
my flesh
and let everyone
see my pain

"We commit Emily Marie McGardle Spencer's body to the ground," the Priest was saying. Pez began to sob violently. He couldn't seem to get any air into his lungs. His mother put her arm around him. She too was crying lightly.

"Goodbye, Mom," Pez heard one of his aunts say.

"She's not here!" Pez screamed so suddenly he hadn't even realized he had screamed it. "She's not in that box!" he screamed. His mother tried to quiet him, but he pushed her off. "You all keep talking to her like she's still here, but she's not!" he screamed, throwing himself against the casket. He knocked the flower bouquet off the top of it. "She's gone! SHE'S GONE!" he screamed. He felt arms wrapping around him and pulling him back, away from the crowd of people. He watched in amazement as the priest replaced the flowers on her casket and started speaking again, as if nothing happened.

"She can't hear you," Pez whispered. "SHE CAN'T HEAR YOU!" he screamed. He felt his mother's hand close over his mouth.

"Quiet down, David," she soothed, removing her hand from his mouth. He was done; they would never listen to him. He fell limp into the arms that held him.

"She's gone," he whispered.

"You didn't need to cry that much, baby," Carole whispered, referring to his grandfather's funeral. She laughed gently.

Pez laughed a little at her joke. Carole kissed his forehead.

"Let's get him in the car," Carole suggested.

Pez turned his head to see his Uncle Wally and his Uncle Jimmy supporting him, one on each side. Uncle Jimmy smiled sadly and winked. His tear-streaked face reflected the sadness that Pez felt.

They helped Pez into the station wagon and then talked to Carole for a few minutes.

"*They can hear you, you know,*" Wolf's voice rang out into the empty station wagon.

"I know. I just wanted to see her one more time, to say goodbye," Pez replied, trying not to move his lips. He laid his head down on Wolf's leg; he could feel Wolf absently playing with his hair.

"*That's what last night was for,*" Wolf explained softly.

"I didn't really get to say goodbye, though," he told Wolf.

"*You may not think that you didn't say goodbye, but you did,*" Wolf assured him.

"Why did I see her after she died and how is it I can still feel you?" Pez asked.

"*It's your gift,*" Wolf informed him.

"What GIFT? I never asked for a gift!" Pez snapped. "What is this gift everyone keeps talking about, anyway?" Pez asked, turning his head to look up into Wolf's ghostly face.

"*I thought it would be obvious by now.*" Wolf laughed. "*You're psychic Pez. Just like your father was; just like your grandmother was. I knew it when I was alive. I didn't need Nanah to tell me about it.*"

"I'm psychic?" Pez asked.

"*Specifically, you're a medium,*" Wolf clarified.

"Psychics come in different sizes?"

"*No, silly. A medium is someone who can communicate with the spirits of the dead,*" Wolf explained, gesturing to himself.

"So, I'm not going crazy?" Pez asked, but his head collapsed against the cushion as Wolf disappeared.

"Did you say something?" Carole asked.

"I just said I'm sorry I ruined the funeral," Pez lied to her.

"You didn't ruin it," Carole comforted him. "You can't help how you feel. I am actually kind of glad that you let your feelings out. It's not healthy to bottle it all up inside. You end up breaking down, just like you did out there.

27

"Can I take you someplace special?" Pez asked Rae softly over his cappuccino.

Rae met him at the café after she got off work. She had covered for Pez so he could go to the funeral. He had just finished telling her all about his horrible funeral meltdown.

"That depends on where you're going to take me," she replied, laughing a little.

"You'll see," he said, taking her hand and leading her from the café. They walked in silence until they came to the bridge. Pez stopped and gazed out onto the city.

"I tried to kill myself here, once. I was going to jump. I almost did, but I heard my mom's voice in my head. Strange, you would think that would make me want to do it even more with the way we are now."

"Oh Davie, I just want to make it all better for you," Rae said, hugging him. He shivered as the smallest memory flashed in his brain. His grandmother had said the same thing to him after his father died.

"She hates me, you know," Pez murmured softly.

"Your mom?" Rae asked.

"Yeah," he replied.

"No she doesn't!" Rae argued.

"Yes she does. Why else would she give me to Nanah and Poppy so that they could raise me?" he asked. "Look, I don't want to talk about this right now," Pez deflected. He looked at Rae and wondered why he had brought her out here. He had no idea what made him stop on the bridge and tell her what he did. "Come on," he said pulling away from her. "We're not there yet."

"Where are we going?" Rae asked softly.

"To see Wolf, if that's OK with you?" he asked.

She nodded, smiling.

They walked in silence to the cemetery, where Wolf and his sister were buried. As they began to walk towards the Waverly plot, Rae gasped.

"Is that Wolf?" she whispered, pointing at the headstone where Wolf sat.

Pez nodded. "You can see him?" he asked in relief. Rae nodded. "I'm glad I'm not the only one. I thought I was going crazy," he explained, as they both watched Wolf fade away before they reached the grave, where his dead body lay.

"Where did he go?" Rae asked.

Pez shrugged. He wasn't exactly sure where Wolf went when he disappeared; maybe he was still there listening.

"That's where his grave is; his sister is buried right next to him. Over to the left is where Eddie is buried. This is the Waverly's family plot. All of the Waverlys and their grandparents are buried here. These two plots were originally for their parents, but Wolf and Diamond died first," Pez explained, as he sat down in his usual position between the two graves. As always, a memory took him immediately.

Pez watched in silence not knowing quite exactly how to feel. This was his first funeral outside of his own family. Diamond and Wolf were completely distraught at the death of their grandfather. Pez felt ashamed that he did not feel the same way, but he hadn't even known the man. As he looked at Wolf, a feeling of grief washed over him. He hated to see Wolf in such pain.

Pez stood as motionless as a statue and watched as all of the family members including Diamond walked away, leaving Pez and Wolf alone in the cemetery. As soon as the members of Wolf's family were gone, Wolf collapsed to the ground, sobbing loudly. Pez ran to him and sat down, throwing his arms around Wolf to support him in his hour of need.

"I... I... I...," Wolf stammered, trying to speak. "He... He hated me. He hated me because of what I am, because of who I am. No, he hated me because of who I love. I never got to tell him I loved him. I tried, but he wouldn't listen. He was too stubborn. He couldn't even forgive me for being me. Why did I hurt him? Why am I like this? This goes against everything he ever stood for," he ended. His face reddened slightly when he realized he had been screaming. "I'm sorry Pez. It just bothers me that he felt that way. I never got to know him as well as Diamond or Mokey did. I wasn't even allowed at his house anymore after I 'came out'. The worst part is even though he disowned me, I still loved him."

Pez just sat silently as Wolf rambled on about his past and how he hated what he had done to his grandfather. He wasn't listening as well as he should have been until he heard Wolf utter the phrase. "Sometimes I think... I feel like I'll be buried here instead of my parents. It's like somebody or something is going to kill me before I get to live my life."

"His real name was David?" Rae asked, breaking his memory trance. She was standing behind him, taking everything in.

Pez nodded. "Yep, luckily, we both had nicknames to differentiate between the two of us: Wolf and Pez," he said sadly.

"Why do people call you Pez?"

"I was named after my father, so when I was little my parents started to call me D, so they wouldn't mistake me with my father. The name stuck so when I started going to school, my nickname was D. I would sign all my papers 'D. Spencer' and when the teachers would call out my name for roll call, they'd call out D. Spencer and I would answer. My friends found that funny so they stared calling me Pez dispenser as a joke and somehow that name fit me more than D ever did."

Rae smiled. "Can we see Eddie's grave?" she asked.

Pez stood up and they walked towards the mount that Eddie was buried under. "Edward William Stanton," Rae read out loud. "I think I knew him. Did he work at the café?"

"Yeah, he got Wolf a job singing there." Pez smiled. "That's all Wolf wanted to be was a singer."

"I recognized him in your picture."

"What do you mean? What picture?" Pez asked, turning to look at her.

"That picture you left in my car; I recognized Eddie in it."

"I left a picture in your car?" he asked in confusion.

"Yeah, the one of you and your friends… the ones that… died," she said, bursting into tears.

"Rae, what's wrong? Why are you crying?" Pez asked, hugging her close.

"I just… It just… I can't… I can't believe all that you've been through. I can't believe how much pain you have suffered. I can't imagine how it would feel. I can't even come close to imagining how I would survive the pain you have survived."

"I'm the one who was hurt, but you're the one who's crying," he said, echoing her words from before.

She smiled that luminous smile that warmed Pez and made him smile too. Her smile faded as she began talking again. "It's just… I can only imagine how you feel. Nothing even close to that has happened to me. I… kind of… take my mother's death and multiple it by ten or twenty and it feels like… You must feel like your whole world was ripped out from under you," she said through fresh tears.

"I do feel that way. Everyone I have ever loved or cared for is gone. I lost all of them, even Mike, Sal, and Amber. Mike and Amber are both druggies now. I don't even recognize them. Sal's in a coma and I doubt he's ever going to come out of it." Pez paused, swallowing back his tears. "He told me once that if he ever lost Penny, then life wouldn't be worth living. I know how he felt… feels. I know because I lost my Wolf and life just doesn't seem to be as good as it was, now that he's gone. He was everything to me. He was my life… and now I'm dead inside," Pez said, not realizing how much of what he said was affecting Rae. She began to cry even harder.

"I'm sorry," Pez said as he stood there holding her. Finally she stopped crying.

"No Pez, I'm the one who's sorry. I shouldn't have asked."

"If it helps any, you've given me something to live for," he assured her. She smiled, but the tears still fell.

"I shouldn't have brought you here. Do you want to go somewhere else, somewhere less emotional?" She nodded. "We have to dress up, I think."

"Dress up how?" she asked.

"Dress nice. It's an award ceremony."

"Really? For who?"

Pez shrugged. "The winners are going to be announced there. I was entered into an art contest. My teacher told me to be there. Maybe I won," Pez said, as they started walking away. "It starts at five o'clock, so be at my house at four thirty. You can meet my mom." Rae nodded. They walked together until the bridge, where they parted company

28

"Aww Mom, do I have to wear the suit?" Pez whined.

"David, it's an award ceremony everyone has to dress up," she advised him.

Pez smiled maliciously. "Remember what happened last time I wore it?" he said, fake crying.

"Shut-up and put the suit on," Carole laughed. "You can go without the tie, if you promise to be good."

"I promise," Pez said

"Stevie, put those noodles back in the fridge. I told you we are going to eat there," Carole yelled, as she walked into the kitchen.

"But mom, I'm not going to eat them," Stevie said, running out of the kitchen.

"What exactly are you going to do with them?" she called after her youngest son.

"Stevie! You little shit! Stop throwing noodles at me. What the hell do you think you are doing? GOD DAMN IT, STEVIE! MOM! Make him stop!" Pez screamed.

"David, you watch your mouth and Stevie get your little a... fanny back into the kitchen before I spank it and PUT THE NOODLES AWAY!"

"What's wrong with Stevie?" Pez asked, bewildered by his younger brothers behavior.

"He thinks we're going to a wedding," Carole explained.

"So he throws noodles at me?" Pez asked, picking noodles off of his father's suit jacket.

"Well noodles... rice, same thing," his mom rationalized as she helped him pick noodles out of his hair, which was pulled back into a debonair ponytail. "He thinks it's your wedding."

"My wedding?" Pez asked. "Who am I marrying?"

"Rachael, of course," Carole replied, smiling.

The doorbell rang.

"Stevie, Honey, get the door." A few seconds later they heard two screams: one of terror and one of hysterical laughter. They both ran into the living room to find Rae standing in the doorway covered in noodles. A bowl lay at her feet and Stevie was nearby rolling on the ground with laughter.

"STEVEN THOMAS SPENCER!" Pez's mom roared, her face turning purple. It was a nice shade that overshadowed the shades of red on Pez and Rae's faces.

"Come on in," Pez said as his mom dragged Stevie from the room cussing up a storm.

Rae stepped in and shook her head. A shower of noodles fell to the carpet around her. "Does your brother always greet people by throwing noodles at them?" Rae laughed. She picked up the bowl and set it on the table. Then, she began picking noodles off of her dress and dropping them into the bowl.

"He thinks he's going to a wedding," Pez explained, helping to pick the noodles off of her.

"What does that have to do with noodles?" she asked.

"I have no idea." Pez laughed, as he finally stood back to admire her. "You look beautiful," he complimented truthfully.

"So do you," she replied, blushing a little at the compliment.

"You've got a noodle in your hair," he pointed out. He reached up and picked it out.

"So do you," she laughed and picked one out of Pez's hair. Pez hadn't realized how close they had gotten. He couldn't help but kiss her. They kissed until they heard a small voice whisper.

"Hey mom, are they going to have sex?" Stevie's voice interrupted their kissing.

They stopped kissing and looked over in the direction the voice had come from.

Carole replied, "No honey, they're just kissing. Please don't let us stop you. Continue." Pez's mom was awestruck by the romance of the two.

"Mom!" Pez said, embarrassed.

"What?" Carole replied innocently.

"Shouldn't we get going?" Pez asked.

"Yes, but before we leave…," Rae started, "I have a score to settle with Noodle Boy." She picked up the bowl and started towards him. He ran from the room screaming. Rae laughed, setting the bowl back down on the table.

"We should probably pick the noodles up off of the floor before we leave," Pez's mom suggested. "You two start in here. I'm going to make sure Stevie's not getting into anything. Then I'll get the noodles in the bathroom." She turned and left the room.

Both Pez and Rae squatted down and began to pick the noodles out of the carpet.

"Don't be mad at Stevie. Sometimes he's just a little weird. He was born premature and the doctors said that might have damaged his brain a little. I think…," Pez's voice dropped to a whisper, "that even though he was in the womb at the time. I think somehow he saw our father's death and that traumatized him…" Pez abruptly stopped talking when his mother walked back into the room.

"Hey mom, I'm gonna ride with Rae, OK? I don't want to be late," he informed his mom.

"OK sweetie." She smiled. "Don't be late, D," she said, winking.

"She thinks we're going to have sex," Rae said as the door closed behind them.

Pez laughed, knowing full well that that was exactly what his mom thought.

"Oh, hey, now that you're here and I remember it, you left your picture in my car." She opened her door and reached into the car. She pulled out the picture and slid it across the roof to Pez.

He picked it up and sank to the ground staring at the picture.

It was a framed picture of all his friends. Mike, Wolf, Pez, Diamond, and Eddie stood behind Wolf's couch. All were smiling. Matt, Amber, Sal, Penny, and Glenn were all smashed together on the couch. In front of the others and lying on the floor, was their friend Brendan who lived in Ireland now. He had been visiting for the week and Wolf decided to set up his camera and take the picture so that Brendan could remember his friends back in America. Pez began to cry as he held the picture close to him.

"What's wrong, Davie?" Rae asked, circling the car to stand above him.

"Wolf gave me this," Pez explained through his tears.

"Oh," she replied.

"No, you don't understand. He gave me this in a dream I had in your car yesterday," he explained timidly, not knowing how she would react.

"Get in the car, Pez," Rae said sounding angry. Pez obeyed her immediately.

"Are you mad at me?" Pez asked, surprised at how angry she had sounded.

"No, I'm not mad. I just don't want you to be late." She paused as she started the car and drove away. After a few moments of silence, she began again. "Look, I can believe that you see him, but I just can't believe that he gave you something in a dream," she said, sounding angry again.

"It wasn't actually a dream. Wolf said it was real. He said I would believe him when I saw what he gave me. He gave me the picture. You're making me want to cry. I just feel like I'm going crazy."

"Pez, you're not going crazy. How can you be? If you didn't bring that picture into my car, and I didn't have it in here, then it must have actually happened. Unless someone slipped it in here while we weren't looking. I know you, Davie. I know you wouldn't lie about things like this. You're not crazy." She stopped talking as they pulled into the parking lot of the hall where the awards ceremony was taking place.

"Do you really believe me?" Pez asked in a small voice.

"Like I said, what else can I do, but believe." She leaned over and kissed him on the forehead. "Now pull yourself together.

We've got an award to win." She smiled so brightly that Pez found himself smiling back.

"You are so beautiful," he whispered.

"Thank you," she said, her cheeks reddening. "You're not so bad yourself," she laughed.

29

They found their seats and they sat waiting, hoping Pez's mom would arrive before the awards ceremony started. It had already begun when Pez's mom ran in late. Stevie was dressed in a sweater and pants instead of the suit he had been wearing. His mom wore a different dress.

"What happened?" Pez asked.

His mom had no time to answer as the winner of the pencil drawing was announced.

"David Spencer in first place gets a scholarship to the art college of his choice."

Pez's mom cheered and Rae smiled hugely. Pez walked up to the stage and through his own excitement, he saw a vision of himself pulling off what he did at the party, in front of this more sophisticated and less stoned crowd. The thought passed as he noticed his art teacher smiling proudly.

"I am so proud of you, David," Carole said, as he returned to his seat.

"Me too! You are so lucky," Rae said, beaming proudly.

"Yeah, lucky," Pez whispered sadly. He didn't want to go to college. He wasn't even sure if he was going to graduate from high school.

"So what happened to your outfit?" Rae asked.

Carole laughed. "Finger paints again." She rolled her eyes. "Stevie decided that his new suit wasn't colorful enough," she sighed. "I hope I can get the stains out... of both outfits."

"My dad's girlfriend works at the dry cleaners, maybe she can help," Rae offered, but Carole was not paying attention. She was staring at something in the distance. Pez looked over to see what she was staring at. Mr. Robertson was walking towards them.

"David!" he called out as he neared the table.

"Mr. Robertson," Pez said in greeting.

"Congratulations," he said holding out his hand. Pez shook it.

"Um... Thanks," Pez replied, but Mr. Robertson was too busy staring at Pez's mom to hear.

"Travis," Carole said, blushing.

"Carole," Mr. Robertson, said taking Carole's hand and kissing it. "It's so lovely to see you again."

"You too," Carole replied.

"Rae, would you like to go look at the entries?" Pez asked.

Rae nodded, standing up quickly. Mr. Robertson took her seat, placing himself next to Pez's mom.

"Honey, why don't you take Stevie with you," Carole suggested.

"Great. Sure thing," Pez responded disappointedly. He had wanted to be with Rae alone.

"So, which one is yours?" Rae asked as they approached the art gallery.

"I am assuming it's the one with the blue ribbon," Pez quipped. He tried to direct her away from it, but she broke away from him and ran over to it. "Please Rae! Don't!" Pez begged. "It's too morbid," he whispered.

"What are you talking about?" Rae asked. "It's beautiful," she praised. Pez could hear tears in her voice.

"No it's not. It's horrible," he argued. He looked up at the drawing and gasped in shock.

"What is it?" Rae asked.

"That is not the drawing I did. I mean, it is, but it looks different. A lot different," he explained.

"Maybe it's the lighting," she rationalized.

"Yeah, that's got to be it," he agreed, humoring her. But inside he was shaking in fear and sadness. The drawing was now a self-portrait. He was sitting on Sal's couch in the exact same way Wolf had been. In the drawing his eyes were filled with tears. The scenery of the apartment was the same as he remembered it, but the action that was taking place in the background was somewhat different. Instead of his friends faces filled with agony and pain they were filled with joy and happiness. They were dancing in the background, just as they loved to do when they were alive. There was also a white longhaired cat sitting next to Pez on the couch. Pez had never seen the cat before and wondered where it had been hiding in his brain.

Above Pez were the words "Sitting There" written in a beautiful, but creepy spidery font.

"It's... It's," he paused, not knowing what to say.

"Beautiful and poignant," an unfamiliar voice expressed, "you're the artist?" the man inquired.

"Yes," Pez replied.

"I'm one of the judges," the man explained. "This is the best drawing I have seen in a long time."

"Yes, me too," the woman standing next to him chimed in. "But why do you look so sad in it?" she asked.

Rae glanced at Pez, afraid of his reaction. But Pez explained to them, in a clear voice, "It's a tribute to my friends. All the people in the background were killed in a car accident." He turned and walked away from them.

"Davie!" Rae called out as she followed him out of the building. She was dragging Stevie along behind her. He was occupied with his Game Boy.

"Are you alright?" she asked when she finally caught up with him.

"Yeah, I just needed some air," he replied softly. He paused for a moment. "You know that picture I drew: the one I remember?" he asked, but didn't wait for a reply. "In the original one that I drew, everyone in the background was dying. I drew them the way they looked on the night they died. I drew the night of the accident," he informed her quietly. "That's how I saw it anyway," he said, shrugging.

Rae hugged him gently.

"Hey, is that your mom and your teacher?" she asked.

Pez turned to check, and sure enough his mother and his teacher were hiding, away from prying eyes, or so they thought. They were making out, just inside the coatroom.

"Great!" Pez exclaimed. "That's exactly what I needed to see!"

"Aw, come on. I think it's sweet," Rae giggled.

"You would," Pez said. He realized then that he was finally alone with Rae. Alone except for Stevie, but he was so engrossed in his video game he was oblivious to his surroundings.

Pez smiled slyly and pulled Rae closer to him and kissed her lips. She giggled again.

"Like mother, like son," she whispered.

Pez rolled his eyes, but any other reply he had was lost in their kiss.

P𝖠RT S𝖨𝖷: G𝖮L𝖣

30

For the first time in months, Pez was actually excited to be going to a party. He found his baggiest pipe-style raver pants and his giant paperclip chain that he used as a wallet chain. He pulled on his uniform Pez shirt. He thought about putting his hair in ponytails, but decided to go for just one ponytail, to keep his hair out of his face while dancing. He looked for his jacket, but couldn't find it. Instead of his jacket, he pulled on Rae's zippy. He was pulling on his shoes when the doorbell rang.

He pounded down the stairs three at a time. Stevie beat him to the door and swung it open. Rae ducked to the side to avoid any flying noodles.

She had her long hair tied back in pigtails. Pez was glad he had decided against them. She was wearing a tight half shirt that showed off her belly button, which was pierced. She had on pants that were just as baggy legged as Pez's, but hers were black. Holding up her pants was a shiny blue belt. Her wallet chain was a chain of metal flowers. She too wore a zippy over the whole ensemble.

Pez smiled the biggest smile he had smiled in a long time. She had completely transformed herself into a little raver girl.

Stevie began running around the room singing, "D and Rae-Rae sittin' in a tree..."

"So Rae-Rae, are you ready?" Pez asked over the racket.

As they walked towards Rae's car, Stevie stood on the porch screaming the song as loudly as he possibly could. Rae's face got a little pink and Pez's turned bright red.

"Shut-up, PUNK!" Pez yelled.

"Stevie! Get in here and shut that door. Leave your brother alone! It's bedtime!" Pez heard his mother call from inside the house. She had not seen him off because she and Travis were watching a movie in the living room.

He folded himself into Rae's tiny car.

"How come you can't drive?" Rae asked.

Pez sighed. "My license has been suspended until I turn twenty one," he explained.

"Because of the accident?" she asked.

"Yep," he responded.

They slipped into an uncomfortable silence.

"So where's this party at?" Rae inquired in an attempt to break the silence. Apparently it worked.

"It's in an abandoned school house on the corner of South and Blanchard in Hickory." He directed.

"I know where that is. I went skateboarding there last summer," Rae said to Pez's surprise. He didn't know she skateboarded.

Rae bit her lip trying to think of a way to state her next thought carefully. She didn't want Pez to know how long she'd had a crush on him. "You used to skateboard there too, didn't you?" she asked.

"Not me, but we hung out there. Amber and Eddie were the skateboarders."

Rae closed her eyes trying to visualize the skaters. "I don't think I recognize her from skateboarding," she said finally.

"You probably wouldn't, she looked a lot different then," he said sadly. He wished she would quit bringing up his friends.

"Rae, there's something I need to talk to you about," Pez began, regretting it immediately, but he had to talk to someone about this. It was eating him up inside.

"What is it?" Rae asked. She was afraid he was going to break up with her.

"I think I need help," Pez admitted.

"Help with what?" Rae asked. She glanced over at him, and then looked back at the road.

"You know *help*," he repeated. "I think I'm going crazy."

"You're not," Rae responded automatically.

"You don't know," Pez sighed.

"What don't I know? Please, Davie, explain it to me," she implored.

"OK, you know the other day when I told you that waitress helped me." Rae nodded. "I didn't see a ghost," David confessed.

"What did you see?" she asked.

"I saw a little boy. I walked up to him and asked him if he needed help. When he looked up at me, I knew who he was," Pez paused.

"Well, who was he?" Rae asked.

"It was me, Rae. I saw myself as a child and that wasn't the first time. The other day I saw myself as a douche bag junkie. Those aren't ghosts, something's wrong with me. Something's wrong inside my head. There's a voice in there and sometimes it tells me to kill myself," he gushed. Once he started he couldn't stop. "Sometimes when I see Wolf I know it's his ghost, but sometimes he's cruel to me and I don't think it's really him. I mean, are people really supposed to see ghosts? Is your dead boyfriend supposed to follow you around and torture you?"

"I didn't know I was torturing you." Wolf's voice came from the back seat.

Pez turned to look at him. "You are Wolf. It hurts me too see you everywhere I look. It hurts me not to be with you."

"I'll go," Wolf suggested.

"I don't want you to," Pez whispered.

"Maybe we should get you home," Rae suggested. She pulled the car over.

"No you have to go. You have to save Amber," Wolf pleaded.

"No, I'm sorry. I shouldn't have brought this up," Pez apologized. "Now you know for sure that I'm crazy."

"Davie, I knew you were crazy from the first moment I met you," Rae rationalized. "That's why I love you. We'll find someone to help you." She kissed him tenderly. She took both his cheeks in her hands and stared into his eyes. "You are not alone, don't ever think you are," Rae whispered and kissed him again.

"Thank you," Pez whispered.

"And Wolf... Maybe if you don't show up unless it's absolutely necessary or if Davie calls you, maybe that would help him," she directed towards the back seat.

"It must be love," Pez laughed. "You're scolding my delusion."

"I don't think he's a delusion," Rae admitted as she pulled back onto the road. "I think you're a psychic, but you need to figure out what's real and what's only in your head."

"How do I do that when what is real isn't even real?" Pez asked.

"I don't know," Rae laughed, "but we'll figure it out."

"Well, when I was visiting Sal at the hospital, this guy showed up. He tried to talk to me about seeing ghosts, but he scared me so I ran away. Maybe I should find him. Maybe he can help."

"Sounds like we have a plan. We'll go to the hospital and find that guy," Rae laughed.

"But first we party," Pez agreed. "Then save Amber. Then save me."

Pez closed his eyes and dozed until Rae shook him awake.

"Is this the schoolhouse you were talking about?" she asked, but the cars parked on the lawn and the people packing into the building answered her question for her.

"This is it. Look, there's Amber and Mike," Pez pointed out as Rae parked the car. He rolled down the window and yelled to them. They were gathered with a few other people, one of whom Pez recognized as Phil. The other two looked vaguely familiar, but were otherwise unknown to him. The five people walked towards Rae's car. Pez and Rae got out and met them on Pez's side of the car. He introduced Rae to them. Then Mike introduced Amber and Phil to Rae and the two other people to the both of them. "This is my boyfriend, Javier, and of course you remember Brendan."

"Brendan?" Pez asked smiling. "I barely recognized you. It's good to see you again," Pez said, giving Bren a big hug.

"It's nice seeing you again too," Bren said. Pez somehow knew that Brendan was glad that Pez was not messed up like Amber was. He had never been really close to Bren, but then again, he hadn't had time to get close to him. Bren's mother sued for custody and took him back to Ireland with her a few months before the accident.

Rae was enchanted with his accent. "I like your accent." she said, smiling at him.

"Why, thank you Lass. I like your navel ring." Rae smiled and looked down at her belly button. It seemed as if she had forgotten she was wearing one.

"This is probably not the best time to ask, but were you in the accident too?" Rae asked nervously.

"No, not me. I was in Ireland. Mike and I were saved by fate."

"Mike, you weren't in the accident either?" Rae asked.

"Nope, I was at a convention with my parents," he replied.

"I was," Amber admitted. "But you probably already knew that," she said sadly, absently tracing her facial scar.

"I did," Rae nodded. "I'm glad you survived."

"Me too," Amber agreed. There was a smile on her face, but Pez could tell from her eyes that she was lying. He could see almost as much pain as he felt raging behind them. She turned to Mike, her eyes pleading.

Mike pulled out a baggie filled with pills.

"E, anyone?" he offered, pouring the baggie into his hand and holding it out to each one of them in turn.

Pez shook his head, Rae followed his lead, Amber took a couple, Javier took one, and Phil and Bren both declined. Mike shrugged and popped one into his mouth and put the rest back into the baggie.

Pez looked around and wondered how many other people were going to be high. Probably all of them, and that realization sickened him. He pushed the thought away as the group began to walk towards the building.

He turned and smiled tentatively at Rae. She smiled back.

"Don't worry, I'm used to that," she assured him. "I don't do drugs," she whispered to him.

"Neither do I... anymore," Pez agreed with her. "I was sort of addicted at one time."

Rae leaned closer to Pez's ear. "With these guys, I can see why," she said, glancing at the group.

Pez nodded. "The rest were worse," he replied, sadly. Rae nodded and kissed his cheek. Pez brightened up. He kissed her on the lips. She blushed.

"Cheeky," she whispered.

He noticed Mike rolling his eyes. "I'll be right back." He kissed her again and walked up to Mike.

"Hey Mike, before we go in, can I have a word?" Pez asked, taking Mike's elbow.

"Sure, I guess," Mike said, resigned to the fact that he had no choice.

"So, I want the truth." Pez began as soon as they reached the side of the building.

"What truth?" Mike asked.

"Where were you?" Pez demanded. "On the night of the accident" he clarified, before Mike could say anything.

"I told you, I was at a convention." He stuck with his most recent lie.

"LIAR!" Pez accused. "Last time you said it was a funeral and the time before that what was it a wedding?"

"What? I did not."

"Yes, Mike, you did. Every time you've been asked it's been some other excuse."

"Why do you care anyway?" Mike asked.

"Because I don't like to be lied to," Pez replied.

"Neither do I!" Mike retorted.

"What? When did I lie?"

"You seduced him!" Mike accused.

"What?" Pez asked. Mike was not supposed to know about that night.

"Knock off the dumb routine. I was there. I saw everything! Next time, check the stalls before you steal someone's boyfriend!" he yelled, leaving Pez staring at him open mouthed. "And to top it all off you're not even GAY!" He screamed the last word, gesturing at Rae who was standing in line with Bren. "What was Wolf, just some experiment? You wanted to know what I had? I hate you Pez. I've hated you since that night."

"I knew it," Pez whispered. "I knew you hated me."

"Well, what do you expect? You destroyed my life!" Mike yelled. "I didn't show up that night because it was YOUR birthday and Wolf told me what he was going to give you for a present. I didn't need to be there for that. He told me everything

256

about you. He never stopped talking about you. I don't know why I even stayed friends with him after he dumped me. I guess I just thought he would come to his senses and get over you and come back to me. Whatever! That's beside the point. I only invited you tonight and tried to be your friend because Amber wanted me to. She was lonely."

"Well...," Pez began.

"No! I don't want to hear it. You're a selfish, overdramatic, whiny little bastard," he fumed. Pez stared back at him with tears forming in his eyes. "You've always been like that. I read the letter and I still don't see what Wolf saw in you."

"What letter?" Pez asked.

"I'm not done yet Pez!" Pez hated the way Mike said his name in that venomous way. "You play the victim card whenever you want something. 'Boo hoo my dad died gimme love.' It happened eight years ago! Get over it already! And with Wolf and them, you are not the only one who lost them! I LOST THEM! I LOST WOLF TWICE! They had families, friends. Amber lost them! Bren lost them! We're all hurting Pez! It's not just you!"

"I'm sorry," Pez replied with the only words that would come to his head.

"It's too late. I'm done with you! I'm done with AMBER too! You take care of the little junkie, she's all yours now. I hope you've got the money to afford her!"

"Davie?" Rae called out from the line. "They're letting people in now."

Pez nodded and signaled that he would be there in a moment.

"What about that night at your house, in the tub?" Pez asked pitifully.

"I washed your hair. Get over it."

"No, not that. Afterwards," Pez whispered.

"I dried you off."

"No... the... the s-s-sex," Pez stammered.

"What the fuck are you talking about?" Mike asked with a confused look on his face.

"We had sex," Pez explained.

"No we didn't. I put you to bed and I left. You're delusional, Pez. You need help. I wouldn't have sex with you for all the money in the world," he spat harshly.

"So you don't remember?" Pez was in shock. How could he forget something like that?

"Nothing happened," Mike assured him.

"But...," Pez interjected.

"Goodbye Pez!" Mike said with finality and stormed off.

Pez walked back over to Rae.

"Are you OK?" Rae asked.

"Yeah I think so."

"What happened?"

"I just got my ass handed to me. I caught him in a lie and he flipped out." Pez replied, unsure of how he should feel about everything Mike said to him. "Let's just forget about it," Pez smiled.

Bren joined Pez and Rae in the line.

"What was that all about?" he asked.

Pez shrugged. He was still processing what Mike had said to him.

"I know we used to do drugs and all, but how long has this junkie thing been going on?" he asked quietly.

"Pretty much since you left," Pez replied sadly. "I was like that too, but after the accident I sobered up," he continued.

"I would too, after something like that happening," Bren replied softly. "It's a damn shame what happened, a damn shame," he said with tears in his eyes. Pez nodded. He was glad that there was finally someone who he could share his pain with, someone who was not obsessed with drugs.

"I'm glad you're back," Pez informed him.

"Unfortunately it's only for the month. Da filed for custody, but I don't think it's gonna work," Bren explained. "As soon as I turn 18, I'll be back to stay though. I miss living here."

"I hope so," Pez told him.

"Davie?" Rae asked.

"What Rae-Rae?" she smiled at the use of the nickname that Stevie gave her.

"How much is this going to cost?"

Pez shrugged.

"All I have is five dollars," she let Pez know.

"Don't worry, I'll pay for ya both," Bren promised. "Da felt bad about the custody thing so he gave me a bunch of money."

"Thanks."

"Yeah, thanks, Bren," Pez agreed.

"Not a problem. That's what friends are for," he declared as he paid for their entry.

Pez and his friends danced together in a group, minus Mike and Javier, until about 2:00 when they all split up and went their separate ways, leaving Pez and Rae alone. Pez stopped suddenly. He had a strange thought enter his head.

"Where's Amber?" he asked.

Rae shrugged.

"Is there anything to drink here?" Rae asked, distracting him from his thoughts. "I'm thirsty."

"I don't know," Pez answered. "I think I saw some water in the other room. You want to go look?" he asked, holding out his hand to her.

"Sure," Rae answered, taking his hand. There was a huge crowd of people gathered around the doorway to the second room.

"Wanna just forget it?" Rae asked.

"Nah! Let's shove our way through, I'm really thirsty," Pez suggested. He was actually hungry, but he thought if he could have something to drink, maybe he'd feel better. There was a bad feeling settling into his stomach.

He shoved his way through the crowd with Rae hanging onto his arm. He soon realized that the crowd was gathered around a person. He made his way closer and realized Amber was laying on the ground. Brendan was holding her head and scanning the crowd for a familiar face.

"PEZ!" he screamed, panicking. "HELP HER! OH GOD, SOMEBODY HELP HER!"

Pez pushed the rest of the way through the crowd and kneeled next to Bren.

"What happened?" Pez asked as Rae's grip tightened on his arm.

"I don't know. She just collapsed," Bren replied, still panicking.

"You go find Phil. We'll get her outside. Come on, Rae."

Rae just stood there covering her mouth, her eyes open wide.

"Rae, pull yourself together. She just passed out." Pez reassured, not quite believing his own words. "We have to get her out of here."

She took a deep breath and stepped forward to help Pez. Amber was so small and light that Pez didn't need any help carrying her. Rae pushed people out of the way. She had never been so rude in her life, but she had just cause.

They made it outside and lay Amber on the grass. "I'm gonna go get Bren. Stay with her, I'll be back." Rae nodded and sat down on the grass next to Amber.

Pez went to go back in, but the doorman wouldn't let him back in. He checked his watch. It was only 3:00. He ran back over to Rae.

"They won't let me back in. What should we do?" Pez asked.

"We need to wait for Bren. He needs to get the others and we can just let them deal with her, if she's only passed out," she stated. Somehow her panic had disappeared.

"What do you mean 'if'? What else could it be?" Pez asked.

"Well, I don't want to worry you, but she could be ODing," Rae warned.

"How do we know?" Pez asked, his voice filling with panic.

Just then, Bren ran out of the door with Phil in tow.

"I was looking for Amber," Phil told them, wondering what was so urgent that they had to drag him out of the party. "Oh God!" he exclaimed as he saw Amber.

"Davie?" Rae's voice sounded. "PEZ!" she screamed. He whipped around to find Amber had gone into convulsions.

The guys ran to Amber's side.

"Bren, call 911!" Pez commanded. Bren scanned the parking lot and finally found a pay phone. He ran towards it, not even looking to see if cars were coming as he crossed the street.

"What's wrong with her?" Phil asked.

"We have to keep her from swallowing her tongue," Rae said, trying to remember what else they were supposed to do.

"You need to cool her down," Wolf whispered.

"She's so hot. We need to get some ice or something cold," Pez suggested.

Phil handed him the water he had been bringing to Amber.

"See if you can get more ice water. You need them between her legs, under her arm pits and on the front of her neck. That way her blood will help cool her body."

"I need more water bottles!" Pez called out. "Does anybody have any water?"

A few people handed him some water, but must of them just stood there and stared.

Amber stopped convulsing and began gagging. They turned her on her side just as she began to throw up.

When she stopped coughing, they laid her on her back. Her eyes rolled back into her head. Pez began to stick the water bottles where Wolf told him to put them.

"I think she's dead," Rae said in a quiet voice.

"No she's still got a pulse, but it's faint," Pez assured her as an EMS pulled up beside the schoolhouse.

The three teens sat on the curb, watching as their friend died and was revived by the EMS crew.

"We're losing her!" one of them kept shouting.

Pez looked down, away from his dying friend. He noticed a shiny shard of glass lying on the ground in front of him, and then his eyes focused on his bandaged wrist.

It was time. He had to go. No more dying for him, now only death. He picked up the piece of glass and began to scrape through the bandage wrapped around his wrist.

"Pez! What the hell are you doing?" Bren shouted. Rae whirled around to see why Bren was yelling at Pez.

"Davie!" Rae grabbed his arm, frustrated and scared. "It's not worth it, dammit! Don't you leave me, asshole!" she shouted in anger.

"It's not worth it," Bren agreed sadly, holding up his wrists to show scars where he too had tried to kill himself. Seeing the scars on Bren's wrists shocked him into dropping the shard.

"Come on, they're taking her to the hospital now. Let's go with her." She pushed him up and led him to the ambulance.

"Who are you?" the paramedic asked.

"I'm her best friend. Can I come? Please?" he begged. Some best friend he was, letting her OD like that.

The paramedic nodded. "You can come, but stay back out of our way."

"OK," Pez said, climbing into the ambulance.

"I'm coming too." Phil said as he climbed into the ambulance, without giving the EMT a chance to disagree.

"We'll meet you there," Rae called as the door slammed shut.

The ride to the hospital was frightening to Pez. All his other rides to the hospital had ended in death. He hoped this ride would be different, but he had a sinking feeling that Amber was going to die. No one could possibly do as many drugs as she had that night and survive.

He sat on the bench and watched as the EMT worked to cool Amber down.

"What did she take?" he asked Pez, but Pez wasn't sure. He just shook his head.

Phil sighed, "Ecstasy. Cocaine. Who knows what else." Phil shook his head.

"This is your fault you know," he turned to stare at Pez.

"What? Why me?" Pez squeaked.

"You and your friends got her into drugs." he accused. "She was fine before she met you. Now she's dying and it's all your fault. You did this. You ruined her life."

Pez turned away from Phil, wondering what the EMT thought. He was busy helping Amber, but he looked up at Pez and shook his head. 'Don't believe him,' the EMT's eyes said.

"Whose idea was the water bottles?" he said instead.

"Mine," Pez mumbled as Phil pointed to him.

"It was a great idea. She's overheated. If you hadn't done that she might not have made it," he explained.

"So she's not going to die?" Phil asked.

"Not if I can help it," the EMT replied.

By the time they reached the hospital, Amber had come around enough to smile at Pez. She gestured for him to come closer. "This is not your fault." she whispered. She had heard the whole conversation.

31

The waiting for news was horrible, because the ghosts of the hospital still haunted him. He tried to pretend he didn't see them, but somehow they knew he could. Rae noticed his face looked rather pale and she asked him if he wanted to take a nap. She gestured for him to put his head in her lap and sleep. Pez smiled numbly and laid his head on her thigh.

"I hope everything turns out OK," Phil said as he paced before Bren, Pez, and Rae.

"Me too," Pez mumbled as he slipped into slumber.

He was standing in a field, alone; or so he thought. The grass was tall enough to hide his feet completely. He wiggled his toes and found that his feet were bare.

He felt a hand on his shoulder and swung around to see who it was, only to find that no one was there. When he turned back to face the way he had been facing, he saw all of his friends that had died, lounging in the grass. Amber stood up and walked towards him. She smiled. She looked like she had before the accident. Her hair was long and brown. She wore a white dress that billowed softly in a nonexistent breeze. Her face was perfect; even the scar was gone. She was no longer skinny and emaciated. She had meat on her bones and she was even a little chubby.

"I'm sorry, Pez," she began. "I just couldn't take it. I didn't know what to do when I lost everyone I loved... even you," she said, tears rolling down her cheeks.

"I can't take it either," Pez mumbled.

"But you have to. You were meant to survive. I should have died with my parents," Amber informed him honestly.

"But I'm so alone." Pez whispered. Suddenly, his friends were surrounding him giving him strength as they circled him. He couldn't help but notice that Penny wasn't there.

"Where's Penny?" he asked, but the question was futile, because as the words escaped his lips the circle parted and through the open end he saw Sal's hospital room.

"She's with Sal," Matt whispered in his ear. "Sal's dead, man." His words gave Pez a jolt, but he wasn't sure what frightened him more: how plainly Matt had said them or what they meant.

Pez turned to look at Matt. "No, he's not!"

Matt said nothing. He only nodded knowingly.

"Yes, love, he is, but he's trapped by that damn machine," Wolf said, caressing Pez softly.

Pez spun slowly to look at each one of his friends in turn. All of them seemed to be affirming what Wolf and Matt said.

They were all startled as Amber groaned and fell to the ground clutching her chest.

"Amber what is it?" Wolf asked.

When Amber looked up at him she had her old look back. She reached up and touched her face to find her scar was back.

"No!" she screamed as she was literally dragged across the field. The friends grabbed at her and tried to catch her, but they failed.

Pez chased after her. Amber disappeared and Pez found himself falling. He saw below him his sleeping body with his head still resting in Rae's lap. He fell into his body suddenly and jumped violently as he woke.

His violent awakening startled Rae.

"Are you OK?" Rae asked.

Pez nodded. He had to find Amber. He stood up and started to walk away.

"Where are you going?" Bren asked suspiciously. He replied with the first place that came to his mind.

"Bathroom," he lied. He knew where the bathroom was, but he walked right by it. He followed the voices of his friends. At times, it was hard to differentiate between the hospital voices and the voices of his friends, but somehow he still managed to find his way to Amber's room.

The hallway to her room seemed to be deserted.

"I knew you would come," Amber whispered weakly as Pez entered the room.

Pez smiled. "I'm glad you're better."

"I'm not," she replied.

She sat up and tried to get out of her bed.

"Help me up," she requested.

"What for?" Pez asked.

"I want to see Sal," she pleaded sadly. "I haven't seen him since the accident." Pez knew that was true. Heidi would have let him know if Sal had any visitors besides his family and Pez.

"OK," Pez replied.

"Put my IV on the stand, please," she commanded, pointing to the wheeled IV stand in the corner. "We have to move fast. The others set up a diversion for us."

Pez nodded. He didn't need to ask who the others were. He helped Amber out of the bed. He led her into the hallway and with his help she ambled quickly down the hallway. He led her to the room that held Sal's comatose body.

Penny was standing near the bed. She looked up when they entered the room. She moved back from the bed with a knowing look in her eyes.

"You'd better go now," Amber warned.

"What are you going to do?" Pez asked.

"I'm going to set him free," she said with determination.

"Amber, no," Pez begged.

"Please Pez, just let her," Penny pleaded. *"It's torture to keep him here like this. He's dead, but he's still alive. It's torture for him and for me,"* Penny continued with tears falling down her cheeks. Pez didn't know that ghosts could cry.

Amber moved to the other side of the room next to Penny.

"It would be better if you weren't here," Amber explained. "That way when the police question you, you won't be able to tell them anything."

Pez stayed put, staring at her in shock.

"What are you going to do?" he asked.

"You know what I'm going to do," she said, locating the heart monitor electrodes.

"Don't," Pez begged.

"I have to," Amber explained. "It's time for him to go. Now, get out." she demanded.

"No," Pez argued standing his ground.

"Get out!" Amber growled.

Pez gasped as what felt like cold icy hands clasped around his arms and dragged him towards the door.

"Let her do it," Eddie growled in his ear.

"No!" Pez tried to pull away from Eddie's grasp. As he struggled, more hands tugged at his clothing, keeping him away from Amber and Sal.

"Amber, please," Pez pleaded. He watched helplessly as Amber quickly pulled off the electrodes off of Sal's chest and placed them on her own chest. She reached across the bed began to unhook every piece of equipment that was keeping Sal alive.

Pez watched in awe as Sal stood up, leaving his body on the bed. He rushed over to Penny and threw his arms around her.

"Thank you so much!" Sal exclaimed as he and Penny vanished.

"Get out!" Amber demanded. She had her IV stand and she was swinging it towards the heart monitor.

Pez turned quickly and left the room. He walked back out to the waiting room and found his mother and Stevie out there. He forgot all about calling her when they arrived at the hospital.

"Oh, D." Carole ran over to Pez and took him in her arms.

"What's going on?" Rae asked, panic filling her voice.

"What do you mean?" Pez asked nervously.

"The doctors and nurses have been running around like crazy," Bren explained.

"I don't know," Pez replied. "I was in the bathroom," he lied.

They all jumped as the sound of breaking glass echoed through the hallways.

"What the bloody hell was that?" Bren asked.

"I have no idea," Pez lied again. He sat down on the couch and started rubbing his temples. Rae sat next to him and began rubbing his back. Carole was sitting on the couch across from them. Stevie was lying down with his head in her lap. Phil started his pacing once again.

32

About an hour later a doctor entered the waiting room. "Excuse me?" she asked. Everyone turned to look at her.

"Are you the family of Amber Weber?" she inquired.

"Um…," Pez said, glancing around.

"Yes," Carole replied.

"I have some bad news," the doctor informed them as a team of cops entered the hospital and headed down the hallway leading to Sal's room. "There's been an accident. Amber… um…," she paused, at a loss for words.

"Is she alright?" Bren prompted.

"I'm afraid she's not. It seems that after we revived her, she left her hospital room and found the room of one...," she paused, looking down at a chart that she held in her hand. "Salvador Carroll and she um... m-murdered him and then she committed suicide."

"What? How?" Carole asked.

"She suffocated Salvador and then she broke the window open and threw herself out." the doctor replied. Pez gulped. He knew they were on the fifth floor; there was no way she should survive that.

A pair of cops approached the group.

"Excuse me," the cop started. "Are you the family of Amber Weber?" he asked.

"Sorry, no. We're just friends," Carole informed them.

"But you just told me...," the doctor began.

"I lied," Carole revealed.

The cops questioned them all, but left when they realized that none of them had seen or heard anything, including Pez, to their knowledge.

"I guess we better be getting home," Carole announced. "David, darling, will you carry Stevie to the car?" she asked, but the tone of her voice told Pez she wasn't really asking a question.

"No," Pez answered her defiantly.

"David," Carole warned.

"He's too heavy. Wake him up and make him walk," Pez demanded.

"David, he's just a child."

"He's eight years old! He's old enough to walk himself to the fucking car!" Pez spat out angrily.

"You watch your mouth," Carole warned him.

"No! You're always babying him! You keep saying that he has brain damage, but no doctor has ever told you that! You treat him like he's a god-damned king and you treat me like shit!" Pez screamed.

"David!" Carole gasped.

"No Mom, I can't take it anymore and I won't. I met Sierra and both her and Nanah say Stevie doesn't have brain damage. They say you should have him tested for Autism."

"Shut your mouth!" Carole yelled. "Don't lie like that."

"No, you shut it! I saw them. I DID! I see people all the time; dead people. Sometimes they are everywhere I LOOK!" he screamed.

"Nobody believes you," D's voice echoed into his ear. *"They all think you're crazy and they're right"*

"I'm not crazy!   I'm not CRAZY!!   I AM NOT CRAZY!!!" he screamed, slamming his fist into the wall.   He turned and ran from the hospital.

Carole looked around, embarrassed by Pez's emotional breakdown. She was at a loss for words.

"Don't worry about him," Carole uttered softly with tears in her eyes. "He'll head home once he's cooled down."

"I'm not so sure of that Mrs. Spencer," Rae began through tears of her own. "He tried to kill himself again earlier."

"Well, let's just head home and I'll wait for him. I'll call you when he shows up," Carole declared. She couldn't believe that her son would go anywhere but home.

"I'd like to come over and wait for him, if that's OK?" Rae asked.

Carole nodded. "That might help us both."

"I'd like to come to, if you don't mind too much," Bren requested.

"Yes, of course, but he'll probably be there when we get there." She turned and walked towards the elevators.

"I don't think I can drive right now," Rae whispered.

"Give me your keys and I'll follow Mrs. Spencer," Bren offered.

"You will?   Thanks," Rae said as they watched Carole fidgeting with the elevator button.

"Maybe I should ride with her, in case she loses it in the car," Rae suggested.

"That sounds like a good idea," Bren agreed. He scooped Stevie off of the waiting room couch and joined the ladies waiting for the elevator.

33

Pez ran all the way to the bus stop and hopped onto the first bus. He exited as close to his house as he could. Once he reached his house, he bypassed it entirely and headed into the backyard. He headed behind the house to the only place of sanctuary that he could think of.

He climbed the ladder into the tree house without a second thought, his hand throbbing with pain. He was reminded of a cartoon he once saw where someone had accidentally hit their thumb with a hammer and it grew large and throbbed. He laughed as he entered the tree house, gasping for breath. He hit his head on the ceiling as he tried to stand fully erect. The last time he had been in there was over five years ago. It looked mostly the same, but a lot of the toys that were in there now belonged to Stevie.

It seemed as if the place had shrunk, but he knew he had grown considerably in the past five years. He hunched over and walked forward a couple of steps. It felt almost as if someone was in there with him, but he knew that was impossible. Stevie was still at the hospital with their mom and Pez's friends. He stopped in front of the curtain that separated the two rooms of the tree house. The area behind the curtain was the sleeping area for those rare times when he had been allowed to sleep out there.

Pez reached forward and pulled aside the curtain with his good hand. The hand that he had punched the wall with was swollen and sore. He wished that he had some ice to put on it.

Pez got down on his hand and knees. He felt along the back wall of the sleeping compartment. He was searching for the secret spot in the wall that Daddy had made just for him to hide stuff in. When his fingers finally found the latch he popped it open and dragged out the garbage bag that was inside. He reached into the garbage bag and pulled out his old blankie and his old teddy bear. The teddy bear was tattered and crusted in his father's dried up blood. He shoved the garbage bag and its contents back into the wall. He closed the door and latched it, dropping the window curtain back over the top of it so Stevie wouldn't find his secret spot.

Pez crawled over to the foam mattress and curled up in the pile of blankets that were on it. He hugged his teddy bear and his blankie close to him. He popped the thumb of his good hand in his mouth. His other hand was throbbing madly. He fell asleep like that; hugging his childhood security items and sucking his thumb.

34

"Why don't you lie down and take a nap, you must be tired," Carole suggested to Rae as she pulled out of the hospital parking lot. Rae nodded and laid her head back against the headrest. She closed her eyes, but all she could think about was Pez and her thoughts had intruded on her dreams.

In her dream she found herself standing in a field. Unknown to her at the time, it was the same field where Pez had found himself in his last dream.

A crowd of people were standing before her. They looked familiar. She thought for a moment, trying to remember where she had seen them before, and then it came to her. She had seen them in the photograph of Pez's friends that she had found in her car.

They were standing about twenty feet away from her. They were surrounding something or someone. She started to walk over to them, but it seemed to take forever.

"Hey!" she called out.

Amber was the only one that looked over at her. "You're not supposed to be here!" Amber accused.

"Neither are you," Rae retorted.

Amber seemed to blush a little. She sighed and waved her hand in Rae's direction.

Suddenly Rae found herself standing next to the crowd of friends. They were slowly parting so Rae could see what they were hiding.

It seemed to be a small boy with a grown out bowl cut. He was wearing the same clothes she had last seen Davie wearing. He was lying on the ground sleeping, clutching a teddy bear and a blanket in one arm. He was sucking his thumb.

"Davie?" she asked.

The boy stirred and woke. He sat up to look at her, but Rae was surprised to find Pez looking up at her instead of the boy.

"Davie?" she asked again.

Amber reached down and took one of Pez's hands. Wolf did the same with the other hand. Together they pulled him up into a standing position.

"Davie?" Rae repeated.

Pez just looked over at her and smiled sadly. He turned away from her and started walking away.

"Davie, NO!!" Rae yelled as his friends turned to follow him. "Davie, come back!" she screamed. Slowly they all disappeared leaving Rae standing alone in the field.

"NO!" Rae screamed, sitting up to find herself in the passenger seat of Carole's station wagon. Stevie and Carole were both staring at her in shock. She smiled shyly. "Bad dream," she explained in answer to their questioning looks.

"It sounded pretty bad," Carole remarked.

"Did I say anything else?" Rae asked.

"No, you were just moaning and groaning. It's a good thing we were parked when you woke up. Otherwise we could've gotten into an accident. You scared the bejesus out of me," Carole admitted.

"Me too," Stevie agreed, rubbing his sleep weary eyes. He turned and climbed out of the car. He waited by the front door while Carole got out her keys. Rae was closing her door when Bren pulled up in her car.

Carole led Rae and Bren into the kitchen. Stevie pushed past them and went tearing into the house screaming at the top of his lungs.

"CAN IT, STEVEN!" Carole yelled after him. Stevie was quiet, but he was still running through the house.

"He's got so much energy," Rae commented. "Does he have ADD?" she blurted out.

"ADHD?" Bren suggested.

"I don't know. I've never really had him tested for anything. The doctors just told me he had brain damage. I lost a lot of blood before they had to take him out... c-section," she whispered the last word as if it caused her pain to say it. She walked over and started to put on a pot of coffee.

"Davie isn't lying about when he saw his Nanah," Rae defended Pez tentatively.

Carole didn't seem to be listening. She turned and left the room.

"Mom!" Stevie yelped in laughter.

"Ha-ha I got you." she laughed. "Why don't you watch a movie sweetheart? Mommy needs to talk to D's friends."

"OK," Stevie answered, running out of the room. He was singing the theme song to his favorite TV show.

Rae and Bren sat at the table in awkward silence.

"So, um how long have you and Candy-Boy been going out?" Bren asked nervously.

"Just a couple of days, but we've worked together for a long time," Rae replied, just as nervously.

Carole walked back into the room and saved them from any further efforts at conversation.

"You two look exhausted. Would you like some coffee?"

"I would love some, Mrs. Spencer," Rae responded.

"So would I," Bren agreed.

"Please call me Carole," she insisted. "Mrs. Spencer makes me feel so old," she laughed. She set a mug in front of each of them.

Rae nodded and smiled gratefully as she took a long sip of her coffee. "It's good. Thanks, Carole," Rae said softly.

"Really good," Bren agreed.

"So," Carole began, "do you guys have any idea where David might have gone?"

Rae shook her head. "No...," she said thoughtfully, "... wait a minute... he might have gone to the park."

"The park?" Carole asked.

"Sam Johansson Park," Rae clarified.

"He hasn't gone there since...," Carole paused. She seemed unwilling or unable to say the words.

"We went there a couple of days ago," Rae confessed quietly, afraid that Carole would be angry that they had visited the park where they used to take D.

"Well I suppose we should go to the park then," Carole replied sadly, sounding more reluctant than angry.

35

$\mathcal{P}$ez awoke to the sound of a child's laughter. It sounded almost like Stevie's voice, but somehow he knew it was Sierra's voice. He opened his eyes, wondering where he was. The midday sunlight hurt his eyes so he closed the curtain above him. He pulled back the curtain that separated the two rooms, pausing momentarily as he wondered if he had actually closed it before he fell asleep.

He looked over at the small girl. She was playing with some of Stevie's toys. She looked so young and innocent. Pez could almost believe that she was real. He could almost believe that she was alive and had been the entire time, but the innocence surrounding her was too overwhelming. She had never lived through the hardships of life, you could tell that in her manner.

He noticed a pad of paper and a box full of pencils and crayons near him. He sat up and reached slowly for them. Sierra stopped and turned to look at him. Pez froze, afraid that she would disappear. She smiled, and giggling, she went back to playing with Stevie's toys.

Pez dug through the box until he found a pencil and a sharpener. He sharpened the pencil and started to draw. Almost immediately, he was lost in the drawing trance. He drew for what seemed like hours, holding the pad steady with his left arm. The fingers on his left hand were so swollen now that he couldn't even move them.

He drew a bunch of pictures of Sierra. Then he began to draw other people: Rae, Wolf, his mom, and his dad. In his delirious state, the sketches wouldn't stop coming.

He was jarred out of his drawing trance by the sound of a cat purring next to him. He blinked and looked around the tree house. Sierra was gone and the sun was fading from the sky. He flipped through the pad of paper and found that he had almost filled the entire notebook with his sketches.

Pez heard a tiny meow next to him. He set the notebook down, leaving it open to a drawing of Sierra's face.

He reached out his good hand and began to stroke the stray cat. He gasped in surprise as he realized that it was the cat that was in his mysteriously altered drawing.

"I think I'll call you Fuzzy," Pez whispered. The cat nuzzled against his hand. Pez marveled at how friendly and well groomed the cat was, it being a stray and all. "Where did you come from?" Pez asked. He knew none of his neighbors had cats, so this one couldn't be any of theirs.

He curled up next to the cat and closed his eyes. He couldn't believe how tired he felt.

Pez followed the cat to the cemetery where his father was buried. Next to Nanah and Poppy's fresh graves was another one. Fuzzy nudged him forward to look at the headstone. It read 'David Allen Spencer III -We will always remember you, Pez.'

He heard footsteps behind him. Then he heard his mother's voice saying "three generations of Spencers gone." A chorus of sobbing followed. He turned to see his mother, Rae, Stevie, and Bren standing in front of his grave crying. He saw shadows behind them, but in the coming dusk he couldn't quite make them out.

"Don't cry," he said, starting to move towards them. "I'm right here." Fuzzy stepped out to block his path. "Please," Pez called out to them.

"Won't do you any good," Eddie's voice said. Pez turned to see his friends were all standing around his headstone.

"I know, don't tell me," Pez spat out before anyone could say what he knew was coming. "They can't see me or hear me, right?"

"You got it," Glenn replied.

"Come on," Wolf beckoned.

"Let's go," Matt prodded him.

"Where are we going?" Pez asked, confused.

"To the other world, of course," Amber answered.

"Some call it heaven, some call it hell, but we call it home," Glenn added.

"Why?" Pez asked. He was beginning to get nervous.

"What do you mean, why?" Matt asked.

"Why are we going there?" Pez asked, backing away from his friends.

"Because that's where we belong now," Sal informed him.

"Why?"

"Why what?" Eddie asked, frustrated at Pez's stupidity.

"I don't belong there," Pez said, shaking his head and backing away.

"Yes, you do," Glenn argued.

"No," Pez replied. He had backed up right into a tree. "I don't."

"You're dead now," Penny explained softly.

"Just like us," Amber said.

"N-n-no I'm not," Pez argued.

"Yes you are, look." She pointed at his arms. He lifted up his arms to look at them. His wrists were cut open.

"I didn't do that," Pez said, wiping at the blood. "I don't want to die!!!" he screamed.

"Too late, buddy. Let's go," Matt said as he reached his hand towards Pez.

"NO!!!" he screamed, looking at Rae. She was still standing at the foot of his grave. "No!" She looked directly at him with a sympathetic look on her face. "I'm not dead!" he screamed. She reached out her hand towards him. Just as he *reached out his hand towards her she vanished, but so did all his friends.*

hands reaching, grabbing
from the ethereal beyond
from the blackened abyss
reaching for me
striving to pull me
under
drag me below
groping outward
towards me
I scream
try to outrun them,
but again
I am caught

Pez woke up from the nightmare panting heavily. He never could tell if that one was real or just something his mind had made up.

36

"I guess we can call the police now. It's been over twenty four hours," Carole said calmly. Rae was surprised at how calm she had been all day and night. She hadn't even cried once, at least not that Rae had seen. Rae on the other hand couldn't seem to stop crying. Carole tried to calm her down as best she could and then they would continue searching.

Together, the four of them searched the cemetery (where Rae had a strange feeling that Pez had just left that very spot), the library, the school, the bookstore, the café, the hospital, the corner store, and the bridge (Rae had even forced Carole to stop the car so they could walk along the area under the bridge to look for Pez's body).

Carole picked up the phone off the charger. As she dialed the numbers, her hands began to shake.

"911, what's your emergency?" a monotone voice asked. Carole seemed to lose all of her composure then. All of her courage and strength ran out of her as she heard that voice asking her what her emergency was. That is when it struck her—this really was an emergency. Her son really was missing. It felt like reality slapped her across the face. She burst into tears and dropped the phone on the floor, sinking to the floor next to it.

Rae jumped up and ran over to pick up the receiver.

"Hello... Hello?" the voice on the other end repeated.

"Hello?" Rae said tentatively.

"Do you have an emergency?" the voice asked.

"Yes," Rae answered, "umm... my boyfriend is missing. He's suicidal and I want to report him missing," she repeated.

"OK, I'll connect you with the police," the operator replied.

Rae answered as many questions as she could about Pez, trying to stress that he was suicidal and possibly dangerous to other people.

Rae hung up the phone and sank onto the floor next to Carole. "They're sending a car," she explained as she wrapped her arms around the older woman. Hugging Carole like this made Rae miss her own mother.

"Do you really think he'll kill himself?" Carole asked through her sobs.

"I don't think he will," Bren answered seriously. "Not after losing Amber. Watching her OD seriously affected him, you know, in a good way." Bren crossed the room and sat down in front of Carole.

"You two are such good friends for David," Carole expressed.

"Pez is a good guy. He's just a little hurt inside," Bren remarked.

"A lot hurt," Rae amended.

"Aye, you're right, he is a lot hurt," Bren agreed.

"He is a big ball of pain," Carole added. "He has been ever since his father died." She wiped her cheeks. "I've never known what to do to help him. I just wish there was something I could do to ease his pain."

"There's not much anyone can do to stop pain like that," Bren told her. "He has to work it out on his own."

"The most important thing for you... for all of us... is to show him that we're here for him; that we are sensitive to his pain," Rae said.

"Aye, and we've got to assure him that he's not crazy. He's gifted; anyone can see that, if they know how to look," Bren informed them.

"Gifted?" Carole asked.

"He's a medium. He can see spirits," Rae explained.

"A very strong one, at that," Bren added. "But, he needs validation. He needs to know that he isn't alone."

"How did you get to be so smart?" Carole asked.

"I'm studying the mind... psychology, parapsychology, ghosts, poltergeists, and that sort of thing. Ever since I heard about the accident, I've been obsessed with the grief process and the afterlife," Bren disclosed. "I think I finally found my calling," he smiled.

"He told me that he's seen Wolf. I saw him too, but my gift isn't that strong," Rae divulged.

"That's how he knew about Sierra," Carole whispered. "He told me Nanah introduced them, but she had already died. I didn't believe him. I yelled at him. I was so angry."

"He probably did see her," Bren explained.

"I'm such a bad mother," Carole sobbed.

"No, you're not," Rae soothed. "You're a great mother."

"One of the best," Bren agreed.

Part Seven: Secret

37

Pez awoke again to the sound of the tree house door slamming shut. He jumped up. His heart was racing. His mind filled with fear until he felt Fuzzy gently lapping the side of his face. He had thought he was dead.

He sniffed at the air. Something smelled yummy. He waited a few seconds until he was positive he could not hear anything else. Painfully, he raised himself up to look out the window.

It was raining quite heavily, but he could still make out Stevie's rain slicker, as he ran back into the house. He smiled as he pressed his hot face against the cold glass window. If only he could be as young and innocent as Stevie. He pushed the curtain separating the sleeping area aside. Once again, it had been closed while he slept. This time, he figured it was Stevie who had closed it.

Pez found a plate with a buttered croissant and a glass of orange juice lying just inside the door. He greedily ate the food and drank the juice.

He wiped his hands and picked up Fuzzy. He sat down in the ratty old armchair. It had been Pez's father's chair. Pez knew the real reason that his father had built his tree house was so that he wouldn't have to throw out his beloved chair. The one that Carole claimed didn't match any of the other furniture in the house.

Fuzzy purred and shoved his head into Pez's hand to remind him to keep petting him. Pez decided at that moment that he didn't care whose cat this was. He was going to keep it. It was his cat now. Again, he fell asleep, clutching the cat as if it were his sanity. It was much more comfortable to sleep in his dad's chair.

In this dream, he found himself in a forest, following Fuzzy again. The sun was setting and darkness crept through the trees covering the forest in nocturnal bliss.

Pez could just barely make out the shape of the white cat ahead of him, beckoning for him to follow. He wanted to quit following and turn back—he was afraid of the dark forest around him—but something inside of him made him press on. He was terrified of getting lost in these deep dark woods. It seemed like the only thing that was keeping him sane was the silhouette of the cat delicately picking its way through the forest.

"Fuzzy?" he called out. The cat stopped and turned to look at Pez. "Where are you taking me?" he asked, knowing full well that cats couldn't talk.

The cat sat down and began cleaning its paw. Pez caught up with him. He knelt down and picked the cat up. He buried his tear-streaked face in the cat's soft fur.

"Shh!" a voice hissed. Pez looked up. It was his mother; a younger version of his mother. Her stomach was round and he knew that Stevie and Sierra were in there.

In his arms, he was now holding his beloved teddy bear, not the living, breathing cat that he had been holding.

"We have to be quiet, now," Mommy whispered softly.

In the distance D could hear the sounds of people struggling. The noises grew closer and D whimpered in fear.

"Shh!" his mommy whispered, as she pressed him tightly against her round body.

"Don't say anything," she whispered, her arms tightening around the smaller D. In this dream memory, D could hear the unborn twins crying inside of Mommy's womb.

"Shh!" he whispered to the babies. Young D didn't know why he had to be quiet, but Pez knew. He knew that somewhere in the woods ahead of them, the mean men had Daddy tied up.

D watched in fear as the clearing became visible to him. He watched as Uncle Jack and Uncle Harry dragged his father into the clearing, right in front of their hiding spot.

Harry shoved Daddy and he fell to the ground. Harry kicked him in the side. Jack leaned in and punched Daddy's face.

"Call your wife!" Jack demanded. He backhanded Daddy. "I said: call your wife!" he demanded again.

"NEVER!" Daddy screamed back.

"Daddy?" Pez whispered. "Dad...," he began to call out. But his mother's hand quickly covered his mouth.

D felt his mother shaking in fear for her husband and her children born and unborn. D tried to push away from her, but only succeeded in moving to a clearer spot in the trees, where he could see the whole horrible scene unfolding before him.

"You shouldn't have taken the money, Spencer," Jack said, aiming a gun at Daddy's head.

"I didn't...," Daddy tried to protest, but the gun colliding with his mouth cut him off. Daddy coughed and D could see blood dripping down his chin.

D was filled with rage; no one was allowed to hurt his Daddy this way. He couldn't just sit there and watch as the bad men tortured his father. D began to sob uncontrollably as Uncle Jack proceeded to hit Daddy with the gun over and over again.

"Tell me where the money is!" Jack demanded again.

"I don't have it," Daddy growled, spitting out teeth and blood.

"Harry, find Carole and D!" he shouted. "Then he'll talk."

"You'll never find them! I told them to run. They're probably long gone by now," Daddy lied. D thought it was the bravest thing he'd ever heard.

"Carole?" Uncle Harry called. "Carole where are you?" he asked. "D," he called dragging the name out in a singsong way. "Come out, come out wherever you are!" he called. "Come out Carole and we'll let him go," Uncle Harry lied.

"Don't listen to him, honey!" Daddy yelled. "Take D and run! Get out of HERE!"

"Shut-up!" Jack yelled. He smacked Daddy's slowly swelling face. D whimpered and bit his lip. "FIND THEM!" Jack barked at Harry. "They're still here, I just heard them."

D could hear the trees around him begin to shake as Harry searched the underbrush for the two of them. D could hear the twins screaming in fear inside mommy's belly. D wanted to hold them close and tell them everything would be all right.

Uncle Jack was still talking and hitting Daddy, but D and Mommy couldn't pay attention. Harry was circling around the other side of the clearing. Mommy used the noise he was making to mask the sound as she covered them with dead leaves. She tried to burrow deeper into the space between the roots of the big tree they were hiding under.

The smell of dead, rotting leaves filled D's nostrils as Mommy covered his head with them. Everyone froze in surprise and fear as the first gunshot rang out.

"NO!" D screamed. Mommy's hand clamped over his mouth again. Sobs racked her body and D could feel her tears landing on the top of his head.

"Jack!" Harry yelled. He had stopped just before he reached the spot where Mommy and D hid. He turned and ran over to where Jack was standing above Daddy. The gun was still smoking.

"What the hell are you doing?" Harry asked.

Jack shrugged and shot Daddy again, this time in the chest. "You said we weren't going to kill him," Harry yelped. "Did you find out where the money is?" he asked.

"He didn't know," Jack replied nonchalantly. He turned and started to walk away. "Besides, he's not dead," Jack rationalized.

D breathed a sigh of relief.

Harry bent down and checked Daddy's pulse. "He's dead, Jack!" Harry called out after him. "You killed Spencer!" he accused.

"He took our money," Jack defended himself.

"That was no reason to kill him!" Harry argued.

D's body shuddered with rage and hurt as he bit Mommy's hand and broke free. He ran from their hiding spot and threw himself at Uncle Harry, kicking and screaming at the top of his lungs. Harry yelped in surprise and tried to push D off of him.

Jack turned and fired one shot at D. Pez cried out in his sleep as phantom pain tore through his body.

"No!" Mommy screamed in horror as D fell to the ground. She struggled to get out of the underbrush to save her son.

Jack turned his gun and shot Mommy in the stomach.

"Dammit Jack!" Harry shrieked. "What the hell are you doing? You could have shot me."

"I didn't, did I?" Jack yelled back.

"You killed a kid, Jack," Harry pointed out.

"Yeah, I killed a pregnant lady too," Jack said proudly.

The sound of sirens startled them into movement.

"Cops! Let's go!" Harry shouted. The two took off into the woods in the direction of their car.

D lay with his head on his father's side. He smelled the sweet smell of his father's cologne. He also smelled some other awful smell that filled his nostrils and made him gag. Pez remembered another time in his past when he had smelled that same smell: the accident. It was the iron-like smell of blood; lots of blood. D stared down at Daddy's still face and into his glazed over eyes.

He wanted to cry, but the pain in his stomach was so bad. The last thing D heard was Mommy screaming for help. He listened to her voice as he slid into a world of darkness.

38

Rae was sleeping on Carole's couch, where she had slept for the past couple of nights. She was awakened by the sound of the doorbell ringing.

"Rae? Are you awake?" Bren asked.

Rae opened her eyes and looked at Bren. He had also spent the last few nights there, sleeping on the floor.

"Yes," Rae answered sitting up.

"Mr. Robertson, who is apparently Carole's boyfriend, is here and she wants to look for Pez some more," Bren informed her. "Do you want to come along?"

"Yeah, just let me get dressed," Rae replied. She sat up and reached down on the floor next to the couch. She gathered some clothes from the bag that was down there. She had brought it over from her house when she stopped by to check in with her father.

She took the clothes and disappeared into the bathroom. After a few minutes, she emerged looking refreshed, but not feeling refreshed at all. She walked into the living room to find Mr. Robertson, Bren and Carole sitting around the coffee table eating donuts and drinking coffee.

"I just can't believe he hasn't come home yet," Carole was saying. Mr. Robertson was rubbing her back.

"We'll find him," Mr. Robertson assured her.

Suddenly, Carole noticed Rae standing in the doorway; she sat up straighter and wiped her cheeks.

"Alright, let's go back to the park. He's probably there. In fact I'm almost positive that's where he went," she said, standing up.

"We already looked there," Rae complained.

"I know, but we didn't check the nature trails," Carole replied.

"Why the nature trails?" Bren asked.

"Because that is where his father died," Carole replied sadly.

39

Pez awoke again with the light of the early morning sun shining into his sleep filled eyes. He took his purring bundle and went back to the sleeping area, pulling the curtain closed behind him. He flopped down as softly as he could and pulled the blankets over himself as fever chills began to overcome him.

Madness

madness

madness
pain
reflecting off
walls
blinding me
with black
light
chaos
erupting
from my
eye sockets
pain
in every
nerve
twitching
in despair
madness
madness
deep in
despair
struggling to
stay afloat
riptide pulling
me under
taken
taken
Inside the
hurricane
I awaken
I am madness
madness is me
madness
madness

He smiled, thinking maybe if he just lay there, eventually he would just die. He would just stop eating the food that Stevie was bringing out to him. He was being selfish; he knew it and he didn't care. He didn't care about any of his loved ones right now. He just wanted to die. The guilt he felt in his heart was too painful to live with.

He fell into a fitful sleep filled with fragmented dreams and lost memories.

He opened his eyes when he heard his mother's voice filled with panic say: "What are we going to do?"

He was lying in his bed. He was ten years old again. He snuck out of his room and slowly made his way into the hallway. He looked down into the living room where his Mommy and Daddy were talking quietly.

"What do you mean?" Daddy asked. "What are we going to do about what?"

"David, they are going to repossess the house!" Mommy exclaimed. "We're going to be homeless."

"We won't be homeless. We can just move in with my mom and dad," Daddy assured her.

"With two babies on the way?" Mommy challenged. "I don't think they would like that very much."

"We'll get through it, we always do," Daddy promised.

"Not this time, David!" Mommy argued. She was getting angry. "This isn't like getting the electricity turned off! They are going to take this house... our house away from us."

"I know that," Daddy sighed. "We can just move in with my parents," he repeated.

"That's not the point!" Mommy shouted. She lowered her voice as she remembered that D was supposedly sleeping. "I love this house! I don't want to lose it!"

"I don't want to lose it either!" Daddy agreed, keeping his voice low. "I just don't know what we can do about it right now."

"Maybe we can borrow some more money from your parents," Mommy suggested.

"I don't think that's a good idea. We still owe them money from buying the house."

"What are we going to do?" Mommy asked again. D was nervous about the anxious tone of his Mommy's voice.

"Look Care, there's this thing I've been meaning to talk to you about. Jack and Harry have gotten into something major. I'm not sure what, but I don't think it's entirely legal. Well, there's an unusually large amount of money in the safe at work," he reported quickly.

"David," she began, but Daddy cut her off.

"I... um took the keys and made a copy. I keep them in my desk. We could... I could... I don't know. If I took the money, we would never have to worry about money again."

Mommy gasped. *"You'd be stealing from your friend's, David!"* she said in shock.

"I know, but they got it in a shady way...," Daddy started.

"All the more reason why we shouldn't do it. It wouldn't be right."

Daddy sighed. *"I know, but it would be nice to have money again."*

Mommy nodded. *"It would be, but we can't do it. We don't even know where it came from,"* she explained.

"Maybe I can sell my bike," Daddy resigned.

"That might be a good idea," Mommy approved.

"Don't worry, baby. We're going to be all right. No matter what happens, as long as we stay together." Daddy assured her. He was hugging her as close as he could with her belly so big.

40

"Carole, I did what you asked me to. I talked to the principal," Travis began.

"What did he say?" Carole asked.

"He said all of D's teachers are suggesting that we hold him back," Travis replied sadly.

"What?!" Carole asked. Her surprise was only partly real. She had suspected something like this was in the works.

"He's missed too much school and he's not making it up like he said he would," Travis informed her.

"I know," she replied. "Is there anything we can do?"

"The only thing he can do is go to summer school."

"He's going to hate that," Carole said sadly.

"I know," Travis agreed.

"MOM!" Stevie screamed. "I spilled my juice!"

"Hold on a minute, Travis," she said standing up from the couch. She disappeared into the kitchen.

Travis turned his head as she left. He noticed a sketchbook lying on the floor. He picked it up and thumbed quickly through it. Every picture was perfectly drawn. He was in awe at the sheer talent D had.

"Sorry about that," Carole apologized him as she reentered the room. "Rae and Bren should be coming home soon. Bren is such a good friend. He worked it out with David's boss, so that he can take David's shifts."

"Have you ever had Stevie tested?" Travis asked as he watched the small boy run up and down the hallway.

"For what?" Carole asked. She was slightly offended, but she knew that Travis meant well.

"I don't claim to be a psychologist or anything, but I've done a lot of research on it. See my nephew has this disability called Asperger's Syndrome. It's a mild form of Autism," Travis stopped as Carole gasped.

"David told me that at the hospital. He told me he had a vision…," Carole trailed off. She didn't really want to talk about this in front of her relatively new boyfriend.

"A vision?" Travis prompted.

"He's um… psychic," Carole choked a bit on the word.

"That explains it," Travis said as recognition struck him.

"Explains what?" Carole asked.

"Just certain things that happened in class," he paused, wondering whether or not he should explain it to her more. "He once drew a picture of an older man. I don't think he was aware of it at the time, but the man he drew was my grandfather."

"I got so upset when he told me about Stevie." She swallowed, not believing that she was continuing with this conversation. "He told me he had talked to Sierra. She was the baby I lost the night my husband was murdered… Stevie's twin."

"Your husband was murdered?" Travis asked in surprise. He put his arm around her shoulder. Carole smiled. She hadn't felt this safe since before her husband died.

She snuggled into his warmth and took a deep breath. She recounted the entire story about her husband's death. She started with the night they found out the bank was repossessing their house.

"Do you think your husband took the money?" Travis asked, after she finished her story.

"He must have, who else could have? Unless someone else robbed them and Jack and Harry just blamed it on him. I just don't understand how they could have done that to him. They were his best friends."

"Did they get caught?" Travis asked.

"Yes. They barely even made it out of the park. The cops got them. Jack got life and Harry got fifteen years." She swallowed. "Both D and I had to testify at their trials. They had the audacity to try and say they were innocent. It was horrible."

"But you're OK now?" Travis asked.

Carole looked up into his eyes. "I am now." She sighed. "I don't think D is though."

41

Pez smiled as he drifted into the darkness again. He smiled because he remembered that saying—"When someone dies they see their whole lives flashing before their eyes." With all these memories he kept having, maybe he was finally dying now.

He opened his eyes to find himself standing in the clearing. From the looks of things, he had arrived just as Harry was dragging his father into the clearing.

Pez screamed out as Harry pushed Daddy to the ground. Pez had to stop this. He couldn't let his father go through this pain again.

"NO!" he screamed, running towards his father. He threw himself at Harry, but he just slid right through him, as if Harry was nothing more than fog. Yet Harry looked solid enough. Pez realized that he was falling to the ground right towards Daddy. He closed his eyes in anticipation with the pain that was sure to come.

"Call your wife!" a strange voice demanded. Pez felt pain blossoming across his face. It shocked him into opening his eyes. He tried to move his hands to block any more blows, but they were tied behind his back. He was lying on the ground staring up at Glenn, not Jack... Glenn. Somehow he had become his father and Jack was now Glenn. He glanced at where Harry was standing, but Sal had now taken Harry's place.

"What?" Pez whispered in fear.

"I said call your wife!" Glenn demanded again.

"NEVER!" Pez shouted out the logical response. He thought he could hear his younger-self whispering, but the voice was shushed immediately. Panic filled his mind as he realized that his younger self and his mother were hiding out in the woods somewhere.

"You shouldn't have taken the money, Spencer," Glenn said holding the gun against Pez's head.

"I didn't...," Pez tried to protest, but the gun colliding with his mouth cut him off. He coughed and felt blood dripping down his chin. Deep inside the consciousness of his father, Pez was again filled with rage. He wanted to fight back or try and escape. He wanted to save Daddy's life, but he knew that Daddy wouldn't fight back. The only thought in Daddy's head was protecting his family.

Pez groaned as Glenn hit him with the gun repeatedly. He drifted between the darkness and the light of flashlights shining in his eyes.

In the darkness, he watched in horror as another scene unfolded. He snuck into Jack's office and pulled out the key. The safe stood open before him, almost menacingly, taunting him with what lay within. He reached forward slowly, glancing over his shoulder to make sure that Jack was still occupied. He reached into the safe and quickly took the money out and shoved it into his bag.

"Tell me where the money is!" Glenn demanded, jolting Pez back into the light.

"I don't have it," he replied, spitting out teeth and blood. His face was on fire; his lips so swollen he could barely move them.

"Sal, find Rae and Wolf!" Glenn called out. "Then he'll talk." Pez gasped in horror. He stared directly at the place where he and his Mommy had hidden. He could just make out the silhouette of Rae's face. He followed her hand down and saw that she had her hand covering Wolf's mouth.

"You'll never find them! I told them to run. They're probably long gone by now," Pez lied.

"Rae?" Sal called. "Rae, where are you?" he asked. "Wolf," he called, dragging the name out in a singsong way. "Come out, come out wherever you are!" he called. "Come out Rae and we'll let him go."

"Don't listen to him, Honey!" Pez yelled, taking Daddy's place entirely. "Take Wolf and run! Get out of HERE!" Pez screamed. He wanted them to run; to get out of there, but he knew they couldn't. They would get caught if they tried.

"Shut-up!" Glenn yelled, smacking Pez's aching face. Pez heard a whimper come from the woods where Rae and Wolf were hiding.

"FIND THEM!" Glenn yelled at Sal. "They're still here. I just heard them."

"They're gone," Pez whispered; a weak attempt at lying. He knew how absurd the words sounded. He knew Glenn had heard Wolf just as well as Pez had.

Glenn knelt down next to Pez's body. Pez looked up at him through his swollen eyes.

"He was calling for you. Did you hear him?" Glenn whispered, his face unbelievably close to Pez's. Pez drew in a deep shaky breath and spat blood in Glenn's face.

Glenn wiped his face and backhanded Pez all in the same motion. Pez wasn't sure which parts of what he was experiencing actually happened and which parts were only his imagination filling in the gaps. He had a strange feeling that all of this was exactly how it actually happened. He was reliving the murder through his father's eyes, just like he had with Diamond.

"Wolf wants you to tell me where the money is. He is going to die otherwise, along with your wife and her babies," Glenn threatened in a voice so different from his own. He had a crazed look in his eyes.

"I didn't take it," Pez maintained. He tried to say more to convince him, but he couldn't say anything as Glenn grabbed a handful of his hair and pulled his head upwards.

He put his lips to David's ear and whispered so quietly Pez had to strain to hear it. "I believe you, Spencer. Forgive me, but it's your life or ours." Glenn laid Pez's head back on the ground gently. He lifted his hand and aimed the gun directly at Pez's neck. He sighed, and before Pez had a chance to protest, he heard the loudest sound that he had ever heard. It was so much louder than the gunshot he had heard as a child.

Pez felt his father's lips move, trying to speak. He heard the words "tree house" barely squeak out through the frothy, bubbly mess that was pouring out of his mouth and neck. He felt more pain as Glenn turned and shot him again. Pez watched in silence as Wolf ran out into the clearing and was shot. Wolf fell and landed directly on Pez's side. Pez's head was bent down and he could see directly into his lover's eyes. He looked up and watched helplessly as Rae ran out into the clearing and she too was shot, right in her pregnant belly.

Pez looked back at Wolf and stared into his eyes, just as Wolf's eyes closed, so too did his own eyes as he slipped into darkness again.

"You can wake up now," a voice suggested. Pez obeyed and opened his eyes. He found himself standing in the empty courtroom where Jack and Harry were convicted. He was standing in the main aisle.

"This is where your father stood," the voice explained. He turned and saw that Wolf was standing next to him. "He watched the whole trial."

Pez was disoriented for a second as Wolf took him in a blink over to the witness stand.

"This is where your father stood when you were testifying," Wolf whispered as ghosts of the past began to fill the courtroom. He saw his mom and Nanah sitting with most of his relatives. Uncle Jack and Uncle Harry's relatives were there too. Like a wedding, they all sat on separate sides of the courtroom, sitting behind the lawyers that represented their family members.

Pez noticed his ten-year-old self was sitting in the witness stand. Wolf stepped forward and placed his hand on the small boy's shoulder.

"He stood just like this, he was giving you support." Wolf turned back to Pez. "You did a good thing for him... taking his pain away from him." He smiled. "You did the same thing for

Diamond. It helped her cross over; maybe it will help your dad, too."

The smaller version of Pez lifted his hand and pointed across the courtroom. "That's the man that shot my daddy." He paused and looked at the judge for approval. The judge nodded and smiled. "Uncle Jack shot Daddy. Uncle Harry helped, but he didn't shoot Daddy."

Pez blinked as the scene changed to the sentencing. He was standing again in the main aisle. Nanah and his mother were sitting in the aisle next to where he stood. Little D was sitting on Nanah's lap. Mommy looked pale and sickly.

He watched in pain as they sentenced Glenn to life in prison. They gave Sal fifteen years. Watching this he knew how his father felt as his best friends were sent to prison. Pez was surprised to find that his father held no anger at them for them killing him. He had only forgiveness in his heart.

"Why can't I see my dad?" Pez asked Wolf.

"He was angry and afraid," Wolf clarified.

"Angry? Why?" Pez asked.

"I don't know," Wolf replied.

"Afraid?"

"Afraid that you hated him for leaving you," Wolf replied sadly.

"I don't hate him," Pez stated. "I could never hate him."

"I know," Wolf acknowledged.

"I want to see him," Pez begged.

"I know," Wolf replied. "It's time to wake up now," he commanded.

Wolf kissed him gently as Wolf and the courtroom faded away, leaving Pez in darkness.

42

"I don't know why she wants to check here again," Rae whispered sullenly to Bren as they made their way through the woods of the park once more. They had returned to that spot at least five times in the time that Pez had been missing.

"She seems to think that this is where he would go," Bren replied. He held a branch up so that Rae could pass underneath it.

"Thanks," Rae said smiling. If she weren't utterly in love with Davie, she would be totally crushing on Bren.

"No problem," Bren replied.

"Stevie, settle down!" Rae commanded. Stevie was running through the underbrush into the clearing. He stopped and sat down under a tree. Carole gasped in horror.

"Why are you sitting there?" she demanded.

"This is where we were hiding," Stevie pointed out. "D was telling me everything would be OK." He paused. "Sierra was really scared. I think she knew what was going to happen to her."

"How do you know this?" Carole asked. She was afraid that both of her sons had the strange gift that D had somehow acquired.

"I remember it," Stevie claimed.

"You remember it?" Carole asked incredulously.

Stevie nodded. "Not very well though. Sierra remembers it more. She tells me about it," he explained.

"Is she here now?" Carole asked, looking around, trying to see the daughter she had lost.

"No, I haven't seen her in a long time," Stevie replied sadly.

"Carole!" Travis's voice called out. "You better come see this."

Carole turned and walked out into the clearing. Travis and Bren were crouching down near the ground in the middle of the clearing. Rae was standing off to the side looking pale.

"What is it?" Carole asked. She was alarmed by the silence that had fallen on the group.

"Blood," Bren replied.

"A lot of it," Travis added.

"David's blood?" she asked.

Travis shrugged, "There's no way to tell."

"Are those…?" Carole began.

"Teeth," Bren confirmed.

"Can we use those to tell if it's David's blood?" Carole asked.

"Maybe," Travis replied. He took a handkerchief out of his pocket and picked the teeth up out of the blood. He wrapped them up and put them into his pocket.

"Maybe we should call the cops," Rae suggested. She was now sitting next to Stevie, trying to distract him from seeing all the blood.

43

Pez woke up with the smell of blood and Daddy's cologne. He pushed aside the curtain and found a bowl of macaroni and cheese sitting on the floor of the outer room. He licked his lips as his mouth watered for it. He gasped in pain. His mouth and lips hurt so badly. He knew there was no way he would be able to eat it.

Tenderly and cautiously, he probed the wounds on his face. One eye was so swollen he couldn't even open it. His lip was split in multiple places. He probed his teeth with his tongue and found that two of his lower ones were missing. He couldn't move his jaw without stars filling his eyes. The pain was so horrible. He rolled over onto his side and cried out in pain. It felt like his ribs were broken; it even hurt to breathe.

Pez gasped in horror as he looked down at his chest. He was wearing his father's jacket. Not the one that he always wore. This one was almost brand new. The blood on it was still fresh. This was the jacket his father died in.

What the hell had he just gone through? Was this penance for all the guilt he felt? He didn't know. He didn't care. He no longer cared about it or anything else. He sighed. The pain outside finally matched the pain inside. He closed his eyes and willed himself to die.

306

44

Carole sighed and turned off the local news. They aired her story three days ago and no one had called to say they saw him. The police had determined that the teeth they had found were indeed David's, but they had no leads on his whereabouts.

She was beginning to think they would never find him. He had already been gone for two weeks now.

Rae poked her head into the living room. "The macaroni is done, Carole."

"OK, thank you dear," Carole replied. Rae had been such a big help through this whole ordeal. She cleaned the house when

Carole was busy making phone calls. She did some light cooking and kept an eye on Stevie.

Carole walked into the kitchen to find a bowl sitting on the table waiting for her. She sat down next to Rae and numbly began to eat. Every day that D didn't come home, was another day closer to Carole accepting that her son had been killed in the very same spot that her husband died.

Rae smiled at Carole. She was glad that Carole was letting her stay here. She missed her own mother greatly and Carole's presence helped ease that pain.

Rae tried hard to keep her mind on menial things. She no longer wanted to talk about Davie or even think about him. She just wanted to live in this pretend family that had formed through Davie's disappearance. She imagined that Davie was just off at college and he would soon come home for summer break. Rae wanted desperately to believe this, but she knew he was probably just lying dead somewhere. She shivered at that thought. She tried to think about other things, but it was so hard when everything reminded her of Davie. She tried to focus on what Carole was saying.

Carole was sitting next to her babbling about little things, not really knowing what to talk about. She didn't really know the girl she was eating with, even though Rae had been living at her house for two weeks.

"So, do you have any brothers and sisters?" she asked Rae.

Rae shook her head and swallowed her food. "Nope, it's just me and my dad. My mom died almost a year ago." Rae regretted the words as soon as they left her mouth. Anytime Rae said anything about dead, death, or dying, it usually set Carole off.

This time was no different. A look of sheer horror crossed her face. "He's not dead, you know," she paused, staring at Rae, looking for any hint of opposition from her. "He's not dead." Rae kept her face as neutral as possible. She wondered who Carole was trying to convince, Rae or herself. "I would know if he were dead. I would know. I would feel it. A mother knows these things," Carole ranted as she pushed her chair back from the table and stood up. "He's not dead!" she accused. "DAVID IS NOT DEAD!" she screamed and ran from the room.

Rae, whose emotions were as messed up as Carole's, if not more, began crying into her mac & cheese.

"Rae-Rae?" Stevie's small voice asked. She ignored him and continued to cry. She wasn't in the mood for his incessant chatter.

"Rae-Rae?" he repeated and she felt a tug on her sleeve at the elbow. "Rae-Rae?" The voice got more desperate.

She stopped crying and looked over at him. Stevie's big, angelic, Davie-like eyes gazed back at her.

"Why are you crying?" he asked quietly.

"Because I'm sad," she answered truthfully.

"Why for?" he asked.

"I miss Davie," she replied sadly. "I'm worried about him."

"Why for?" he repeated.

"Because he's so sad," she answered and thought a moment before she spoke again. "I'm afraid that he is dead."

"Do you love him?" Stevie asked.

"I like him a lot," she paused. "Yes, I love him. I love him more than anything. Why for?" Rae asked, turning the tables on him.

"He loves you. I know he does," Stevie informed her.

"How do you know that?" Rae asked.

"He drew your picture in his sketchbook. He drew it a lot," Stevie said, handing the book over to her. Rae gasped as she looked at the sheer number of sketches that Pez had drawn of her.

"Who's that lady?" Stevie asked.

"What lady?" Rae responded.

Stevie reached over and turned the book to one of the last pages. Rae felt the tears falling down her cheeks as she stared at the picture.

"Who is it?" Stevie prompted.

"It's my mother," Rae clarified sobbing.

"Did she die?" Stevie asked.

Rae nodded miserably, still staring at the haunting sketch.

"My sister died too," Stevie told her matter-of-factly. "She died before she was born. The mean men shot her right in my mommy's belly. I almost died too," he stated as he turned the pages of the sketchbook. "He drew a picture of Sierra too." Stevie pointed at the sketch of Sierra he had stopped on.

Rae smiled at the laughter that Davie had caught in his sister's eyes.

"I tried to show it to Mommy, but she wouldn't look," Stevie told her sadly.

"She's sad too," Rae explained.

"I know," Stevie replied. "He's not dead ,you know," Stevie said, smiling as if it were funny that Rae thought D was dead.

"I want to believe that…," Rae began.

"It's true!" Stevie asserted.

"But, how can you be so sure?" Rae asked.

"Because, I know where he is."

"CAROLE!!" Rae screamed. Stevie jumped almost a foot and a half. "Sorry, buddy, I didn't mean to scare you," she apologized. "Carole!" she called again, quieter this time so she didn't startle Stevie again.

Carole came running in after the second desperate plea for her. "What is it?" she asked as she entered the room. Her eyes were red and puffy from crying.

"Stevie, tell your mom what you just told me," Rae commanded.

"Look, Mom. D did a picture of Sierra for me," Stevie announced, holding out the sketchbook to her. Carole took it and stared at the picture with new tears falling down her cheeks.

"She's beautiful," Carole said in awe.

"Not that!" Rae scolded. "Tell her what you said about Davie," she prompted.

"David?… What about David?" Carole asked. She was rather afraid to hear the answer.

"D's not dead," Stevie announced. "At least I don't think he is. He might be though, because he didn't eat the food I left there last night. I found it still on the plate when I took the macaroni and cheese to him," Stevie revealed. He seemed oblivious to the state his mother was slowing falling into. He didn't notice the panic and fear filling her eyes.

"Where is he, Stevie?" she said, grabbing him by the shoulders. "TELL ME WHERE HE IS!" she screamed, shaking him violently.

"Carole!" Rae yelled.

"Mommy!" Stevie cried out and begin bawling.

Rae grabbed Carole's shoulders and tried to pull her away from Stevie.

"Calm down, getting angry won't help," Rae soothed. Carole stopped and pulled Stevie into a warm embrace.

"I'm so sorry, baby. Momma's sorry. I didn't mean to yell at you." She hugged the sobbing child until his tears subsided. "Where's David at, sugar?" she asked in an overly sweet voice. "Can you take us to him?"

Stevie nodded and sniffled softly. He turned to go. "Come on," he beckoned. The two women followed the child obediently. They expected him to lead them out to the station wagon; instead he led them into the backyard. He stopped and looked up into the air. Carole was so afraid he was going to point at the sky and say that he was in heaven.

"Up there," he said, pointing to the tree house.

"Are you kidding me?" Carole asked in relief.

"No," Stevie said, shaking his head with a hurt look in his eyes.

"Has he been up there the whole time?" Rae asked in awe. The tree house was the only place that none of them had even thought to look for him.

"Yep," Stevie replied. "I've fed him every day and I gave him clean clothes, but I don't think he wanted them," he admitted as he climbed up the ladder. Rae and Carole followed.

"Davie?" Rae called softly into the seemingly empty tree house.

"D?" his mother called a little louder.

Both women closed their eyes as they listened for any sound whatsoever. They wanted to hear some sort of reply, but to their knowledge no one was in the tree house. Could Stevie be lying? Did he really know where David was?

"I don't think he's here," Rae said, but Carole shushed her.

"Did you hear that?" she asked. Both were silent once more. Then they heard it: a tiny whimper coming from the area behind the curtain.

"David?" Carole asked again.

"Mommy?" a small voice returned.

Carole rushed forward and pushed aside the curtain. She looked into the dim sleeping area. For a split second, she saw her son the way he looked when her husband was murdered. She gasped as her vision cleared and she saw David lying in a bundle of tattered blankets, clutching a blood encrusted teddy bear to his chest. His face was bruised and his lip was split in numerous places. His left hand was a bloody swollen mess. D had it propped up on a musty old pillow.

Pez looked up at them with glazed over eyes. He seemed to be shivering in fear.

Rae stared at his jacket in shock. Somehow he had gotten blood all over it, yet despite the blood the jacket seemed crisper, newer then it had been before. The thought was pushed out of her head as Pez opened his mouth.

"LEAVE MY DADDY ALONE!" he screamed.

"Oh my God," Rae shuddered. "What's wrong with him?" she asked, panicking. "What happened to him?"

"I don't know," Carole replied, pushing her own feelings of fear and panic aside. "We need to get him to the hospital," she said as she crouched down next to her child.

"D, darling can you stand up?" she whispered in his ear.

"I'm sorry Daddy," Pez mumbled, closing his eyes.

"Come on, sweetie, stand up," Carole said, reaching her hand down and putting her arm under his side. She tugged a little.

Pez howled in pain, but helped to stand himself up.

"Watch your head, D," Carole warned. She moved her arm to prevent him from standing up completely.

"Mommy?" Pez asked, opening his eyes and seeing her as if for the first time.

"Oh, God!" Rae breathed as the tears rolled down her cheeks. She had never seen anyone who looked this lost before.

His head jerked in her direction. Upon seeing her, his eyes seemed to clear. He came back to himself.

"Rae?" he asked, smiling slightly—all that his swollen lips would allow. Rae noticed the spaces in his teeth where the two teeth had fallen out.

"What happened to you?" she asked.

Pez sighed, somewhat painfully. "I took away his pain."

"Whose pain?" Rae asked.

"Daddy's," Pez replied. He ran his finger across his neck and found a bullet wound scar there. "I took away all his pain, see," he pointed to the scar.

"I think Bren is here," Carole announced.

"I'll go get him, maybe he can help us get him down from here," Rae suggested. She turned and ran out of the little house and down the ladder. She jumped off of the third step and used her momentum to carry her into a run. She ran to the front of the house where Bren was just parking her car.

"BREN!" Rae called. "We found him!" she shouted gleefully.

"Are you serious?" Bren asked.

"Yes, he's in the tree house," Rae answered.

"In the tree house?" Bren asked in astonishment.

"Yeah, and we need your help to get him down," Rae explained.

Bren followed her around the house to the back. Carole was standing on the balcony with Pez and Stevie. "I got him this far," she called down to them.

"Bloody Hell!" Bren exclaimed. "What happened to him?"

"We don't know," Rae answered.

Bren ran over and climbed the ladder.

"Start going down, Pez and rest your weight on me," Bren instructed from the ladder.

Pez slowly followed his directions and climbed down the ladder using Bren as a brace.

"Let's get him to the hospital," Carole said as she climbed down the ladder, followed by Stevie.

They guided Pez into the backseat of Carole's station wagon. Rae climbed in next to him and Stevie sat next to her. Bren sat in the front seat with Carole. Stevie laid his head in Rae's lap and fell asleep. Rae started absently playing with his hair.

Pez stared out the window; he seemed to be in a daze again. Carole kept stealing glances in the rearview mirror to check on him.

"What do you think happened to him?" Rae asked.

Pez didn't care to listen as his mother babbled about gangs and skinheads. The word homophobic came up a few times. Pez just stared out the window, watching the road fly by as they drove. They were stopped at a red light when Pez saw something that made him gag.

"FUZZY!" he screamed, opening the car door and jumping out. He dashed over to the cat and ran his good hand across its head.

Carole pulled the car onto the side of the road.

"He's lost his mind!" Bren said as they all got out and ran over to Pez. He was now burying his head in the cat's blood-stiffened fur.

"Honey, that cat's dead," Carole whispered softly as she put her hand on his shoulder. Rae crouched down next to him.

"It's not dead. It was just with me," Pez pleaded.

"Candy-Boy, that cat is dead," Bren agreed.

"No! No! No!" Pez cried, shaking his head violently.

"Davie, he's right. This cat has been dead for a long time, "Rae added shuddering. "It has no eyes left. Please let it go. Please," she begged him, trying not to gag.

Pez lifted the stiff, light body of the cat up. A look of repulsion crossed his face.

"No, it can't be dead!" Pez told them. "It can't be!"

"Why not Davie?" Rae asked, humoring him as best she could.

"Because, if this cat is dead, then I am definitely going crazy," he said, dropping the dead cat and running back to the car. He noticed as he climbed into the station wagon that this intersection was the very same one that all of his friends had died in.

He no longer cared that they hadn't actually all died here. It was the accident that had killed them all; even Amber and Sal. They both died in the accident even though their bodies lived on.

45

"Well, Mrs. Spencer your son is an extremely lucky boy." the doctor stated.

"Lucky?" Carole spat out.

"Bad choice of words," he scratched his head. Carole could see the wheels turning. "Has your son been having hallucinations?"

"No!" Carole answered indignantly.

"Yes, he has," Rachael corrected her. "They need to know everything, Carole."

"Fine, yes. He's been 'seeing' things."

"Fever... weakness... agitation... confusion... fatigue... headaches?"

"Yes, all of those," Carole nodded in agreement.

"Have you noticed his personality changing at all? Has he seemed like himself lately?"

"Well no, but I mean he's been through a lot. His... his friends died, he lost pretty much everyone he knew."

"That explains a lot. I said he's lucky in the sense that if he hadn't had these head injuries. We probably wouldn't have found the encephalitis."

"Encepha... what?" Carole asked.

"Encephalitis, it is a swelling of the brain. It causes all of the symptoms I mentioned."

"Is he going to be alright?" Carole implored.

"I think so. We've got him on fluids, anti-inflammatory drugs, anti- viral drugs. He should be fine. I think we caught it in time."

"So he's had that this whole time," Rachael asked. "I thought he had the flu or something."

"Well, encephalitis can present itself like the flu. In most cases, it goes away without need for medical attention, but in rare cases such as his...," the doctor shrugged.

"How do you get something like that?" Carole asked.

"Well there are two ways. One is by a mosquito carrying one of many viruses, but we've tested him and his is caused by Herpes."

"HERPES!" Carole shouted.

"Herpes Simplex 1 to be exact... Oral Herpes. About 50% percent of adults have it. It's spread from sharing utensils, using someone else's toothbrush. Even just a caress can spread it."

"Wow." Carole was in shock. "My son went insane from herpes."

"He's not insane, but this course of treatment, won't cure what his brain perceives as real. He'll have to undergo serious therapy... physical... emotional... speech..."

"When can he go home?"

"We're going to have to keep him here until the brain swelling goes down. Then he can go home, but I would start looking for somewhere he can get therapy. I can give you the names of a few places as well."

"Excuse me, Dr. Hanson?" a male nurse asked.

"Yes, Jon."

"Um, I hate to say I was listening in, but um... Ms. Spencer, I think you son would be perfect for this program we offer at a place called Fairhaven. It's covered by insurance and, well, it's a really good place." He handed Carole a flier.

"Thanks, both of you." Carole smiled.

46

"How you doing, Davie?" Rae asked, smiling.

"Better," Pez mumbled through his teeth. His jaw was wired shut.

"Bren's coming over," Rae informed him.

"I know," Pez replied. "Can you scratch my leg?" he asked.

Rae happily obliged. Pez's wrist was in a cast. He also had a broken nose and three broken ribs. The worst part of all was that he wasn't allowed to have any painkillers stronger than over the counter aspirin. His mother gave him two aspirin every six hours. She was very strict about it. She didn't want him to get addicted to any drugs again. Rae and his mom had gone through the house and hidden all the medications.

"D?" Carole asked from the doorway. Pez looked up.

"Travis and I have been talking to your social worker," Carole announced. She entered the room and sat on the chair across from Pez.

Pez gulped. He knew what the social worker had said. She had told them to send him back to rehab. What else would she have suggested?

"She suggested you get therapy" She paused taking a deep breath. "Inpatient therapy. At the hospital. One of the nurses told us about this place," Carole began and there it was... another rehab hell. "It's not exactly a hospital. It's um...," she paused.

"A mental rehabilitation center," Travis supplied from the doorway.

"We think it would be good for you to go there. It's out in the country... in the woods. The nurse assured us it would be like summer camp compared to the place where the court sent you."

"The thing is...," Travis began.

"I'm eighteen," Pez interrupted.

"That's right," Carole confirmed. "So we can't force you to go. It has to be your decision."

"I'll go," Pez agreed, to their surprise. "As long as I can get out for a day or two if something happens, like a funeral... or a wedding or something." He didn't want to tell them that during his time in the tree house he had had a vision about Travis and his mom getting married.

"I'm sure we can arrange that," Travis assured him.

"We can leave as soon as you're ready," Carole informed him.

Pez nodded. "I just need to get something out of the tree house though," he said with tears in his eyes.

"OK, but don't run away again, please," Carole begged.

"I won't," Pez pledged. "I know that I need help and this place may be the only place I can get it."

Carole nodded with tears in her eyes.

Pez turned to Rae. "I'll be back to say goodbye." he promised her. She nodded, biting her lip to keep herself from crying. She didn't want Pez to leave her again, but she knew that it was for his own good. "Don't leave."

"I won't," Rae said, wiping a tear away.

47

Pez climbed carefully into the tree house. He wrapped his good arm under each bar and pulled himself up. He knew this would be the last time he saw the tree house for a long time.

"*You made the right choice,*" Wolf assured him. He was waiting for Pez in the tree house.

"It's not fair," Pez mumbled.

"*What's not?*" Wolf asked.

"I can see all these ghosts or spirits or whatever, but I can't see the one I want to see the most." Pez elaborated.

"*Pez, he's an earthbound spirit. I can't reach him,*" Wolf explained.

"I know, and it's not fair!" Pez yelled through his teeth. He winced in pain.

"Nothing in life is fair, Pez," Wolf scolded him.

"I just really want to see my dad." Pez replied sadly.

"I can talk to Daddy," Pez heard another voice. He turned to find Sierra sitting across from Wolf on the floor.

"Can you bring him here, Sierra?" Pez asked.

"No," Sierra replied.

"Why not?" Pez said in anguish.

"Because, silly, he's already here." She pointed to the sleeping area.

"DADDY!" Pez yelled, throwing the curtain aside. "He's not back here!" He turned to yell at Sierra, but both she and Wolf were gone.

He glanced at his father's chair. His father's ghost was sitting in it.

"D?" his father asked. *"Is that you?"*

Pez nodded, choking back tears. "Daddy!" Pez cried. He watched in fascination as his father stood up and walked towards him.

"Son," his father said, as his arms folded around Pez's body. It was an awkward hug in a room with such low ceilings, but he was real and solid. Pez sobbed and felt himself sinking to his knees. His father followed and the hug was less awkward as they both knelt on the floor.

"I miss you Daddy," Pez said, feeling as if he were ten years old again.

His father laughed gently and lifted Pez's face up tenderly to look into his eyes. *"David, I haven't left you. I've been with you or your mom the whole time."*

"Why didn't you go where Nanah and Poppy went?" Pez asked.

"I didn't realize that I was dead," he replied.

"But you do now?" Pez asked.

"Yes," his father replied. *"I realized it when you did what you did for me. When you took my pain, I was taking yours. It was strange to see the world through your eyes."*

Pez smiled a little. "It was weird for me too," Pez agreed.

"Don't try to kill yourself anymore, OK?" Daddy asked.

Pez nodded. "Will you ever forgive me?"

"Forgive you for what?" Daddy asked.

"For letting you die," Pez answered, "for killing you."

"I don't feel that way son. I never have. The only person you need to ask forgiveness from is yourself."

"I love you Daddy," Pez whispered.

"I love you too, D," Daddy replied.

"Is there any way that you can go and be with Nanah? She looks happy where she is," Pez asked.

"Yes," Daddy assured him. *"First I need you to do something for me."*

"What is it?" Pez asked, anxious to help his father.

"It will be very hard for you to do it," Daddy stated.

"What is it?" Pez asked. "I'll do it. I swear."

"Set things right with your mom. She needs to know the truth," Daddy explained. Pez knew exactly what he meant.

"That's what I came up here for," Pez explained.

"Good, I'm proud of you, D," his father beamed. *"Tell your mother that I love her... and give her my blessings on marrying your teacher. Tell Stevie I love him and I'm sorry I couldn't be there for him when he was growing up. Make sure he knows that I will always be watching him, and that I will always be proud of him."*

"I will," Pez promised.

"It's time for me to go now," Daddy said. He turned his head and looked to the side. *"Help me to cross over, will you D?"*

"I will," Pez assured him. "Will I see you again?" he asked.

"If the fates allow, you will," Daddy promised.

"How do I cross you over?" Pez asked.

"You need to concentrate and visualize the other side," Daddy instructed.

Pez closed his eyes and visualized the garden where he met Nanah.

"Oh D, it's beautiful," Daddy breathed.

Pez opened his eyes to see the most brilliant white light he had ever seen.

"Mom? Dad?" Daddy asked in disbelief.

"I can't see them." Pez said sadly.

"They're there and they want me to join them now. Sierra's there too." His father was smiling the biggest smile Pez had ever seen on his face. He kissed Pez's forehead and stood up. He walked towards the light and disappeared.

Pez sighed and set about his original task. He pushed the sleeping curtain aside again. He walked over to the window and pushed aside the curtain and felt around for the secret compartment. He pulled out the garbage bag. He reached inside and pulled out his old backpack. Then he stuffed his blankie and the teddy bear back into the bag and replaced it in the wall.

48

"*D*, is that you?" Carole asked as he opened the back door.

"Yes," Pez replied as loudly as he was able to.

"Are you OK?" Carole asked. She was sitting at the table with Travis, Rae and Bren. They were drinking coffee.

"Yeah, I think so," Pez shrugged. "I finally saw Dad," he blurted out.

"Did you?" Carole asked excitedly. Pez was surprised at her reaction. She seemed like she actually believed him. "What did he say?" Carole asked.

"He said that he's been watching over us. He didn't know he was dead. He said he loves you and misses you, but he gives you his blessing in you and Mr. Robertson's wedding."

"I didn't tell him, Travis, I swear," Carole cried out in surprise.

"I know," Travis replied. "I asked your mom yesterday. I know it's sudden and all, but we really love each other. I hope that it's OK with you."

"It is," Pez assured him.

"Candy-Boy, what do you have in the sack?" Bren asked.

Pez paused, looking at each one of them in turn. Was he really going to do this?

"It's proof," Pez replied, tossing the bag on the table.

"Proof of what?" Rae asked.

"Open it," Pez instructed. "It is proof that even if I didn't kill my friends, without any doubt whatsoever, I caused the death of my own father," Pez sobbed.

Carole gasped in horror as Rae dumped the contents of the bag on the table.

"I never counted it," Pez told them. "You can have it. I don't want it," he said, shoving one of the many bundles of money at his mother. "I don't think the people Uncle Jack and Uncle Harry stole it from will miss it."

All of them sat there staring at the money with their mouth's hanging open.

"He was the only man who has ever truly loved me for me. Wolf only loved a shadow of the boy I used to be. I took the money. I walked into his office and stole his key. Then I went to his work and took the money out of the safe. I just wanted to help you pay the mortgage. I didn't expect any of that to happen. I didn't know any better. Uncle Jack might have pulled the trigger, but I killed my father."

EPILOGUE

$\mathcal{D}$avid blinked as he finally came back to the present. He heard Mokey crying, but he also heard something else. It was the sound of many people whispering. He looked around.

"I hope you don't mind; my boyfriend called a few other people," Mokey informed him. She gestured to the young man sitting next to her.

"No, I don't mind," David replied as he focused on her boyfriend. He looked strangely familiar. "Do I know you?" he asked.

"Have I really changed that much?" the boy asked. "I'll give you a clue… Davie and Rae-Rae sitting in a tree," he sang.

"Stevie?" David asked. He stood up and walked over to him. Stevie stood up and hugged him.

"I'm just Steve now. Mom's here too," he informed David, pointing to the other side of the table.

"Mom?" David asked. Carole ran over and threw her arms around him.

"I am so sorry about everything!" Carole apologized.

"It's OK. It's all in the past. I'm sorry too. It was mostly my fault. I took everything you said the wrong way," David admitted.

"Hey Candy-Boy! Don't forget about us!" David heard Bren's voice call. He pulled away from his mom and turned to see Rae and Bren. Rae was holding a sleeping baby. David winced as he remembered getting the letter a few years ago. Rae married Bren, mostly so he could stay in the states, but also because they loved each other. David was hurt, but he knew Rae wouldn't wait for him forever.

"You had a baby?" he asked.

Rae nodded. Her face reddened. "I had four," she laughed as she pointed across the room to a table filled with laughing teenagers. "Diamond!" she called out. "Come here and bring your friends."

David sat down in the nearest chair to him. This was not the homecoming he was expecting. The children ran over to her.

"What is it, Mom?" the young girl asked.

"Davie, these are your daughters," Rae said. "Remember that night at the wedding?" she paused. "I tried to write you a million times, but I could never find the right words," she sighed. "Girls, this is your real daddy."

"What are their names?" David asked.

"I'm Diamond, and this is my twin sister, Penny," the one standing in front of Rae introduced herself and her sister. She looked almost exactly like David, but she was still feminine. Penny looked more like Rae, but she still had David's eyes.

David offered his hand to each one. "Sorry, I wasn't there for you," he said nervously.

"Please, it's Mom's fault she never told you," Diamond laughed.

"Besides, Bren's been our Da for as long as we can remember so we didn't miss out or anything," Penny agreed.

"Good," David smiled.

"So, who are these other ones?" David asked.

"I'm your half-sister, Sierra." the little girl replied, winking. David smiled. He always wondered what happened to his ghostly sister. It seems she decided to give life another try. David laughed and threw his arms around her. "I'm pleased to meet you, Sierra."

"Where's um… Dad?" David asked, smiling. It was still weird to call Travis Dad.

"He's at work," Carole replied. "I'm sure he wants to see you. Are you staying for a while?"

"I'm home, mom. For good," David replied.

Carole nodded with tears filling her eyes. "That's good to know, baby."

David hugged her once more and then turned back to Rae. "What's the baby's name?" he asked.

"Glenn," Rae replied. "Bren picked out the names."

"I like them," David said, smiling.

She smiled again. "This is my other boy, David," she introduced a boy who looked to be about 8.

There was another boy standing among the children. He seemed to be slightly older than the rest. "Who does this one belong to?" he asked.

"He's mine," a voice claimed. He turned and found even more people he knew sitting at the table next to him. Lisa was waving to him.

"Hey, you were in the Lodge with me. When'd you have time?" David asked.

"I had him before I went in. I couldn't tell you, I was embarrassed. I… um named him after you, sort of." She shook her head. "His name is Raphael David."

"He's not mine, is he?" David asked. He couldn't remember sleeping with Lisa, but who knew what he had done back in his drug days.

"No," she paused, swallowing. "His father died in the um… incident that eventually led to me joining you at the Lodge," she clarified. "I named him after his father, Raph."

"Was, it scary in there? In the Lodge?" Mokey asked.

"Not really," David said, shaking his head. "I mean when I first went in I was still in a fog from the Encephalitis. The first year went by in a blur. Wolf told me that I was pretty much iv

catatonic. I would just stare off into the distance; I didn't talk to anyone..." David stopped as he realized Mokey was no longer listening.

"You really have seen Wolf," she whispered, crying.

David nodded, chewing on his lower lip.

"Can you see him now?"

"No, he's gone. I think he finally crossed over," he replied after he thought for a moment or two.

"I wish I could talk to him." Mokey wiped viciously away at her tears.

"You can." Pez smiled. "You can talk to him in your dreams."

"What?" Mokey asked in wonder.

"Yeah, the dead are always talking to us in our dreams; it's just that nobody ever listens," David explained, looking around at the people who had gathered to hear his story. His eyes focused on a booth across the café from them. It seemed for a split second he saw his old friends gathered there, laughing and joking. He waved to them, but hid the gesture by rubbing the back of his head again.

"Hey!" David called out as his eyes focused on a face that was from his present and not his past. "What are you doing here?" he called out.

The man who had just entered the café waved and walked over to Pez's table. "I heard through the, um... grapevine...," he started, making air quotes around the word grapevine. "That you finally got back to the states."

"Everyone!" Pez called out to the little crowd of people gathered in the café. "This is my best friend and savior, Spooky. He taught me everything I needed to know about my gift."

Spooky waved to everyone.

"I really can't say enough good things about this man. He saved my sanity. He taught me what was real and what was just in my mind."

"Please David, I didn't do that much," Spooky said humbly.

"But you did Spooky. You saved me; I would still be in the Lodge if it wasn't for you. You even got me into the Hutchinson School. I couldn't have done that without you."

"I'm just glad they accepted you. I wouldn't have been able to help you if it weren't for them teaching me everything I know."

"Hi," another voice chimed in. "Sorry to interrupt, but I wanted to make sure everyone had drinks."

"Mercury?" David asked.

"I remember you. I haven't seen you in forever. Pez, right?" Mercury smiled.

"Pez is in my past. I'm David now," he nodded. "I can't believe you still work here," he blurted out.

"I don't work here anymore. I own it," she replied.

"I like what you've done with the place," David complimented.

"Thanks," she smiled proudly.

"I don't believe we've met," Spooky said, smiling. "I'm Jon. People call me Spooky though. I'm a medium." He extended his hand.

"My name is Mercury." She smiled back, taking his hand. "I'm an empathic aromatherapy Reiki master."

"Impressive," Spooky commented.

"I had a cameo in David's story," Mercury pointed out.

"Me too," Spooky agreed.

"David, do you think you could walk me home? I have something for you, at my house," Mokey asked.

"Do you guys mind?" David asked the impromptu gathering.

"No, we'll be here when you get back," Carole smiled. "Go, we're just glad your home. Take my car, you'll get back faster."

David took the keys and handed them to Mokey.

"You still can't drive?" Rae asked.

"I can. I just choose not to," he smiled. "Be right back."

They arrived at Mokey's house faster than David thought they would.

"Everything seems different now," he remarked. "Like, the city used to be so much bigger and wider. I feel like I didn't fit before. It was too big for me."

"And now?" Mokey asked turning off the engine.

"I think it's starting to fit." He smiled. "What do you got for me?"

"It's up in my room... Wolf's old room." Mokey got out of the car and headed for the house. David stepped out of the car and looked up at the house.

"Can I come with you?" he asked shyly.

"Sure." She ran back and grabbed his hand. She pulled him up onto the porch and into the house. "Let's go. It's important."

David wanted to examine every change that had happened in the house that the Waverly's had grown up in, but he followed Mokey as she pulled him up the stairs into Wolf's old room.

"OK, so this is really weird, but if anyone is going to believe me, you will," Mokey started. Her excitement was contagious. "I was sitting on my bed reading yesterday night," she paused, steeling her nerves. "And that picture of Wolf, the one right there." She pointed to a portrait of her older brother sitting on the front edge of her dresser. "It fell behind my dresser."

"It fell behind it?" David asked.

"Yeah, it was just where it is now. I heard a noise, I looked up and it was gone, behind my dresser."

"That's it. That's what you wanted to show me?" he asked.

"Nope," she said, smiling gleefully. "So I get up and I can't reach it behind there. So I moved the dresser. Go ahead, pull it forward."

David shrugged and edged the dresser forward.

"What is that?" he asked. He pulled the dresser out further.

"My thoughts exactly, so I pulled the dresser out more and I found a secret door. I think Wolf made it. It's so invisible, but his picture fell on it; like he was telling me about it. So I opened it." She opened the secret door. "And I found this." She reached in and pulled out what looked like a letter. "It's to you, from him. I couldn't open it. I knew you'd come back someday so I put it back in there and I waited." She smiled her quirky smile. "Guess I didn't have to wait long," she laughed.

"He knew I was coming home," David said through tears. "Can I read it alone?" he asked as he sat down on the bed.

"Sure, I'll be downstairs. Take your time."

David waited until Mokey left the room before he carefully opened the letter. A cassette tape was wrapped in the letter and he laid that next to him on the bed. He straightened out the letter and began to read…

My Dearest Love,

Tonight you shared with me a very special and sad secret. Something I don't think you have ever told anyone at all about it...ever. So for that reason I thank you. Thank you for loving me enough to tell me about something so horrible that happened in your past. Thank you for trusting me with the sanctity of it. I will keep it forever locked in my heart.

With that said I need you to know, that you can't blame yourself. Not for any of it. You didn't 'kill' him. Yes what you did led to the events causing his death, but it was your 'uncle' who pulled the trigger. He had a choice and he made the wrong one. Greed can do that to people. It can turn people into monsters. It can make the sweetest person go sour.

You were a child then. You had no way of knowing what was going to happen when you took that money. You were just trying to help your parents. Who can blame you for that? You were scared. It's a very scary thing for children to see their parents so vulnerable.

So, please Pez, please forgive yourself. You don't deserve the punishment that you are putting yourself through. You deserve to be happy. You deserve to be loved.

If it's the money that's holding you back from forgiving yourself; then for God's sake get rid of it, donate it to charity. Give it to another family facing the same crisis that your parents were. You can do it anonymously. That way no one would ever know what you did.

I do think you should tell your mom. She needs to know the truth. Does she really deserve to live her life thinking that her husband was a thief and a liar? She won't hate you for it. Moms are like that; she will forgive you.

Besides you told me the truth and I don't hate you. In fact, if anything, I love you more. It was a very noble thing you did at such a young age. You were trying to support your parents and your future siblings.

So please, love, don't hate yourself.

I love you too much.

You are my life. I couldn't bear to lose you. So don't ever even think about suicide again, ok? I could not live without you.

I made you a mix tape. It's mostly songs that remind me of you, but one side of it is songs I recorded at the recording studio. I wrote them for you. I hope you like them.

I should get some sleep now, we've got a big day tomorrow. I hope you're rested well and I hope you like the shirt I got for you.

I love you, David. I knew it from the first time we kissed, the time at Sal's party when I first met you. I've loved you since them and I will always love you.

Hugs & Bugs,
Wolfie

David folded the letter back up and wiped away his tears. He picked up the tape and wondered if it would still play.

"David," Wolf's voice came from over by the dresser.

"I thought you left me for good," David replied.

Wolf laughed, "I thought I did too."

"What happened?"

"After I left, I realized I missed you too much. So I came back," he laughed again. *"I told you. I can't live without you."*

David rolled his eyes.

"There's more," Wolf pointed out. *"I want you to have them."*

"Where?" David asked softly.

Wolf pointed across the room to the other dresser.

"Mokey!" David called out.

He stood up and walked over to the door. "Wolf's here," he informed her when he saw her on the landing.

"He is?" she asked, entering the room. She looked around in disbelief. "I don't see him."

"Not everyone can," Pez explained. "We need to check behind the other dresser."

"What? Why?" she asked, but she was already clearing off the dresser.

"Wolf said there's more he wants me to have," David replied, as the pulled the dresser away from the wall.

"There's something for Mokey, too," Wolf whispered.

"Did you just whisper my name?" Mokey asked.

Pez smiled as he dropped to his knees. "That was Wolf. He said there's something for you in this one," David told her. He felt along the wall until he found a finger hole. He swung the door open. He stuck his head in the tiny doorway. "There are a few boxes in here. It's a big space. Almost like a low ceiling room, but I can't see much," David announced.

"Can you reach the boxes?" Mokey asked.

"Let me crawl in there. Do you have a flashlight?" David crawled into the hole while Mokey found a flashlight.

"There's a light switch to your left." Wolf was with him in the room.

David felt around on the wall until he found the switch. "Never mind the flash light," he called out as the small room filled with light.

"This is where I used to hide, when I wanted to be alone," Wolf explained.

"What the hell?" Mokey's voice exclaimed as she crawled in after David.

"He said this is where he used to hide." David stood up, the ceiling was sloped dramatically, but he found he could stand up if he leaned against the wall. He helped Mokey up. She could stand without hitting her head.

"Is that a mattress?" she asked, making her way around the boxes.

"Wow," David uttered. "You think you know someone."

"You had your tree house. I had my attic," Wolf laughed.

"I think it's kind of cool," Mokey laughed as she watched David maneuver his way around the boxes. She collapsed on the mattress; a huge cloud of dust engulfed them both. David collapsed next to her causing another dust storm. They both ended up coughing and laughing.

"How the hell did he get this in here?" Mokey asked, still coughing a little.

"Very carefully," Pez replied and they fell into gales of laughter again.

"There's another door in the closet. It's full size," Wolf explained.

"Why the hell did you make us crawl through the hole then?" Pez asked laughing.

"I didn't expect you to crawl all the way in."

"Are you talking to Wolf or me?" Mokey asked.

"Sorry. Wolf told me there's a full size door to this room in your closet."

Mokey laughed hysterically at that one.

"This is for her," Wolf said, placing something in David's hand.

"What the hell?" Mokey whispered, her laughter stopping suddenly. "Where did that come from?"

"I found it on the bed," David lied.

"Bull shit!" Mokey cried. "It just appeared out of thin air."

"It's called an apport. Spirits can make things move or appear. It takes a lot of energy, but Wolf loves to make a point."

"It's cute," she said, taking the stuffed animal from David. "What is it?" she asked, caressing its mauve fur and feathery hair. "It looks like a Muppet," she pointed out, running her hand up and down its soft tail.

"It is… sort of… It's a Fraggle," he paused, noticing the blank look on her face. "It was a TV show in the 80's that Wolf loved: Fraggle Rock. It was made by Jim Henson, so Fraggles were Muppets."

She turned the toy over and looked at the tag sewn into its butt. "Mokey Fraggle," she read.

"No one ever told you?" Pez asked. "About your name?"

"No, I just thought it was something my parent's made up."

"I can't believe no one ever told you."

"You tell me," Mokey requested.

"When you were born, your parent's didn't know what to call you, so they asked Wolf and Diamond what to name you and they, in unison, said Mokey Fraggle," he laughed. "Your parents kept the Mokey, but dropped the Fraggle."

"Named after a Muppet," Mokey laughed.

"It could have been worse."

"Really?"

"Sure, they could have picked Boober." Mokey laughed and hit David with her Fraggle. "You should watch it some time. Mokey's a real cool Fraggle. You'd like her."

"I will. So what's in the boxes?" She hugged her namesake toy close to her.

David stretched and pulled a box closer to them. He lifted the lid and found it was filled with notebooks. He pulled one out and opened it. "It looks like a journal. It's got songs... drawings... lists..."

"So a whole lot of Wolf," Mokey suggested.

"Yes," Pez smiled. "A whole lot of Wolf."

"This one is the same," Mokey said, opening a box of her own. "I wonder if all of them are just filled with journals."

"Probably, except maybe this one." Pez picked up a box that was a lot smaller than the others. He opened it and the contents made him gasp.

"What is it?" Mokey asked. She stuck her hand in the box and pulled out some old receipts.

"I can't believe he kept all this junk," David said, combing through the box. "It's like a memory box." His hand closed around the Humbug massager and he pulled it out. He clicked the button, but the batteries were either dead or corroded. He hugged it close as he went into the box for something else. "This is everything from when we were going out. Receipts... one of my hair bands... wristbands from raves... ticket stubs from concerts... everything. I never knew he did this." David was smiling sadly. He pulled out a Mokey Pez dispenser and handed it to her. "Here this one is for you," he laughed.

"Aw, it'll remind me of both of you." She pulled out a dried rose. "Who knew my brother was such a romantic?"

"I did," David replied sadly.

"I'm sorry," Mokey apologized.

"Don't be. It happened a long time ago." Mokey put her arm around his shoulder. "Besides, I don't think I'm ever going to be rid of him, entirely."

"Is he still here now?"

"Yes, but he's very weak right now from that apport. I can't see him, I can only feel him." He looked around the tiny attic room. "Let's get out of here and go back to the café and get some food. I'm starving."

"Sounds good to me. Let's find that closet door though."

"Great idea." Pez stood up and helped Mokey up and together they made their way through the mini-attic and found the door that led to her closet.

Mokey tripped on the way out of her closet.

David caught her. "You OK?" he asked.

"Yeah, I tripped over that stupid box." She pointed to the box the she had inadvertently kicked into her bedroom.

"You mean the present?" David asked, picking it up. "To: Mokey, Happy 10th Birthday," David read. "Wolf died before he could give it to you." He handed her the present.

"Should I open it?" Mokey asked nervously.

"Yeah, why else would you have tripped over it," David laughed.

Mokey ripped the paper off. "It's an empty box!"

David dropped the humbug to the floor. He pointed to the name on the box.

"Mokey Fraggle," she read. "Are you trying to tell me, that the doll you gave me in the attic was in this box." David nodded. "And my brother magically took it out and gave it to me?"

"The box is still sealed." David said weakly.

"If you're doing this, David, you need to stop. You're freaking me out," Mokey accused.

"It's not me. It really is your brother. He likes to show off."

Mokey laughed. "Well, he was like that when he was alive. I guess he'd be like that as a spirit too," she conceded.

"It took him a long time to convince me too, but Mokey, when people die, they don't go away. They're still with you all the time. You may not feel them, but they are."

"I guess I have a lot to learn," Mokey said sadly.

"Stick with me kid. I'll teach you everything I know," David suggested.

"I think I will. That way you won't be the only crazy one in town," Mokey laughed.

David surprised himself when he threw his arms around her. She squealed. "What's this for?"

"I'm just so glad you came to the cemetery today. Really, today has been amazing. It's like a weight I have been carrying for years has finally been lifted off of my chest." He paused, releasing her from his grasp. "Thanks."

"No problem. Us Spencers need to stick together," Mokey responded.

"Us Spencers?"

Mokey lifted her hand and wiggled her fingers at him.

He grabbed her hand and stared at the engagement ring.

"How come I didn't notice that before?" he wondered.

"I just put it on. I forgot to put it on this morning. He just proposed last Thursday, so I'm not used to wearing it yet."

David picked her up and spun her around. She squealed again. "Welcome to the family," he congratulated, smiling widely.

"Thanks. Steve's different than anyone I know. He's special and I'm not talking about his Asperger's Syndrome. He just gets me. You know?"

David nodded. "Yeah, I know."

"Well, we better get back or we're going to miss the party."

"The party?"

"Ooops," Mokey blushed. "It was supposed to be a surprise Welcome Home party."

"When did you plan this?"

"While you were greeting everyone," she pulled out her cell phone. "Your mom, Rae, and I were texting away."

"Really?" David was touched. He honestly believed that no one would even notice that he had come home.

"Just act surprised, please," Mokey requested.

"I will," he agreed, kissing her on the forehead. He walked over to the bed and picked up the letter.

Lying on the bed next to the letter was a CD with the word "Sessions" written in the middle of it.

"Mokey?" he asked, picking the CD up. "Is this yours?" He held it out for her to see.

"I've never seen it before," she responded. "Was it wrapped in the letter?"

"It wouldn't have fit in the envelope."

"It's probably Wolf showing off again." She paused, a puzzled look crossing her face. David shivered at her next question. "What do those letters mean?" She pointed to the letters written on the out edge of the CD like a secret code.

She sounded the words out.

"You're not reading it right," David corrected. "It's the first letters of the words from Treasure, it's a Cure song." He closed his eyes and recited the words he loved more than any other song he had ever heard.

The End

A Murder of One is a fictional novel, but it deals with some very real problems. If you are suffering from any of these problems there is help. There is a light. Suicide is never the answer. If you are contemplating suicide or if you suspect someone you know is, please call the National Suicide Prevention Lifeline any time 24/7…
  1-800-273-TALK (8255)
or visit their website..
  http://www.suicidepreventionlifeline.org/

If you or any one you know is struggling with drug or alcohol abuse Call Substance Abuse and Mental Health Services Administration or SAMHSA any time 24/7 …
  1-800-662-HELP (4357)
or visit their website…
  http://www.samhsa.gov/find-help/national-helpline

Self Injury or Cutting is a very real disease. It is not a healthy way to deal with your feelings. I should know I used to do it. I conquered this disease with therapy and a book called:
'Bodily Harm: The Breakthrough Healing Program for Self-Injurers' by Karen Conterio and Wendy Lader, Ph.D.

For more information on S.A.F.E. (Self Abuse Finally Ends) Alternatives. Call…
1-800-DONTCUT (366-8288)
or visit their website
www.selfinjury.com

Coming Soon....

Shattered
by Patti Keno

His lips were soft and so exquisite. He kissed her so passionately that she forgot she had just met this man. Maggie whimpered softly in pleasure as his hand gently touched the back of her neck. Tears began to well up in her eyes, as she realized that this was exactly what she had wanted to do since the moment she first laid eyes on Josh. She whimpered once more in sorrow as he finally pulled his lips away.

Maggie gasped for air, surprised that she had been holding her breath for so long. She looked into his eyes and saw a rapture that echoed her own.

"That...was...Amazing," she told him, still trying to catch her breath. She had never been kissed so deeply; so passionately before this moment. "I never..." She tried to speak the words that were in her mind, but they melted away before she could. She struggled to explain what she felt inside, but stopped as she noticed the tears in his eyes. "What is it Josh?" She asked, "You felt it too didn't you?" Maggie demanded softly.

Josh nodded slowly, a tear rolling down his cheek. "You don't remember do you?" he asked cryptically.

"What?" Maggie asked.

"I'm sorry," Josh whispered painfully.

Those words filled Maggie with confusion, sorrow and rage. She started shaking her head. "No," she whispered softly, knowing what was coming next – rejection– the only thing, in Maggie's eyes, that could ruin this perfect evening. "Don't say you're sorry," she begged, still shaking her head.

She hadn't noticed him moving until his lips touched hers once more. She whimpered again at the raw passion behind his delicate kiss. Slowly, he kissed his way to her ear. The feeling of his stubble against her cheek and neck made her feel week.

"I really loved you," he breathed into her ear. His warm breath sent chills down her spine and throughout her entire body.

Again, his lips found hers and she was swept away with emotion; swept away with love and lust for this man she had just met. It felt as if that missing part deep inside of her had finally been filled. How could she love this stranger so much? How could she have such feelings for a man she had never met before?

His tongue began to explore every part of her mouth; she sucked it gently and melted into the arms that held her. She had lost herself his kiss…his tongue…. her tongue…. there was no difference. They had become one in the passion of the kiss.

His tongue seemed to probe deeper into her mouth, she could feel it gently caressing her molars. She sucked his tongue harder, more passionately as she longed for his hand to move to her breast. She hadn't felt like this in so long. She hadn't been kissed like this in…. well she'd never been kissed like this before.

All at once, she began to feel something much deeper than anything she had ever felt. It was something more primal than sex or lust. His kiss had awakened an insatiable longing deep inside her soul. It was as if with his kiss, Josh had touched the very core of her soul.

Once again her knees went weak with the glory of the rapture that filled her. Thankfully, Josh's loving arms supported her as her knees gave way. She began to cry openly, no longer caring what happened to her as long as she could remain in Josh's arms forever.

She felt his hot tongue pushing deeper and deeper still into her mouth. She sucked his tongue with a needy desire, unable to control herself anymore. She was accepting him, accepting anything he wanted to do to her.

She heard his voice once more, but this time it seemed as if it was coming from inside of her own mind. Somehow they had connected so deeply that they could communicate mind to mind. Maggie couldn't even stop to think about the craziness of that idea as she thought it.

The voice inside her head pushed all thoughts out of her head. "I love you," it said. His voice was raw, aching and saturated with real emotions.

She was not surprised when the orgasm overtook her. She wanted to scream out in sheer ecstasy of his kiss. She dug her nails into Josh's back. She was shaking in awe as she was pushed even further past the point of orgasm, pushed to a point of perfection that could never be matched. She had never imagined that there was anything better than an orgasm.

She felt as if her soul had lifted out of her body and taken flight. This had to be love; had to be real. Josh was the one. After spending only a few hours with him, she knew she wanted to spend the rest of her life with him. Anyone who could bring her to orgasm with a simple kiss was not to be given up, but why was he so sorry? He couldn't still be thinking of leaving…not after this kiss.

Suddenly, pain ripped through her very soul. She shuddered in horror as she tried to pull away, but Josh's hand held her locked to him in an iron grip. He would not let her break the kiss.

The pain was exquisite, sensual and raw, Maggie couldn't help but to give in and let go. She let the pain sweep through her entire body. She was sobbing now, but Josh didn't care. He continued to force the kiss upon her.

She felt like she was spinning faster and faster at an alarming rate. She longed to open her eyes and see if she actually was spinning, but she no longer had control of her body. 'Is this death?' she wondered as she lost all feeling in her body. Her soul began to panic as she realized that Josh was killing her; he was suffocating her with his kiss. He was sucking the very air from her lungs. She couldn't move she couldn't breathe. She was surely dying.

She wanted to scream out in horror and pain, as the sickening sensation of vertigo swallowed her. She began to lose herself once more. This time she lost all touch with reality as she spun endlessly. Just as she thought she could no longer take it, the feeling disappeared. She found herself standing on the boardwalk gasping madly for air.

His lips were gone and his arms pushed her away. The kiss was finally over and she was still alive. She had thought she would never breathe again. Her lungs were burning as she sucked the sweet autumn-chilled air into them. Her entire body throbbed and ached with the power of his kiss. She licked her lips sensuously, savoring his taste on them. It felt odd as she did this. Something felt different, felt wrong. It felt as if somehow the kiss had changed her in some way.

"Wow." She breathed. Her voice sounded strange; maybe she hadn't said anything at all. Maybe it was Josh who said it. She opened her eyes. She was filled with the sudden urge to see his eyes. She had to know if he had felt it too. She wanted to know if what she felt was real or if she had imagined it all.

As her eyes adjusted to the dark night around them, she noticed that somehow her vision was crisper. She could see things so much clearer than ever before.

She started to feel nausea creeping up into the back of her throat as she focused on the person standing before her.

Instead of seeing Josh standing there, Maggie saw a girl. In fact the girl was a mirror image of herself. She smiled, but the mirror image's face remained still. Tears began to roll down the mirror image's cheeks.

"I'm sorry," the mirror image whispered. Her eyes lifted up to look at Maggie. She was shocked to see Josh's essence staring up at her from behind her own eyes. This was not just a mirror image of Maggie; this was a complete duplicate of her body.

"What the hell?" Maggie asked. Josh's voice came out of her mouth. Realization dawned on her and she felt as if the world had just dropped out from under. This couldn't be real… The body standing before her was not a mirror image and it was not a duplicate. It was her body. Her own body stood before her with Josh looking out of **her** eyes.

Maggie's panicked breathing sped up until she was literally gasping for air. She looked down at her chest and found Josh's chest heaving in time with her breathing. She felt as if she were hyperventilating. She couldn't seem to catch her breath…his breath.

"What happened?" Maggie asked in a pitifully small Josh-voice. "What did you do to me?" she demanded without conviction. She was crying again. She moved her hands to touch her chest, Josh's hands moved at her command. This was real, somehow Josh was inside her body and she was in stuck in his.

"Put it back…put it back," Maggie began a feeble chant. "Put it back…put it back…put me back…put me back," she demanded between sobs.

The mirror image…Josh…stood before Maggie. He toed a crack in the boardwalk with Maggie's cross trainer-clad foot. He was staring intently at the lake. Josh bit her lip trying to stop the tears welling up in his stolen eyes.

Josh turned his gaze onto his former body. He stared deeply into the eyes that used to be his. He was staring directly at the part of the man before him that was Maggie. Josh reached Maggie's hand up and touched the face that used to belong to him. Maggie recoiled from his touch…no her touch.

"I'm sorry," Josh repeated through Maggie's lips.

"No, It's not real," Maggie argued. The masculine voice she heard was hoarse from crying so much. "This is not happening," Maggie whimpered. "This can't be happening."

"I'm sorry," Josh repeated. "I love you, I really do." Maggie felt the body she now occupied trembling as she heard her own voice whispering his words.

Maggie watched in horror as her body moved closer. She panicked again as Josh placed Maggie's own hands on her new Josh shoulders. The reality of the situation hit harder with the touch of her own former hand. Maggie's breathing sped up again. She wanted to scream, but all that came out was a whimper.

Josh kissed Maggie gently. Shocked, Maggie stood frozen as the lips that once were hers kissed the hollow of Maggie's unfamiliar cheek. Josh lingered, softly breathing into Maggie's new ear. Maggie whimpered once more, crying as she heard Josh's voice whimper instead of her own.

Josh backed away slowly, regretfully even. He reached up and wiped the tears away from Maggie's new cheeks. Josh smiled a small, sad smile. He shook Maggie's head and opened her mouth as if to speak. Suddenly, he turned and ran, leaving Maggie to deal with the situation alone.

"WAIT!" Maggie screamed in a desperate Josh voice. "JOSH! COME BACK!" She started crying again…no… he started crying. Maggie knew no amount of tears could ever change what had happened, as strange as it all seemed.

All she wanted to do was go home and sleep. Then, when she woke up in the morning, this entire nightmare would be over. She would be back in her own body again. 'This has to be a nightmare,' her mind rationalized. 'It just has to.' She took a few steps forward getting used to his footing. A few steps more to get used to his stride, then she started to run, pumping his legs as fast as she could. She needed to go home. Everything would be fine, if she could just make it home.

Available now:

Patti Keno lives in Belleville with her family and her two fur babies. She has been writing since she was ten years old. She has written many poems and many stories waiting to be turned into novels. When she isn't writing she likes crafting, bowling and ghost hunting. She is a spirit medium who, like her main character, can speak with the dead. She likes creating her own cute crochet stuffie patterns and playing cards with her family. When she can, she volunteers at local animal rescue groups and urges everyone to support their local rescue groups: Don't shop…Adopt!!

Follow her on…

Twitter: @PattiKeno
Facebook: www.facebook.com/authorpattikeno
Blog: www.pattikeno.com

Contact her at:
pattikeno@gmail.com

To check out her ghost hunting group visit:

www.facebook.com/michiganghostswatchers
or
www.michiganghostwatchers.net